EVERLASTING LOVE

"Zeke . . ." Abbie spoke in a near whisper. "Without you there would be no life for me. With you I can bear anything that happens, but without you I am nothing."

He leaned down and kissed her neck, unbuttoning the front of her gown at the same time. "It's the same for me," he said softly. "I need you, Abbie." His lips found the soft sweetness of her skin, and he began to move more quickly, hungry for her now, enjoying being alone with his woman.

Their bodies seemed to melt together naturally, in tune to one another's needs; this lovely excitement never really changed for them. His lips searched her mouth, and she gloried at how gentle he could be with her as his hands caressed and explored. Abbie had seen the vicious side of Zeke Monroe, had seen what he could do to his enemies when provoked. But she alone knew the side of him that others hadn't imagined existed.

"Abbie, my Abbie," he whispered, his lips moving against her flesh, drawing out her passion. She touched his hair, breathing deeply, allowing herself to enjoy the moment fully, never knowing what tomorrow might bring. She wanted him as much today as always, and she would love him forever. . . .

SAVAGE DESTINY

#5

CLIMB THE HIGHEST MOUNTAIN

F. ROSANNE BITTNER

ZEBRA BOOKS

KENSINGTON PUBLISHING CORP.

ZEBRA BOOKS

are published by

Kensington Publishing Corp.
850 Third Avenue
New York, NY 10022

10 9 8 7 6 5 4 3

Printed in the United States of America

To Beverly Cole, Marilyn Arent, Kim (Kime) Karnes, Russ Kime, Donnalee Houser, Jane Hollacher, and Nancy Zausner, loyal fans before I was even published. True friendship and support are precious gifts, and people who care are human treasures. Thanks to all of you for the hope that kept me going.

Each novel in this series contains occasional references to characters and places that existed and to events that occurred during the time period it covers. Such references are based on factual printed matter available to the public. However, the primary characters in this series are purely fictitious, a product of the author's imagination, and any resemblance of these characters to actual persons, living or dead, or of author's fictitious events to any events that may have occurred at that time, is purely coincidental.

The major portions of this novel take place in present-day Colorado and its surrounding territory. Fort Laramie is in today's southeast Wyoming; Fort Lyon, called Bent's Fort before it was purchased by the War Department, is in southeast Colorado. Fort Robinson is in northwest Nebraska. The Arkansas River, along which our main characters live, is in southeast Colorado and is near Fort Lyon. The Treaty of Little Arkansas (1865) ships the Cheyenne to a new reservation along the southern border of Kansas, several hundred miles from their natural habitats in Colorado, northern Kansas and Nebraska.

This novel covers the years 1864 through 1866. A massacre actually occurred at Sand Creek on November 29, 1864.

Please note that the Fort Lyon referred to in this novel is the old Bent's Fort. It is not to be mistaken for the Fort Lyon in the fourth novel of this series, which was in New Mexico.

With grateful acknowledgment to the inspiring authors, Will Henry and Dee Brown, and thanks to the University of Oklahoma and the University of Nebraska for the wealth of resource information I have derived from the historical books they publish; as well as to the St. Stephen's Indian Foundation, Wyoming, for their very informative publication *The Wind River Rendezvous*. Facts about the massacre at Sand Creek were derived from *The Southern Cheyenne* by Donald J. Berthrong, *Life of George Bent* by George E. Hyde, *The Sand Creek Massacre* by Stan Hoig, and *Bury My Heart at Wounded Knee* by Dee Brown.

Betray me not, my love,
Tho others come to tempt us
And hardships make us tired.
Neither death, nor war, nor the pain of parting
Should beat us into resignation.
The pathway could be easy,
If we would choose it.
But the easy path means the sacrifice
Of our love, and so would bring more pain
Than all our sufferings from being together.
We are one, my love,
And we know not the meaning of betrayal.

—F. Rosanne Bittner

Prologue

Some called it the Battle of Sand Creek, some the
Chivington Massacre—Chivington led the Colorado
Volunteers that day—but most people call it the Sand
Creek Massacre. Whatever its title, it is a shameful
chapter in American history. On November 29, 1864,
an uncalled-for attack on the Cheyenne peacefully
encamped at Sand Creek left grotesquely mutilated
bodies of Indian women and children strewn across the
village and the surrounding area. The reason for the
Volunteers' attack is debated to this day, but the actual
event and its consequences cannot be denied. The Sand
Creek Massacre gave the Indians cause to retaliate,
perhaps more cause than all the broken treaties had
given them.

This massacre and other such brutal assaults
eventually devastated the Plains Indians, despite the
desperate last stands of the red men. Yet to this day
their mourning cries can be heard on the west wind as it
groans through canyons and howls across the open

11

plains. Red men's bones lie beneath concrete sidewalks and deep reservoirs, but they do not rest. Such greatness and spirit never die, just as great love never dies. This is a story about that kind of spirit, that kind of love . . . the spirit of the red man, the love between Zeke and Abigail Monroe. . . .

Chapter One

He stood at the hotel window, a glint from the afternoon sun accenting the hard lines rugged living had etched into the dark skin of his handsome face. His sleek black hair was braided down his back, bereft of the Indian ornaments he usually wore in it. He was in town—in civilization. He must not look too "Indian," although that was almost impossible, for everything about him was Indian. The most he could do was don the cotton pants and shirt of a white man, and leave off the paint and decorations he so dearly loved to wear. But he longed for the softness of his normal garb—buckskins—longed for the peace and quiet of his ranch along the Arkansas River, longed for the days when he rode wild and free with his next of kin, the Cheyenne.

"What are you thinking?" The soft voice came from the bed. He turned to look at his woman, his Abbie girl, who had just stirred from an afternoon nap. It had been a hard journey to Pueblo from the ranch, and it irritated him that she had had to come at all. But that was the law. Abbie was white. He was half Indian. Only Abbie could sign the papers to ensure that they retained ownership of their ranch. His eyes drifted from her lovely face back to the window, down to the

13

rutted streets over which wagons clattered amid the bustle of a growing town.

"I'm thinking about Lean Bear . . . shot down in cold blood by soldiers while riding toward them with a white flag in his hand. I'm thinking about the rumors of moving the Cheyenne to Kansas. I'm looking down on the streets of Pueblo and seeing the end of the People. It's only a matter of time, isn't it, Abbie? Soon Colorado will be rid of all its Indians. Look at me—standing here in white man's clothes because I don't dare come to town dressed as an Indian." He met her eyes again. "And you have to wear that tight, uncomfortable 'proper' white woman's dress instead of the tunics you like so well, just so you aren't scorned in the streets."

She lay on her side watching him, studying the lean, muscular body that remained hard and strong despite his forty-four years. There was nothing soft or aging about Zeke Monroe, except perhaps a few extra lines on his face. The thin scar that ran from temple to jawbone down his left cheek had not faded over the years, and it reminded her of the savageness that lay beneath the white man's clothes. A Crow Indian had put the scar there, and Zeke had acquired many other scars over the years: for he was accustomed to living by fists, knives, and guns; to dealing out his own form of justice; to living off the land and setting his own rules. Yet it was that side of him that brought out her wildest passion.

That was also the side of him she understood best, which was why she understood the pain he was suffering because his way of life, the way of his Cheyenne relatives, was fast disappearing. This was 1864, and as the Civil War was drawing to a close, more and more white people were arriving in the West. Abbie and Zeke knew that when the war ended the

14

westward surge of whites would surpass anything they had seen so far. Too many families had been displaced by the war, too many had lost their homes and land—lost everything they had ever known and loved. Changes would come. People would leave the south and look for new horizons, for new places in which to settle. There was only one direction they could take.

"Come lie down, Zeke," Abbie spoke up. "We have enough on our minds, what with getting those papers signed. Attorney Dearborn has to get them ready so let's rest until five o'clock when we can go and sign them."

He sighed and ambled over to the bed, his animal grace reminiscent of wild things and the outdoors. He unbuttoned his shirt and began to remove it, revealing a broad, firm chest and muscular arms. White scars marked his dark skin, souvenirs of numerous battles and of the torturous Sun Dance ritual he'd endured when very young.

"You mean when *you* can sign them," he answered, bitterness in his voice. He threw down the shirt and lay wearily down on the bed, stretching out on his back.

She sighed and reached over, lightly tracing her fingers over his high checkbones and finely etched lips, then trailing them down over his muscular chest and resting her hand lightly on his firm, flat stomach. "There's nothing we can do about it, Zeke. It's the law."

He laughed sneeringly. "White man's laws stink," he grumbled.

Abbie just smiled. "Now you sound like Swift Arrow," she teased, referring to his younger full-blood Cheyenne brother who now lived and warred with the Sioux in the north.

"I'm right and you know it," Zeke answered.

She sighed and lay back on her own pillow, staring up at the ceiling. "I know. But what else can we do?

15

Those tax men have told us to file a legal claim or get out. With seven children and only the ranch to keep us going, what else can we do? We certainly can't live with the Cheyenne any more. It's not like the old days, Zeke, much as I hate to think about it myself. Remember when we first came here and we lived with the People? We were always warm, always had full bellies. Not anymore. And if they want to survive at all, they'll have to go wherever the government tells them to go." She pulled a comb from her lustrous dark hair, hating to wear it in the uncomfortable bun. "Surely they are going to move them, Zeke. Why else are we expected to file this silly claim? Our ranch is on reservation land. This can only mean that soon it won't be reservation land anymore. It will be open to anyone who wants to settle there. Suddenly the papers William Bent signed years ago verifying our claim are no good. Suddenly everything is changing, and it frightens me. But we've been threatened before. We've fought and suffered and been apart, yet we've never been beaten . . . and we won't be beat this time."

He rolled to his side, resting on his elbow and looking down at her. She always felt dwarfed beneath his tall, broad frame. He had inherited his powerful body from his white father, who had been a very big man. His hard-edged leanness came from his Indian side, as did his dark skin and the piercing dark eyes that sometimes could almost hypnotize her, even after all the years they had been together. He ran his fingers lightly over her throat and chin.

"Still the scrapper I married, I see," he told her, forcing a smile for her. Things had been hard enough on them the last two days. At least he could try to keep his mood even. "Every time you talk like that I think about the fifteen-year-old girl I met on that wagon train, and how she shot those Crow Indians and how

16

she took that arrow and then let me cut it out of her."

She smiled sadly at the memory. She'd lost her whole family on that trip west, but she had found Zeke Monroe. She studied the provocative smile that he still flashed quickly and unexpectedly, the smile that had made her melt when she was fifteen, that still made her melt, nineteen years and seven children later.

"Well, I don't like what's happening any more than you do. And I especially don't like having to be the one to sign those papers, just because I'm white. You're my husband. You're the man, and you're the one who runs that ranch—with more intelligence than most white men I know." Her brown eyes began to glitter with anger. "Imagine! After all the years you've run that place, with all your knowledge of horses and ranching, you can't even sign as owner! It's ridiculous! Everybody in Colorado Territory knows you raise the finest Appaloosas in the West!"

Now it was she who was getting upset, despite her intention to calm down her husband.

"They're even saying Indians aren't citizens!" she said in a louder voice. "Can you imagine? They've been on this land for centuries, and they aren't citizens?"

She met his dark eyes and they were dancing as he studied her lovely face. Her skin was still soft, thanks to the creams she used, and her thick, dark brown hair showed no sign of gray. Her breasts were full and firm, her form trim. With seven children to care for in an untamed land, a woman didn't have time to get soft and fat. Zeke's Abbie girl was still firm in the right places. He moved a big hand down over her breasts and rested it on a protruding hip bone that he could feel through her dress.

"Why on earth are you smiling, Zeke Monroe?" she asked with a frown.

"Because I enjoy seeing you get angry," he answered.

"You're prettier when you're angry." He leaned down and kissed her lightly. "Besides, if we can't see a little humor in this damned life, we might as well end it here and now, Abbie." His smile faded then. "Things are going to get worse, I'm afraid. The day is coming when it will be a lot harder to smile."

Their eyes held, a million memories flashing through both their minds . . . years gone by . . . those first years spent with the Cheyenne until he built the cabin for his "white woman" . . . the hardships of surviving in a wild land . . . the pain of birthing children . . . her near death from some of those births. The operation in Denver, five years ago, had ended her ability to bear children. Her depression over that had lasted a long time.

There had been so many tragedies, so many deaths since she'd come west and had fallen in love and married the half-breed scout who'd led her father's wagon train. Fate and necessity had separated them far too many times, but always he'd come back. Always her Zeke had returned to hold her, protect her, provide for his children.

But their last separation had brought the most pain. The Civil War had torn them apart, sending Zeke east and leaving Abbie vulnerable in a lawless land. Their eldest son, Wolf's Blood, had tried to save her that fateful day; he'd risked his life to help his mother. But there were too many, and the outlaws paid by the wealthy Winston Garvey had whisked her away to the place where Garvey and two of his men had tortured and raped her in an effort to obtain information about the half-breed son Winston Garvey had fathered by a Cheyenne woman. Stubborn and proud, Abigail did not tell where the child was, only she and Zeke knew. She held out against pain and horror, trusting Zeke to find and rescue her. And not longer after Zeke

Monroe's return home, Winston Garvey had mysteriously disappeared, never to be seen again. Only Zeke Monroe and his son Wolf's Blood knew what had happened to the man; only they knew just how cruelly Winston Garvey had died. For Zeke Monroe's big knife was as much a part of him as his skin, and when he was out for vengeance, the blade did a fine job of prolonging pain and suffering.

Even though she'd been hidden away in a cold, deserted mine shaft deep in the mountains of Colorado, Zeke had searched out his woman, whose body was almost lifeless by the time he'd found her. That had been sixteen months ago. She had been a long time recovering, and there were times when he could tell that ugly memories tortured her. She loved Zeke, heart, soul, and body; but to have had men force themselves on her had been devastating despite her strong countenance and the bravery she had shown living in this land. She still could not sleep without a lantern lit. If she awoke to darkness, her mind would race with fear. She imagined herself in that horrible cave again, thought that Garvey and his men would come to hurt her.

Zeke's pain at not being there in her most dire time of need could be read in his dark, loving eyes, especially in their intimate moments. Over all their years together, he had always protected her. He'd risked his life for her more than once, and he'd always sworn he would not allow her to be hurt. Yet he had failed her that one time, and he would never forgive himself, never forget it. Abbie! His beautiful, faithful Abbie-girl, abused by other men! He wished he could kill Winston Garvey all over again, torture him, dismember him piece by piece! In times of vengeance, Zeke Monroe was the Cheyenne Indian, Lone Eagle, a man capable of inflicting the worst torture on a foe. Winston Garvey's screams for

19

mercy had rung like music in Zeke's ears, as had the screams of the other two men who had helped to create Abbie's days of horror. He had left the other two to Wolf's Blood, only sixteen at the time, a boy almost totally Indian in nature and beliefs. It had been the first time Wolf's Blood had killed, but doing so had come naturally to him. He had sought vengeance. The men had abused his mother! There could be no better cause for making them suffer. Still, what Zeke and Wolf's Blood had done could not obviate what had happened to Abbie. Even now as Zeke leaned down to kiss her again, she could see the remorse in his eyes, feel it in his lips as they suddenly searched deeper.

So much! They had been through so much together . . . and survived! Always it seemed that their pain and loss came through in their lovemaking, mingled with their joy and laughter. Each time they made love the experience was enhanced by the deep secrets they shared, the special things that only two people who had been through what they had and who had survived could appreciate.

He was removing her dress, and she let him. She always let him. This was Zeke. Only in the last few months had she been able to give herself this way again, and he still moved carefully, always afraid of bringing back some terrible memory. The first time after her ordeal had been very difficult, but she had forced herself to open to her husband again, determined that men like Winston Garvey were not going to destroy her marriage and the deep and special love she shared with Zeke Monroe. After all, she had never given herself willingly to anyone but Zeke . . . her Zeke . . . her first man—her only man. He had taken her one lonely night in the wilds of Wyoming. She'd been only fifteen. She had belonged to him ever since.

His sweet kisses smothered her, and within moments

they were both naked and touching. How many times had they done this? Why was each time as good as the last, even after all the children? It was as though this was all, as though this was the only way they could prove that as long as each had the other everything would be all right. This was something no one could take away. No one!

His hands moved gently over her, fire in his fingertips, sweet Indian words of love on his lips as they caressed her throat, her breasts. In these moments it was difficult to picture him violent and vengeful. But others knew just how violent Zeke Monroe could be. How well they knew! Still, when bedding his woman there was nothing violent about him, although he took her more passionately than usual when he thought about other men using her body. Then he needed to ensure that his brand was burned into her forever.

"Ne-mehotatse," he whispered, using the Cheyenne word for "I love you" in his passion. He moved on top of her, parting her slender, white legs and pressing against her flat belly, its flesh soft from bearing many children but not protruding.

He thrust himself deep and she cried out. He felt her tense, and he knew she was thinking of the cave. "Look at me, Abbie," he whispered.

She clung to the hard muscles of his arms as he invaded private places, his eyes glazed with passion.

"It's me, Abbie girl. It's only me," he told her, his voice gruff from heated desire. "Nobody else will ever touch you."

Their eyes held then, hers taking on a look of provocative passion that fed his urgent lust for his woman. He lowered his head and met her lips, parting them hungrily as she arched up to him. In these wonderful moments all sorrow and pain were left behind. The precarious future was not to be thought of now. The fate of the Cheyenne must not get in the way of their moments of ecstasy. The unpredictable future of their children must be set aside temporarily. First they must have this, for being one gave them strength, relieved the awful tension, told them that at least they were still alive and still together. Here, in each other's arms, lay their power, their determination to survive against all odds. This great love could endure.

He felt her climactic contractions and she shuddered with sweet abandon and cried out his name. He held himself in check as long as possible, wanting her to enjoy the union, always trying to erase her ugly memories and make her think only of these times—the good and beautiful times that were right and wonderful and pleasurable. Her eyes were closed now, and he studied her beautiful face, the thick hair now escaping from the neat bun and falling onto the pillow and her shoulders, the soft white skin of her shoulders, the fullness of her breasts, and the pink fruits at the tips of them. One breast still bore the scar from the arrow wound she had suffered on the wagon train years ago. He remembered how he'd felt when he'd thought she might die, how he'd felt when he'd removed the arrow and burned out any infection, how brave she had been, and how terrified he had been that she would die. It was then he'd given his love to the woman-child, Abigail Trent, and when he'd asked her to marry him, there had been no doubt what her answer would be. In her childish innocence she had made it very clear to the scout "Cheyenne Zeke" that she was in love with him.

He smiled as he watched her take him inside herself, her face nearly as innocent looking as that first time when he had stolen her virginity. It seemed amazing that after all the years he could derive just as much pleasure from her as he did then—even more for their love had been made richer by years of shared tribulations, terrible tests of their marriage, the agony of having to be apart.

His life poured into her. That life could no longer be nurtured into a child inside her body, but it didn't matter. Her life was more important to him. Indeed, the operation had brought him welcome relief by removing the worry over another pregnancy and what that could do to her. Besides, she had already given him seven beautiful children, all waiting for them now at their ranch on the Arkansas. The first-born was Wolf's Blood, seventeen, all Indian, the only child who had refused to take a white name after being told he must do so and be baptized to prevent his being taken from the parents and put onto a reservation. Not that Zeke Monroe would let anyone take away his children, nor would Abbie. But fear and worry about the future had made them want to ensure their safety.

Margaret Elaine, Blue Sky, was fifteen; LeeAnn Bonita, Young Girl, twelve. Jeremy Trent, Little Wolf, was eleven; and Ellen Lynn, Rising Sun, nine. Lillian Rose, Summer Moon, was seven. Little Jason Ezekiel, Yellow Hawk, was five. All were different. Wolf's Blood seemed to have no white blood at all, nor did Margaret, a dark beauty, always a shy child. LeeAnn on the other hand seemed to have no Indian blood. She was a blond-headed, blue-eyed beauty who looked very much like Abbie's dead sister, who also had been fair. Jeremy looked like any other white boy, and had nothing in common with his older brother. He was always a problem to Zeke, for he didn't seem interested in any of the things Zeke thought important to survival, nor was he interested in the ranch or horses. The boy seemed to be afraid of animals and of guns. Ellen was a bright, happy girl, dark but blue eyed. Lillian was the weak one, always sickly and a worry to her mother, but a shy, sweet, gentle child, with pale

23

brown eyes, light brown hair, and no outstanding features. Zeke felt Abbie overprotected the girl because of her fragility, but he never said so. Indeed, he often found himself doing things for the child to keep her from overexerting herself. Last came Jason, a happy, zealous child, daring and energetic, already riding horses and asking endless questions about animals. All were educated by their mother. All could read and write and work figures, except Wolf's Blood. He had never had the patience to sit still long enough to learn anything. Wolf's Blood preferred riding free, the wind in his face and the sun on his back, and it had not taken long to lose him almost completely to his Cheyenne relatives, with whom he lived a good deal of the time.

Zeke stretched out beside his woman, caressing her breasts as she quickly pulled a blanket to her waist.

"Do you realize it's the middle of the afternoon!" she said, suddenly blushing and reaching up to pull the combs and pins from her hair.

Zeke just grinned. "Is there some kind of law against a man taking his woman in the afternoon?"

She met his eyes slyly, then laughed lightly and snuggled against him. "I suppose not." She sighed. "I hope the children are all right."

"Lance can take care of them," he answered, referring to one of his white brothers. Lance had come from Tennessee to help Zeke run the ranch after he'd served with the Confederates in the Civil War. "And with Wolf's Blood around, who's going to bother them? Our eldest is meaner than that damned wolf he keeps as a pet."

Abbie smiled and looked up at him. "No meaner than his father can be when necessary, but just as gentle and sweet when it's called for."

He kissed her lightly. "I'm sure all's well at home, my

love, and we'll be back there ourselves by day after tomorrow. We'll get those papers signed in a couple of hours and head out in the morning. I'll be glad to return to the peace and quiet of the ranch and get back into my buckskins. I just hope the snows hold off until we get there. I feel the bite of winter in the air. No doubt there's plenty of snow in the mountains already. We're lucky that snow we had last week has melted."

She kissed his chest and pulled the blankets up over her shoulders. "I think Wolf's Blood stays warm just thinking about Morning Bird," she answered. "She seems to be all he talks about anymore."

Zeke grinned and ran a hand through her now-undone hair. "He's almost a man—he already is a man in most ways—and Morning Bird is the prettiest girl on the reservation."

"Zeke, he's only seventeen."

"More like twenty-five if you go by white man's standards. The boy has always seemed older than his years, Abbie girl. You know that."

She moved back and met his eyes. "Sometimes I wonder if he was ever a child. He's the only one that I have difficulty remembering as a child. It seems since he could walk he was riding horses, naked in the sun; trying to throw a lance, his long black hair blowing in the wind. I never got to hold him often. It was like trying to wrap my arms around the wind." Her eyes teared. "Sometimes it hurts to think about him, Zeke."

He kissed her eyes. "I know. But that's life, Abbie girl. Everybody gets older. The children come up to take the place of the parents."

She ran her fingers lightly over his handsome mouth. "I don't want to think about that . . . about us getting older . . . my children getting older."

"Well, before you know it, some of them will be

25

married and having children of their own. Then you'll have grandchildren and you'll have babies to fuss over again."

She smiled through her burgeoning tears. "Oh, I look forward to that!"

He grinned and ran a hand over her smooth skin beneath the blanket. "I know you do. But when I touch you, look at you, it's hard to believe you could ever have grandchildren. All I see is my pretty little Abbie, and you're still like a young girl in bed."

She blushed again and buried her head against his chest. "Zeke Monroe, I'm hardly a young girl anymore."

"You are to me. And you're, by God, beautiful enough that I have to keep a close eye on you in these wild towns."

They snuggled down to rest before dressing to go see the lawyer. Outside the streets of Pueblo remained busy. A fine, polished coach clattered down the main street, its rich elegance posing a stark contrast to the common farmers' wagons, its fine horses making those on the street look broken down. A man stepped from the coach, wearing a well-fitted tweed topcoat, an expensive silk hat, and rich leather gloves. His boots were polished and well cut. He was tall and handsome, dark and well manicured, a man of obvious wealth, education, and elegance.

"We're at the bank, Sir Tynes," the driver of the coach told the man.

Tynes shut the door of the coach and nodded. "Well then, I shall go inside and take care of the purchase of the rest of that land," the man replied. He looked up at the driver. "Hank, what did you say was the name of that fellow whose land adjoins mine now?"

"Monroe. Zeke Monroe."

26

"H'm." The wealthy Englishman pursed his lips in thought. "I don't suppose he'd sell, too?"

The man called Hank laughed. "In all due respect, sir, I wouldn't even bother asking. That ranch is pretty important to Zeke, and if you have any thought of using force to get it, I'd think twice. Nobody messes with Zeke Monroe. He's a half-breed Cheyenne, and what he can do with a knife would make you pass out if I told you the details."

Sir Tynes shrugged. "So be it. I shan't worry about it at the moment. But I'm not too excited about having a blood-thirsty half-breed living along my borders."

"Depends on how you treat him, sir. He can be right friendly if you're honest and up front with him. But he can be right nasty if you try to do him wrong."

Sir Tynes grinned. "Well, then, I shall have to meet this Zeke Monroe. I look forward to it." He strutted into the bank and disappeared through the door. The driver laughed and shook his head.

"What a mixture," he mumbled to himself. "Zeke Monroe living right next to Sir Edwin Tynes." He laughed again and jumped down from the coach. "Wonder what Tynes will think of Zeke's white wife? I hope I'm around when they meet."

He shook his head at how fast Colorado was growing. Now every type of person was pursuing every manner of occupation, all hoping to build personal empires by using whatever talents they possessed. The stage lines were busy, and hot on their heels was talk of railroads coming west. This was a good place for the adventurous sort, and Sir Edwin S. Tynes was certainly that. He financed his whims with "old" family money and a bold spirit, from what Hank could see. But like many such men, Tynes appeared to have little concern for the natural balance of the land, nor did he respect its people. He appeared to run roughshod over those who sought to stand in the way of his spirited enterprises, and beneath his fine clothes was a man accustomed to having whatever he wanted. He was a boy in a forty-five-year-old man's frame, a "man" who had no conception of how it might feel to be denied his will.

Chapter Two

Zeke and Abbie exited the lawyer's office, Abbie clinging to the precious piece of paper that declared for once and all that the land they lived on belonged to them. Now the government could not take it away, nor could new settlers claim it. It was not a large spread, not by comparison to what some people were claiming now. It was eight hundred acres of good green grazing land along the Arkansas River, some of it rocky and hilly but most of it flat. The river provided a good water supply and they had a view to the west, of the magnificent Rockies. They had been able to add another three hundred acres to the original five hundred they had claimed years ago, thanks to a letter from William Bent verifying that the additional three hundred acres Zeke would like to add were unclaimed.

William Bent was one of the founders of old Bent's Fort, and he had always been a helpful friend to the Cheyenne. Now, with all the Indian troubles, the rebuilt fort had been purchased by the government and turned into an army post called Fort Lyon. But William still lived nearby with his Cheyenne wife, Yellow Woman, and their half-breed children—Mary, Robert, Julia, George, and Charles. William was now an Indian agent, known and respected in the area, and his letter had helped swing the lawyer in Zeke's favor. Thus the three hundred acres of badly needed grazing land had been acquired. But Zeke and Abbie both knew that the lawyer had acceded grudgingly, only because William Bent was well known and because Abbie was white. The man's distaste for Indians was as obvious as most people's in these parts, except for old traders like William Bent and former mountain men who remembered the "old days" and who had dealt with Indians for years. But Colorado was becoming populated by newcomers, people who had had no experience with Indians. These folks had heard numerous stories back East and had formed opinions based on them. In their eyes, Indians were dirty, worthless, lazy, drunken, and savage, and little could be done to change their attitude.

It hurt Abbie deeply to know how these people felt, for she had lived among the Indians when she and Zeke were first married, and she had been shown only love and kindness. That was before the white man's rotgut whiskey had come. Then the Indians were strong and proud, hunters and warriors of unmatched skill. Many still were, but others had fallen into the whiskey trap. Zeke's own half brother, Red Eagle, had sold his own wife for whiskey and then had shot himself because of it. His wife had ended up in the hands of Winston Garvey, the wealthy rancher and businessman, the Indian hater. Garvey had made a sexual slave of her until Zeke had found her and brought her back home, after which she had borne Winston Garvey's crippled half-breed son. Then she had died. Only Zeke and Abbie knew the boy lived in the north with a dear friend, Bonnie Lewis, a missionary and nurse who had adopted him. That was the information Abigail Monroe had refused to reveal to Winston Garvey, the information for which she had suffered torture and rape. But Garvey was dead now. The public only knew that he had mysteriously disappeared after an Indian raid. He was presumed dead, but Zeke and Wolf's Blood knew he was.

"How about some supper?" Zeke now asked as he took Abbie's arm.

"Yes. I'm hungry," she replied, folding the paper and shoving it into her handbag. She met his dark eyes, seeing the hurt there that she had been the one required to sign. It tore at his Indian pride and his manly nature. "At least we got the extra land, Zeke. With even more horses now, we'll need it badly. Be grateful for that much."

His eyes glittered angrily. "Sure," was all he said. He wanted to go back inside and strangle the attorney for the insinuations the man had made about their relationship, the remarks he had made about Indians. "Let's go eat," he added, almost pulling her down the boardwalk as he walked in long, angry strides. Just past the saloon several men sat on a bench, leaning forward and watching them approach as though they had been waiting there for them. Zeke's keen senses alerted him before they even reached the men, and he stopped.

"Get off the boardwalk and we'll go the rest of the way on the other side," he told Abbie.

She looked up at him with a frown. "Why?"

"Just do like I say," he urged, turning with her. But the men, six of them, were suddenly up and coming toward them.

"Where you goin', Injun?" one of them shouted out at Zeke, who by then was in the middle of the street.

Zeke stopped, not being one to turn tail on any man. But this was Pueblo, civilization. It wasn't good for an Indian, and it was even worse for a half-breed, to get

31

into trouble. There was no justice among these people, and he had Abbie to think about. He looked down at her eyes, which pleaded with him to remain calm. He began walking again.

"Hey, I asked you a question, red man!" the man repeated, as he and the others started across the street. "By God, you better answer when white men talk to you!" The man picked up a rock and threw it. It glanced off Abbie's shoulder, and she barely stifled a small, startled scream.

Zeke whirled, giving her a shove toward the other side of the street as he did so. Since her ordeal with Winston Garvey, he could not bear to have her hurt in any way, and the hurled rock had brought on an instant, killing fury.

"Zeke, please don't!" he heard her beg in a small voice.

"Get on across the street!" he ordered, glaring at the men as he spoke. Three of them came closer, grinning, some chuckling. The other three hung back, wary of Zeke's size and the wild look in his eyes.

"We don't ordinarily hurt women," the apparent leader sneered. "But then any white woman who runs with an Injun' ain't got much worth. How'd you get her, red man? Capture her on some raid awhile back? Rape her, maybe?"

Zeke's foot instantly struck the man's privates, and he kicked again as the man bent over, smashing a booted foot into the man's face and sending him sprawling backward unconscious.

Abbie put a hand to her throat and clung to a porch post, trembling with fear as the other two men pounced on Zeke. She knew that he could handle himself, for Zeke Monroe was not one to tangle with, especially when his woman had been insulted; but she feared the law and what it sometimes did to Indians. White men had the right to insult, beat, rob, and even kill Indians. Yet Indians had no rights whatsoever. It was always assumed they were the instigators of conflict. Now Zeke had struck the first blow, and the other three men looked ready to join the fight.

The first two men knocked Zeke to the ground, but in the next moment they were shoved off and Zeke managed to get to his feet, growling like a bear. He wore white man's clothes, but he was not carrying a gun or rifle. However, he did wear his knife, a huge blade with a buffalo jawbone handle that he had carried for years, a knife that had sunk into the flesh of many men. Abbie prayed he wouldn't use it now, and she cringed as Zeke whirled when the two men pounced on him again and tried to hang on to him, kicking at him cruelly.

Zeke bashed his head against the head of one of his attackers, and the man grunted and slumped away. Then Zeke rammed a big, angry fist into the face of the last man. People were gathering around by then. Most of them were shouting and rooting for the white men, but some were laughing at their inability to take down the "wild Indian."

The first two men were up again and coming at Zeke. Abbie gasped, clinging helplessly to the post, her heart aching for Zeke. She started toward him, determined to dive into the fray herself, but a gentle hand grasped her arm.

"I wouldn't," came a voice. "If you get mixed up in it, you will look as bad as those men want you to look. Don't grovel in the dirt with them, ma'am. You're too lovely."

She looked up into a handsome, dark face, then pulled away, her eyes tearing. "I have to help him," she whimpered.

Her companion looked out at the fight. The man

33

Zeke had bashed with his fist lay unconscious, and the other two were now bloodied and staggering. "I don't see that he needs any help," he answered, his strong English accent obvious. "My, this is bloody exciting! What a magnificent specimen of man! Who is he?"

She blinked and stared at the newcomer. He was immaculate, his clothing tailored perfectly, his hands too clean for anyone who lived in these parts.

"He's my husband," she answered.

His eyebrows arched, and his eyes roved her body. "I thought perhaps . . . he was just a friend . . . perhaps you were a missionary of—"

"I am his wife," she interrupted, taking on a proud stance. "I have been his wife for nineteen happy years, and Zeke Monroe is more man than all the men in this town put together!"

The man smiled at her fiesty response, his eyes moving over her again. "Amazing!" he commented. "You are Mrs. Zeke Monroe!"

"I am!"

"Incredible!"

She turned away, irritated by his presence and concerned only with Zeke. All three men now lay in the street, bloody and covered with the mud that had resulted from the recently melting snow. Zeke had blood on his lower lip, and he rubbed his side as he watched the three men closely. Not one rose, so he brushed off his clothes, angry that his shirt was torn in front and his jacket muddy. He bent to pick up his hat. Fury consumed him. He wanted to rip each man open with his blade, take his scalp. It would serve them right for insulting his Abbie. He turned to leave the melee, but two of the three who had held back faced him. The crowd turned their attention to this new confrontation, worked up now. They wanted more, and the "Injun" was exciting to watch.

Both challengers held out knives. Leering at Zeke, they waved the blades. "Good with the fists, are you?" one of them sneered. "How about with a blade, red man? Want to show off some more for your white squaw?"

"How is she, anyway?" the other badgered. "Are the white ones more fun than your dirty Indian women? Maybe the fun comes when you take the white ones by force, or is she just one of them loose white whores that likes to lay with big bucks?"

Zeke whipped out the big blade, his speed startling. The crowd jumped back as, in an instant, the knife slashed across the second man's lips, whipping upward, then flashing downward and jabbing directly into the man's arm, ramming deeply and making him cry out and drop his knife. Zeke jerked his blade out of the man's arm and stood there menacingly.

The other man with a knife stood transfixed. Beads of sweat appeared on his face as he stared at Zeke in astonishment, obviously amazed by Zeke's speed and accuracy. As Zeke's dark eyes turned to the man, the first attacker fell to his knees, making jerky groaning sounds as blood poured from his lips and his arm.

"Abigail Monroe is the best woman in the territory!" Zeke hissed at the other man. His eyes quickly scanned the crowd as blood dripped from his knife. "Anybody else want to insult her?" His lean body was arched for a fight, his jawbone flexed in anger. Power emanated from his huge frame.

"You fools!" someone spoke up. "That's Cheyenne Zeke!"

A man stepped forward. It was Hank Buckley, the driver of the fancy coach. He stepped up beside Zeke. "I'll vouch for what he said. You sons of bitches just insulted the finest woman I've ever known! And Monroe is one of the best men I've known. Those

35

bastards who fought with him are damned lucky their hides aren't ripped from stem to stern and their innards laying out in the sun to dry!" He turned his eyes to the last man still holding a knife. "Put that thing away you dumb bastard! Haven't you ever heard of Cheyenne Zeke? There's not a man west of the Mississippi who doesn't know what Zeke can do with a blade. You itching to find out?"

The man swallowed and backed away, then suddenly threw down the knife and ran off, followed by the sixth man, who had never joined in the fighting. By then a sheriff broke through the crowd, brandishing a rifle and Abbie's heart pounded with fear. The man Zeke had stabbed was still squatting on the ground. He looked up at the sheriff, literally crying.

"Look what he did to me!" the man bellowed. "Look at me! Look at my lips! My arm! That stinking redskin ripped me up with his knife, Sheriff! And look at my friends there! He hurt them bad!"

The sheriff glanced around at the first three men. Two were staggering to their feet, but the one Zeke had hit with his fist still lay unconscious. The sheriff turned his attention back to Zeke, who stood panting, teeth clenched, ready to fight again, fight his way right out of town if necessary. How he hated towns and civilization!

"That true?" the sheriff asked, holding the rifle pointed at Zeke.

"They started it! They insulted my woman! They hit her with a rock, and the one I cut up there pulled a knife on me! I didn't come here looking for trouble, but I won't walk away from it either!"

The sheriff looked down at the big blade still in Zeke's hand, stained with blood. "Maybe you'd better come with me, Indian."

"Now wait a minute!" Hank spoke up. "The man is

telling the truth, Sheriff. He's got no fault in this."

"That's exactly right!" The wealthy Englishman moved off the boardwalk where he'd been standing near Abbie and approached them. Zeke glanced at Abbie, trying to tell her with his eyes not to be afraid. But he could see her fear, and it made him angrier at the men who had caused it.

"Sir Tynes," Hanks was saying to the well-dressed man who came through the crowd. "This here is Zeke Monroe, the fella I was telling you about earlier."

Zeke glanced at the elegant Englishman, confused by this sudden turn. Why had Hank Buckley been telling this stranger about him? The man called Sir Tynes took inventory of Zeke with his eyes. "I can see you were right, Hank, about this man being capable of being quite nasty with a knife when he needs to be." Tynes turned to the sheriff. "My driver here, Hank Buckley, is right, Sheriff. This Indian man didn't ask for any of this. He is perfectly innocent, and these other men deserve everything he gave them. May I ask if it is legal for six or eight men to gang up on one man in this great country of America?"

The sheriff blinked in confusion. "Of course not, but—"

"Then there's nothing more to be said. It is the other men who were in the wrong. I daresay this Indian man had every right to kill them, and I am surprised he didn't. I'd say he did right well, leaving them alive as he did. Doesn't that show you he's trying to abide by the law? He could have done much worse, considering his reputation with that"—Sir Tynes glanced down at the ugly, bloody blade and shivered—"that weapon he carries, wouldn't you say, Sheriff?"

Their eyes held. The sheriff could see that the Englishman was a man of great wealth, perhaps a man who could make trouble if he arrested Zeke Monroe.

He lowered his rifle and scowled.

"Get going!" he told Zeke.

Zeke glared at him and bruskly shoved his knife into its sheath. "Thanks for your kind justice!" he sneered. He turned, barged past Sir Tynes and the others, and headed toward Abbie. She could see the pain in his eyes. How he hated it when she suffered because of him! For nineteen years he had fussed and fumed, thinking that she probably never should have married him, that he'd had no right to make her his wife, not when he knew how hard it would be for her. Yet for nineteen years she had argued back that it didn't matter, that she could not live without Zeke Monroe . . . and that was true.

"Zeke, are you all right?" she asked quickly, running her hands over his arms.

"I'm fine!" he grumbled, wiping the blood on his lip with his shirtsleeve. He winced and held his side for a moment.

"Zeke?"

"Just that damned old bullet wound. It never bothers me unless somebody lands into it just right."

She frowned. Apparently some old wounds never really healed. He had been hit by the bullet back on the wagon train years ago, when he had saved her from a band of renegade Crow Indians led by white outlaws. She had taken the bullet out herself, a fifteen-year-old child who knew nothing of such things, because she knew if she didn't remove it he would die. She always wondered if she had done something wrong and that was why to this day the wound sometimes bothered him. He forced a light smile for her and pressed her shoulder.

"I'm all right, Abbie. I'm just sorry—"

"Don't be!" she spoke up quickly. "What do they know about us, about what we've been through and all?

They're ignorant fools!"

He sighed deeply. "Let's go back to the hotel and get cleaned up. I just hope we can get to a place to eat without any more problems."

They started to leave when the Englishman called out to them. "Monroe! Zeke Monroe, I wish to talk to you!"

Zeke turned, having almost forgotten the man. He put out his hand. "I'm sorry, mister. You stuck up for me over there. I should have thanked you."

Sir Tynes shook Zeke's hand and glanced out into the street. Two men were picking up the one man who was still unconscious, while others helped the man Zeke had cut toward the doctor's office. Bystanders grumbled and mumbled as they headed back into saloons and stores.

"Ah, well. You have a lot on your mind, Monroe. I must say, that was a dandy fight! You're marvelous to watch! Marvelous! God, how I love this wild country! And you fit it perfectly!"

Zeke couldn't help but grin, and Abbie smiled. Zeke beat some dust from his hat and put it back on. "So who are you, and why do you want to talk to me?" he asked.

"This here is Sir Edwin Tynes, from England," Hank replied for the man. Buckley stood beside Tynes and pushed his hat back as he nodded to Abbie. "I work for Sir Tynes now, on a big ranch right next to yours, ma'am."

Hank moved his eyes from Abbie to Zeke, whose dark eyes studied Tynes closely, taking in the well-cut clothes and neat appearance. Wealth, education, and power emanated from the man, who, at the moment, was eying Abbie carefully, his look one of utter admiration.

"Next to mine?" Zeke asked pointedly, wanting to

get Sir Tynes's eyes off of Abbie and to direct his attention elsewhere. Jealousy was stirring deep in his soul. Tynes looked up at him then and flashed a quick, handsome smile.

"Yes! I was just talking to Hank this morning about you, Mister Monroe. I own five thousand acres now, and I am told your place is right on my border."

Zeke frowned and put an arm around Abbie, suddenly feeling as though he must protect her against something. "Five thousand acres? All the land around me is reservation land, Sir Tynes."

Tynes paled slightly, unsure of just what might rile this half-savage man. "I am afraid that inside sources tell me it won't be reservation land for long, Mister Monroe." He swallowed. "I am sorry to tell you that, but it's true. The Indians are going to be shipped to Kansas. A treaty is in the making at this very moment. The Cheyenne have simply caused too much chaos in these parts—burned ranches, stolen cattle and horses, stolen women—"

"Not the southern Cheyenne!" Zeke glowered, his temper rising again. "The Comanche and Kiowa and a few northern Cheyenne have caused all the trouble, not my people! And what are they expected to do anyway, when they're shot down in cold blood by soldiers while standing helpless and waving a white flag, like what happened to Lean Bear?"

Tynes smiled a soft, kind smile. "Don't take it all out on me, Mister Monroe. I've had nothing to do with it. I only came out here to buy land and make my fortune in the great American West. If the government is willing to sell me that land, what can I do? I have no say in what has been going on with the Indians."

"Just the presence of people like you, taking over their land, killing off their game, has plenty to do with what goes on with the Indians."

40

"And because of Indian raids along the Overland Stage Route, the whole Platte River road was closed half the summer," Tynes retorted. "I am sure you noticed how high the prices of food climbed during that time, Mister Monroe. Some people in the mountain towns nearly starved to death. Everything had to come by sea to San Francisco and then be shipped overland to Denver. To make matters worse the grasshoppers devoured what crops the people around Denver had grown. It was very bad for them. I know, I lived in Denver this past summer."

"I suppose it's all right, though, for white settlers to starve out the Indians. It's the same thing, Sir Tynes. Wild game is disappearing, and the lands on which they can hunt are shrinking. They attack the supply trains for survival. They're forced into it because their women and children are dying; the government rations don't come half the time, and when they do, they're usually rotten. On top of that, soldiers badger them everyplace they go. Most of the troops out here don't know one Indian from another, so the innocent ones suffer for what the raiding ones do."

"And the price of flour goes up from nine dollars to twenty-five dollars for a hundred pounds," Sir Tynes replied.

Zeke studied the man's fine clothes. "I highly doubt the price of anything troubles you much," he answered. "You foreigners come out here to a country you know nothing about and try to run it! You take advantage of people who have lived here for centuries and—"

"Zeke," Abbie interrupted quietly, putting a hand on his arm. "This isn't the time or place. Sir Tynes just helped convince the sheriff not to haul you off to jail."

Zeke rubbed at his lip again. "I'm sorry, Sir Tynes. You did help me just now, and I owe you for that. But people like you don't know anything about the

41

Indians—nothing about their culture and spirit. I have family among the southern Cheyenne. I have a half brother and a nephew with them and another half brother with the northern tribes."

Tynes's eyes roved over Zeke's amazing physique again. The two men were of equal height, but Zeke's body was much more muscular, although Sir Tynes was a well-built man who had traveled the world and had tried his hand at many things. "So, you're only part Indian?"

"My mother was Cheyenne. My father was from Tennessee. I was born out here but I was raised in Tennessee among whites. When I was old enough I came back out here to find my real mother; then I lived with the Cheyenne."

Tynes nodded, moving his eyes to Abbie again. He was captured by her stunning beauty, and was surprised that she had survived so well in this violent land. His gaze returned to Zeke. "Your wife is a lovely woman, Mister Monroe. And I admire her courage, living out here as she does." He looked back at Abbie again, deep admiration in his eyes. "I don't doubt that I am looking at the kind of woman a man needs in this godforsaken country. You are to be envied, Mister Monroe."

Zeke wasn't certain how to take the compliment. He didn't like smooth, wealthy men admiring his wife. "Thank you," he answered grudgingly. "Abbie is the best. We've been together a lot of years," he added, a ring of possessiveness in his voice.

Abbie blushed lightly and Sir Tynes smiled and folded his arms. "I'm told you're very good with horses, Mister Monroe—that you raise them and are good at doctoring them and so forth."

"Zeke is the best man around with horses," Hank declared. "No one else in the territory raises finer animals."

Sir Tynes grinned and nodded. "Well, it's to be expected. I'm told Indians are marvelous with horses."

"What are you after, Sir Tynes?" Zeke asked, growing impatient.

"Well, since our land adjoins, and since I am told you have . . . uh"—his eyes took in Abbie's small frame again—"that you have several children . . ." He turned to Hank. "Seven did you say?"

Hank nodded and Zeke scowled, a little upset that Hank Buckley had been so free with information about the Monroes. Zeke had known Hank a long time. He was a drifter who hung out at Fort Lyon, doing odd jobs. He was a good man, but shiftless. Now he apparently had hit on a good job, working for Sir Edwin Tynes. The name was beginning to sour in Zeke's mouth. He looked back at the Englishman, who continued talking.

"Well, since you have so many children to support, Mister Monroe, and since your ranch is so much smaller than mine, I thought perhaps you'd be interested in additional work. I am having some very fine thoroughbreds shipped out here from the South. I would enjoy your expertise in caring for them. I could pay you well."

Zeke bristled. His pride had been injured enough today. He didn't like Sir Edwin Tynes offering him work, and he didn't like the way the man looked at Abbie.

"I don't need the work," he answered. "I have enough to do on my own place, and I do just fine with my own herd. I have a white half brother who helps me—Lance. The two of us and my older children and Abbie and I put in a lot of hours. I wouldn't have time to tend to your horses, Sir Tynes."

Tynes's eyes again took inventory of the mass of power that was Zeke Monroe, feeling a jealousy of his own as he tried to imagine how the small, lovely

Abigail lived with such a man. She seemed so happy and contented, and so ready to defend her husband. The man nodded to Zeke.

"So be it. But the job is there, any time you want it. Just come and see me and we'll talk about it."

Zeke nodded, his dark eyes cautious and wary. "I hope you aren't considering trying to get my land, Sir Tynes. Your stay here in Colorado might be cut short."

Tynes chuckled and shook his head. "No, Mister Monroe. I shan't bother your place. I have all the land I want now . . . and in just the right spot. It's a big country, isn't it? An ideal place for adventurers like myself who come here to build empires. You realize, of course, that a railroad will be coming through our land one day. That's part of the reason I bought up what I did. I will make quite a profit selling rights to the railroad, let alone being able to use the railroad to ship my cattle and horses to Denver and Santa Fe. I have no doubt that there will be rails to every major town in the West in the not-too-distant future."

Abbie's eyes widened in alarm. "A railroad! I thought talk of a railroad had died out."

Tynes studied her again, wondering how she would look with fancy curls and with ribbons in her lustrous hair, wearing a low-cut ball gown and a light touch of makeup. She would be ravishing! Even in her plain clothes and hairdo, her beauty could not be hidden. Her skin had a golden glow from the Western sun, and her dark eyes were large and framed with thick lashes. They were true eyes, determined eyes, and he was suddenly overwhelmed with curiosity about her. How had she ended up in this savage land, married to a half-breed Cheyenne?

"Oh, there will most certainly be railroads out here in the next few years," he told her. "That shouldn't upset you." He looked back at Zeke. "You'll probably

44

get rich!" he exclaimed with a smile. "Your property lies right in the heart of a possible railroad line."

"I have no interest in getting rich off the railroad," Zeke answered. "And trains are among the Indians' worst enemies. They frighten away all the game, and they bring in more settlers."

Sir Tynes shook his head. "There's no fighting that, Mister Monroe. Surely you realize that. Colorado is growing, and we can help it grow."

Abbie's temper flared then. "I highly doubt that it is in the interest of helping Colorado grow that men like you come here, Sir Tynes!" she snapped. "It is more likely your pocketbook you wish to grow and prosper, is it not?"

Tynes repressed his anger. Eying her with even deeper admiration, he replied, "I can see you are a woman who speaks freely."

She closed her eyes and sighed. "Forgive me, Sir Tynes, but I have been through things that would shock you, and most of the hardships have been brought on by white men, not Indians. I consider the Cheyenne my friends and family, just as Zeke does, and I have personally seen atrocities committed against them that I never believed civilized men could carry out—all in the name of power and progress."

The man frowned, removing his hat and studying her closely. For some strange reason he suddenly wanted her, wanted to tame her pride and defiance. She was a challenge, and Sir Tynes liked challenges. "I take my hat off to you, Mrs. Monroe." He looked up at Zeke. "And I apologize if I have offended you. It was not my intention. I assure you, you have the wrong impression of me. I am only here for the excitement and adventure. I want to be a part of the things that are sure to take place in this great land of yours and to do my share to aid in its growth. It so happens I find America a

45

wonderful place, and this Colorado Territory is some of the most beautiful country I have ever seen."

"It is," Zeke replied. "I love it too, Sir Tynes. But I love the Cheyenne more, and I hate seeing what white man's progress is doing to them. It was their land first. Do men like you understand that? I don't think so."

Tynes nodded. "Perhaps you're right. Perhaps we can visit more and you can explain it to me." He flashed a smile then, glancing at Abbie again. "You both must come to see me. I am lonely and want to make friends, and I can see that both of you are people worth knowing. Come and see the mansion I am building. It will be fun for you. A castle in the desert, I call it. All stone. That's the coolest building material, you know, for the summer heat of the Plains. When it is finished I shall have a grand party. I will be sure to invite both of you." He looked up at Zeke again. "You have a most beautiful and remarkable wife, Mister Monroe. I must talk to you more, learn about how the two of you got together. I find this entire situation utterly fascinating. I shall have to write home about it. Actually, I am quite pleased to find out that you two are my neighbors. Such a wonderful specimen of man you are, Mister Monroe! You shall have to show me some tricks with a knife! And I'd like to meet all those children of yours. Oh, and I'd like to take a look at the horses you raise. I might buy a few. What do you have available right now?"

"I sold most of what I had available at Fort Lyon this summer. I've got a few geldings and some mares left. Each one has its own worth, according to age, sex, and castration. But they're all quality horses. I have some of the best brood mares and stallions in these parts."

Tynes studied the man, thinking that Zeke Monroe was himself a grand stallion, and his wife a gentle brood mare. "Fine," he told Zeke. "I shall come and see them." He turned to Abbie. "I am honored to have met you, Mrs. Monroe. No doubt it is women like you who create legends in this great West."

Abbie only blushed, and Zeke kept an arm about her waist. "Thank you for your help earlier," he told Tynes, "and for the job offer. I didn't mean to be rude about that, but this hasn't exactly been a good day for me. I'd like to wish you luck with your own place, Sir Tynes, but in my position that's difficult to do. Just don't do anything underhanded to the Cheyenne. Right now, it looks like the government is going to ship them off for you." There was bitterness in his voice.

Sir Tynes nodded. "I'm sorry, Mister Monroe. As I say, we shall have to get together again some time and talk." He turned to Hank. "Shall we go?"

Hank shrugged and glanced at Zeke. "See you around, Zeke. Take care of that family now."

Zeke gave him a cautious look. "I always have," he said defensively.

Hank nodded to Abbie, and then he and Tynes walked toward the grand coach. Zeke turned and took Abbie's arm, saying nothing all the way back to their room. There, he pulled off his jacket and shirt and walked to the washbowl to cleanse his lip. Abbie sat down on the bed where not long before they had made passionate love. There were so many contrasts to Zeke Monroe. One moment he had been gently bedding her, the next he'd been wielding his wicked blade in the street.

"Zeke, are you all right? What about that old bullet wound?"

He wiped his face and shrugged. "Today was nothing. I've been through a hell of a lot worse, and you know it." He put on a clean shirt. "The whole thing makes me mad enough to want to go down there and kill every man on the street! Taxes! Land claims!

Railroads! Insults and injustice! And foreigners, like that Sir Fancy Man, coming over here and forcing themselves on us, pushing out the Indians! It all makes me sick!"

She sighed. "I'll be glad to get home. You're always in a better mood at home."

"That's because I feel free there." He buttoned his shirt and studied her closely. "I think what made me madder than anything else was the way Sir Edwin Tynes looked at you," he grumbled.

She looked up in surprise. "At me?" She laughed. "Don't be silly!" But her smile faded at the possessiveness in his eyes.

"He's infatuated with you. It was obvious."

"Oh, Zeke, I'm sure a man like that has better things to do than to pursue a middle-aged rancher's wife, one who has seven children and wears tunics!"

She rose and walked to the window, and he tucked in his shirt and came to stand beside her, touching her cheek with the back of his hand. "He saw the beauty in you, without the fancy clothes and hairdo, just like I see the beauty in you. Any red-blooded man can see it, Abbie girl. You underestimate yourself."

She laughed lightly. "I couldn't care less what other men think of me. You matter. I simply don't think about anyone else." She turned to meet his eyes, seeing the little boy that sometimes made an appearance in them when Zeke Monroe feared the white world would take his woman from him. She wanted to chide him, but she knew his worry stemmed from her suffering during the years she'd been married to him, despite their deep, abiding love. She had silently endured all hardship, for no man could love her more than Zeke Monroe. Together they had shared the joys and tragedies that create an unbreakable bond between two people.

"Zeke, I am sure Sir Edwin Tynes has all the ruffled, painted women he wants," she said quietly. "He's just trying to make some friends, that's all. I'm not at all sure that I even like him, and I feel uncomfortable that he owns so much land right next to us. But he seems to want to understand, to do things right. And he might be a good resource for selling more horses. We shouldn't judge him too quickly." She smiled. "He's actually quite amusing. He doesn't fit this land at all." She rested her head against his chest. "Not like you fit it."

He grasped her shoulders, pushing her back slightly and looking down into her soft brown eyes. "I love you, Abbie. I'm so goddamned sorry for what happened down there in the street."

"Stop saying you're sorry. They're the ones who should be sorry, not you. What do you have to be sorry for? For all the times you risked your life for me? For all the times you've given me joy in the night? For all the beautiful children your seed created? For our lovely ranch? For giving up your Indian life to settle in one place because you married a white woman? You've made as many sacrifices for me as I have made for you, Zeke Monroe. It's been compromise all along. And we've made them because we love each other. We both knew it that first night we saw each other, when you came to scout for our wagon train. It can't be any other way, Zeke, so we both put up with what comes."

She could feel him trembling. "But . . . someone else . . . could have offered you such a better life, Abbie girl."

"What good would that have been? What good is life without my Zeke? You're so much a part of me that I would not be able to breathe without you. Now let's go eat so we can get to bed early. I want to leave at first light and get home to my children."

49

He bent down to kiss her, a hungry, possessive kiss; and she knew why. She returned it just as possessively, as his strong arms wrapped around her and pressed her tight against his chest. He parted her lips, searching, branding. Then his lips moved to her cheek, her throat. "I need you, Abbie girl," he whispered.

"And I need you." She hugged him tightly. "Oh Zeke, I was so afraid they'd take you away like they did that time in Denver."

He kissed her hair and finally released her. "Well, it's obvious that cities and I do not mix, not that I try to get in trouble."

She sighed and turned to the mirror to repin her hair. "Maybe it will get better, Zeke. There's just so much tension now, so much happening. Colorado is simply growing too fast. And this talk of railroads . . . It's just so overwhelming. Everybody is on edge, and Black Elk and the others are so confused."

He dug for a flannel shirt, unable now to wear his muddied jacket. "Yeah. Well, they're laying low up at Sand Creek for the winter. They figure the less trouble they make, the better off they'll be. My brother is with Black Kettle's band. He should be pretty safe. Black Kettle has that medal President Lincoln gave him, and he flies that big flag over his tipi. But I don't trust Colonel Chivington and his Colorado Volunteers. I've heard Chivington is half crazy. The Cheyenne call him Zetapetazhetan, Big Man, Squaw Killer." He met her eyes. "You know what that means."

Her heart tightened and their eyes held. "I know. And with Wolf's Blood living with them half the time, I worry even more—especially after what happened to Lean Bear."

He came to her and put an arm around her shoulders. "Let's try not to think about it for now. Let's just hurry up and get home."

They left the room, just as Sir Tynes's coach rattled out of town. Unbeknownst to any of them, Colonel John Chivington was that very day marching his Colorado Volunteers through southeast Colorado, with orders to kill any Indians they found. All redmen outside the confines of their reservation were to be considered hostiles.

Chapter Three

The wind howled, ruthlessly stinging their faces with a mixture of sand and a light sleet. Abbie pulled her buffalo robe closer around her face just as Zeke tried to tell her something, but his voice was carried away in the wind. He urged his horse closer to hers then, grasping the throatlatch of her bridle.

"Get on behind me!" he hollered. "My body will shelter you more from the wind!"

"But what about you!" she yelled back.

"You almost died on me last year, Abbie, and I'm not going to risk your getting sick again. Now get on, damn it!"

It was too cold to argue. The short respite from winter that the Plains had enjoyed was over, and their journey was hampered by the cold wind that swept down across the Plains, the barren Colorado Plains that offered no shelter. Abbie dismounted and climbed up behind her husband on the big Appaloosa; then she took the reins of her own horse and they were off again.

She hunkered down behind his broad shoulders, one arm about his waist, grateful for the shelter from the wind but sorry that Zeke had to face it. Still, nothing ever seemed to bother him. She could not remember his being sick, except when he'd been wounded. The elements never seemed to phase him. It was as though he were a rock or a tree. She was glad he had made her bring along her knee-high winter moccasins; the warmth of the buffalo hair was welcome now. She reflected on how ingenious the Indians were at using every last part of the buffalo for survival. However, the buffalo were disappearing. When they were gone, what would the Cheyenne do for warmth and food and shelter?

They rode for several miles, saying little, and she'd almost fallen asleep against his back when he suddenly pulled his horse to a halt. She straightened to look around, thinking they might be near home yet knowing enough time had not passed. Zeke was studying the ground, and she noticed several places had been torn up as though a herd of buffalo had been through. Piles of horse dung were scattered as far as she could see.

"What is it, Zeke?" she asked.

"Stay put," he answered, dismounting.

Her face and chest were suddenly cold when he left her, and she shivered as he walked around for several minutes, stooping down occasionally to look at the tracks. Finally he gazed at the barren horizon, a worried look on his face. Then he mounted up again.

"What's wrong?" she asked, leaning up near his shoulder.

"The way I read it, Army troops have been through here, maybe five or six hundred men, maybe even more."

Abbie's heart pounded with apprehension, and there seemed to be a mournful wailing in the wind. "Are you sure it couldn't be something else?" she asked, knowing this was a foolish question.

"All the horses are shod, and there are wagon tracks besides, some deep and close together, like the kind made by the contraptions that pull mountain howitzers. I don't like it, Abbie. Soon as we get home I'm riding to Fort Lyon to talk to Major Anthony—see what's going on."

"But Black Kettle and his band are at peace. They've been waiting at Sand Creek for Major Anthony to bring them final word on the peace treaty."

"Something's in the wind, Abbie. I can smell it just as sure as I can smell a skunk. After what happened to Lean Bear, how can the soldiers be trusted, especially the Volunteers? They're all Indian haters, mostly rabble—undisciplined men with nothing better to do than kill Indians."

She hugged him tighter, feeling an unexplainable urgency. "Zeke, let's get home. I'm worried about the children."

He nodded. "So am I, especially Wolf's Blood. I hope he has sense enough to stay at the ranch until we get back. He's so infatuated with Morning Bird it would be just like him to go to Black Kettle's camp to see her, even in this weather. It isn't safe for him to be with the Cheyenne right now."

He urged his horse into a moderate gallop. Abbie hung on tightly, not to stay on the horse, but from fear . . . for her children, for her very Indian husband, and for her eldest son.

Finally they crested the low hill that looked down on the ranch. Fear had filled their hearts all day, for the tracks of the large troop of military men had followed the same route Zeke and Abbie were taking. Zeke could see that most of his prized horses were corralled as usual, and in the dim dusk of evening they made out a curl of smoke coming from the chimney. All looked peaceful, but the fact remained that a huge body of troops had gone right through the ranch. They headed down to the cabin, and before they reached it, the door

55

opened and Zeke's half brother Lance stepped out, brandishing a rifle. He lowered it when he realized who was coming.

"Zeke! Thank God you're back," the man called out.

Zeke came closer, dismounting and reaching up to help Abbie down. Her legs were stiff, her knees cold. "Let's get inside," he told her. "Damn it, you're shivering." He looked at Lance. "We followed the tracks of one hell of a big army battallion all the way here," he said, quickly tying the two horses.

"That's why I'm glad you're back, Zeke. They came right through here. Must have been seven hundred of them. They were led by that John Chivington."

Zeke halted his movements at the mention of the name. "Chivington!" he exclaimed.

"Oh, no," Abbie whispered.

Zeke kept an arm around her. "Let's go in," he muttered, helping her up the steps and through the door. The house was warm and welcome, and they were greeted by a barrage of excitement as six children inside surrounded them, helping their mother remove her robe and coat, bringing her over by the fire to warm herself, and all the while talking nonstop about the hundreds of men who had ridden through.

Lance added wood to the fire. Zeke's brother was a welcome addition to the ranch, since Zeke's former hand had been murdered by Winston Garvey's men over a year ago when they had raided the ranch and kidnapped Abbie. Disillusioned by the Civil War, Lance, at thirty-one, had come west six months ago to help Zeke with the ranch. He was dark haired and dark eyed, with a sturdy build, but shorter than Zeke. The white father they both shared was dead now, as was their brother, Lenny, and the old farm in Tennessee had been sold, though it had been run-down by then and worth little.

Zeke fingered the buffalo jawbone handle of his big blade as he paced about, telling the children to quiet down and talk one at a time.

"Father, Wolf's Blood is out there somewhere!" Margaret spoke up first. The second child and eldest daughter, she had always been close to her older brother, often riding with him to visit their Cheyenne relatives. However, she had always been shy and easily frightened, and fear shone in her eyes now as she talked. "Those men were terrible! I know they'll shoot every Indian they see! What if they see Wolf's Blood!"

Zeke still gripped his knife, and Abbie could see his own apprehension building, as well as his determination to protect his son at all costs, for if ever a father had a favorite child, Wolf's Blood was Zeke's. They shared the same spirit of freedom and adventure. Zeke looked at his brother, who rose from the fireplace and stood with his hands on his hips.

"Where's Wolf's Blood?" Zeke asked anxiously.

"The damned kid rode off a couple of days ago, Zeke. You know what he's like. He stays around for just so long, then he gets that itch to feel the wind in his face and he's gone again. He kept talking about that little filly that's got him all glassy-eyed lately. I think he went up to Sand Creek to see her again."

The children all started talking at once and Zeke raised his hand to silence them. "Let Lance tell me," he told them, angry that the Army had ridden through his property as though they owned it. "What's this thing about Chivington and his men?"

Lance shook his head. "They came through here not long after Wolf's Blood left. They're a bad bunch, Zeke. Must have been seven hundred or so, like I said. They aren't even regular army—just a bunch of miners and shiftless outlaws. The worst of the lot, all of them. No uniforms, nothing. And it's a damned good thing I

57

was here because they looked ready to ride off with Margaret just because she looks so Indian—figured her to be my squaw or something. I swear, if there hadn't been a white man in charge here, there would have been trouble. It's probably a damned good thing Wolf's Blood wasn't here. His Indian looks and his temper would have created a problem. That Chivington fella looked right at me with them crazy eyes of his and told me I'd best not be telling anyone I'd seen him and his men or it would go bad for this ranch. He said he was on a secret mission."

Zeke glanced at Abbie, already angry that she had been subjected to the terrible weather just because white men had said they had to file a claim in Pueblo and she had to sign it. Now she had come home to learn that their eldest son could be in danger. He wondered if she was shaking from the cold or from fear for their son—that or the knowledge that he would have to ride to Fort Lyon to see what was going on and perhaps on to Sand Creek to find Wolf's Blood. She hated it when Zeke was gone. But there was no way around it. Zeke looked back at his brother. "What do you think he's up to, Lance?"

Their eyes held.

"I heard some mumbling when they camped here overnight . . . some of the men talking about wanting to find some Indians because they were anxious for some target practice and they wanted to take some scalps for souvenirs. They talked about how much better off Colorado would be when it's rid of its . . . its lice."

Zeke's eyes grew darker then. "I heard talk about this Chivington in Pueblo," he told Lance. "Some say he's crazy. The Indians call him Squaw Killer."

"Zeke, Black Kettle's band is peaceful," Abbie put in hopefully. "They're under Major Anthony's protection. Anthony and everyone around here knows Black Kettle is one of the most peaceful and least trouble-making of the Cheyenne. Surely if Wolf's Blood goes to Sand Creek he won't be in any danger."

"To men like Chivington and the ones with him, an Indian is an Indian. It makes no difference what tribe, no difference how peaceful he's been. To them killing Indians is like stamping out a plague or killing off a nest of rattlers. First thing in the morning I'm heading for Fort Lyon."

"They knocked down the east fence, Father," Margaret spoke up. "I heard one of them say a . . . a half-breed didn't have any right to claim land. They talked about stealing your horses, but then they just rode out."

"Why do they want to go and kill all the Indians, Father?" LeeAnn asked. Zeke glanced at his third child, a blond-haired, blue-eyed beauty that certainly did not look as though she belonged to Zeke Monroe. She had a way of referring to the Indians remotely, as though she had no Indian blood of her own. Already Zeke could see that the girl didn't like having Indian blood. Her blond hair and blue eyes made her feel safer, and she sometimes acted uncomfortable when she went to the fort with her father. It pained his heart that already the girl was half denying her heritage.

"At least you don't look Indian," Margaret muttered to LeeAnn.

"What did you say?" Abbie asked sharply.

Fifteen-year-old Margaret looked at her lap. "You know what I mean, Mother. At least LeeAnn doesn't have to worry about being shot down for nothing. Those men were thinking of shooting me, I know it. If Uncle Lance hadn't been here to convince them I have white blood in me, they would have. They might have done worse things. I saw how they looked at me and it

59

scared me."

"Sons of bitches!" Zeke hissed. Life was hard enough for his children without this. Just the year before Margaret had been attacked by a soldier when a troop of Confederates sent to secure the West had bivouacked at their ranch. Luckily she had not been raped, but the memory of the man's insults still weighed heavily on her young mind and heart. He wondered if she would ever get over the humiliation.

"Don't ever be ashamed of your Indian blood—any of you," Abbie commanded. "It should make you proud and brave. I'll not have any children of Zeke Monroe's blood and my blood be afraid or ashamed!" She scanned all their faces, meanwhile lifting little Jason to her lap and holding him close. "Tell me your Indian names," she told them all.

LeeAnn frowned. "Why do we have to do that?"

"Because I want you always to remember who you are!" Abbie answered. "Because your father is a fine, proud man who loves all of you and who has risked his life for you more than once. Because you were created from his seed and are therefore part Cheyenne. Tell me your names." She looked at Margaret, who blinked back tears of fear.

"I am Moheya, Blue Sky," the girl said quietly.

LeeAnn spoke up grudgingly. "I am Ksee', Young Girl," she said in an almost inaudible voice.

Abbie's eyes moved to Jeremy. "I am Ohkumhkakit, Little Wolf," the eleven-year-old answered. He, too, often spoke of wishing he were not Indian. None of them looked all Indian except Wolf's Blood and Margaret, but Jeremy and LeeAnn had the least Indian features of them all.

Abbie looked then at Ellen, a fine mixture, with dark skin and hair but blue eyes. The nine-year-old girl answered proudly, too young to realize the consequences of being part Indian. "I am Ishiomiists, Rising Sun," she answered in her small voice.

Abbie smiled and looked at Lillian—shy, quiet, pale and thin Lillian, with such mixed features that she seemed to have no features at all, her hair light brown, her eyes light brown, her skin light brown. The girl coughed before answering. "I am Meane-ese, Summer Moon," the girl answered quietly.

Abbie hugged Jason and looked down at him. "And what is your Indian name, Jason?" she asked, giving him a tickle. The boy giggled.

"I am Eoveano," he answered in perfect Cheyenne. "Yellow Hawk."

Abbie smiled and looked at Zeke, determined he should never feel guilty that any of his children or his wife might suffer because of his Indian blood. He looked at her lovingly, but the guilt was still there, mixed with anger and worry.

"And your father is Lone Eagle," she told the children, still looking at Zeke. "A respected warrior among the Cheyenne in spite of his white blood." She looked at Margaret then. "Help me prepare some supper, Margaret. Your father and I have had a long journey and we're hungry. Zeke should eat as soon as he can. He'll want to start for Fort Lyon early."

The girl nodded. "Don't get up, Mother. I can do it all myself. You must be tired."

Abbie leaned back and patted Jason's bottom. "I am. Thank you, Margaret. Jeremy, you go out and get more wood, and, LeeAnn, you help Margaret. The rest of you go into the spare room and play some games or something. I'm just glad to be home and to know you're all right."

Margaret looked at her father. "What about Wolf's Blood?" she asked. "I'm afraid for my brother. Sometimes he's wild and foolish like some of the other young Cheyenne boys. It would be just like him to ride right up to those men and taunt them."

Zeke sighed. "I know, Margaret. I'll do my best to find him."

"You're the only one he listens to, Father. Make him come back home."

"I'll try."

The girl moved around the table and pulled a gunnysack of potatoes from under the cupboard. Zeke met Abbie's eyes, and it was all said in that one look. "I'll go tend to the horses," he told her.

Little was said the rest of the evening, and soon all were bedded down for the night. Abbie wanted desperately to reach out to her husband, to hold him and be held by him, but he stayed up long after she had gone to their bedroom and crawled into the bed of robes on which they slept. He sat by the fire smoking a pipe, thinking, planning. She knew Wolf's Blood was heavy on his mind. The boy was Zeke Monroe's whole world, their only child totally proud to be Cheyenne, the only one who had been half raised by the Cheyenne, taught the Indian ways by his Uncle and Zeke's half brother, Swift Arrow, who now rode with the Sioux in the North. Zeke had just two full-blooded Indian brothers left, borne by Zeke's Cheyenne mother, who had married a Cheyenne man after Zeke's white father had deserted her and gone back to Tennessee. Swift Arrow was the most warlike. He was a Dog Soldier and had married but once, only to lose his woman to a white man's disease. That had been many years ago, and the continued settlement of Indian lands by whites had fanned the man's bitterness over his wife and son's deaths to all-out hatred. Now he stayed in the north with the war-making Sioux, participating in raids and killings. The second brother, Black Elk, was peace-loving, and dwelt among the southern Cheyenne with Black Kettle's band, now camped at Sand Creek. A third brother, Red Eagle, had succumbed to the evils of whiskey, had sold his wife, and then killed himself.

Abbie gave up trying to stay awake until her husband came to bed, but deep in the night she was awakened by a gentle hand rubbing over her hips and soft, warm kisses to her throat. She stirred, moving onto her back, only to have his lips cover her mouth hungrily while one hand pushed up her flannel gown. Then his lips moved to her throat again.

"I'm sorry to wake you, Abbie girl," he whispered. But she knew he wasn't, nor was she, for he had never left her without making love to her on their last night together. There was too much danger in this land, the risk of his not returning was too great. How she hated to have him go away when Indian killers were roaming the land!

"Zeke, I'm afraid for you—afraid for Wolf's Blood," she whispered. But her fear only seemed to enhance their lovemaking, for she returned his kisses with possessive passion. He opened her gown and pulled one side down to expose a breast. His long hair was unbraided and fell across her bared skin as her powerful savage moved over her almost desperately, as though this might be the last time they shared their lovemaking. He pushed her gown to her waist and moved on top of her, his hard manliness pressing against her belly almost painfully, needing relief. Always when he sensed imminent danger his love-making was more forceful. There was a light scent of whiskey on his breath, and although he seldom drank, she knew he had done so this night because of his worry over his precious son.

He pushed inside her then, with a shuddering groan,

63

and she was lost beneath him as he took her almost desperately due to the worry and the agony of having to leave her. Her nails dug into his upper arms as she forced herself to remain quiet, and her breathing came in deep gasps. At times she whispered his name in exhaled breaths. She could not help but cry out lightly at the last almost vicious thrust, and then he went limp, pulling away as she rubbed at her stomach.

He sighed deeply, pulling her into his arms and kissing her hair. "Damn it, I hurt you," he groaned. "I'm sorry, Abbie girl. Sometimes I get so damned angry I take it out on you in the night."

"It's all right, Zeke."

"No it isn't!"

"You're just worried about Wolf's Blood." She snuggled into his shoulder. "You must get some sleep, Zeke. You have a long day ahead of you. I know you. You'll ride all day and all night and half the next day to get to the fort faster than it usually takes."

He kissed her hair again. "You're right there." He ran a hand over her belly himself, gently massaging it. "You okay?"

"I am when you touch me that way," she answered. She moved to kiss his scarred cheek, grateful that he had left the lantern dimly lit. "Bring our son back, Zeke."

He met her eyes. "You know I will."

When Zeke reached Fort Lyon he was immediately alarmed at the absence of a good share of the troops. An uneasy silence hung over the fort, and a hawk called out a lonely cry as Zeke rode through the gates of the fort. Only a skeletal garrison was left, Zeke noticed as he rode to the supply post and dismounted. He went inside and greeted the trusted white trader, John Wilkens, who looked up from an inventory sheet as Zeke entered. Wilkens immediately put down his quill pen and extended a hand to Zeke.

"I was wondering when you might show up, Zeke," he said.

Zeke shook his hand. "What's going on, John? Where are all the troops?"

Wilkens sighed. "They've gone to Sand Creek, Zeke. I think that Chivington fella intends to wipe out every Cheyenne and Arapaho—every Indian there."

Zeke's blood ran cold. "You sure?"

The man let go of his hand and nodded. "Afraid so. Chivington was here just two days ago. It was a real surprise to Major Anthony. You know the major has been workin' real hard on a peace settlement with Black Kettle's band because they've made no trouble. Chivington came riding in here like he owned the place, said as how he was on his way to Sand Creek to kill every Cheyenne in sight. There was a big argument between him and Anthony. I mean to tell you, it was one hell of a fight. But Chivington won. That man has been given almost total authority over Colorado, Zeke. And he's an Indian hater. He must have had seven or eight hundred men with him—all worthless rabble just itching for a slaughter. Chivington ordered Anthony to join him, so they're about a thousand strong now, all well armed. They even have mountain howitzers with them, and he forced poor young Robert Bent to go along as a guide. It will be bad for the Cheyenne, Zeke. They must have already got there by now."

Zeke's jaws flexed in anger. "Have you seen Wolf's Blood, John?"

The man's eyes saddened. "He out makin' hay again?"

65

Zeke couldn't help but grin a little. "I'm afraid so." He sobered again. "The worst part is he's got a yen for a little Cheyenne girl. I'm afraid he might have gone to Sand Creek."

The man frowned. "Then you'd best get up there. Ain't nothin' but bad times comin' for them people. Orders are to kill all Indians, take no prisoners. Them words is right out of Chivington's mouth."

Zeke gripped his knife. "I'd like to get my hands on the bastard!"

"You'd have to go through about a thousand men to do it."

Zeke's eyes glittered with hopeless rage. "Thanks for the information, John. I'd best head out right away."

The man nodded. "Good luck, Zeke. I hope you find your son okay."

Zeke hurried out. He didn't care what the orders were regarding Indians. He'd worn his buckskins and left his hair loose, decorating it with ornaments. He always felt happiest when he rode as an Indian, using no saddle, only a blanket over a rawhide seat stuffed with buffalo hair. He wore a buffalo coat and winter moccasins. His soul was Indian, and he had prayed to the spirits that morning for his son's safety and his own.

"Help me, Maheyo," he prayed now as he eased himself up onto his Appaloosa with a young man's agility. He headed out of the fort at a fast gallop.

There was no sound but the howling wind as Zeke's mount moved silently through the deep snow toward the edge of the bank that looked down on the Cheyenne village below. Zeke was already alarmed because he had seen no smoke. Any village in the dead of winter would put out smoke from the warming fires of every

66

tipi, and there should be at least a hundred lodges at Sand Creek. When he'd climbed the bank, his chest filled with pain at the sight below.

"Ihaveseva!" he gasped. "Wolf's Blood! Nahahan!"

He could only pray that Wolf's Blood was not among the bodies that lay strewn and mutilated throughout the now-burned village below. There were too many to count. As he rode forward, shuddering with fear that Wolf's Blood's corpse would be among them, his eyes filled with tears at the horrible sight. This had been the most peaceful band of Cheyenne. They had been waiting faithfully beside the creek for instructions from Major Anthony. From the looks of the half-naked bodies, they had been attacked at dawn, before they had a chance to dress.

He dismounted as he rode closer, knowing he must perform the gut-wrenching chore of inspecting each body to see if Wolf's Blood or his brother Black Elk and his family might be among them. He looked down into the faces of women and small children, noting the huge gashes on their limbs and chests. He groaned at the sight of women's bellies riped open, their female organs removed. Some children were dismembered, and some lay naked, sprawled where they had run with little feet to get away from the huge men thundering down on them atop big horses, men wielding sabers and guns. Parts of bodies were still inside the remains of tipis that had been hit by howitzer shells.

Zeke could scarcely believe his eyes. He spotted a huge, battered flag lying next to one tipi. "Black Kettle's," he muttered. The banner lay wrinkled and matted on the frozen ground. The flag had been presented to Black Kettle by President Lincoln himself. The Indian leader had trusted the white man's promises. Had Black Kettle escaped? Zeke walked among the frozen bodies that lay in grotesque positions, stuck to the ground by their own frozen blood. He walked along the creek, where it was obvious some of the Indians had run for shelter. Everywhere around the camp he saw signs of shod horses. The village had apparently been totally surrounded. Bodies were strewn in the creek. Apparently soldiers had lined up on both sides of it to kill off the fleeing victims as though they were merely rooting out a pack of wolves. Many women and children lay in the creek bed, some women hunched over their children as though to protect them. Never had he seen anything like it, not even in the Civil War.

Then he noticed a familiar red headband. With pounding heart, he approached the body, then threw his head back and emitted a long cry of sorrow. It was his brother, Black Elk. Nearby lay his wife, Blue Bird Woman and their son, Bucking Horse. How they had prized their seven-year-old son, for he was the only child Blue Bird Woman had been able to have. Now they were dead! All dead!

Zeke fell to his knees and grabbed up the stiff, frozen body of his brother, holding the man and rocking him. Then he gently laid him back down, again crying out, angrily this time, and pounding his fists into the cold snow and cursing John Chivington, the white settlers, progress. Was this then the price of settling the West? He pushed up his coat sleeve and angrily removed his knife from its sheath. Quickly, he cut a long gash into his arm in his sorrow, letting the blood flow onto his brother's body. He knew he would have to bury them, even if it took all day to break open the frozen earth enough to do so. Then he would have to keep looking for Wolf's Blood. He screamed out to Maheo, begging his God that he would not find his son among these bodies; then he hunched over and wept as he had never wept before. It was not just for his brother that he cried, but for the entire Cheyenne nation.

"Wolf's Blood," he groaned. "Where are you, my son!"

His only reply was the moaning wind. Already the blood that had dripped onto Black Elk was frozen, and snow had drifted across the dead man's face.

Chapter Four

It took hours to dig a hole deep enough to hold Black Elk, his wife, and child. Zeke wished he could bury them all, wished he could erect proper platforms for a proper Cheyenne burial, but there was not enough material and not enough time. He had to find Wolf's Blood. At first he suppressed the fear that the boy would be among the bodies scattered about. He didn't want to think he could be there. He wanted to delay finding his son as long as possible if Wolf's Blood was among them.

The wind howled at his back as he covered the bodies of his brother and sister-in-law and nephew. But his own numbness was from grief rather than the cold. He threw down the small spade he had salvaged from what was left of the village; then he began the grim process of looking at all the bodies. He wanted to throw up and wondered why he didn't. The bodies were those of the very old, of women and of small children—the weakest ones who could not escape fast enough and who could not defend themselves.

The horror of what was happening to his people engulfed him. Nearly all the bodies had been mutilated, before or after death he would never know. Many

71

were scalped. He recognized some of them: Cheyenne friends he had known for years, some old ones who had known his own mother. How grateful he was now for her own early death. She could not see what was happening now, could not know that one of her sons had shot himself after selling his wife for whiskey, that another lay dead and mutilated along with his wife and son, and that still another rode in the north, making war with white settlers. His mother's name, Gentle Woman, had truly fit her. How heartbroken she would be to see this!

He was startled to see that one of the bodies was that of old White Antelope, an aged and peaceful chief who had been to Washington just the year before to meet President Lincoln. One old woman he found was totally scalped, her face covered with blood. That could only mean she had been scalped while still alive, otherwise the blood would not have run over her face. His head pounded with the reality of it. Surely then, others had been mutilated while still alive. His eyes teared so that he could barely see as he stumbled about amid the bodies, afraid, so afraid one of them would be Wolf's Blood.

To his relief he did not find the boy or the young girl Morning Bird of whom Wolf's Blood was so fond. Zeke found his way back to his mount, glad Abbie was not with him. This would have been too much for her, and too much for any of the children to see. If this indicated how much Indians were hated, what lay ahead for his own children? He climbed wearily onto his Appaloosa and looked around the camp again. The bodies were strewn about for over two miles, and he had walked the entire area looking for Wolf's Blood. He had noticed faint tracks that continued into the distance from the creek bed. Apparently a few had survived and had gotten away.

72

There was only one direction in which they could go, to the headwaters of the Smoky Hill River, where many more Cheyenne were camped. That was a good fifty miles away, and most of them were probably on foot. If the soldiers overtook them, there would be no hope for them. And even if they didn't, how could these Cheyenne survive when most of them were half naked in the winter cold.

He took one last look around the village before leaving. "Fools!" he growled. "They think this will end the Indian fighting. But after this it will be worse than ever! There will be no hope for peace now!"

It seemed he could hear cries of death and pain in the wind. The People lay dead on the ground, and soon their bones would be one with the earth, as they had been even in life. Perhaps the bodies were dead, but their spirits were not dead, nor would they ever be. They would go on forever, blooming with the prairie flowers, falling in the spring rains to greet the buried bones. These Indians would speak forever, perhaps not in voices, but in other ways.

He headed at a near gallop toward the Smoky Hill, hoping he would not run into John Chivington and his Third Colorado Cavalry, the "Denver Roughs" as they were sometimes called, one hundred-day volunteers who joined up just for the fun.

Abbie raised the old Spencer that was once her father's and took aim. The big buck stood as though in a trance, looking straight at her. In these days of scarce game, one did not pass up such precious meat, and although she had only been walking and had not planned on hunting, the good fortune of coming on the mule deer could not be passed up. The gun she had brought along for protection would now be used to

73

keep food on the table.

She squeezed the trigger and fired. The deer slumped down, then tried to rise. It struggled to its feet and, while Abbie quickly reloaded, ran for several yards before it fell again. Abbie hurried to where it lay. The animal did not stir. Blood covered the white hairs of its chest. Abbie sighed and stooped down, petting the deer's neck.

"There was a time, long ago, when I was too soft-hearted to shoot something like you," she said aloud to the animal. "But out here we have to be practical, as Zeke would say. According to his beliefs animals were put here by his God to feed his children, yet we are all one in spirit. So I'll do what Zeke would do and say thank you, deer spirit."

She rose and looked back toward the cabin. It was much too far away for her to drag the animal, but she could see Lance already running toward her and she could make out a rifle in his hand. He had heard the shot and probably had thought she was in trouble. He had argued with her about going out alone, but she had needed to get away, to pray for Zeke and Wolf's Blood, to remember the good times and to try to keep her sanity until Zeke returned.

"Halloo!" someone called to her from the ridge behind her. She turned, rifle ready, only to see a man riding down toward her on a grand black stallion. He was sporting the best of riding clothes and a warm, tweed coat.

"Sir Tynes," she muttered to herself. She was suddenly aware of her appearance. She looked all Indian. Her hair was braided down her back, and she wore winter moccasins, a long tunic, and a heavy elkskin robe. The man came closer and smiled.

"By God, it is you! I wasn't sure. I don't believe it! You shot that deer yourself, Mrs. Monroe! What a woman!"

She blushed slightly and pushed back a piece of hair that hung loose on her forehead. "It was nothing, Sir Tynes. Just a few more meals on the table."

"Nothing!" He laughed and dismounted, stooping down to look at the dead animal. "Where did you learn to shoot like that?" He glanced at her rifle. "And with such a relic! What is that, an old Spencer?"

She cradled the gun in the crook of her arm. "It was my father's. I kept it after he died coming west. As far as how I learned to shoot, I've been using this gun for twenty years, Sir Tynes. Out here a woman has to know how to use a gun. I killed two Crow Indians with this gun when I was only fifteen."

Lance came closer, panting from running. He looked warily at the fancy man with the fancy horse. "Abbie, you okay?"

Abbie smiled at him. "Yes. The gunshot was mine. I killed us a few meals, Lance."

Lance trudged his stocky, muscular body over to the deer. Bending down and looking at it closely, he laughed lightly. "By God, you sure did! You're something, Abbie. Wait till Zeke hears about this one. He'll tease the hell out of you for the way you carry on, feeling sorry for every dead animal he brings home."

She smiled softly. "I know. But as he says, we must be practical." Lance met her eyes, and their thoughts were the same.

"He'll be okay, Abbie."

She nodded, pressing her lips together to keep from crying.

"Why, where is your husband, Mrs. Monroe?" Sir Tynes asked. "I've come to see him, look at his horses."

Lance stood up, several black curls of his thick hair sticking out from beneath his beaver hat. "Who the hell are you?"

75

"Lance, this is Sir Edwin Tynes, from England, the man we told you about meeting in Pueblo."

Lance looked the man over, almost wanting to laugh at the man's perfect horse and gear and clothing. He nodded then. "I'm Lance Monroe."

"Ah, yes! Zeke's white brother." The man put out his hand and Lance shook it, surprised at the strong handshake. "I am glad to meet you, Mister Monroe." He turned to Abbie. "And you, madam, would do well on one of my African hunting expeditions. How exciting it would be to have a woman like you along when hunting big game like lions and tigers!"

She laughed lightly. "I only know about lions and tigers from reading books to my children, Sir Tynes. And I have no interest in the place called Africa. Colorado is wild and dangerous enough for me, thank you." She turned to Lance. "Can you go get a horse and come back and get the deer, Lance? I'll help you clean it if you'll get him strung up for me."

"Sure, Abbie." He turned and headed back toward the cabin, and Abbie looked up at Sir Tynes.

"Would you like some tea or coffee, Sir Tynes?" she asked. "Our cabin is quite small and humble, but it's warm."

"I'd be delighted!" he replied, tipping his hat. He took his horse by the reins and walked beside her through the deep snow. How utterly different and delightful she was! A survivor in the greatest sense! He liked women like Abigail Monroe, wondered what it took to master such a woman. But he had only to picture the man Zeke to know that, a man sure and strong and rugged. But then wasn't he also all of those things, with the additional attribute of being rich? He smiled at the contrasts fate could provide. There she was, walking beside him in common Indian clothing, her hair plain and braided; yet he could visualize her

76

walking gracefully in a full ball gown, her breasts billowing above its low bodice, her dark hair cascading in curls, her large dark eyes and lashes accented with just a hint of color, her full, sensuous mouth enhanced with lip rouge. Abigail Monroe knew not her own beauty, and apparently she did not care about it. That made her even more attractive.

"Your husband has a fine-looking ranch here, Mrs. Monroe," he declared.

"We built it up ourselves," she answered. "We started with just a few horses and set up house in a tipi on the bank of the river. It took a while to get the cabin built; we had so many other problems. Then the children kept coming, one after another, and after the cabin was built it soon became apparent we needed even more room, so we added an extra room, and it still seems crowded."

He thought it no wonder that the children had come one after another. Zeke Monroe seemed to be the type of man who would be as active in bed as he was out of it, and who wouldn't be, with such a woman in his arms at night?

They reached the cabin, and when they went inside, to his surprise six children sat around a large table in the main room, all with books in front of them, all obviously well disciplined, for they had apparently been sitting there while their mother was gone. An older girl, very dark and beautiful, very "Indian," looked up at her mother.

"Uncle Lance said you shot a deer, Mother!" the girl exclaimed. The other five children all looked at Abbie and Sir Tynes then, and the littlest one clapped his hands.

"Mamma got a deer!" he exclaimed. "Can I go with Uncle Lance to get it, Mamma?"

Abbie smiled and set her gun in the corner. "I

77

suppose, but first I want you to meet someone."

They all stared at Sir Tynes as Abbie removed her outer garments. "This is Sir Edwin Tynes, from England," she told them. "He owns a very big ranch next to ours." She looked up at Tynes. "This is their reading time. All of my children can read and write very well, Sir Tynes. I have educated them myself. The only one who can't read well is Wolf's Blood." Her face fell at the mention of her eldest son's name. "He's always been the untamable one. Zeke is out looking for him now. The boy rode to the Cheyenne camp at Sand Creek and we heard soldiers might be preparing to attack it. We're worried about him."

Tynes frowned. "I'm sorry." Then he brightened. "But please introduce me to each child. They're lovely, so well mannered. You're a wonder, Mrs. Monroe."

Margaret frowned. She didn't like the way this fancy, apparently rich man looked at her mother. Abbie smiled proudly and named each child seated around the table: Margaret, LeeAnn, Jeremy, Ellen, Lillian, and Jason. Jason jumped up then, and pulling on a pair of winter moccasins and a little deerskin jacket his mother had made for him, he ran out the door to chase down his Uncle Lance. Abbie offered Sir Tynes a chair, and the man sat down, feeling suddenly awkward as the rest of the children stared at him curiously.

"Margaret, please get the tin of tea," Abbie told her daughter. She herself took down a porcelain cup and draped gauze over it. She held it as Margaret opened the tin of tea and spooned some onto the gauze. Then the girl went to the hearth, where a kettle of water was always warming. The girl picked up the kettle after wrapping a rag around the handle to keep from burning her hand. She brought the water to her mother, slowly pouring it through the tea and gauze.

"This is the best I can do, Sir Tynes," Abbie was explaining. "It will keep the tea grounds from swimming in your cup. Do you take cream? We have a little cow's milk."

"Yes, I would like that, but you mustn't fuss, Mrs. Monroe." He studied the firm roundess of her hips beneath the common tunic, the luster to her thick, braided hair. Lovemaking must be very rich and rewarding with such a woman, he thought.

"It's no bother," she replied, her back to him. "But we don't drink much tea around here. I hope this is fresh enough for you. We drink mostly coffee or plain hot water."

Sir Tynes looked away quickly when Margaret gave him a dark look for staring at her mother. The man looked at the rest of the children and smiled. They all smiled back.

"Where is England?" Ellen asked.

"Oh, it's very far from here, clear across the Atlantic Ocean," he replied.

"Don't you miss it?" Jeremy asked.

"Oh, quite often."

"Why did you come here?" Margaret asked almost accusingly.

Abbie set the cup of tea in front of him and handed him a spoon to stir it with.

"Well, now, young lady, I happen to be the adventurous sort, you see. I've been everywhere, done just about everything. So I thought I'd try this wonderful American West I have heard so much about. I have five thousand acres north and west of you, and I'm building a mansion there. I thought it might be amusing to have an English mansion sitting in the middle of the Colorado Plains, and it will make me feel more at home. When it is finished, I shall have all of you come to a grand dinner and show you around."

The other children's eyes lit up, but Margaret just scowled and went into the other room. Abbie sat down then, pushing at the stray wisp of hair and feeling strangely uncomfortable under his gaze. "I am sure we don't have the proper clothing for such an affair, Sir Tynes. Besides, we really wouldn't be interested in such things. We are plenty busy right here."

"Nonsense. You don't need any special clothing. You're a beautiful woman and your children are beautiful. Just dress as you always do. It would be quite fun, really."

"Mother," Jeremy put in, "I've never seen an English mansion. We could go, couldn't we?"

She gave him a warning look. "I highly doubt it, Jeremy. We have more important things to worry about at the moment than whether we should go to a time-wasting dinner party. God only knows what has happened to your brother and father. Now take your books, all of you, and go to the loft and finish at least one more chapter. I'll be asking each of you questions, so don't try to cheat."

Jeremy sighed with disappointment and scowled at her; then he took his book and climbed the ladder to the loft. The other four followed but Margaret stayed in the other room, listening attentively to the conversation.

"You have a lovely family, Mrs. Monroe," Tynes was telling her. "I am very impressed. I didn't mean to speak so lightly when you have so much to be worried about."

Abbie sighed. "And I didn't mean to be rude. Your offer is very kind. Perhaps by then things will be back to normal, but right now Zeke is out looking for our eldest son, and a huge army of Colorado Volunteers is scouring the countryside looking for Indians to kill." She rose and walked to the hearth, taking a pot of coffee from it and pouring some into a tin cup for herself.

"Tell me about yourself, Mrs. Monroe. How did you end up out here?"

She walked to a back window to look out, hoping to see Zeke coming. "My father brought us out, after my mother died back in Tennessee," she said quietly, almost as though speaking just to herself. "There was my father, my older sister, and my little brother. When we reached Independence, a man came to offer his services as a scout for our wagon train. His name was Zeke, Cheyenne Zeke he was called by most. And the minute he stepped into the light of our fire, I was in love." She turned to look at Tynes then, her cheeks flushing. Sir Tynes felt a pang of jealousy at seeing the expression on her face. She looked like a young girl talking of her first love. "At any rate, we had various tragedies along the way, and I lost my family. It just seemed that it was supposed to happen that way, that I was supposed to be left alone, supposed to end up with Zeke." She sat down again. "He fought it, but I made it known how I felt about him. He was afraid because I'm white. He had already married a white girl when he was very young, back in Tennessee. She and their little son were murdered by white men who were angry that she had married a half-breed. Zeke hunted them down and killed them all; then he fled out here to search for his real mother. He was a wanted man for a long time back in Tennessee, but that's been long forgotten now, at least by others. Not by Zeke. He'll never forget it." She ran her fingers around the edge of her cup. "But I helped him forget a little. Then, when I was wounded by a Crow arrow, Zeke saved my life. After that, it just seemed natural that we should get married." She met Sir Tynes's eyes. "So we did, and I came to Colorado with him to meet the only family he had then—the

81

Cheyenne. I lived with them for a while, in a tipi, all of it. It was wonderful. Those were good times, happy times, days of freedom for the Cheyenne." She blinked back tears. "But it isn't like that anymore."

She sipped some of her coffee, and he stirred his tea. "So, you are both from Tennessee?" he asked.

"Yes, but I never knew Zeke then. And we no longer feel any attachment to Tennessee. Colorado is our home now, and the Cheyenne are our friends and family." She pulled her braid around over her shoulder and fingered it nervously. "Zeke's white father returned to Tennessee after Zeke was born, taking Zeke with him. He married a white woman and they had three sons, so Zeke had three white half brothers. One was killed in the Civil War. Then there is Lance, whom you have met. The other was also in the war but he's probably back up north by now, at Fort Laramie or thereabouts. He was going to rejoin the Western Army. He had served in the Dakotas for a long time before the war broke out, then he fought on the Confederate side and was wounded. If Zeke hadn't gone east to find him, he might be dead now."

Sir Tynes wondered about the rumor Hank Buckley had told him, that while Zeke was searching for his brother Abigail Monroe had been taken by outlaws and later rescued by her husband. It was said she'd been raped and tortured, for what reason no one knew. But those who knew about her abduction were all certain of one thing: whoever had manhandled Zeke Monroe's wife must have suffered terribly. Sir Tynes didn't doubt that. But he would not ask her about the affair. It was too personal. Still, he admired the woman's obvious courage and stamina.

"His name is Dan," she was telling him. "He resembles Zeke in build, but he certainly doesn't look like him in any other way," she said with a smile. "Dan

82

has very blond hair and very blue eyes, like his white mother. He's a wonderful man with a lovely wife and daughter."

She sipped her coffee again.

"And Zeke has full-blood Indian brothers?" Sir Tynes asked.

She nodded. "One is dead now. Another, Black Elk, lives among Black Kettle's band. I'm worried about him too. He is at Sand Creek. The other brother is Swift Arrow. He's very warlike, lives in the north with the Sioux."

Tynes smiled softly. "What an interesting family you have, Mrs. Monroe. I feel very lucky to have you for neighbors, especially upon hearing how good your husband is with horses. I'll be getting those thorough-breds soon. If he won't work for me, I do hope he will at least come to my aid if I have a problem with any of them."

She tossed the braid back behind her. "I am sure he would help if you needed it, Sir Tynes. He might appear savage and ruthless to you, but I know another side of him. He's a very good man, a very loyal husband and father. It is only his enemies who know another side of him, so I would suggest you don't do anything to make him your enemy."

There was a warning look in her eyes, and Margaret caught the inflection in her mother's voice and smiled. She had nothing to worry about from the fancy Sir Tynes. Tynes himself studied Abbie's dark eyes and felt a chill at the thought of Zeke Monroe having it in for him. Certainly if Monroe were aware the Englishman had an interest in his wife, that would be more than enough reason for the man to use the big blade on him. Still, that made the challenge presented here even more tempting. He finished his tea and rose.

"I thank you for the tea and hospitality, Mrs.

Monroe. Your cabin is charming, your children lovely. You are an admirable woman." He bowed slightly. "By the way, I have a bolt of cloth I brought along, something I was going to use for curtains but I changed my mind. I don't suppose you might have any use for it?"

She raised her chin slightly. "Not if it is in the form of charity or bribery, Sir Tynes. I don't need either one."

"On the contrary, it is neither. I simply—"

"I don't need your gifts, Sir Tynes," she said quickly. She frowned. "If it is simply friendship you want, if you are lonely," she added, "then we are here, and we can help you with any problems you have with your horses. But you must be honest with us, Sir Tynes. Zeke will know if you're being honest, and you will know it if he thinks otherwise. I hate to keep sounding so rude, but it is men of wealth, like yourself, who have given us the most trouble and who pose the biggest threat to Indians. We find it difficult to trust such men."

The man smiled nervously. "Well, you do have a way of putting things openly, Mrs. Monroe. I assure you I am an honest man. I have no connections with the wealthy political machinery of Colorado. I am simply here because it is exciting and beautiful. Since my wife died fifteen years ago, I have done nothing but travel and try new things." His eyes saddened. "Perhaps, I suppose, to help me forget."

She nodded. "I'm sorry about your wife. And I am sorry that things have happened to us—to me—that come through rather bitterly at times. I would show you some horses, since that is why you came here, but I have no idea which ones Zeke would be willing to sell, so you'll just have to come back after he is home. I can send Lance for you if you like."

Her full breasts looked soft beneath the tunic. How he wanted her! But such a woman was impossible to have. "Yes. I would like that. And thank you again for the tea."

He put on his hat and went to the door, and she followed him. When they went outside, Lance was approaching, dragging the deer. "Get a couple of knives, Abbie, and we'll have this thing carved up in no time."

She smiled. "I'll get them and put my coat on. It's too bad Zeke isn't here. He'd have that thing opened up and sliced into steaks in one quarter the time it would take both of us."

Lance laughed, and Sir Tynes felt a chill at the stories he had heard about Zeke Monroe and his knife. If he was going to be interested in any man's wife, he had certainly picked the wrong one. He nodded a good-bye to Abbie and mounted his horse, turning and riding away while Lance threw a rope over a clothesline crossbar and pulled until the deer hung by its front hooves. He counted ten points on the sprawling antlers and grinned at the thought of Abbie showing Zeke the rack as proof of her catch.

Abbie closed the door and went to get her buckskin jacket, glad for the diversions that Sir Tynes and the deer had brought to her day. They had helped her to forget her increasing worry over Zeke and Wolf's Blood. She touched a jacket that hung on the wall hook next to hers; then she buried her face in the thick sheepskin lining, breathing in her husband's scent.

"Zeke," she whispered. "Please be all right."

When Zeke rode into the camp along the Smoky Hill, his heart was torn by the weeping and wailing that could be heard throughout the village. Even some men were crying, a sight seldom seen among Indians. But the losses had been too great: wives, husbands, sons, daughters, grandmothers, grandfathers, aunts, uncles, nephews. The slaughter had been sudden, uncalled for, and had left the survivors in shock. Some now sat around campfires warming frostbitten toes and fingers.

Zeke rode up to Blue Bear, an old man who had been a friend of his mother's. The old man had tears on his face and rubbed at a shoulder that was caked with dried blood.

"Zeke!" the old man said in a weak voice. "Our . . . village . . . the soldiers came—"

"I know," Zeke said quickly. "Have you seen Wolf's Blood?"

The man shook his head. "Some survivors . . . are still coming in. I saw . . . your son once . . . before the attack . . . saw him fighting some of them off to protect Morning Bird . . . saw them push a saber . . . through the girl. Then I got hit. I don't know what happened then. We all . . . fled. Those of us who . . . got away . . . spent the night on the open plains . . . with hardly any clothing and the wind biting into our skin. Many more . . . died." The old man coughed.

"Wolf's Blood!" Zeke repeated. "I didn't find him at the scene of the massacre, Blue Bear. Are you sure you haven't seen him?"

"I . . . don't know. You'll have to . . . search the village. I was in much pain. I didn't pay much attention. Some of the others . . . who managed to get right away on horses . . . they came here and gave the alarm. Our Cheyenne and Arapaho friends here . . . rode back to look for survivors . . . brought clothing, food, and extra horses. If they had not come, we would all have died . . . out there in that awful wind. Some may still die . . . others will lose their feet and hands to the cold. Perhaps your son . . . is among the survivors. I do not know. You will . . . have to search."

Zeke patted the man's shoulder. "Can I do anything

for you, Blue Bear?"

The old man touched his hand. "Not now. I have what I need. Go and look . . . for your son."

Zeke sighed and rose. It seemed everyplace he walked there was weeping and groaning. Some sat with gashed chests and arms, letting blood in mourning for lost loved ones. He knew most of them, had once ridden with some of them on buffalo hunts and even on raids against their enemy the Pawnee, Crow, and Utes. But that time seemed long ago.

He searched throughout the camp until he found one old woman who nodded and pointed when he asked about his son. Zeke's heart pounded when she pointed to two bodies lying near a fire and wrapped in blankets. He forced his legs to move, afraid of what he would find. When he came closer, he knew it was his son.

"Wolf's Blood!" he groaned, kneeling down to touch the young man's shoulder. The boy lay with his arm around a girl, whose back was to him. The boy turned his head slightly at the sound of his name and opened bloodshot eyes to look up at Zeke.

"Father!" he whispered. "How . . . did you find me!"

"I heard about Chivington and those bastard volunteers out hunting for Indians. I was worried about you."

"Father, they attacked us. It was . . . terrible."

"I know. I've been to Sand Creek. Are you hurt, son?"

The boy's forehead and hair were soaked with perspiration in spite of the cold. "Morning Bird. She is hurt. Help her first, Father. I tried to stop them . . . from hurting her . . . but there were so many!"

"Be still, son." He reached over to touch Morning Bird's forehead, then felt the chill of sorrow sweep through him. He knew immediately she was already dead, probably had been for quite some time. Perhaps

87

Wolf's Blood knew also but didn't want to face it. Zeke sighed and gently pulled the boy's arm from around her body. "She's dead, Wolf's Blood."

The boy's eyes widened and he put the arm back. "No. She is not dead! She is not dead!"

"Yes, she is. Calm down, Wolf's Blood. Let me tend to your wounds."

"No! I love her. I am going to marry Morning Bird!"

Zeke's eyes teared. "I'm sorry, son. The girl is dead. I'll bury her for you just as soon as I tend to you."

A shuddering sob exited his son's lips and ripped at Zeke's heart. "Why?" he groaned. "Why did they . . . do that? They rode right down on her . . . for no reason! They pushed a big sword right through her—and laughed!" The boy rolled back to his side and put his arm around the girl again. "Why did they do that?"

Zeke rubbed at his eyes. "Who can explain it, son? Please let me help you."

The boy's shoulders shook in great sobs, and Zeke gently pulled him away. He helped the boy to his feet, unable to carry him because at seventeen Wolf's Blood was just as big as his father, only slightly more slender. He was a handsome, powerfully built young man, and just as Abbie had said, Zeke wondered himself if this son of his had ever been a child.

He led the boy to a tipi, sitting him down beside it and lifting the entrance flap to look inside. Two wounded women lay there, along with four wounded children, all tended by an old woman and a middle-aged warrior. Zeke asked in the Cheyenne tongue if he might come inside and share the warmth of the tipi so he could nurse his wounded son. Sad eyes greeted him in reply as the pair nodded their approval, and Zeke half dragged and half carried Wolf's Blood inside, laying him down on a buffalo robe offered by one of the others.

Zeke's chest tightened when he saw the blood stains on the front of Wolf's Blood's sheepskin jacket. The boy had apparently been sleeping at the time of the raid, for beneath the jacket that had been loaned to him by the rescuing Cheyenne, he wore only leggings. His chest was bare of clothing, and blood was clotted thickly on his belly. It would be difficult to find and treat the wound, since it was already a couple of days old.

"Wolf's Blood, was this caused by a gunshot or saber? And is this your only wound?"

"Bayonet," the boy moaned. Then he began crying again. "Morning Bird! She was so . . . innocent!" He gritted his teeth in anger and pain. "I will kill them! I will kill them all! I will go north and make war with my uncle, Swift Arrow! There shall be . . . no peace for the . . . soldiers . . . or the white settlers!"

Zeke did not advise him otherwise. How could he do so at this moment, when the boy was so full of sorrow? If he were in the boy's place, he would be saying the same things.

"I'll have to clean out this wound somehow, Wolf's Blood. It will be painful."

"I . . . don't care! I want to feel pain!" The boy wept. "They . . . killed her! They killed . . . so many! So many! We were all sleeping . . . doing nothing wrong!"

"I know, Wolf's Blood. This will leave a stain on the hands of Colorado politicians and peacekeepers for a long time to come, perhaps forever."

"And it will bring more war!" Wolf's Blood growled. "They will see! They will . . . regret that they . . . deceived us! They told Black Kettle . . . to wait there and remain peaceful. Then they came . . . and slaughtered us!"

"What about Black Kettle? Is he still alive?"

"He is . . . somewhere in the camp. He is alive . . .

but his wife is badly wounded. She fell . . . while she was running. Black Kettle . . . thought she was dead . . . so he kept running. Then soldiers came . . . and while she was lying helpless . . . they put many bullets into her and rode on. Black Kettle . . . went back . . . found her still alive . . . brought her with him . . . carried her on his back."

Zeke fought his own rage. It would do no good at this moment. He had to help his son. "Try to relax, Wolf's Blood. I know it's hard. And I'm damned sorry about Morning Bird. You're young, Wolf's Blood. You will find another."

"Never! I want no other! How did you feel . . . after those white men killed your first woman . . . back in that place called Tennessee!" the boy sobbed. "You wanted . . . to kill! You did kill . . . all of them! It is the same . . . for me!"

Zeke closed his eyes and nodded. He would never forget the horror, nor his own need for revenge. "I know, son," he said sadly. He started to rise to get his parfleche which contained the items necessary to treat the wound, but Wolf's Blood grasped his wrist.

"Father, the one who stabbed me . . . as I fought those who rode down on Morning Bird . . . I recognized him."

Zeke frowned. "Who?"

"I looked deep into his eyes . . . as he pushed the bayonet at me. He could not push it deep enough . . . to kill me. I shoved my lance deep into his thigh. He was not . . . at a good angle. I was on foot. He was on horseback . . . but I managed . . . to get my lance into him. He is . . . badly wounded . . . I am sure. If he lives . . . he will be crippled."

"Who was it, Wolf's Blood? You said you recognized him. Someone from the fort?"

"It was that same boy . . . the one I fought back in

90

Denver a long time ago . . . the one whose father we killed for hurting my mother."

"Garvey's son? Charles Garvey?"

"*Ai.* The same one. He must . . . hate Indians as his father hated them. He rides . . . with Chivington. And I could see him killing them . . . great joy on his wicked face."

Zeke's own eyes glowered with hatred. How well he knew Charles Garvey! The day Zeke had gone to the Garvey mansion years ago to rescue his own sister-in-law from Winston Garvey's clutches, the younger Garvey had kicked at him and cursed him, spouting all kinds of obscenities against Indians even at a very young age. Now the boy had grown up to ride with the Colorado Volunteers. The father was dead, at Zeke's own hands. But what of the son? He was as bad as the father. Zeke wondered what Charles Garvey would think if he knew he had a half brother with Cheyenne blood in him, if he knew that his own father had slept with an Indian woman who had borne him a son, a crippled boy who now lived with their missionary friends in the north. Zeke would love to see the look on Charles Garvey's face if he knew, but he didn't dare let him find out, for Charles Garvey would try to find his half brother and have him murdered. Abbie had suffered greatly to keep that information from Winston Garvey, and now that he was dead, the secret must die with him. Zeke looked down at Wolf's Blood.

"You say you wounded him badly?"

The boy grinned wickedly. "I buried my lance deep into his thigh. I heard the bone snap. It was a good sound!"

Zeke smiled himself. "Maybe he'll die," he answered.

"I hope he does!" Wolf's Blood sneered. "And I hope he suffers greatly first!"

Zeke shared the same hope, even though Charles

Garvey was not much older than his own son. The boy was evil and the world was better off without him. Zeke laid a robe over his son to keep him warm until he would be able to wash the wound.

"Where's your wolf?" Zeke asked his son, referring to the pet wolf the boy had raised from a cub.

Wolf's Blood's eyes teared more. "I think he is dead. I am not sure. I saw him leaping at a soldier, who shot at him. I saw him fall, but then I had to help Morning Bird. After that I could not find Wolf." That was all the boy called the animal, simply Wolf.

Zeke sighed and put a hand to the boy's face. "He probably went off to die someplace."

A tear slipped down the side of the boy's face and trickled into his ear. He pressed his lips tight and did not reply. Zeke squeezed the boy's shoulder in a reassuring gesture. "I'm going outside to get some supplies to treat your wound."

Zeke rose and went to get his parfleche. So, Charles Garvey rode with the Volunteers. It was no great surprise. The boy's father had come west years ago, first setting up an empire in Santa Fe, then moving to Denver when the gold strikes there presented a need for saloons and businesses. The man had been a senator in Washington, D.C., and he had gotten involved in politics in Colorado. But he'd met his end at Zeke Monroe's hands, a terrible end that no one but Zeke and Wolf's Blood knew about. However, he had left a son who had been reared to hate Indians and to do whatever it might take to rid the territory of them because they stood in the way of progress and riches.

Zeke went back inside to find Wolf's Blood crying. That tore at his guts, for Wolf's Blood was proud and brave and would never let anyone see him cry. But the girl Morning Bird had meant very much to him, and he had seen horrors that he would never forget. Zeke sat

92

down beside his son and pulled him into his arms, holding him tightly, not knowing what else to do to comfort him. The two were close, always had been, and now Zeke could feel his son's great anguish. He would not tell the boy yet that his uncle Black Elk was dead. The sad news could wait, although the boy must already suspect it to be so.

And even as they sat there together, Chivington and his Colorado Volunteers headed for Denver, searching for Indians to kill along the way, disappointed that they found no others. Soon they would be in Denver, and when they arrived they would be greeted by cheers for the "brave soldiers" who had daringly attacked the "savage Indians" and won a "great victory." They would be paraded down the street to the accompaniment of shouts of praise and admiration, and some of them would carry Indian scalps with them as they accepted the gratitude of the settlers who would now be "safe" from warring red men. But no act could have done more to increase raiding than the unwarranted butchery at Sand Creek.

Before long, stories would begin to filter in about what had really happened there, but the damage was already done. There was no changing it. And in those moments Zeke wanted only to comfort his son, to save the boy's life, and to get back home to Abbie.

been pushed over those same fields and jerked to their knees and beaten and what he had found out had been devastating. The Cheyenne village at Sand Creek had been attacked by Colonel John Chivington. That was all they knew. There had been no word from Zeke or from their son, and their imaginations ran rampant. Didn't they know the awful outcome of the battle — how many had been killed, how many had suffered? Had Zeke been there when it happened, or had he arrived later? And Wolf's Blood — would he too turn a boy to man through the ugly bloodshed that was the soldier's way with his Indian. And there were

Chapter Five

Abbie pulled her robe closer and walked behind the cabin, brushing snow from the wooden planks that covered her outdoor vegetable bin. She pulled up one board and set it aside, then reached down inside the hole where potatoes and carrots were kept beneath the earth to preserve them yet keep them from freezing. She felt through the straw and took out some potatoes and a few carrots, putting them into a burlap bag. Snow stung her face. It was warmer in the vegetable pit, but cool enough to keep the food fresh. She pulled out some more carrots, holding one to her nose and smelling the sweet odor of fresh earth. Its scent made her long for spring and warmth.

That thought brought memories of the past summer, when the family was reunited after her terrible ordeal at the hands of Winston Garvey. It had been a time for quiet loving and for being together, a time for her and Zeke to pick up the pieces of their lives and to find one another again, in body and in spirit.

A harsh gust of wind brought her back to reality, and she tied the bag and placed the board back over the vegetable pit. She shivered, wondering where Zeke and Wolf's Blood were now and if they were alive. Zeke had been gone over three weeks. She had sent Lance to Fort Lyon for news, and what he had found out had been devastating. The Cheyenne village at Sand Creek had been attacked by Colonel John Chivington. That was all they knew. There had been no word from Zeke or from their son, and most people around Fort Lyon didn't even know the actual outcome of the battle—how many had been killed, how many had survived. Had Zeke been there when it had happened or had he arrived later? And what about Wolf's Blood? He was not a boy to run. He would fight back if attacked. That was the hell of it. So would his father. And there were others she worried about: Zeke's brother, Black Elk, and his family; and an old and dear friend, Tall Grass Woman, who had befriended Abbie years earlier when she came to live among the Cheyenne with her new husband.

She had spent many sleepless nights, and her eyes burned from being so tired. She had prayed so hard she was sure God must be tired of listening. When she managed to nod off, she always awoke with a start, and her anxiety for her husband and son would overwhelm her, plunging her into a painful depression, especially in the wee hours of the morning. Where were they? Were they hurt? Were they warm enough? She refused to believe they were dead. She dared not let herself believe it or she would lose her mind and be useless to the rest of her children. Her emotions were still too tender. She hadn't recovered from her own ordeal. It was hard enough just to sleep alone, to be unable to turn to Zeke when the terrifying nightmares woke her, but at least if she continued to believe he would be back, she could bear it.

She rose, holding the bag of vegetables in one hand, and pulling the hood of her heavy robe tighter under her chin with the other, she started back around the house to go inside when she saw the movement—a small, dark figure against the bright white of the snow on the distant hill. It was some kind of animal, too small to be a deer, too big to be a skunk or fox or any of the smaller animals found around the ranch. It kept coming, and she kept staring, squinting her eyes against the blinding whiteness. It moved slowly but deliberately toward the house, and her heart pounded harder when it came even closer.

"Wolf!" she whispered. She scanned the horizon desperately. It was her son's pet, she was sure of it. Wolves traveled in packs, and seldom ever came this close to the house and barns. This one was alone and seemed to know exactly where he was going. Surely if Wolf was coming, his master would not be far behind, but there was no sign of Wolf's Blood or of Zeke.

She hurried to the house and set the sack of vegetables on the table; then she ran back outside. Some of the children bounded out behind her, having noticed the concerned look on her face when she came in and hurried out again.

"What's wrong, Mother?" Margaret asked.

"Wolf is coming," Abbie replied, going down the steps. "Get back inside and wait where it's warm. And if Wolf comes into the cabin, don't go near him. You know how unpredictable he can be. I don't want the little ones to try to touch him."

Margaret herded the others back inside, her own heart racing. She all but worshiped her older brother. Why was his pet wolf here without Wolf's Blood? Was her brother dead? She fought tears of fear while Abbie ran to the barn calling for Lance. Her brother-in-law came out, young Jeremy at his side and holding a pail of milk.

"I think Wolf is coming," Abbie said. She looked at Jeremy. "Get to the house with the milk, Jeremy," she told the boy. He hurried to do as she bid, milk splashing from the pail. Jeremy was afraid of his big brother's "wild animal" pet.

Lance took Abbie's arm and they walked to the corner of the house. Wolf was closer now, obviously limping. They stood very still as the silver gray animal stopped and stared at them with steely black eyes. He growled at first, then slunk closer, sniffing Abbie's winter moccasins. There was dried blood on his left hip, and Abbie wondered if there was a bullet in the animal or if the wound was from a saber. She would probably never know, for she was not about to approach him to find out. Wolf was touchy even when healthy, but in his wounded state it could be dangerous to try to handle him. He had never harmed anyone in the family. He seemed to understand that they were to be trusted because they were people his master loved, but only Wolf's Blood could actually hold and pet the animal. Now that Wolf was wounded, he would be more distrustful.

"Lance, why is he here alone like this?" Abbie asked, clinging to his arm.

"Hard to say. Just stay back from him, Abbie."

The animal left her and hobbled up the steps to the door of the cabin, scratching on it. Abbie hurried up behind him and carefully pushed open the door. "All of you children stay back," she called out. As the wolf entered the cabin, followed by Abbie and Lance, the room was silent. All the children stared at their brother's pet while the animal casually walked to the wood-burning potbelly stove that heated the cabin and lay down in front of it. His black eyes looked up at the children, scanning them carefully before closing.

"Mother, why is he here without Wolf's Blood?" Margaret asked.

None of them wanted to think the worst, so Abbie

suddenly gave them a reassuring smile.

"As far as I am concerned, this can only mean that your brother is alive," she told them.

"But Wolf's Blood isn't with him," Lillian spoke up, her thin, pale face looking sad.

"Exactly," Abbie answered, going to the table and dumping out the potatoes and carrots. "We already know something terrible happened at Sand Creek. Wolf is wounded. Somehow he and Wolf's Blood must have got separated. If your brother was dead, Wolf would never have left the boy's side. He would have stayed beside the boy; even if it were buried he would stay by the grave. Your brother must have escaped somehow. Wolf probably went off to tend to his wounds, as wild animals often do. He has come here now to wait for your brother."

"Are you sure, Mother?" Margaret asked.

Abbie glanced at Lance, warning him to go along with her. She buried her own panic at the real reason the animal might have come home. She would not let herself believe it.

"Of course I'm sure," she answered, pouring some water from a bucket into a shallow pan. "Now come and help me wash the potatoes, Margaret. From now on we will fix a fine supper every night. We can't be sure just when your father and brother might show up, but there is no doubt they'll be looking forward to a good hot meal when they get here."

She turned and set the bucket of water back on the counter, biting her lip and breathing deeply to keep from breaking down in front of them.

Dan Monroe looked up from his desk when the door to his office opened letting in the noises of the parade grounds outside. With Indian hostilities increasing daily in Nebraska territory and the nearby Dakotas, Fort Laramie was bustling with soldiers, government agents, scouts, and Indians. Dan was grateful for being assigned to the place where he'd served in the Army for so many years before the Civil War. That war still raged in the East, but he no longer wanted to be a part of it.

A woman entered, her soft blond hair shielded from the strong prairie wind by a shawl, her blue eyes smiling at him as she closed the door and came inside. The years had not detracted from her gentle beauty, but she looked tired.

"Bonnie!" he exclaimed, rising from his chair. He walked slowly around the desk, his severe war wounds still not totally healed. "How long have you been here?"

"About five months," she replied, coming closer and taking his hands. "How are you doing, Dan? I was so worried after Zeke left to take you back home to your father's farm in Tennessee. You really weren't healed enough yet, but Zeke was so anxious to get back home to Abbie . . ."

"Apparently I'll live," the man told her, leading her to a chair. "Thanks to the skills of you and your father. Is he here, too?"

"Father stayed behind. There's still a war going on, you know, and plenty of wounded men need attention." She sat down and removed her shawl, studying Dan as he walked, with some difficulty, back to his desk. How much he resembled his half brother, Zeke! He had the same height, the broad stature, yet he was so unlike Zeke in coloring. He had thick blond hair and handsome blue eyes.

Zeke . . . Occasionally she allowed herself to think about him, when she dared risk acknowledging her secret needs and emotions. It had been eleven years since he'd rescued her from the horrible men who had

100

intended to sell her in Mexico—eleven years since she'd first set eyes on his masculinity and had been awakened to true desire for a man, eleven years since she'd quietly and secretly fallen in love with Zeke Monroe. But there was only one woman for Zeke, his Abbie. Bonnie had known from the beginning that her rescue had been a simple act of chivalry on the part of Zeke. She knew her love was unrequited, so she had returned to her missionary work after Zeke had saved her. That had been in New Mexico. Since then she had married a missionary, a preacher—a marriage that had been expected of her, one with cool love and almost no passion. They had come north to Fort Laramie to doctor and teach among the settlers and Indians, and later Bonnie had agreed to take in Zeke Monroe's crippled nephew, little Crooked Foot, now called Joshua, the half-breed son born of Zeke's now-dead sister-in-law and the hated Winston Garvey.

"And how is your husband faring?" Dan was asking her. "Still on the preaching circuit?"

Her face saddened. "Rodney was killed by Sioux Indians ten months ago, Dan. I didn't know myself until I came back."

Dan frowned. "I'm damned sorry. I just got here a few days ago, Bonnie. I didn't know."

She smiled softly. "Of course you didn't." She sighed. "I guess I almost expected it. I wanted him to come East with me and father and Joshua, but he said he would stay and tend to the spiritual needs of the people here while I went East and tended to the physical needs of the wounded soldiers. With all the raids and uprisings, I wasn't totally surprised Rodney died at the hands of Indians." She looked at her lap and toyed with her shawl. "Rodney was a good man, brave in his own way, but he could be very stubborn. I pleaded with him several times to stay close to the fort, yet he insisted on completing his circuit and visiting the settlers no matter what. He was a very passive man and would not have fought back when attacked. I can only hope he didn't suffer too terribly, still I can't fully blame the Sioux for what they're doing. They've simply been driven beyond the point of reason." She met his eyes again. "If the government doesn't start treating the Indians fairly, things will just get worse. I will continue to teach the peaceful ones what I can, and I'm staying right here in spite of the danger. I feel safe here at the fort."

Dan studied her pleasant form, still firm although she was in her mid-thirties. He knew little about Bonnie Lewis, except that Zeke had once saved her from outlaws and that several years later she and her preacher husband had taken in the half-breed boy fathered by Winston Garvey. During the Civil War, Bonnie and her father had set up a clinic back East to doctor wounded soldiers, and it was there Zeke had taken Dan after he had been wounded at Shiloh. There, too, Dan had determined that Bonnie was secretly in love with Zeke. While Zeke had waited for Dan to recover from his wounds, Dan had noticed how Bonnie watched his half brother, a look of near worship in her eyes. Dan knew Zeke would never return Bonnie's love, but he couldn't help but wonder about her inner torture.

"I suppose you think I'm terrible for not blaming the Indians for Rodney's death," she was telling him.

Dan took a pipe from his drawer and began stuffing it. "Not at all. I've seen what the Indians can do to their enemies, yet I don't blame them for calling us their enemy, Bonnie. That's partly why I rejoined the Western Army, to help see that they get a fair deal, at least within the extent of my power."

She watched him light the pipe. "I was so surprised

when I heard you were here, Dan," she told him. "What happened after Zeke left to take you to Tennessee and the old farm? I thought you would stay there."

He puffed the pipe quietly for a moment. "Well, to make a long story short, Pa was killed. Zeke, of course, had no intention of staying at the farm, and my younger brother, Lance, he'd been wounded in the war too, and had lost his enthusiasm. Zeke left right away, and once I was healed, Lance left too. Said he was going to Colorado to help Zeke on his ranch. That was about six months ago. Far as I know, that's where he is right now. Me . . . I sold the farm and left too. With our older brother dead, there wasn't much point in staying around. I'd lived out here in the West for so long that I was used to Army life and I didn't feel like I belonged in Tennessee anymore. The only bad part is after stopping in St. Louis to be with my wife and little girl, I couldn't convince Emily to return to the West with me. She's always been afraid of this place, afraid of the Indians. And with everything that's going on right now I suppose she is safer where she is. She has her father's big, rambling home to live in, and she and my little Jennifer are comfortable and happy there."

She saw the sadness in his eyes. "You miss them terribly."

He puffed his pipe and nodded. "The ironic thing is that Emily traveled all the way to Zeke's ranch to plead with him to come and find me after she'd learned I'd been wounded at Shiloh. Zeke went through hell to do it, and now she won't come west to be with me."

Bonnie sensed the bitterness in his voice. "I'm sorry, Dan. Perhaps when things calm down she'll come."

Dan studied the blue curl of smoke from his pipe. His marriage had always been fragile. He'd fallen in love hard and fast, to a frail child who was exquisitely beautiful but inept. Afraid of hardship, Emily was

103

unwilling to brave the challenges of the West to be with her soldier husband. She seemed afraid of everything, even of sex. Dan had managed to break through that barrier somewhat, but that part of their marriage had never been truly fulfilling, for Emily had never been able to give herself to him with total abandon. He often wondered if she preferred to stay in St. Louis because doing so meant she could avoid sex. It shortened their time together. It angered him, for he had never been anything but careful and gentle with her, and he was certainly not unpleasant to look at.

"Perhaps," he now said in response to Bonnie's suggestion that Emily might come west. His eyes scanned her lovely form again. Bonnie Lewis was a fine specimen of womanhood, and if her own marriage had been less than satisfactory, it could only have been Rodney Lewis' fault. Bonnie Lewis was a warm, strong, giving woman, the kind of woman Dan would have married if he'd not been so struck by Emily's enticing beauty. Dan didn't know much about Bonnie's personal life, but the few times he had met Rodney Lewis he'd sensed a coldness about the man that did not match Bonnie's warmth. He guessed that Bonnie was not suffering long-term grief over the loss of her husband, that she might miss him for the good and dedicated man he was but not for any loss of friendship or affection.

"You shouldn' be out here all alone, Bonnie," he told her.

She shrugged. "I'm surrounded by soldiers, and I have the children of the fort families to teach, as well as a few Indians. And Joshua is with me, of course."

Dan leaned forward, his elbows on the desk. "How is the boy?"

"He's doing fine," she replied, her face lighting up. "He walks almost normally since the last operation, but he'll always wear the brace of course."

"Zeke would be real happy about that. You should take the boy down to see Zeke and Abbie sometime and let them see how he's doing."

She blushed at the mention of Zeke's name and looked at her lap again. "I . . . don't think so. It would be too dangerous a trip, and besides, it might endanger the boy if the wrong people discovered his identity. It's best we all remain far apart."

"You're probably right," Dan answered. "Have you heard from Zeke?"

She swallowed. "No. I doubt he knows either one of us is back yet."

"Well then, do me a favor, will you? Write Zeke and Abbie a letter and tell them everything that has happened. They would want to know. And tell them I'm here at Fort Laramie again. I'm so busy I don't have time for a letter, and I'm not much good at that sort of thing anyway. Ask Abbie to write back, will you? I want to know everything that has happened over the past twenty months or so since I first joined the damned Confederate Army." He puffed the pipe again. "Pardon my language, Bonnie, but I sometimes wish I hadn't let my Tennessee pride get in the way of wise thinking. I know now there is no way the South is going to win the war, and a divided country is useless. After Shiloh I lost all my enthusiasm and Southern pride. I just wanted to live and get back out here to the country I've learned to love. I can see why Zeke never returned home after coming out here." He chuckled then. "Of course, being a wanted man in Tennessee had a little to do with his decision at the time."

Bonnie laughed lightly herself then and their eyes held. She suddenly realized how handsome Dan Monroe was, and she thought Emily a fool. Fate was often cruel, bringing people together who did not belong together, keeping people apart who would make perfect partners—except for Zeke and Abbie. How many people experienced that kind of love? How she envied Abbie! But she loved the woman, nonetheless, because Zeke loved her. And she loved the boy Joshua because he was kin to Zeke. Seeing Dan Monroe was stirring deeply sleeping emotions in Bonnie's soul, for there was so much about him that was like Zeke: his stature, his voice, the way he smiled. Both men had inherited these traits from their white father. But their coloring on the outside and their deeper beliefs on the inside were miles apart, for Zeke Monroe was much more Cheyenne than white. He often participated in Cheyenne rituals, he practiced the Cheyenne religion, and he was much more prone to violence. At times only revenge could soothe his rage. Still, Dan was as much a man, more reserved only because of his gentler white upbringing. Back in Tennessee, Dan had never known the cruel rejection and abuse Zeke had suffered for being an Indian in a white man's world, but he had seen how Zeke had suffered and he'd sympathized with him. The two had been close brothers when Zeke had lived in Tennessee. Indeed when Dan had joined the Western Army at a very young age, he had intended to find his Indian brother who had fled west never to return to his home. Dan's search had led him into the Mexican War, during which an act of valor had earned him a rapid promotion to lieutenant before he'd left to join the Confederates.

"So, you're wearing a blue uniform again—and you're a lieutenant again," Bonnie said pleasantly.

Dan grinned. "Thanks to the Indians. If the Sioux weren't so belligerent, I wouldn't be sitting here now. But men with experience are needed out here, and I've got that experience—with Indians, that is. So, my 'sins' were forgiven and I was given a second chance, so to speak. But it will be rough for a while. Most of the men here are Northerners, and that war is going to leave very hard feelings for a very long time. I'm hoping the men out here can stop thinking North and South and just think West. The problems out here are a whole different matter."

"I hope you aren't expected to go out on patrols right away. You're still much too weak, Dan."

He laid his pipe in a metal ashtray. "Thank you for your concern, Nurse Lewis," he said with a wink. "No, I won't be going out of the fort for a while."

She smiled and rose. "I'm just glad Zeke found our clinic and we were the ones able to help you, Dan. That was a very bad wound, and I'm surprised to see you looking as good as you do. If you need anything, let me know. Are you in pain?"

He rose himself and made his way around the desk. "Sometimes. I am tempted to consume a little whiskey to help, but I had a small problem with that stuff a few years back when Emily and I weren't—" He stopped and ran a hand through his hair, looking a little embarrassed. "At any rate, I try to stay away from whiskey," he finished, "especially if I'm upset over Emily. I need her right now and she's not here."

Bonnie walked closer, putting a hand on his arm. "I can get you medicine for the pain, Dan. And you be sure to tell me if there is anything else I can do, or if you think something isn't healing properly. Remember that I can be a very good friend."

Their eyes held again, saying everything while their mouths said nothing. They were both starved for love and affection, yet each was bound by social etiquette not to display such feelings. She was a widow and a missionary; he was a married man. He turned away then, walking back behind his desk.

"I'm . . . glad you're back here, Bonnie," he told her, affecting a smile. "Will you write that letter for me?"

She smiled back, but there were tears in her eyes. "Of course."

"And thank you for your offer, Bonnie. If the pain gets too bad I'll be sure to come and see you."

"Good." She put the shawl back over her hair. "We're in the little cabin next to the church school. And if and when I get word back from Zeke, I'll let you know the latest."

He nodded. Their eyes held for another moment, then she turned and hurried through the door. Dan sat down wearily. Although he had little time for letters as he had told Bonnie, there was one letter he knew he must write—to Emily, pleading with her to come to Fort Laramie.

Crowds thronged the streets of Denver, cheering the Third Regiment of Colorado Volunteers who paraded through the streets. Some sported Indian scalps dangling from poles. Others displayed more hideous items, pieces of flesh that the crowd did not even recognize. Had they, they would have realized that some of the "brave" Third Regiment were dangling the reproductive organs of Indian women and that some of those stalwart men secretly carrying other parts of Indian bodies, parts that they had deftly removed from old men and women and children: ears, breasts, noses, genitals. Some of the men also carried valuable jewelry, all of it taken from the dead bodies of peaceful Cheyenne Indians, some of the rings procured only after cutting off fingers to get to them.

But these were surely brave and skilled men, daring men who deserved the glory the citizens of Denver now gave them. The *Rocky Mountain News* had already

108

reported the Sand Creek "battle" as a brilliant feat of arms in Indian warfare, yet at the sight of the massacre the dead bodies lay silent, some already ravaged by wolves.

One woman stood watching the parade, secretly sympathizing with the Indians and wondering what had really happened at Sand Creek. She dared not voice her doubts, for she feared the frenzied crowd would probably beat her to a pulp. But she didn't like John Chivington after listening to him make a public speech two days earlier. The man had arrived in Denver well ahead of his troops to report the event, and he'd been basking in boastful glory ever since. But he was such an obvious Indian hater the woman found it amazing that people swallowed the man's story word for word.

"I'd love to know what Zeke thinks of this," she thought, turning to go back inside her boardinghouse. She closed the door against the noise outside and breathed deeply, her heart aching as it always did when she thought about Zeke. If it were not for Zeke, she would never have given up her lucrative saloon and house of prostitution to try to make something decent out of what was left of her life. She was still beautiful, her hair still thick and black, her eyes still a vivid blue, with only a few lines at the corners. But the way she dressed now and the way she wore her hair and left the paint off her face, few would suspect she was once the notorious Anna Gale. Her life had been wicked and selfish, her goal money. Her poor and terrifying childhood as an orphan in the East had made her hard and grasping. It was Winston Garvey who had set her up out West and who had kept her indebted to him and under his thumb for many unhappy years. Anna Gale had been a callous woman who'd cooperated with Winston Garvey's scheming to the fullest because she'd wanted all the money she could get her hands on.

Now she was rich, and with Winston Garvey dead, she was free of his command, free to do something different with her life. After all her years of prostitution she had not really intended to change her way of living . . . not until she'd met Zeke. Somehow his approval was important to her, even though she could never have the man, even though she might never see him again. To hope he might ever reenter her life was futile, for he had his Abbie. How Anna wished she could have been like Abigail Monroe. But Anna's life had been destined to be hell ever since she'd been raped as an orphaned child. Only her envy of the kind of woman Abigail was and the fact that she was rid of Winston Garvey moved her to finally sell her saloon and quit prostitution. She liked having the boarding-house. It was a respectable business, and it kept her quite busy. Indeed, with Denver growing so fast, it was even a lucrative endeavor.

But she was lonely. What else could she expect after leading the kind of life she had led? No decent man would have her. It had taken her months to begin to win just a little friendship from some of the more reputable women in town, but the extent of her social life was a few short visits over the fence. It was a far cry from the wild, noisy saloon life, but it felt good— except for the loneliness. Yet even at the height of her barroom life she had been lonely, so it made little difference.

She picked up the day's paper and scanned the headlines.

"CHARLES GARVEY, SON OF WINSTON GARVEY, WOUNDED AT SAND CREEK," the headline read. Anna smiled. "Well, well. So the little bugger got what he had coming." She was glad he'd been wounded. "If we're all lucky, he'll die and we'll be rid of the Garveys once and for all," she added

110

to herself.

She felt a momentary disturbance at the thought that Zeke Monroe had killed the boy's father. Anna suspected that Zeke had killed Winston Garvey. The man's body had never been found. That would be like Zeke. Perhaps the body wasn't even all in one piece. That would also be like Zeke. Anna had known that it was Garvey who had kidnapped Abigail Monroe, and it was Anna who told Zeke the best time to attack the Garvey ranch so he could get his hands on Winston Garvey without being found out. She would never tell the law what she knew because she loved Zeke Monroe, and because she detested Winston Garvey and was glad he was dead.

She read the article about Garvey's son, Charles, an Indian hater and a powerful young man who had his father's money to back him up. It was certain the boy would do all he could to destroy the Indians.

She sat down at the dining-room table and read quietly on, while the cheering continued outside. So, Charles Garvey had been severely wounded in the thigh. It had been feared that his leg would have to be removed, but it was now believed that would not be necessary. However, the man would be crippled for the rest of his life.

"Wonderful!" Anna hissed. "Good for the Cheyenne!"

That thought reawakened the memory of the first time she had seen Zeke Monroe, years ago, when he had come to her saloon down in Santa Fe in search of his sister-in-law who had been taken by outlaws to be sold into prostitution. Anna had given Zeke the information he'd needed. She'd told him the girl was the slave of Winston Garvey, but she had not given him that information without demanding a high price first . . . a night with the handsome, powerful Zeke

Monroe in her bed. He paid the price coldly, almost viciously, wanting nothing more than to get it over with and find his sister-in-law. He'd paid with his body because he'd had no choice, for Anna Gale had been well guarded and he'd been in a civilized town where he would have been promptly hung had he hurt her. But Anna had known by the look in the man's eyes that if he'd had her alone he would have cut her to pieces to get the information. Out of pure necessity, he'd kept his part of the bargain, hatred in his dark eyes the whole time. The odd part, and the part that still hurt her and made her hate herself, was learning that later Zeke had cut off part of a little finger, as a Cheyenne sacrifice for doing something against his will and beliefs—for betraying his beloved Abbie.

Anna sighed as she walked to a window to peek out at the scrubby, worthless-looking bunch of men that called themselves brave soldiers. None of them could hold a candle to Zeke Monroe. She actually chuckled to herself at the thought of any man cutting off a finger for being untrue to her. She had had so many men in her life she had lost count long ago.

No. Women like Anna Gale did not find men who cared like that. Only women like Abigail enjoyed that kind of love. She swallowed back the lump in her throat, suddenly worried about what had really happened at Sand Creek. Zeke often lived among his people. His oldest son's nature was all Indian. Had they been involved in the massacre? She decided she would hire a man to go to Fort Lyon and quietly inquire. She could not have any direct contact with the Monroes. They had their own life to live, but she must know if they were all right, especially Zeke.

A man rode by in buckskins, laughing and holding up the long hair of an Indian woman's scalp.

112

"Bastards!" Anna whispered. But she was in the minority. Not many people in these parts were on the side of the Indians, and those who dared voice such feelings usually suffered for it.

She walked to her large kitchen to start the evening meal for her boarders.

Chapter Six

Zeke returned to the campfire, carrying the religious pipe he used in his private worship. This was a time to thank his God for saving his son's life, and it was a time to pray for wisdom for Wolf's Blood, whose heart was aching and confused.

"We should be home in just a couple more days," he told the boy who sat near the fire, an elkskin robe pulled around him. Zeke sat down and reached for his pouch of special tobacco and herbs, called *kinnikinnick* by the Indians. Opening it to extract a chunk of the very special mixture, he placed the tobacco into the red stone bowl of the pipe.

"Hoimaha will come to stay long this winter, I think," Wolf's Blood answered, speaking of the God of cold and snow as he pulled his robe closer and winced at the aching pain in his belly.

"You're probably right," Zeke replied. "But at least this is a sunny morning, and both of us need the peace and strength of the Gods, Wolf's Blood. You speak of going north to fight with your uncle, Swift Arrow, but right now your heart is full of hurt. I love you and I don't want you to go, but a man must do what his heart tells him. I want you to pray and think and be sure,

115

Wolf's Blood. You know how it will hurt my heart to be apart from you."

Their eyes met, and the boy nodded, tears in his eyes. How he worshiped his father! But there was a need in him now that was stronger even than that love—a need for revenge, a need to kill and plunder.

"And your leaving would be very hard on your mother," Zeke continued, looking back at the pipe as he pushed the tobacco into the bowl. "You were the one child she could never really get close to, you know, never hold and cuddle and baby, even when you were small."

Wolf's Blood smiled lightly and shook his head. "White women are strange in the way they treat their children, always looking at them as if they are babies. Indian women are just the opposite, always looking at their babies as grown men and women, training them to be so at an early age."

Zeke smiled. "Well, your mother is kind of a happy medium, I guess. I think she's done a pretty damned good job of teaching all her children strength and independence. All they have to do is model themselves after Abbie, and they'll be okay."

The boy's eyes saddened as he remembered his mother's beaten, starved condition when he and his father had found her after she'd been held by Winston Garvey's men. He had enjoyed raiding Garvey's ranch, enjoyed helping his father drag off Garvey and two of the men who had abused his mother, enjoyed carving them into pieces out of revenge. Those had been Wolf's Blood's first killings, and now with Sand Creek to add to his memories of unfair tortures, he needed to kill more. The men who had abused his mother were Indian haters, as were those who had attacked the Cheyenne at Sand Creek. He would not forget what had happened there, nor would he forget sweet

116

Morning Bird. He thought of how his mother had looked when they'd found her at the cave. He had sensed that it had taken many months before his father and mother could be one again in body, but Abigail Monroe's resilience and stamina always brought her back from disaster. She had a fighting spirit like some Indian women he knew. But he guessed that most of her strength and spirit came from his father, just as his father's strength was drawn from Abbie. The boy had once dreamed of having that kind of relationship with Morning Bird, but that could not be now, and every time he thought of her there was a pain in his chest. And Wolf! If only he had his precious pet, that would help to ease his hurt. They were one in spirit, man and beast.

"Let's pray to the animal spirits, Wolf's Blood," Zeke suggested as he lit his pipe. "You draw your strength and wisdom from the wolf, I draw mine from the eagle. Our animal spirits were shown to us in our own separate visions. Now there has been suffering, and it is a time for hard thinking and praying, especially for you, son."

The man drew on the pipe, then held it up to the sky in honor of Heammawihio, the Wise One Above. He exhaled the smoke, considered a breath of prayer, then drew on the pipe again, exhaling the prayer smoke as he pointed the pipe toward the earth, toward Ahktuno-wihio, the God Who Lives Under the Ground, then offered the pipe to the four directions, east, west, north and south, in a sacrifice called Nivstanivoo, in prayer for long life. He closed his eyes then and handed the pipe to his son, breathing deeply and allowing the spirits to fill him as his son performed the same ceremony with the pipe. The sweet odor of the *kinnikinnick* hung in the still air. Both prayed quietly for several minutes before Zeke finally tamped out the special tobacco and slid the precious prayer pipe into its soft, deerskin covering to protect the polished stone bowl and delicately carved cottonwood stem from scratches.

He drew the pipe bag closed and sighed. "If not for Abbie and the children, I'd go with you, Wolf's Blood," Zeke told the boy, already knowing there would be no stopping his son. "But I would know, just as you must already know, that it would be a pointless battle. I would go anyway, because it is right, and because a man must do those things. But I see the Cheyenne dying, Wolf's Blood; I see all Indians dying. Those who are not shot down by white man's bullets will die of starvation, for just as the white man kills off the buffalo, he kills off the Indian. I am sorry it cannot be like the old days for you. You will grow up in these troubled times, wanting to be part of something that is dying. It saddens my heart, but one day the choices will be made for you and you will have no control over them."

"Then I will fight until that day comes, or until they kill me," the boy replied staring at the flames of the small fire. "It can be no other way for me, Father, at least not for now. Perhaps in time I will be able to come home again. I cannot say."

Zeke nodded, a lump in his throat. They had been so close over the years. From the time Wolf's Blood was big enough to get on a horse and until the last few months when he started spending most of his time with the Cheyenne, he and his father had made a daily ritual of riding off together early in the morning, feeling the wind in their faces, galloping free and far, talking and worshiping. Wolf's Blood had been the only child who had shown a desire to be totally Indian, and he had even participated in the torturous Sun Dance ritual to prove his manhood at the tender age of fifteen.

"You'll never really get over Morning Bird," Zeke was telling the boy, "just as I never got over my first wife's death. But you are young, and you will love again. Love will do much to soothe your aching heart and ease your bad memories. Abbie has brought me great joy and warm comfort. Sometimes I feel that she has suffered from being married to me. I wish I could change that, but she loves me and doesn't seem to mind."

Wolf's Blood poked at the fire with a stick. "How did you bear it, Father, finding your first wife tortured and raped, your little boy dead? I can hardly bear the thought of Morning Bird being dead, and it was so much worse for you."

Zeke stared at the flames for a long time. "Who knows where people find the strength to bear some things. Maybe, at first, it's anger that keeps us going. I had no thought except to find the men who did it and make them suffer . . . and they did, one by one, until I got every last one of them." His dark eyes glittered with remembered hatred. "Then I knew my only hope of having a reason to live again would come from finding my Cheyenne mother, finding my people, so I came out here where I belonged. I hated Tennessee. People there treated me like something less than a dog. But I was Cheyenne, I was proud, I knew I was worth something! I lived for a long time among my own people after that, but fate often led me back into the white man's world and I felt the same prejudices whenever I was around them . . . until I met your mother." His eyes softened. "There are some good whites, Wolf's Blood. You should remember that. Not many, but some. There's my brother, Lance, and my other brother, Dan. There's Bonnie Lewis, who was kind and loving enough to take Crooked Foot and adopt him and see to it that he got those operations. And years ago one of my best friends was white—an ornery mountain man called Olin Wales. I still miss Olin at times. Then, of course, there was our former ranch hand, Dooley, who died trying to protect your mother from Garvey's men. Dooley and I had been friends for a long time."

"But they are just a few. We both know what most whites want—this land, all of it, and they want it free and clear of Indians. To get that they will ride through us and slaughter us like animals. What I saw at Sand Creek will burn in my belly for many years, Father!"

"I know, son. That's why I'll not stop you if you want to go north." He met the boy's eyes again. "But it will bring great sadness to my heart to be apart from you, Wolf's Blood."

The boy blinked back tears and looked away. "It will be the same for me, Father. Yet I cannot stop myself, just as you could not keep from going after those men who killed your first wife, even though you knew every lawman in Tennessee would come after you, just as soldiers will come after me and my uncle and the others I ride with. It does not matter." He looked at his father again. "You once told me we must all be ready to die, that to die in battle was the only honorable way. I am a good fighter, Father. I will be careful and I will not die, but perhaps it will be God's will that I do. If so, I will die bravely and with honor, and I am ready to walk Ekutsihimmiyo."

Zeke reached out and grasped his shoulder. "I'm sure you are. But I will pray daily for your health and safety, and for the day you come back home."

The boy put a hand over his father's. "And I will pray for my father. I—" He stopped talking when Zeke suddenly put up his hand to be still and looked past Wolf's Blood toward a distant hill.

"Someone is coming," he said quietly. "Do you feel the horses' hooves?"

120

Wolf's Blood sat quietly for a moment, then rose and began kicking out the fire. "There are not many . . . maybe four or five," he said as Zeke shoved the pipe into his parfleche.

"That's my guess, too. Whoever it is, let me handle it, son. You aren't healed yet. Any kind of strain could break you open all over again."

They picked up their gear and threw it on the horses, just as four men appeared at the crest of the hill. The men stopped as Zeke and Wolf's Blood mounted their horses. For a tense moment they all just sat looking at each other.

"Don't try to ride off," Zeke told his son quietly. "They'll just chase us down out of curiosity, and I don't want you riding hard. It could kill you. Besides, if they're going to come after us, I'd rather be facing them than riding off with my back to them. See that extra long rifle across the neck of that one horse? That's a Sharp's rifle, the Big Fifty. They're buffalo hunters."

Wolf's Blood's face hardened more and his horse pranced restlessly. Buffalo hunters were probably the Indians' worst enemies. They were slowly, but surely, destroying the very livelihood of the Indian. There was not a waking, sleeping, eating, hunting or fighting moment that the Indian did not use or wear something made from some part of the buffalo. Yet with the need among white settlers and railroad workers for meat, and with the new demand in the East for hides, the whites had allowed professional hunters full rights to slaughter every buffalo they could find.

"I hope they come!" the boy hissed. "It is a good day to kill buffalo hunters."

Zeke grinned. "I agree. But you stay out of it unless I get myself into more than I can handle. You don't have to prove your fighting skills to me, son. You saved my life with them once down in Kansas."

121

The four men moved in a slow trot down the hill, and Zeke gripped his Henry .44 rifle allowing it to rest casually across his lap as he waited for the men to come closer. Wolf's Blood had no weapon. He had lost everything at Sand Creek, except for the fancy Bowie knife Zeke had given him as a gift after he'd endured the Sun Dance ritual. He gripped the knife now, reaching inside his robe but leaving it in its beaded sheath that hung on a belt about his waist. His father had taught him well how to use that weapon.

The men came within several feet of Zeke and Wolf's Blood. All of them were unkempt. They wore buffalo robes made from hides not fully dried and cured, and Zeke could smell them from where he sat. One was a very big man, too big for the poor horse that had to carry him. He was not only tall in the saddle, but wide and fat as well. Two of the others were of medium build, and the fourth was spindly looking. When he grinned at Zeke, he had two teeth missing in front. All sported unshaven faces and hands covered with dirt and buffalo blood.

"Out for a morning kill, are you?" Zeke asked. His horse tossed its head and whinnied as the four men studied him and Wolf's Blood, eying them as Indians, for there was nothing about the appearance of Zeke and his son to suggest white blood.

The biggest man spit tobacco juice. "That's right, Injun'," he replied. "But it don't necessarily have to be buffalo we kill." He looked Zeke up and down. "Kill a buffalo or an Injun'—makes no difference to the white folks. So I expect we'll take back more than just buffalo hides to camp tonight." He looked at Wolf's Blood and grinned. "We might maybe take the young one there alive. With no women in these parts, we could make use of him."

That was all the goading Zeke needed. He had intended to try to convince the men to move on and then just leave, but visions of Sand Creek and the filthy words of the buffalo hunter combined to trigger that part of him that was wild and savage. In a quick flash his Henry .44 fired, its barrel shining in the morning sun as a hole exploded in the big man's throat and he flew backward off his horse. It had happened so quickly that the other three men were confused. One man's horse reared at the sudden gunshot, and the other two whinnied and pranced backward in startled fear. In that instant, Zeke's gun clicked as he reloaded the chamber of his lever-action rifle, and he fired again, suddenly filled with rage at the harm men such as these brought to the Indians. A second man went down. The other two men turned their horses, not expecting this sudden and skillful reaction from one man who faced four threatening buffalo hunters.

Zeke let out a war whoop and charged after the two men, who began riding off, afraid now for their own lives and not caring to stick around and have it out with the Indian. Wolf's Blood merely laughed at the entertainment as Zeke rode down hard on one of the hunters, taking out his wicked knife and slashing out when he got close enough, ripping the blade through the man's neck with one mighty swipe and half cutting off the man's head. The man fell, his hand on a handgun he had been unable to get from its holster in his fright.

The fourth man whirled and managed to fire his Sharp's rifle. A glancing blow to Zeke's upper left arm only tore his robe and the buckskin shirt beneath it, grazing the skin, but its force literally whirled Zeke's body, making his horse whirl with him. The animal stumbled and went down, taking Zeke with it. Wolf's

Blood saw his father go down, and his heart pounded with dread as he headed his own horse toward the confrontation, but before he got there Zeke was on his feet, too far from where his rifle had fallen to reach it before the fourth man started to fire again. Zeke saw the rifle barrel in that quick second and he dove away as the gun boomed again. He rolled to the front legs of the man's horse and quickly rose up before the man realized Zeke was right underneath him.

Zeke reached up and literally yanked the rifle from the man's hands, pulling the man down from the horse when he tried to hang on to the weapon. When the man was on the ground, Zeke tossed the rifle aside and stood there knife in hand, panting and grinning. The man froze and stared up at Zeke.

"Get on your feet, white scum!" Zeke growled as Wolf's Blood rode up beside him.

"Father, are you all right?" the boy asked anxiously.

"I'm just fine," Zeke hissed, his eyes on the buffalo hunter. "But this man won't be for long!"

Wolf's Blood backed off as Zeke held his arms out to his sides in a menacing stance, the big, ugly blade still gripped tightly.

"I . . . I don't want no quarrel with you, Injun!" the hunter pleaded, slowly getting to his feet.

"That's too bad, you smelly bastard!" Zeke rumbled. "Because I have a quarrel with you! The last few days have made me damned angry and I'm not about to leave you alive now to run to the soldiers and tell them who killed your friends! You can go for your gun and die like a man, or you can just stand there and die like a woman! I'll make it easier for you. I'll put my knife back in its sheath!" He shoved the knife into its holder and grinned at the hunter.

The man swallowed and backed up. "Look, I . . . I

won't say nothin'."

"Like hell you won't! Go for your gun, you boy-loving son of a bitch!"

Sweat poured from the buffalo hunter's face in spite of the cold, and there was a long moment of stand-off before he finally decided the Indian was going to kill him so he'd best try to save his own hide. He went for his gun, but Zeke Monroe's reputation with a knife was well earned. Faster than the hunter could draw and fire, Zeke's knife was out and thrown. It landed with a thump in the man's heart. The hunter staggered backward, his eyes wide with horror. Then he slumped to the ground, his eyes still wide and staring.

Zeke stepped forward and yanked out the blade. It had been a long time since he'd had the pleasure of ripping a deserving man from throat to belly. The vision of these men touching his son, and of their killing not just buffalo but Indians, was all the fuel he needed. The big blade tore through the man's torso. Then the Indian in Zeke came to the forefront, and he reached down and grasped the man's long blond hair, deftly cutting off a section of scalp.

He turned and held up the scalp to Wolf's Blood. "Put that in your belt and take it north with you," he told the boy, his voice still hot with anger. "Tell my brother Swift Arrow that your father is still not and never will be totally white, and that at least four buffalo hunters will not live to kill buffalo or Indians again!"

Wolf's Blood took the piece of hair and held it up, letting out a war whoop while Zeke removed a small hatchet from his gear. He took the tool and used it to chop up and destroy the hunters' Big Fifties. Perhaps it was only a small ripple in a large lake of more hunters to come, but he had done what he could for the time being. He shoved the hatchet back into his gear and slid up onto his horse with ease, feeling a hot sting in his left arm where the bullet had fallen short of felling its target.

"Let's go home!" he told Wolf's Blood. "We'll head down and follow the Arkansas for a ways, keeping to the water so if anyone comes upon these bodies and tries to follow, they'll lose our trail. Let the soldiers and settlers wonder who did this." He rode up next to his son. "One good thing about being out here away from the towns is a man can still get away with self-defense without getting hung for it. I'm afraid that won't last forever either, son. This damned open territory is getting more and more settled all the time."

"We should leave quickly then, Father. Perhaps, if we are lucky the vultures and wolves will take care of the flesh so that anyone who finds them won't even know who they are." He tied the scalp into his horse's mane. "I would have helped you, Father, if I'd thought you were in trouble. But I have seen you fight before. I was not too worried."

Their eyes met and they both laughed lightly. It had been a good day after all. They urged their mounts into a gentle gait and faded into the hazy morning horizon.

Abbie curried down her favorite Appaloosa, after taking an afternoon ride to exercise the animal and try to free her own mind of worry. Wolf sat outside the entrance to the stables. He was not allowed to go inside because his presence spooked the horses. The animal seemed to have an uncanny sense of what he could and could not harm, so the Monroe horses were spared his fangs.

The wolf had been home for five days now, five days

of agonizing waiting for Abbie, who tried to sort out in her mind what she would do next. Should she send someone to search for Zeke? She had to have some answers soon. The afternoon ride had relieved her tension and fear only temporarily. Now as the sun began to sink, so did her hopes.

"There, Pepper," she said softly to the mare. "Aren't you beautiful now?" She smiled and patted the animal's rump, admiring the perfection that Zeke Monroe had bred into nearly all of his horses. They were the man's most valuable possession, and they were their security for the future. Abbie was grateful for Zeke's talent with the animals; sometimes it seemed that was what kept the man going. She knew his mind and heart were heavy with sorrow over what was happening to the Cheyenne—to all Indians. But the ranch, the horses, and his large family gave him reasons to go on. Sometimes Abbie suspected if it were not for these things, Zeke Monroe would be out there with the Cheyenne, probably raiding with the worst of them, fighting to the death to keep the freedom they'd once had. That was where a man like Zeke belonged, riding free and wild, and she well knew it. Only love for his woman and the children she had borne him kept him within the confines of the ranch; and even at that, there were times when he seemed to make up any excuse to go riding off somewhere, but never for long—not since their terrible parting during those awful months he'd gone off to the Civil War. For this reason she was even more worried. She knew Zeke would come back as quickly as possible after he found Wolf's Blood. Perhaps both of them were dead, or perhaps one or both of them were wounded.

She set down the brush and walked to the back of the stables to scoop up a generous armful of hay, bringing it back to Pepper and dropping it into the feed trough. "Eat up," she told the horse, petting it again before going out and closing the stall door. She met Lance coming inside the stable then, carrying a pitchfork.

"I brushed down Pepper and fed her," she told her brother-in-law. "I'll send Jeremy out to help you tend to the rest of the horses. Do you need Margaret and LeeAnn, too? They can take care of the horses in the other barn."

"Yeah, there're more out back too. I put them up in that corral behind the barn out of the wind. I got a little behind today when I stopped to split that wood."

She put a hand on his arm. "I'm glad you came out, Lance. Zeke certainly needed the help, and when he has to be gone you're a godsend."

The man shrugged and grinned, studying her lovely face. He was a little younger than Abbie and had been a very small boy when Zeke had fled Tennessee. By the time Zeke had seen him again, he'd been a full grown man. He had the dark hair and eyes of their white father, unlike Dan whose blond hair and blue eyes were derived from their mother, the stepmother Zeke remembered with little affection. She had been dead for many years, and when she'd died, Zeke had already been living with the Cheyenne, away from Tennessee and the bad memories of his boyhood there. But all the Monroe boys had the same even, handsome smile, very masculine but with an appealing gentle side, although Zeke's gentler side didn't show through as readily as his white brother's.

Their eyes held, and he put a hand over one of hers. "You okay, Abbie?"

She forced a smile. "Sometimes. But not most of the time. I'm going crazy trying to decide what to do next, Lance."

He squeezed her hand, then turned and put a strong arm around her shoulders. "Want me to ride out and do some looking?"

She shook her head. "We need you here. I don't want to add you to the list of those who ride out of here and never come back." She swallowed back tears. "I'll just . . . maybe you could just go to Fort Lyon again, find someone there who would be willing to do some searching. I could pay . . ."

Her voice faded in midsentence when she saw Wolf perk up. The animal rose on all fours, looking in the direction of the hill east of the cabin. He was not growling, and he suddenly bolted away almost happily.

"Lance, someone is coming!" she exclaimed, pulling away and running outside. Lance followed, and both looked in the direction where Wolf had run. Two mounted figures appeared over the hill.

"It's them!" Abbie said excitedly. "It must be them, or Wolf wouldn't be running to greet them that way!" She started to pull away, but Lance grabbed her arm.

"Be careful, Abbie. It might not be them."

They both stood there another moment. Then she heard an Indian war whoop and recognized her son's voice. He was yelling because he saw Wolf coming.

"That's Wolf's Blood!" she told Lance. She looked up at him. "Keep the children here for a few minutes, will you, Lance?"

He studied the two figures a moment longer. "I think you're right, Abbie. Go on. I'll keep the others behind so you can have a minute alone before the rest of your brood attacks."

She smiled. "Thank you, Lance." She ran off, half stumbling through the snow, and Lance watched her, breathing a sigh of relief. Then he headed for the cabin.

Abbie ran as fast as she could, her lungs tight from the cold air. But she didn't notice that they ached, didn't notice the cold against her ears. She could only see her son—her husband and her son!

"Zeke!" she called out. He rode forward then at a faster gait. They were still several hundred yards in the distance. Wolf had already reached them, and she noticed that Wolf's Blood dismounted slowly to greet Wolf. In the next instant Wolf had literally knocked the boy down and was licking his face. Then Wolf's Blood's laughter penetrated the clear, crisp air. How beautiful it sounded! The boy very seldom laughed. He'd been a serious, determined child even when very small.

By then Zeke had reached her, his horse pushing up snow in front of its hooves when Zeke yanked it to a sudden stop. She reached up, and in the next moment a familiar strong arm was pulling her up onto the horse and her arms were around his neck, his own firmly around her body.

Nothing was said. There was only being together. She breathed deeply of the scent of man and leather as they clung together tightly for several seconds.

"Take me to my son," she finally whimpered.

He still had not spoken. He turned the horse, and she kept her head on his shoulder as he headed the animal back up to Wolf's Blood who lay in the snow hugging Wolf and burying his face in the deep, thick fur at the animal's neck. The boy sat up when he saw them come closer; then he got to his feet. Abbie could see the pain on his face, and he was so much thinner! Zeke immediately released her and she slid down and ran to her son, hugging him tightly and crying. He hugged her back more out of respect than emotion. He loved his mother deeply, but he was not one to display affection openly and his heart was still full of the loss of Morning Bird.

"Mother, do not hold me so tightly," he finally said quietly. "I still hurt."

She quickly pulled away, looking him over, putting a hand to the side of his face. "Where? What's happened to you, Wolf's Blood? Were you at Sand Creek?"

Their eyes held, and she noticed that he was suddenly struggling to keep back tears. However, his look of terrible sorrow was quickly replaced by one of hatred and vengeance.

"Yes, I was there!" he said almost angrily. "Morning Bird is dead! And so is my uncle, Black Elk, and Blue Bird Woman and"—his voice started to break—"and little Bucking Horse!"

He turned away and wiped at his eyes, and Abbie felt a terrible rush of shock and sorrow. She turned to look up at Zeke just then, seeing it all in his dark eyes. Sand Creek had been much worse than she had heard. She wished there was something she could do about the pain she found in her husband's eyes, but she knew there was not.

"I came upon the scene later," Zeke told her quietly. "If you had seen what I saw, you'd realize how lucky we are that Wolf's Blood is alive." He looked out over the horizon. "I'm not sure I should even tell you the details. Maybe you're not strong enough for it."

"Strong enough!" she exclaimed. "I should let you bear this alone? I most certainly will not! What happens to the Cheyenne is as important to me as it is to you. I am certainly strong enough to share your sorrows, Zeke Monroe." She turned back to Wolf's Blood. "How badly were you wounded?"

He rubbed at his stomach. "Very bad. With a soldier's bayonet. Father fixed me, though. That is why it took us so long. I was not strong enough to ride."

She reached out and embraced him again, this time with less fervor, afraid of hurting him. "Thank you, Jesus," she whispered. She let go and grasped his shoulders. "I'm so sorry . . . about Morning Bird."

His eyes hardened. "There are others who will be more sorry when I am through!" he hissed.

Her heart tightened. "What do you mean?"

"You know what I mean, Mother. As soon as I am strong enough I am going north to fight with my uncle, Swift Arrow! I will not stay here among the timid southern Cheyenne who choose to fight no more!"

She shook her head, her chest painful with fear for him. "It's a losing battle, Wolf's Blood."

He shook his head. "No, it is not a losing battle! And what good does it do to speak for peace? Black Kettle spoke for it! He waited faithfully at Sand Creek for instructions from the white leaders, waited for the government rations, even flew the American flag over his tipi! The day the soldiers came he even raised a white flag beside it! He stood there watching them come, telling us not to fire on them, telling us if we stood together and did not fight back the soldiers would stop shooting at us. But the soldiers did *not* stop firing! They kept coming! By the time we realized what they meant to do, it was too late to get away! The soldiers rode down on us, shooting and butchering women, old people, little babies! Some of them were scalped! The soldiers cut off their fingers to get their jewelry! They cut out the bellies of women, cut off men's organs! I will never forget Sand Creek! Never! And I will ride in revenge until the day I die. I choose to die killing white men rather than die a shriveled old man on a reservation!"

132

"Wolf's Blood, that's enough!" Zeke ordered.

Abbie stepped back, blinking and speechless. She looked up at Zeke. He sighed and dismounted, coming around his horse and taking her into his arms. She broke into tears. He looked at his son.

"I understand exactly how you feel, Wolf's Blood, but you'll not raise your voice to your mother because of it. I intended to find a gentler way of telling her. And I told you to think awhile before going north."

The boy's eyes softened slightly. "I'm sorry," he answered. "But I will not change my mind about going north." He stepped closer to them and put a hand on his mother's shoulder. "Forgive me, Mother."

She reached behind and put a hand over his, keeping her other arm around Zeke. "At least . . . you're alive," she sobbed. "Let's just . . . enjoy each other today . . . this moment. I don't want to talk about you . . . going away."

Wolf's Blood looked up at his father. "I am sorry," he repeated, realizing how protective the man was of Abbie since her abduction the year before. He pulled his hand away and touched his mother's hair. "Mother, how did Wolf get here? I thought he was dead."

She turned from Zeke and wiped at her eyes. "He just showed up on his own—about five days ago. He was wounded." She sniffed. "Apparently the two of you got separated and Wolf came back here thinking he'd find you. He must have gone off to nurse his wounds first." She sniffed and wiped at her eyes again. "I took hope when I saw him. I thought if you were . . . were dead, he'd stay beside you." She half collapsed against Zeke and he held her close.

"Let's get down to the house, son," he said, his voice tired. "For now, let's just be grateful that you're alive and Wolf is alive too. Don't be filling the children's heads with horror stories, and don't tell them right away that you might leave. Margaret will be upset."

"She will be upset, but she will understand," the boy replied. "She is the only sister I can talk to, the only one who understands. Perhaps it is because Margaret and I are the only ones who look and think all Indian."

He took his horse's reins and started toward the cabin. Abbie noticed the scalp then, hanging from the horse's mane. Her eyes widened and she grasped the horse's bridle and stopped walking. "Where did you get that scalp?" she asked, looking from the boy to Zeke and back to Wolf's Blood.

Wolf's Blood only grinned. "My father lost his temper with some buffalo hunters," he answered. "It was a good day."

Abbie's heart tightened. She had seen enemy scalps before on Cheyenne men's belts and gear and in their tipis. But they were always the scalps of enemy tribes, like the Pawnee and Ute. She had never seen a white scalp before, and it frightened her. What did the future hold for her warrior son if it meant going after the white soldiers and settlers? And what of her husband? She had seen him in action many times, knew how vicious he could be. But Sand Creek had apparently had a more terrible effect on him than she realized. He himself had taken enemy scalps, but never a white man's, at least none she had known about, and it had been years since he had done such a thing. She looked up at him in wonder.

"It seemed like a good idea at the time, Abbie girl," he told her casually. He lifted her onto his horse as though she were a feather, and she noticed the tear in his robe where the hunter's bullet had ripped through it. She touched it lightly.

"Are you hurt?"

He gave her a reassuring smile, though a sad one.

"Not physically. I guess it was something they said that set me off, and I won't repeat it. Let's just forget it." He took the horse's reins and walked with it, alongside Wolf's Blood, toward the cabin, where six other Monroe children waited eagerly to greet their big brother and their mysterious father.

Chapter Seven

The Monroes all sat solemnly around the table, trying to grasp the total meaning of what had happened at Sand Creek. Abbie knew by the look in Zeke's eyes that it was much worse than what he and Wolf's Blood had told the children, and Wolf's Blood's earlier tirade had presented a picture she could hardly bear to envision. There was quiet crying, a mixture of sorrow and fear. The older ones who had been closest to their uncle, Black Elk, and to their little cousin, Bucking Horse, wept more openly. Abbie wanted to weep too, and she knew that when the full force of their deaths hit her she would indeed weep bitterly; but she could only handle so much at a time. Right now her heart was heavy for Wolf's Blood, and for Zeke, who had been there, had seen it all, had buried his brother and his family. Wolf's Blood had never been a boy who laughed much. Now she could see that there would be even less laughter in his life. She knew it was difficult for him not to burst out in a fit of yelling and cursing and swearing to get his revenge. He was holding back out of respect for her wish not to further upset the

137

others. But he was tense and sober, his eyes darting around the cabin like those of a caged animal.

The boy did not mention sinking his lance into Charles Garvey's leg. Zeke had already ordered Wolf's Blood not to speak of that in front of Abbie. He did not want the Garvey name brought up in her presence.

"How could they do that?" Margaret finally sobbed. "If Black Kettle flew the American flag over his dwelling, and a flag of truce, how could they attack? Black Kettle's band was peaceful! It isn't fair!"

Zeke thought about his first wife's murder back in Tennessee, about the Trail of Tears, and the many other instances of unfair killings and battles prompted by hatred of the Indians.

"There are a lot of things in this life that aren't fair," he said quietly. He picked up a pipe from the table, one he had already stuffed. He put it to his lips and lit it, puffing it quietly while he waited for some of the sniffling to stop. Abbie watched him carefully. So tired! He looked so tired! She knew he was feeling the strain of not being able to go out and exact his own revenge, at least not by riding with warriors and raiding settlements and supply trains. She thought about the encounter with the buffalo hunters. It worried her deeply. Zeke Monroe had a wild streak that had caused him to kill many men in self-defense and in vengeance, but the land was becoming more and more civilized, was coming under the white man's laws, although many of those could not be called civilized at all. It seemed white men could slaughter Indians and be within the law, but if an Indian laid a hand on a white man, that was an act that was punished by hanging. Zeke Monroe had a large family to consider now . . . and his woman. He would have to be more and more careful. Perhaps he could no longer react to some wrongs in his murderous fashion. To a man like Zeke there was right and wrong, black and white, and wrongdoing meant an eye for an eye. Now it only mattered who did the wrongdoing, and black and white was turning to gray.

His children watched him as he slowly gazed at each one of them while he puffed the pipe. Their father was a big man, a man to be respected, a man whose reputation with his big knife was known far and wide. Many times they had listened with keen interest to the story of how he and their mother had met, and they had heard the adventures of their parents' early years. Only Wolf's Blood, Margaret, and LeeAnn had actually lived among the Cheyenne for a time; and LeeAnn's memories of it were vague, for she had been very young.

"These are bad times for Indians," Zeke was telling them. "But times have been bad for the Indian since white settlers first set foot on the Eastern shores. I've told all of you about the Trail of Tears. Sand Creek was just another form of that kind of senseless brutality. The white settlers want what rightfully belongs to someone else, and they have the strength of numbers and superior weapons. But the Indians won't give up easily so there are many years of hardships ahead." He glanced at Abbie, then at the children, while Lance looked on from where he stood across the room, feeling sorry for his brother.

"Most of you needn't worry," Zeke continued. "I know what you're thinking. You're afraid because of your Indian blood. But white men have a tendency to look only at the color of someone's skin. I find that ridiculous. It is a person's worth that should matter." He puffed the pipe again. "Be that as it may, most of you don't look Indian. Much as it hurts me to think

139

that some of you might deny your Indian blood, it's bound to happen, and I'll not blame you. You're my children and I love all of you, but you're all getting old enough to make your own decisions." His eyes rested on Margaret. "Those of you who do look-Indian, I don't want you to be afraid, and I don't want you to be ashamed. I took a lot of abuse when I was growing up in Tennessee, but I, by God, was never ashamed of being an Indian. It made me angry, but not ashamed." His eyes scanned all of them again. "I just want you to be proud of yourselves and to remember that if you're strong inside, no man, no law, no army can bring you to your knees. You remember that. Don't let people like John Chivington destroy you. Someday the truth about the Sand Creek will be known, and it will be remembered in history as a disgrace to white men."

His underlying, seething anger could be felt throughout the room, and to all the children he looked even bigger than they had remembered him being. They had seen him at times with his Indian brothers, painted and dancing as they were participating in war games and fancy horsemanship. He bore many scars, from battles and from participating in the grueling Sun Dance ritual. He was a man of two worlds, belonging to neither, wanting one life but living another.

"What will happen now, Father?" Ellen asked.

He studied his pipe. "I expect there will be Indian raids and warring on a scale bigger than anything the white men have seen yet," he replied. "By trying to wipe out the Indians they're only making more trouble for themselves."

"They are digging their own graves!" Wolf's Blood growled. He shoved back his chair. "I am going out for fresh air," he told them, walking slowly over to his heavy buffalo-robe coat. He took it from a hook and

140

winced with pain as he put it on.

"You should come back in soon, Wolf's Blood, and lie down," Abbie told him pleadingly, knowing how restless the boy felt. "You must rest."

He looked at her with tears in his eyes. "When I remember lying next to Morning Bird, my arms around her dead body, it is hard to rest, Mother," he replied, his voice choking. He walked slowly to the door and went out, and Abbie knew that if it were not for his wound, he would get on his horse and ride north. She was almost grateful for the wound. It would keep her son with them awhile longer. She looked at Zeke and saw his grief. He was losing his favorite son, and he knew it.

Zeke scanned his children, resignation in his eyes. "Your brother is going through a difficult time," he told them, his voice sounding weary. "Be patient with him. He still isn't healed, not just in body but in heart. Morning Bird was very special to him. Don't be noisy around him, and give him your support. Perhaps some of you don't look or feel Indian, but Wolf's Blood is just the opposite. He is proud of being Indian, and he has a wildness about him that none of the rest of you have."

"He's like his own pa, that's what he is," Lance spoke up. Zeke met the man's eyes and nodded.

"I suppose he is, at least like I was back in Tennessee—young and restless and full of revenge. I know how he's hurting." Zeke looked back at the children. "All of you eat a good supper now. Margaret, help your mother get the food on the table."

"You should eat too, Zeke," Abbie spoke up. "I've fixed a good supper every night, never knowing when you'd get here. And you should get Wolf's Blood back inside and make him eat. You both need

141

the nourishment."

He met her eyes. "I've got no appetite yet, Abbie. I know you're right, and I'll try to get Wolf's Blood to eat, but he needs some time alone." Their eyes held. There was so much to say, and they hadn't had a chance to be alone themselves since Zeke and Wolf's Blood had arrived.

"Will Wolf's Blood be all right?" Jeremy asked.

Zeke looked at the son who was so different from Wolf's Blood. He loved Jeremy as any man loved a son, but he knew the two of them would probably never think alike. He felt that Jeremy Monroe would be one of those who would run from his Indian blood. "He'll be all right, son . . . in time."

The boy swallowed and stared at the big, wild man who was his father, a man he knew he could never be like. "I helped with all the chores, Father, like you said to do before you left." He swallowed. "I worked real hard."

"That he did," Lance put in, walking over to sit down at the table. "He's a hard worker, that one."

Zeke saw the boy's hopeful eyes, hopeful that he had somehow pleased his father. Zeke gave him a smile, aware that the boy always felt he was being compared to Wolf's Blood. It wasn't Jeremy's fault that he was more white than Indian. Each of the children was different, unique in his or her own way. "Jeremy's the hardest worker on the ranch," Zeke said to Lance, his eyes still on Jeremy. Jeremy's eyes lit up and his face reddened slightly.

"I'm not afraid of Thunder anymore," the boy told Zeke, speaking of one of the wilder Appaloosas. "I rode him twice while you were gone, Father." The boy had always been afraid of horses, taking much longer to get used to them and to learn to ride properly than his older brother and his two older sisters.

"Well then, we'll have to go for a ride tomorrow and you can show me how well you're doing," Zeke answered.

"Really? Just the two of us, like you and Wolf's Blood do sometimes?"

Zeke's smile faded. He knew he was guilty of paying more attention to Wolf's Blood than to the other children, but it hadn't been deliberate. It was just that Wolf's Blood was a replica of his father, not just in looks but in nature. Their closeness and keen understanding of one another had been natural and easy. "Yes, just the two of us," he told Jeremy. "We'll talk. Maybe we can learn to understand each other a little better. You can tell me about your studies and some of that fancy book learning your mother has taught you, and I'll teach you more about riding."

The boy smiled and nodded, and Zeke looked toward the door, then rose. "All of you eat now. I'm going out to try to get Wolf's Blood to come back inside."

"Mama killed a deer all by herself!" little Jason spoke up, his young and happy mind oblivious to the gravity of the day. "A great big one with horns!" He put his hands at the top of his head and stuck his fingers up.

Zeke looked over at his wife in surprise and she blushed. "I was just walking, carrying Pa's Spencer for protection, and I just . . . came upon him . . . standing there looking at me. So I shot."

Zeke flashed the handsome grin that always warmed her heart, and the mention of her "kill" seemed to break some of the tension around the table. She thought of telling him about the Englishman coming to visit that day, but she decided not to do so, suspecting it might upset him. There would be a better time to tell him.

Praying that none of the children would bring the subject up just then, she shot a warning look at Margaret and Lance.

"Well, Abbie girl, it looks like you've still got what it takes to survive out here, woman. First it's Crow Indians, then outlaws, now a deer. I told you you'd quit feeling sorry for those animals someday when you thought about all the hungry mouths we have to feed."

She rose to help Margaret put supper on the table. "He was just standing there as though God sent him to me, so I shot him. But I properly thanked his spirit." She met Zeke's eyes and saw a strange sadness there, as though he was sorry she had had to be a part of putting food on the table. She hoped his Indian pride was not injured. Cheyenne men took great pride in being the hunters, the providers. His dark eyes roved her lovely form. "You're some woman, Abbie." He winked then. "Did you save the rack?"

She blushed again and picked up a spoon. "It's in the barn."

"The barn! That's no place for a woman's first hunting souvenir. We'll bring it inside and hang it on the wall for everybody to see."

Their eyes held for a moment longer, then he turned to go out.

"Zeke!" Abbie spoke up. "You didn't mention Tall Grass Woman."

He had already told himself to be prepared for the question, for Abbie and Tall Grass Woman had been close in the days when they could frequently be among the Cheyenne. Abbie had even saved Tall Grass Woman's daughter from drowning that first year Abbie lived among the People, but the little girl had since died from cholera.

"Tall Grass Woman was among the survivors at the

Smoky Hill," he told her. "She and Falling Rock are all right. She said to give you her love. She and a lot of the other peaceful ones will be heading for Kansas soon."

Abbie sighed deeply. "Thank God. I hope I can see her again." She turned back to her cooking and Zeke quickly left. He apparently had fooled her, for he did not intend to tell her yet that he had found Tall Grass Woman at Sand Creek, slain alongside her husband and son, mutilated like the others. He would not put that burden on his wife right now. She had enough on her shoulders. There would be a better time to tell her.

Inside the cabin, Abbie sliced some bread, her heart heavy for her husband. Something was different about him since his return. It was as though some of the fight had gone out of him in spite of his encounter with the buffalo hunters. That was a single fight, but what was happening to the Cheyenne was occurring on a much larger scale. It was something one man could do nothing about. Sand Creek had had a great effect on Zeke Monroe, and it would take some time to get over it. She felt an odd apprehension that she could not put her finger on. It went deeper than the fact that Wolf's Blood might go north, although that would be very hard on Zeke. More had been lost at Sand Creek than lives, something much more important had been trampled there . . . something called spirit. She felt her husband slipping away from her, even though he was present in body. Their love had survived many terrible tests. Could it survive the demise of the Cheyenne?

Several days passed, during which time Zeke threw himself into his work with more fervor than usual. He seemed to be trying to take out his need for vengeance through his work. At night he was too tired and still too

145

full of the recent tragedy to make love. He simply held Abbie, and he seemed to have an urgent need to do so, as though each time might be the last time he held her. He spoke little and slept restlessly, and Abbie often awoke in the night to see him standing at the window. Sometimes he had even gone outside. She knew that the wild side of him wanted to ride north with his son and make war. When Wolf's Blood left, which he still swore to do, it would be very hard on Zeke Monroe.

It was a full week after his return when Abbie noticed some spark to the quiet, withdrawn man who had returned from Sand Creek. The children were sleeping in the loft while January winds howled outside when Zeke sat down at the edge of their bed of robes. That was the kind of bed Zeke had preferred early in their marriage, and they had never purchased a conventional one. He pulled off his buckskin shirt, and in the dim lamplight she studied the broad shoulders of his muscular back. His black hair hung long and straight, and he removed his headband. He sat there for a moment saying nothing; then he turned and looked at her, studying her lovely face, the dark brown hair spread out on the pillow beneath her head.

"Margaret said that Englishman was here while I was gone," he stated with a frown. "What the hell did he want?"

She watched his dark eyes, wanting to smile at the hint of jealousy in them, but he was too serious for her to make light of anything.

"He wanted to look at some horses. I told him to come back when you were here."

"After you served him tea and talked awhile," he answered, standing up and removing his pants.

Abbie sat up straighter. "Zeke Monroe! So far the man hasn't done a thing against us, and he seems to want very much to be on friendly terms. Neither one of us likes the fact that he is here, but he is, and we have enemies enough without creating more deliberately. I may have become more suspicious and careful of people since I've lived out here, but I refuse to totally forget the art of being neighborly. I'm no different now than I was nineteen years ago when I offered you that cup of coffee when you came to offer your services as a scout for our wagon train!"

"Yeah?" He got into bed and sat beside her. "Well, look where that led!" he reminded her.

As he met her eyes, she smiled softly, reaching out and tracing her fingers over his chest. "Yes. Look where that led."

He grabbed her hand, then broke into the wonderful, handsome grin she had not seen since his return. She reached up and touched his face. "Zeke, there are so many terrible things going on around us, and our son might go away. We've been through so much. Don't let a silly thing like Sir Tynes get in the way. I love you, Zeke Monroe. And I've missed you so—need you so."

He grasped her wrist and moved his lips to kiss the palm of her hand. "I guess I just look at someone like the Englishman and then I think about all we've been through, Abbie—all that is to come—and I see what life might have been like for you if not for me."

She leaned closer and kissed the scarred cheek. "Zeke," she spoke in a near whisper. "Without you there would have been no life for me, and you well know it. With you I can bear anything that happens. Without you I am nothing. And you can't tell me it isn't the same for you."

He studied the honest, soft brown eyes of his Abbie girl. Her eyes had never changed over the years. They were still the eyes of the young girl who had been so in

147

love with him nineteen years ago. Abigail Monroe would not be untrue to her man or even think of doing so. But then maybe she didn't know what was best for her. Surely it wasn't a half-wild, half-breed Indian who was followed by trouble wherever he went. Yet their marriage had been good, their love rock strong. Maybe he loved her too much.

He leaned down and kissed her neck, unbuttoning the front of her gown as he did so. "It's the same for me," he said softly. "And I need you, Abbie."

His lips found the soft fullness of her breasts, and he began to move more quickly, hungry for her now, hoping to forget Sand Creek and his other problems for the moment and just enjoy being one with his woman. He pulled her gown over her shoulders and down over her arms, his lips moving over her breasts, her stomach, and down over her body as the gown came off. He threw it aside and removed his loin cloth and pulled her close, enjoying the feel of her softness against his body. It had been so long since they had done this. He wondered why he had allowed so many things to get in the way, for he found his strength and peace with this woman who loved him just the way he was.

Their bodies seemed to melt together naturally, in tune to one another's needs, and the excitement never really changed for them. His lips searched her mouth, and she gloried at how gentle he could be with her as his hands massaged and explored, for she had seen the vicious side of Zeke Monroe, knew what he could do to his enemies. But this was not that man. That man had never been in her bed. She knew a side of him that few others could imagine existed.

"Abbie, my Abbie," he whispered, his lips moving to her breasts again, tasting their sweet fruit, drawing out her passion. She touched his hair, breathing deeply, allowing herself to enjoy the moment, never knowing what tomorrow might bring. He moved between her legs so that she could not close them, but she didn't want to. Even that first time he'd taken her, despite being frightened and unsure and hardly more than a child, she had wanted him this way. She had always wanted him, always would.

"Don't let anything change between us, Zeke," she whispered. "Don't let anything ever change between us. You're my Zeke." She gasped as he quickly entered her then, arching up to him in great waves of love and relief, turning her face and smothering her whimpers of ecstasy in the pillow as her body pulsed in the sweet explosion he forced from her by bringing her such intense pleasure. His powerful shoulders hovered over her while he whispered gentle words of love in the Cheyenne tongue and filled her with his power and masculinity, bringing out all that was womanly about her. In this act they drew strength from one another, shared joy and sorrow, gave and received pleasure. Over and over he pushed himself into the silken softness that welcomed him. She could no longer give him children, but he was glad she'd had the operation that had put an end to her child bearing. To have another baby would have endangered her life, and the seven they had were almost more than they could handle. It was nice to be able to simply enjoy Abbie as a woman, to ravage her, devour her, take his pleasure with her whenever he needed without the worry of pregnancy.

He shuddered and grasped her hair tightly in his hands, then as his life poured into her, he relaxed and pulled her close, kissing her eyes and staying inside of her. He wanted more of her before they slept. That night they would both forget the hardships of living in this land. There would only be Zeke and Abbie. There was no Sand Creek. There was no rebellious son . . . and there was no Sir Edwin S. Tynes.

The children sat around the table listening in awe as they always did when their father played his mandolin. The music was enchanting and magical, made more so by the fact that Zeke did not play the instrument for them very often. He had taught himself to play the instrument early in life, in the lonely moments when he'd retreated to the swamps behind his father's house to get away from taunting whites and a chiding stepmother who'd never failed to remind him that he did not belong in her house. Actually, he had decided she was right. He belonged in the mountains, in the out-of-doors, with the animals and the earth. It was there in the swamps that he'd begun to toy with the mandolin. His father, who had gotten it from a friend, had given the mandolin to him in the hope of interesting Zeke in something, anything, for as a boy he was restless and inattentive in school, wanting only to get back outside, never fitting in with anyone.

Alone, the young Zeke had taught himself to play, and he'd made up his own mountain songs, which he occasionally sang now to his family and Abbie. Mostly he played and sang for Abbie, for when he did he was all Tennessee man again. He knew he took her to her own childhood home through his songs.

Wolf's Blood watched, feeling less a part of the family than ever as his sisters and brothers listened attentively, Jeremy holding a book in his lap. He waited until Zeke finished and told the children it was time for bed before making his announcement.

"I am leaving tomorrow, Father, to go north," he spoke up. "I am well enough now."

The room quieted, and Zeke set the mandolin down, leaning its long neck against the table. Abbie saw the determined look on her son's face and knew she could not hold him there any longer. A wave of despair engulfed her and she looked away. "Get to bed, children," she told the others.

"But we won't see Wolf's Blood again!" Margaret lamented.

"Yes, you will," Abbie replied, looking at Wolf's Blood almost chidingly. "I am sure he will be kind enough to stay around long enough in the morning to see all of you one last time."

Their eyes held. "I will not leave without saying good-bye," he assured his mother. He saw the hurt in her eyes and it pained him, but he refused to let it make him stay.

Abbie rose and herded the children to the loft while Zeke sat watching his son. "You'll have to be very careful, son. You'll be traveling alone."

"That will make it easier for me to hide, and I will do some traveling at night. I know what to watch for, Father."

"Send a runner down and let us know if you arrive safely," Zeke said.

The boy nodded and swallowed. "I will . . . miss you, Father. But I have thought about it . . . for a long time. I must do this."

Zeke's heart hurt so badly that he put a hand to his chest. "I know."

Abbie came back to the table and sat down, looking almost angry as she crossed her arms in front of her. "I suppose you've heard the rumors that white women are being raped and murdered, that some have been taken

151

captive by the Sioux for ransom," she said briskly to her son. "Do you intend to take part in such doings . . . to commit depredations against women who are no different from your own mother and sisters?"

The boy frowned, confused by her sudden anger and chastisement. "I do not believe I would," he answered.

"You might have to," Abbie answered, while Zeke watched curiously, allowing her to get her feelings out, whatever they might be. "If you are riding with a raiding party and they attack innocent women and children and slaughter them or rape them or make slaves of them, do you intend to put up your hand and tell them to stop? They would slay you right along with the whites!"

"I will do whatever I must do!" the boy answered angrily. "I cannot say yet what I will do, except that I have vengeance in my heart that will not let me sleep. I will ride with the Sioux and I will fight, because I am a Cheyenne!" He rose and pulled his knife, stabbing it into the wooden table so that it stuck there. "Cheyenne! Do you understand that, Mother? I am not white, not one bit of me!"

Abbie rose also, her eyes on fire. "You came from my womb!" she said, her voice rising. "A part of you is white whether you like it or not! I understand your need for revenge, Wolf's Blood. Your father has the same need and has killed many men because of it. When those men murdered his wife back in Tennessee, he went after them and got every one of them. But he didn't go around raping white women just because his own wife had been raped! Nor does he do so today, in spite of what happened to me! He kills either in self-defense, or he kills men who do him wrong! But he does not kill innocent people!"

"That is different!" Wolf's Blood hissed, trying not to yell at his mother. "Everything is different now! How can we go against the soldiers who attacked us at Sand Creek? How are we to know who they were? How can we ever find them again? We cannot fight man to man anymore! It is impossible! We must keep the white men out of our land, and we do not have the numbers or the weapons to attack their soldiers and towns and ever hope to win! The only thing left to do is attack the settlements—to try to scare them out! There is no other way for us! How much are the Cheyenne or the Sioux or any of us supposed to take? We tried peace, Mother, and you know it! But treaty after treaty has been broken. The white man does not want peace! He wants our land and he wants the Indian dead! He rapes and murders our women and children, raids and plunders our camps. Why is that any different from Indians raiding settlements?"

"The men who raided at Sand Creek were soldiers, not settlers! They were one hundred-day volunteers," Abbie shot back. "Rabble! They were not innocent farmers, women and children."

The boy's eyes glittered with desperate anger. He did not like arguing with his mother. He worshiped her. But there was a stubborn and, worst of all, a sensible side to her that frustrated him. "That is the white woman in you, Mother," he told her in a quieter voice. "That is the part of you that will never understand what I am talking about. Those innocent settlers are killing off the Indian just as surely as the soldiers do. They just do it in a different way. They take our land, our game, our freedom. They want us dead, just as surely as the soldiers do. And they use the soldiers to do their dirty job for them so they can feel clean and innocent! But they are not innocent! They go where they have no right to go! Father understands what I am saying, and if he were free, he would go north with me and fight with Red Cloud and Swift Arrow!"

Abbie blinked and looked suddenly beaten. She swallowed, her lip quivering. "Promise me you will not harm white women and children. Surely I bred that much civility in you! When you ride down on white women and children, think of your own mother and sisters. Ride against the soldiers, Wolf's Blood, if you must do so, and against the supply trains and miners. Cut the telegraph lines and root out the buffalo hunters. But don't make me envision my son hurting children and innocent women. Do you think those women and children are out here by choice? They are here because that is where their men have taken them. They had no choice! If they could have chosen, they would have stayed in the East, away from this lawless land! The government, the men in power, and perhaps some of the settlers want the Indian wiped out, Wolf's Blood, not little children and gentle housewives!"

Zeke frowned at her remark about the women having no choice. Was that how she had felt all these years? Was she wishing to be back East? He was again overwhelmed with guilt about her own ruthless treatment many months ago. Had that made her finally wish she had never agreed to stay in Colorado with a half-breed Indian?

"Right now I make no promises, Mother," Wolf's Blood told her sadly.

She pressed her lips tightly together and said nothing more, but simply turned and walked briskly into her own bedroom. Wolf's Blood turned to his father, a helpless look on his face.

"Don't worry about it, son. I'll talk to her. You get some rest." He rose and walked around the table. Their eyes held for a moment, and then they embraced. "You can understand how she feels, son."

The boy nodded and pulled away. His watery eyes met his father's. "I cannot help how I feel, Father. Surely she knows I would not bring harm to women and children if I can help it. I remember the day she was taken from here, how I felt trying to keep those men from touching my mother. She sacrificed herself that day so they would not harm her children. She let them take her, knowing what they would do to her. My mother is the finest woman I know. I do not like making her unhappy, but she never seems to be able to accept that I am a man. An Indian woman would never talk to her son in such a way, and when she scolds me it makes me angry and makes me say things I do not mean."

Zeke smiled sadly. "She does have a way of saying her piece. In this case she has damned good reason to say it, after what she's been through." He put a hand on the boy's shoulder. "You should weigh it heavily in your mind, Wolf's Blood. And when you ride with the Sioux and the northern Cheyenne, don't be afraid to do what you know is right in your heart. Get your vengeance in the right way. That's all she's telling you."

The boy nodded. "I am going out to the stables, Father. I want to . . . want to see all the horses once more, walk through the buildings. I will probably sleep out there tonight. Then if you and mother have words about me, I won't hear them." He swallowed. "I will miss the ranch, Father, the horses, my brothers and sisters, most of all you and Mother. Perhaps I will even come back someday. I cannot say now."

Zeke took his hand from the boy's shoulder and nodded. "I know." He sighed. "Give our love to Swift

Arrow. And if you make it back down here, try to get him to come with you. It's been a long, long time since I've seen my brother. Too long."

"I will tell him." The boy picked up his heavy buckskin jacket lined with sheep's wool and put it on. "I will go out now. I must get some things ready for my trip."

He stood there awkwardly for a moment, not knowing what else to say. How many ways did a son tell his father he loved him? How many ways were there to say good-bye. He turned away and went through the door, and Zeke looked at the doorway to the bedroom where his wife was. There were times when he didn't know what to do with Abbie's stubborn streak, and this was one of them. His big frame ambled through the curtained doorway and he walked through to see her already in her flannel gown, sitting up and reading her Bible by the dim lamplight. She looked up at him, her eyes unreadable.

"The boy only answered you that way because you made him feel like a child," he told her. "You have to let go of him, Abbie."

She closed her Bible and looked away. "That's the hardest thing for a mother to do," she answered quietly. "I guess what makes me angry with him is that he never allowed me the privilege of babying him and cuddling him, even when he was small. He's run wild ever since he was able to stand up and walk."

"I suppose much of that is my fault," Zeke answered, coming around to the other side of the bed. "And I don't doubt you blame me for it."

She watched him lovingly. "Oh, Zeke, that isn't so. I love the People, and when he was little we lived among them. I wanted to let him be Cheyenne because it seemed he was born to it from the first day he breathed

156

life. We both let him be what came naturally. But now it's suddenly difficult for me to accept it."

He pulled off his shirt. "They'll all be different, Abbie, and once they're grown we have to let go of them and let them be what they will. There'll be no stopping them, and if and when they go away, it's better they at least leave on good terms and know that they are loved simply for what they are." He turned to face her, an alarming agony in his eyes. "You told him those women aren't out here by choice, that they're here because their men want to be here. Is that how you've felt all these years? I'd take you back East in a minute, Abbie, if that is what you want, in spite of how much I would hate it. I'd do it and I'd be able to handle it. I never meant to make you feel forced to stay here. You know how guilty I've felt all these years for marrying you and subjecting you to life in a wild land. But I've loved you for understanding why I needed to be out here with my people. Now I don't know what's going to happen to them. They might be shipped hundreds of miles from here. It's all different, and if you want to go home to Tennessee before you're old, I'll take you."

Her eyes teared and she reached out and touched his face. "When I married you, Zeke, I was already out here, you were already out here. I knew you belonged here and I married you anyway. When I spoke of those other women, I only meant their husbands married them first and then came west, giving them no choice. I had plenty of choices before I married you, and you did your best to discourage me. I married you because I wanted the scout Cheyenne Zeke for my own, and I knew that no matter where we lived I could be happy as long as I was with Zeke. Don't put more into my words than what was there, Zeke. All these years

157

you've carried an unnecessary burden of guilt for marrying me. I wanted to be Zeke Monroe's woman no matter what I had to do to make that happen. My happiness depends on your happiness, and you'd never be happy back in Tennessee. That's gone now. I deserted that life years ago. Sometimes I wonder if I ever really lived there. It's as though that Abbie never even existed." She leaned back on her pillow and watched him. "And you know how I love the People, know it hurts my heart to see what is happening. I want very much to stay here, to do what I can to help them whatever that might be. Don't let any of this come between us, Zeke. I've seen a strange resignation in you ever since Sand Creek and it frightens me."

He sighed and leaned over her. "I just . . . sometimes I can't get over the guilt of being responsible for your hardships."

"Do you call lying beneath the man I love a hardship? Is living in this cozy cabin with seven healthy, lovely children a hardship? The only real hardship in life, Zeke, is to not be loved, to have no one who cares. I have eight wonderful people who care, and it's the same for you." She closed her eyes. "I'm sorry for getting so upset. I guess it was just my roundabout way of trying to get Wolf's Blood to stay, my way of covering the hurt of his leaving. I wanted him to hurt too, and that's no way for a mother to be. I don't know what got into me. Perhaps I should go out and talk to him."

"No. You gave him food for thought. Let him weigh it in his mind. He should. You can talk to him in the morning." He leaned down and kissed her tenderly. "Thank you, Abbie, just for being my Abbie girl."

She reached around his neck and he pulled her close, pulling the covers over them against the cold. "Try to sleep," he told her, holding her firmly and caressing her hair. "We have to be strong in the morning. Our son is truly leaving us for the first time."

He lay his head on the pillow beside her, and then she felt him tremble slightly. He made an odd choking sound. "My God, Abbie, I'll miss him so much!" he groaned.

Chapter Eight

Abbie dropped the still warm biscuits into a small burlap bag and turned to put it into her son's parfleche, along with the potatoes and carrots she had already put inside, and the leather pouch of pemmican and some jerked meat. It was only five o'clock in the morning and the house was quiet as she prepared food for her wayward son. There was a light tapping at the door, and she went to open it, letting in Wolf's Blood. He stood there in his grandest Indian regalia, buckskins and winter moccasins. Beads and ornaments were tied into his long, black hair. The sight of him quickened Abbie's heart, for at that very moment he looked as striking as his father had the first day she'd set eyes on him.

Their eyes held briefly and then she stepped aside, closing the door after he came inside. She folded her arms and looked him up and down, her son, as tall and broad as his own father, and as handsome. "My, you look grand," she told him with a soft smile.

He frowned and studied her. She was supposed to be angry with him. "I do?"

She walked to his parfleche. "You make me long for my younger days. You're a replica of young Zeke

161

Monroe, you know. I made you some fresh biscuits, Wolf's Blood. I hope you appreciate it. I was up at three-thirty kneading the dough and getting it ready. And I packed you some pemmican and some jerked meat and a few raw vegetables. I'll get Zeke up. He wants to pick out a couple of the better Appaloosas for you take along as a gift for Swift Arrow."

He watched her finish filling the parfleche. "You are not angry with me?"

She stopped and met his eyes. "You're my son. I'll not have you go away with hard feelings. What if you never came back?" She blinked back tears and glanced at the parfleche she had beaded for him herself. "Besides, I only said those things because I was desperate to find a way to make you stay. Still, I gave you some things to think about, and when the time comes I'm sure you'll do the right thing, just as Zeke always does. You are your father's son, which means you are a good boy . . . man, I should say." She met his eyes again. "I will trust in that, Wolf's Blood. You're a fine young man, a fine young Indian man. I understand you and I love you, and I want you to take my love with you when you go, not my anger." She wiped her hands on her apron almost nervously. "I only ask . . . I know you aren't one to express affection . . . but I'll not let you leave without . . . without holding you once in my arms." She looked at him again. "Do you think you can satisfy this white woman's needs just once before you run away?"

He stepped around the table, putting his hands on her shoulders. "I am not running away, Mother. I am trying to know myself."

She closed her eyes and nodded. "Come back, Wolf's Blood, if not for my sake then for your father's. He needs you, in more ways than you know. A little bit of him will die when you leave."

Their eyes held and then he embraced her and she cried quietly against his chest. "I will come back, Mother. I don't know when, but I will come back. It is the same for me. I love my father. But I must go away for a while. I must learn to be strong without him."

She clung to him tightly, wondering if she herself was strong enough to survive without Zeke. She had been able to do so several times when he'd been forced to be away, but she'd known he would come back to her. What if he didn't? What would she do if Zeke Monroe no longer breathed life?

"Don't stay away forever," she whispered to her son, a note of urgency in her voice. "When your father is gone and you are here, it's as though he's here too. You're so much like him, Wolf's Blood." She leaned back and looked up at him, her arms still about his waist and tears on her cheeks. "Every time I look at you, I remember that awful day when Dancing Moon came after me with a knife and you tried to defend me with your lance. You were so small, but you were already a warrior in your heart. I guess I knew then that you would one day ride with Swift Arrow and the others."

He smiled down at her. "You saved my life that day, Mother. That wicked woman was going to kill me after she took that lance away from me. If you had not killed her yourself, I would be dead. You are a warrior woman and you do not even know it."

"That was necessary," she said, sobering. "I would kill for any of my children, and I would die for them if necessary . . . so would your father."

He kissed her forehead. "And I would kill for you and father both," he replied.

Zeke came through the bedroom door then, wearing only his buckskin pants and still shirtless. He stopped and eyed his son and wife. "You two are on speaking terms I see," he stated.

Wolf's Blood turned and walked to the man, his arm around his mother's waist. Zeke gave his son a hard, long look. It was as though he were looking at himself twenty years earlier. "You look damned good, Wolf's Blood. You'll make a good impression when you ride into the Sioux camps. And when they see how well you can use the knife and lance, they'll welcome you readily enough."

"I will never use the knife as well as my father," the boy answered. "Many people speak of Cheyenne Zeke and his big knife. And there are many other ways I will not be as good as my father," he added. "I can only try."

He put out his hand and Zeke grasped it, holding tightly to the boy's wrist. Then Wolf's Blood let go of his mother and the two men embraced. "Goddamn, I'll miss you Wolf's Blood," Zeke said quietly to the boy. "But you aren't a little boy anymore and I can't hold on to you forever. Go your own way, son. But come back to us now and then." He thought about another day, that day long ago when he had left his own home back in Tennessee. He didn't care to think about how many years ago that had been.

Wolf's Blood pulled away then and nodded. "I will come back." He put on a smile and fought an urge to cry. "Mother said you wanted me to take two horses to Swift Arrow."

Zeke nodded. "Let me get a shirt on and a jacket. We'll go pick them out." He went back into the bedroom and Abbie got busy with breakfast as the rest of the children began to sleepily descend from the loft. From then on everything was rush and bedlam—breakfast and packing and tears and good-byes. Margaret cried the most. She was the closest to her brother and had always looked to him for protection whenever Zeke was gone. She and Wolf's Blood had the keenest memories of their early life among the Cheyenne, before Zeke and Abbie were settled on the ranch, when the Cheyenne had roamed freely, when life was happier, and when they sometimes went with the Cheyenne on the summer hunts. That was over now. There had been the Laramie Treaty of 1851, then the Treaty of Fort Wise in 1861. Each had given the Cheyenne less and less room to move around. Now a treaty that would take them out of Colorado altogether was in the making, and Sand Creek had shown them what would happen to those who did not obey. But there were a few, like Wolf's Blood, who would hang on to the bitter end.

Too soon, Wolf's Blood was standing beside his mount. Again he went around the circle of his family, beginning with his Uncle Lance and then the smallest child, Jason. He embraced Margaret longer than the others, telling her to be a proud Cheyenne. Then came the hardest part, saying good-bye one last time to his mother and father. He hugged Abbie for a long time, having to practically force her to let go of him finally. His father he did not embrace. It would be too difficult. They grasped hands and said everything with their eyes, unable to speak. Wolf's Blood turned then and mounted his horse with ease, taking two ropes in hand to lead the extra horses. Wolf had been prancing nervously in circles. He sensed a new adventure coming and was happy to be off, running across the land with his master. This would be much better than sitting inside a house. This was freedom, excitement!

Wolf's Blood scanned the whole brood with tear-filled eyes. "I love you all," he told them. Then he looked at his father and mother. "Not a night will go by that you are not in my thoughts and prayers. Both of you have taught me strength and independence. If I can be nearly as wise, as strong, and as skilled as you, I shall

165

be satisfied. Perhaps one day I can learn to love in the way that you love one another. If I do, I will be a lucky man." He held his father's eyes. *"Nemehotatse."*

"Nemehotatse, Nahahan," Zeke replied. He crossed his arms in front of him, his right wrist across his heart, his left wrist atop the right wrist. He pushed against his chest, giving the Cheyenne hand sign for love.

Wolf's Blood turned his horse then. *"Hai! Hai!"* he shouted, kicking the animal's sides and taking off at a gallop. If it was to be done, it must be done quickly.

Zeke stepped away from the others, watching the boy slowly disappear over a distant hill. A soft morning wind blew his long black hair about his face and shoulders. When he'd been young and free and wild, he had ridden with the Cheyenne, raided enemy camps, gone on the buffalo hunts, and shared warm tipi fires in the winters. Now his Cheyenne mother and stepfather were dead, as were two of his Cheyenne brothers. Perhaps some day the entire race would be gone. If Wolf's Blood could ride relatively free for the few years left to the Indian, then he would let the boy go. He heard a war whoop in the distance and grinned, but his jaw quickly flexed in buried sorrow. Abbie watched him, this man who was as elusive as the wind at times, whose son was just the same. She stepped closer and he turned and embraced her.

"Let's walk for a while, Abbie girl," he told her softly.

Several days later the letter came from Bonnie Lewis. "Dan is back at Fort Laramie!" Abbie told Zeke as she scanned the letter. "He's doing all right, and Bonnie is there teaching again." She read further and her face clouded. "Bonnie's husband was killed by

166

Indians, Zeke, while she was back East. That's terrible! Poor Bonnie!"

She was standing outside beside her husband, who had been cutting wood while she read the letter. Zeke slammed an ax into a log and came to stand beside her. "Rodney Lewis is dead?"

She looked up at him. Both of them knew Bonnie Lewis had secretly loved Zeke for years, ever since he'd rescued her from outlaws who dealt in the buying and selling of white women. Zeke had risked his life to save Bonnie; then he had returned her to her missionary father in Santa Fe. In doing so, he had made an impression on Bonnie Lewis that she had never forgotten. She had never known a man like Zeke Monroe in her sheltered, timid life, and his brawny power and brave skills had overwhelmed her. But there had been nothing between them; Zeke Monroe already had been married to Abbie. It was a one-sided love that could not be requited, and Bonnie Lewis had gone on to marry her preacher husband, a marriage planned for years. She found some consolation later when Zeke and Abbie brought their crippled nephew to her and asked if she would care for the boy.

"Joshua is doing well," Abbie went on, returning to the letter. She sighed deeply. "I'm glad now that she has the boy, Zeke. She would be so lonely without him." Her eyes sought his and they shared a look of understanding.

"I'm glad, too," Zeke told her. "It's too bad about her husband. I don't think they had much of a marriage, but he was a dedicated man who stuck to his beliefs. Apparently he died for them. I just hope Bonnie stays close to the fort. These are bad times, Abbie. You have to be careful too. Some of the Cheyenne you once called friend may not consider you a friend any longer.

I hate to say it, but the anger and hatred is so deep that you shouldn't be too ready to trust the younger ones who don't know you."

She closed her eyes and nodded. "It breaks my heart to think of it, but you're probably right." She scanned the letter again. "Oh, Zeke, Emily is in St. Louis again and won't come west. Poor Dan. I thought they had straightened all that out."

Zeke's face darkened. "I ought to go to St. Louis and kick her ass all the way to Fort Laramie!" he mumbled, going back to retrieve his ax. "I risked my life and you went through hell while I was off in that damned war, just to find Dan . . . and why? Because she came sobbing to us about how much she loved him and how worried she was about him. Then she pulls that trick again, staying in St. Louis. She's spoiled!"

"Zeke, don't talk that way about your brother's wife. Besides, once you knew about Dan you'd have gone to find him without Emily asking you to do so."

He chopped at more wood. "Well, the fact remains I wouldn't have known about it if she hadn't come crying to us. I don't know how she can treat Dan that way. He's a good man, a dedicated husband and soldier, and he's crazy about her. Why, I'll never know, but he is. It's mean of her to stay in St. Louis. He needs her now more than ever." He chopped angrily then, slicing off a piece of fresh cottonwood. "If I were Dan I'd go to St. Louis and drag her back by the hair of the head!"

He slammed the ax down again, and Abbie watched with a smile on her face and a pleasant stirring deep inside. "You would, would you?"

He stopped and looked over at her, then flashed his handsome grin. "I would." His eyes moved over her body that was shrouded by a heavy animal-skin jacket. "No woman of mine would get away with that. Fact is,

168

I'd never have married such a creature in the first place. Trouble is, I got a woman that's almost more than I can handle. You go killing any more big bucks and you'll make me look bad."

She laughed lightly and watched the ax come down hard, noted the strength of the powerful arms that held it. "That will be the day, my husband." She returned to the letter. "Bonnie and Dan want us to write back. They heard about Sand Creek and are worried about us. I'll go start a letter right now and you can ride with Jeremy to Fort Lyon and find someone to take it north."

"Be sure to tell them about Wolf's Blood. Tell Dan to see what he can find out about the boy, whether he got there all right and all. Tell him to have his scouts keep an eye out and give Dan word whenever they see Wolf's Blood so he can let us know how the boy is."

Abbie's smile faded and their eyes held. "I'll tell him."

He nodded and frowned. "You know, it's too bad Dan is married to that slip of a woman. If he were free, he'd be smart to go after Bonnie. She'll be needing a husband now. They'd be good together. If that brother of mine had had any sense, he'd have married a woman like her in the first place."

Her eyebrows arched in mock jealousy. "Oh? Well at the moment I am glad that she is up there and we are down here."

Zeke smiled at her and winked. "Abbie girl, even a woman like Bonnie can't hold a candle to you." He grew more serious then. "That's too bad, though, about Rodney Lewis. I'd better check things out at Fort Lyon when I go, see what I can find out about the Sioux. Things might be worse up north than we thought, and with Wolf's Blood up there, we'd best try to keep informed on what is happening. I know Red Cloud is really on the warpath to keep the miners and settlers out of the Powder River country."

Abbie folded the letter. "Remember the time we rode north for the Laramie Treaty, Zeke? That seems like a hundred years ago."

He nodded. "If the damned government would have stuck to the original treaty, there might not be so much trouble now," he answered. "Word is the Cheyenne are forming a strong alliance north and south now, Abbie. Perhaps Wolf's Blood should have stayed here if he wanted some action, although maybe it's good for him to be in new surroundings. The Dog Soldiers are gaining firm control and the warriors are well disciplined. Leaders like Tall Bull and White Horse are organizing. There'll be a lot of raiding and senseless killing, Abbie, all because the white man doesn't know how to keep his word. I expect Dan will have his work cut out for him up in the Dakotas and Montana. And we'll have to keep a sharp lookout around here. We aren't necessarily safe from the Cheyenne anymore, at least not if I'm not around. But I don't worry about them as much as I worry about raiding Apaches and Comanches. They seem to be spreading out of their own territory. Seems like every Indian tribe east of the Mississippi is on the warpath lately, Abbie girl. They're desperate and hungry and scared. I know you're used to trusting the Cheyenne, but I want you to be more careful; and I don't want the children riding anyplace alone."

She put the letter in her jacket pocket. Her heart felt heavy. It didn't seem right that she should have to worry about the Cheyenne, but past cruelties and broken promises and rotgut whiskey were all working to bring a change to the once-beautiful People of the

Plains. She turned to go inside when a rider appeared in the distance. "Someone is coming," she told Zeke.

Zeke planted the ax into another log and watched, walking to his rifle. It was apparently a lone man, and as he rode closer on a fine black horse a woolen cape attached to the shoulders of his finely cut overcoat flopped with the horse's stride.

Abbie was upset to see that it was Sir Tynes. She had hoped he would not come around again. The man disturbed her, for she didn't want Zeke to be upset by anything. He had enough to worry about without a wealthy Englishman living so near them and reminding them of how settled Colorado had become. As the man rode up to the woodpile, Abbie saw Zeke go rigid with repressed anger.

"Mister Monroe, you're back!" Tynes exclaimed, dismounting and putting out his hand. "I do hope your son is all right. I heard about Sand Creek and I wanted to express my sorrow and to find out if your son and you were all right."

Zeke took the hand reluctantly, seeing sincerity in the man's eyes. "We're all right. My son was badly wounded and a girl he loved was killed. I also had a Cheyenne brother who was killed, along with his family."

Tynes's face darkened. "How terrible!" He looked over at Abbie, genuine concern on his face, mixed with what Zeke interpreted as affection. "How terrible for both of you. I'm sincerely sorry." He looked back up at Zeke, still clasping the man's hand. "Perhaps I have come at a bad time then. Is your son recovered? I should like to meet him."

"He's recovered," Zeke answered, letting go of the man's hand. "He's gone north to make war alongside Red Cloud and the Sioux. I have a Cheyenne brother

171

up there who lives among the Sioux. I'm afraid after what my son saw at Sand Creek, his heart is very confused and bitter. He's gone away to find his revenge, and perhaps to find himself."

Sir Tynes scanned Zeke. The man looked even larger in his heavy deerskin coat. "I've been in touch with Pueblo and Julesberg, Mister Monroe. The Indians, mostly Cheyenne, are making some bad raids. There are even rumors that up to a thousand warriors are headed for Julesberg to wipe out the town, but no one has been able to spot the marauders."

Zeke just grinned. "Good. I hope they're successful. If it weren't for my wife and family I'd be with them." He picked up his ax and sobered. "Whatever you heard about Sand Creek, Tynes, I'm sure the story was distorted if it came from whites, especially from the governor's office in Denver. I was there. I saw the slaughtered bodies of women and little babies and old people, ears cut off, fingers cut off, privates cut off, heads bashed in beyond recognition. I buried my brother and his wife and their little son. It was no battle, Sir Tynes. It was a deliberate, unnecessary slaughter of a band of peaceful Indians. I don't give a damn what the Cheyenne do in retaliation. More power to them."

Tynes eyed him coolly as he chopped more wood. Then the man looked over at Abbie. "How was that venison, Mrs. Monroe? Tasty, I'll bet." He was referring to the deer she had shot the day he'd visited.

"Very good. There is a lot left, smoked and cured. Just last night we—"

"What's your business here, Tynes," Zeke interrupted, disturbed by the way the Englishman looked at his Abbie. "I'm a busy man."

Abbie was tempted to scold her husband for his

172

rudeness, but there were times when it was best not to interfere in Zeke Monroe's actions.

"Well, I . . . I was just being neighborly. I thought you might like to know what I had learned about the Cheyenne . . . and I wanted to find out about your son. The last time I was here your wife was quite worried, and—"

"The last time you were here I was gone."

Their eyes held. "Yes. Well, I didn't know that until I got here."

"Didn't you?"

Sir Tynes's face reddened slightly. "I assure you I did not. If you think I am spying on you and yours, Mister Monroe, you are gravely mistaken. I am here to be neighborly and to look at your horses, and to tell you that if you have any problems because of all this raiding I will be glad to help out. The house I am building is made of stone and will be a virtual fortress. You are obviously a man of great skills and one who has good rapport with the Indians, so you may not need any help. But if you do, my doors are open. You must stop judging all wealthy men by the same standards, Mister Monroe. I judge men by their worth as people, not by their means or race, and I am sure you judge men no less fairly. So please judge me as a lonely neighbor who wishes to be a friend and who admires your magnificent horses. Don't turn me out just because I happen to have money."

"It isn't the fact that you have money, Tynes," Zeke replied, removing his gloves and throwing them down. "It's the fact that you're here at all. I'm sorry, but Sand Creek is still fresh in my mind; and it's people like you who, one by one, are killing off my People."

The man nodded. "You are probably right. But you are not a fool, Mister Monroe, and you know as well as

173

I that the West will be settled, whether it be gently or ruthlessly. Either way it will happen. I am in total agreement that it is a sad and unfair situation for the Indians, but whether I stay or leave will make no difference to what will ultimately happen. It's been inevitable since the Pilgrims first landed on the Eastern shores. I don't say that without feeling, Mister Monroe. I do sympathize with your people. In fact, I am writing a book about them, about the American West and all the excitement out here. And I plan to do great justice to the red man in my writing and to tell both sides. I would be very honored if you would tell me what you saw at Sand Creek so I can add it to my notes. There is quite an investigation going on in Denver, you know, from the governor down to the volunteers who participated in the raid."

Zeke stared at the rapidly talking Englishman. He wondered if the man had any idea what hardships in this land were all about. "A book?" he asked, grinning. He snickered then, the sound building to full laughter. "A book!" He looked at Abbie, who didn't know whether to laugh with him or be angry with him. Sir Tynes drank in her beauty as she stepped closer. He had hoped his desire for her was done, but now that he saw her again it was reawakened.

"Zeke, if Sir Tynes wants to try writing a book about this land, I think we should answer his questions and talk to him. At least maybe the truth will be told. What harm can that do?"

Sir Tynes smiled and bowed. "Thank you, dear lady."

Zeke put a casual arm around his wife and pulled her close. "Tynes, I don't have you completely figured out yet, except that you're amusing if nothing else. I'll answer your questions, and you'd better tell it straight

174

if you ever get anything in print."

Tynes removed his hat and bowed again. "You have my word. Now, may I see your horses? I need some good sturdy ones for keeping my cattle together. Oh, and if any of my cattle should stray onto your property, just shoo them back over, or corral them and hold them until one of my men comes round looking for them. I'll pay you for your trouble if that should happen."

Zeke shook his head. "No need. But if you run across any of my animals on your place, I'd appreciate the same favor. Come on over to the stables and I'll show you some of my better stock. They haven't been turned out yet." He'd started walking, one arm around Abbie, when they heard a gunshot. Sir Tynes was amazed at how quickly Zeke turned and whisked up his rifle, running in the direction of the shot. A young boy came running from a clump of thick cottonwoods down near the river, holding a rifle in one hand and a small animal in the other.

"Father! I got a rabbit! I got a rabbit!" the boy shouted as Zeke ran toward him.

"Oh, Jeremy!" Abbie exclaimed. She looked at Sir Tynes. "That's the first time the boy has ever managed to hit something. He's been trying for so long."

She started walking toward her husband and son, and Sir Tynes followed, envisioning her slender form beneath the mounds of winter clothing. Zeke was laughing and praising his son when they reached them, and Jeremy was beaming with pride. Perhaps he could be a real son to Zeke Monroe after all.

"Jeremy, such a big one!" Abbie told him.

"I know!" the boy said, grinning from ear to ear. "Will you fix it for supper, Mama? Will you?"

"I certainly will. But you have to skin it and clean it first."

175

The boy looked at his father. "Will you show me with your knife?"

Zeke took out the big blade and Sir Tynes grimaced. "I sure will," Zeke answered. He took the rabbit from the boy and cut off the head as though the rabbit's bones were made of butter. He started to hand the head to Sir Tynes as a joke, but the man was studying Abbie's face intently as she watched Zeke. The obvious love and desire in the man's eyes could not be denied. Zeke sobered, set the head aside, and in one quick flash ripped his knife through the animal's belly to slit it open and clean it.

"How can you do that so easily?" Sir Tynes asked. "Your weapon must be very sharp."

Zeke looked up at the man, the bloody knife in his hand. "It is. But a rabbit has fur, which makes it harder to cut quick and clean. I can go through a man a lot faster."

Their eyes held and Sir Tynes swallowed. "Yes. I am sure you can."

The winter was long and lonely without Wolf's Blood. Zeke and Abbie's worries were made worse by the fact that the Cheyenne had built their force to over a thousand warriors, and although Black Kettle still would not fight, there were many others with memories of Sand Creek who would. The raiding and killing had become fierce and hot. Many settlers were slaughtered, ranches were burned, and cattle and horses were stolen. No ranch was safe, and many forts were not safe. Stages were stopped and robbed. In one instance the entire payroll for the Colorado soldiers was ripped from its strongbox and chopped to pieces by the Cheyenne, the little pieces of "green paper" scattered

176

for miles. A train near Valley Station, west of Julesberg, was attacked and twelve men were killed. On February 2, 1865, the town of Julesberg itself was attacked and burned, and hundreds of thousands of dollars worth of supplies were either stolen or destroyed. The Cheyenne fed their starving bellies with white men's cattle and with stolen flour, meats, dried fruits, and molasses. The Cheyenne victory and the plunder they took at Julesberg helped ease their ravaged hearts and minds of the memories of Sand Creek. They had become so powerful and determined that they dared to hold a victory dance after destroying Julesberg, right in front of the soldiers and civilians who huddled inside Fort Rankin. Telegraph poles were cut and used for fires. Indeed, the Indians had become such a force that help had to be sent all the way from Fort Laramie.

Dan was not among those who came to the rescue of the Colorado citizenry. He was busy with the Sioux in the north, which was exactly where many of the southern Cheyenne were headed. Troops were dispatched from Laramie to try to stop that northward movement. Meanwhile the Cheyenne plundered and murdered as they pursued their northward trek. Nothing was safe between the north and south branches of the Platte River. Relief troops headed out of Fort Laramie to back up those already dispatched. These troops were commanded by Lt. Col. William O. Collins, the commanding officer at Fort Laramie. But the efforts of the soldiers were to no avail. The strong force of Indians continued moving north, now and then getting into skirmishes with soldiers. But the soldiers were so outnumbered that the colonel finally decided to go back to Fort Laramie and to cease trying to stop the northward movement of the Cheyenne. The warring southern Cheyenne reached their northern hunting grounds, and soon joined the Oglala Sioux and the northern Cheyenne on the Powder River. Wolf's Blood found himself greeting former friends. The boy was full of excitement and ready to fight. The situation could only get worse, for Congress had granted a charter to the Union Pacific to build a railroad across the Plains, right through the heart of Indian country. The order was given for the "removal" of all Indians from the railroad lands.

Dan Monroe's wounds healed, and he found himself thrust into some of the worst Indian fighting since he'd first come west to join the Army. He only hoped he would not run into Wolf's Blood or into Zeke's Cheyenne brother, Swift Arrow. He had no desire to harm either of them, but it was his duty to protect the settlers as best he could. Scouts kept eyes and ears open for the wild and elusive Wolf's Blood, but so far to no avail. Consequently, Dan was unable to send Zeke and Abbie any news about their son.

Skirmishes turned into all-out war, while the Department of War and the Department of Interior fought their own battles in Washington over the best way to handle the Indians and how to handle and propose peace treaties. In Washington, there were arguments for and against peace offers. Some wanted to "punish" the Indians severely for their hostilities, others argued that this would only make matters worse. There was talk of a new reservation, this one in southern Kansas, far from Colorado and far from the North and South Platte. This talk had been going on for a long time, and men in power began secretly buying up more land along the Arkansas, in preparation for the day when the Cheyenne would be completely cleaned out of Colorado and the territory would be open to settlement.

Zeke and Lance were tired because they had to keep a constant lookout in addition to doing daily chores. In addition, Zeke's mind and heart were torn. His inner spirit wanted to make war alongside his Cheyenne brothers, but he had a family to support so he was forced to keep selling horses at Fort Lyon to soldiers and settlers. His situation confused him, hurt him. There were many men in similar circumstances. Famous scouts who'd once lived and traded with the Indians were now hired by the government to help hunt the red man to death or reservation life. They, too, felt helpless and confused, wanting the old life and ways to come back but knowing they never would.

Abbie watched Zeke become more and more withdrawn. His heart was torn by the wars and by his feelings for his own warring son about whom they heard little. He would have to count on Swift Arrow to watch out for the boy, and on Dan to send him news of Wolf's Blood's well-being. Occasionally Sir Tynes visited them during that long winter and spring, asking many questions and writing down many notes for his "book." Zeke began to think he could probably like the man if he hadn't suspected that Tynes had a yen for Abigail; and more and more Zeke considered what life would have been like for his Abbie girl if he had not married her and subjected her to the dangers of this wild land.

Amid headlines about warring Indians, mingled with more headlines about the progress taking place in the West due to the westward movement of the railroad and the construction of additional telegraph lines linking forts and towns and mining camps, there was a headline that stated that the now-crippled Charles Garvey was going east to college. Then came the headline about the assassination of President Lincoln. The Civil War was over, but a new war was beginning—in the West.

In August of 1865 the Kiowas, Comanches, and Kiowa-Apaches agreed to the Treaty of the Little Arkansas, opting for peace and agreeing to go to Kansas. But the remnants of the southern Cheyenne held out until October 14, 1865, when Black Kettle and six other leaders from his band placed their marks upon that treaty. However, some southern Cheyenne and all the northern Cheyenne refused to recognize the treaty, and that refusal promised future hardships. For those who agreed to the treaty, one hundred sixty acres of land was granted to each survivor of Sand Creek who had lost a husband or parents, such lands to be protected for fifty years. The peacemaking Indians were entreated by the government to convince the warring Indians to agree to the peace, and William Brent promised to live among the Cheyenne who agreed to the treaty for a period of time to see that they remained calm and agreeable.

A few Cheyenne, all half-bloods, were allowed to stay on land they already owned under the Treaty of Fort Wise. Zeke was among them, although he and Abbie had already signed title to the land under Abbie's name. Thus, all the reservation land under the old Fort Wise Treaty was open for settlement, just as Sir Tynes had said would happen. The Cheyenne were cleaned out of Colorado, but there were still hostiles north of the Platte who had to be persuaded to sign for peace. If they did not, the Treaty of the Little Arkansas would do little to stop the continuing Indian wars.

It was in November of 1865, when the few peaceful Cheyenne began a migration to Kansas along with other peacemaking tribes, that the war came to Zeke

Monroe's doorstep, in the form of renegade Comanches who needed supplies and horses, and someone to capture and use as ransom in exchange for rifles. The day started like any other, with Zeke going to open the door to the stables, and young LeeAnn running to the corral to open the gate for her father.

Chapter Nine

The ranch had been scouted for two days by a lone
Comanche warrior on foot. Yes, morning was a good
time to raid. That was when the men came out of the
house; then they would be in the open and easy to kill.
One of the men looked Indian, but perhaps he was only
part Indian for the ranch was a white man's dwelling. It
was a good ranch to raid, for the man's horses were
exceedingly beautiful and sturdy. They would be
excellent to trade for guns, as would the young girl with
the white hair and fair skin that the scout had seen.
Raiding Comanches were not expected in this cold
season, and a light snow that had fallen the night before
muffled their presence.

They were hungry. They were desperate. They were
determined to keep fighting. They needed horses and
women to trade for rifles. The twenty renegades had
moved quietly through the night to the bank of the
river just south of the ranch, where they were hidden by
cottonwoods. They watched patiently as dawn broke.
Finally both the men came out, the white man and the
one who looked Indian. There appeared to be no other

men about, only a woman and several children. The blond-haired girl came out soon after. It was apparently a custom for her to run to the corral gate and open it, then sit there as the two men brought out the beautiful horses.

They thought the white-haired girl belonged to the white man with the dark, curly hair. The Indian man must be a half-breed who helped on the white man's ranch. It made no difference. Both men must die, and the beautiful horses and the white-haired girl must be taken.

Zeke walked to the stables with Lance while LeeAnn ran to the gate. "We've got four pregnant mares now," Lance was telling his half-blood brother.

"Kehilan has been busy," Zeke answered with a grin, referring to his stud horse, called Drinker of the Wind.

Lance laughed. The two men set down their rifles and went to each stall, untying the horses one by one and nudging them out, then leading them to the stable entrance and slapping their rumps. Each horse trotted to the corral as Lance hurried out and began whistling and slapping them in the right direction. It didn't take much urging. They had been raised on this routine, kept in the stables on winter nights and then herded into the corral each morning for exercise. Most of them went willingly. Next came the horses in the bigger barn. The men picked up their rifles and walked to the building. Then Lance saddled a horse while Zeke took more horses from stalls.

"You must be getting tired, boy," he said to Kehilan. In response, the animal actually tossed his head and snorted, and Zeke and Lance both laughed.

"Not a bad life with all those wives, hey Zeke?" Lance joked. "A different woman every night."

"Every man's fantasy," Zeke replied, slapping the

perfectly formed Appaloosa stud on the rear.

"With a wife like Abigail, I doubt you think about it much," Lance teased, mounting his horse.

Zeke grinned, love in his eyes as he pulled out a mare. "I reckon you're right there. Besides, not many women would put up with my wild side, and fewer would want to bother with an aging man who's got so many battle scars he quit trying to count them."

"You're as mean and strong as ever," Lance reminded him, turning his horse. "Head them out, brother. I'll herd them to the corral." He trotted his mount through the door, and Zeke began urging the horses toward the entrance, Kehilan in the lead. All but two of the pregnant mares were through the entrance when Zeke heard the gunshot.

Immediately his body was tense and ready. He grabbed his rifle and ran to the barn entrance, shooing back the last two mares and running outside. Lance lay on the ground next to his horse, a bloody hole in his head and three arrows in his back. Zeke recognized the make of the arrows.

"Comanche!" he whispered. There was no time to allow his terrible grief to spend itself. From behind him he heard war whoops and thundering horses and the jingling of the brass bells Comanche warriors tied to the fringes of their leggings. "Abbie, stay inside and bolt the door!" he screamed, hoping she heard.

He ran toward LeeAnn, who sat frozen on the corral gate staring at the oncoming warriors already swooping around the barn, some with red streaks slashed on their faces, others with their cheeks painted yellow and black circles around their eyes.

"Run to the house, LeeAnn!" Zeke screamed at her, trying to reach her and protect her. But already a Comanche man was thundering up to her and reached for her. Zeke stopped and took aim, quickly firing and knocking the man from his mount.

LeeAnn began to scream as several other warriors circled the corral, tore down some of the fencing, and began to herd the horses away. LeeAnn was frozen, too frightened to move. Zeke could hear shots coming from the house and he knew Abbie was doing what she could from inside with her own rifle.

Zeke reached LeeAnn, who sat staring at the dead Indian in front of her. He grabbed her from the fence, tucked her under one arm, and began running. Then he felt a hot stinging in his back near his right shoulder. He refused to succumb to the pain, but turned and fired his rifle with just one hand. The bullet smashed into a warrior's face and the man jerked backward, yanking the reins with him and causing his mount to whirl and fall. Zeke dodged out of the way. Two more warriors were circling him then and with LeeAnn in one arm he couldn't move fast enough to manipulate his lever-action rifle to get another bullet into the chamber. He threw down the rifle, pulled out the handgun he kept tucked in his waistband and fired, hitting still another warrior before the second man took the club end of his lance and slammed it across Zeke's wrist, making him drop the handgun.

Zeke knew what the men were after besides the horses, and his desperate determination to protect his daughter helped him to ignore the pain of his wounds. A screaming LeeAnn still held in his left arm he grasped for his knife as two more warriors rode up. A rope was tossed around Zeke's neck from behind, but he whisked out his knife and quickly cut it. The three warriors circling him began to laugh and to make remarks about what a good fighter this Indian man seemed to be. They were enjoying the game.

There were more gunshots from the cabin, but there was nothing Abbie could to do help her husband. She dared not unbolt the door and expose the rest of the children to the raiders. She knew instinctively they might give up in a few more minutes and be satisfied with the horses. Zeke had taught her that in such situations she must be practical, no matter how horrifying and cold that might seem, and in this case she could not risk the lives of all the children just because the raiders were after one of them.

She fired several shots, hitting three of the raiders, but soon those herding away the horses were routing them toward the river and were out of range. She could not fire at the men attacking Zeke for fear of hitting Zeke or LeeAnn, so she watched from the window in helpless horror while the children huddled in the loft, shaking and crying.

Three warriors were now poking at Zeke with lances. He hacked off the end of one lance with his huge, sturdy blade, then he whirled and drove the blade into one warrior's thigh. Ignoring the stinging lances, he quickly turned again, ramming the knife into another warrior's side. That warrior fell with a scream and the other two backed off, one of them with a bleeding thigh, both of them amazed at the Indian man's skill and lack of fear. This was a great warrior. It was too bad there was no way he could keep them from taking the little girl he so fiercely protected. But since he was such a brave warrior, perhaps they would not kill him after all.

Two more raiders thundered up then, while the remaining warriors rode off with the stolen horses, yipping and making victory cries as they splashed through a shallow part of the river with their loot.

There was no way Zeke could get away from the

circle of warriors, and no way Abbie could fire at them from the house. Zeke's right shoulder screamed with hot pain, and his whole body protested the numerous jabbing cuts. His right wrist felt broken. LeeAnn's screams had turned to huddled sobs, as she clung tightly to her father, inhibiting his ability to fight in the manner Zeke Monroe normally could. He clung to her, the big blade in his right hand, ready to kill. He cursed the four warriors in the Comanche tongue, calling them women warriors for trying to steal a helpless girl. At that, their faces grew cold and curious so he gestured to them in sign language, indicating the girl was his own daughter. The warriors looked at each other and then began to laugh. They did not believe that the white-haired, blue-eyed child belonged to the dark Indian man.

"Perhaps now that the white father is dead, he wants her for himself," one of them joked in the Comanche tongue. "She is a good prize."

One of the others swung a club from behind, slamming it into the back of Zeke's skull. Zeke fell forward, keeping LeeAnn with him, stubbornly fighting his wounds and struggling to stay conscious as he placed his large frame over his daughter's in an attempt to keep the warriors from getting to her. He felt a foot pushing on him then, trying to roll him over, and somehow Zeke found the strength to bolt upright and ram his blade deep into his protagonist's belly, then rip upward to the warrior's throat while LeeAnn screamed in horror. She had never seen her father commit such a ruthless act. This was the Indian side of her father. This was the Cheyenne in him. It frightened her, yet now he was her only hope of being saved and she was afraid her father was going to die trying to protect her.

The other three warriors began to club Zeke before

he could rip his knife out of the fourth warrior's throat. Zeke finally yanked it out and whirled, slashing with the knife but unable to see because of the blows to his head. He felt himself falling, and he grasped for LeeAnn but felt her being torn from his hand. He heard her screams of terror, then laughter and war whoops and the sound of horses riding away.

Zeke still grasped his knife. He struggled to his knees, his bludgeoned mind thinking he could actually get on a horse and go after his daughter. But when he fought to get to his feet, he could not move. He groaned LeeAnn's name, feeling himself a failure, even though he had been one man against twenty warriors. In addition to the three dead braves Abbie had shot, five others lay dead around Zeke Monroe, a remarkable feat considering the odds and the vicious blow and stabbings Zeke had suffered. But he could not consider his struggle a success. Eight warriors out of twenty lay dead, but his daughter was gone. To Zeke that spelled failure. Zeke Monroe was not used to failure. Rage overwhelmed him at the thought that the Indians had been driven to such desperation that even he had suffered their revenge. Now he would have to go after the Comanche raiders and get his daughter back. Again and again he struggled to rise, breathing deeply, drawing on the inner fighting spirit that had made him a warrior.

He crawled to a fencepost and grasped it, pulling himself up by sheer will! He would not let his wounds stop him! He would pray to the spirits for strength and wisdom and he would get his daughter back from the Comanche.

Suddenly Abbie was there, speaking to him from some distant place for her voice seemed far away. He was barely aware that he draped an arm around her shoulders for support as she walked him to the cabin, where his children gasped and cried out at the sight of their bloodied, beaten father, his coat and clothes ripped by Comanche lances, his body caked with blood. His face was bruised and battered and his right wrist, already swollen, was an ugly purple color. Still, with amazing stubbornness, he still clung tightly to the blade in his right hand.

He heard Abbie ordering one of the children to boil water, and he was aware that she undressed him before he was lowered to their bed of robes. There was frightened crying somewhere, and someone asked what was going to happen to LeeAnn.

"Nothing will happen to her!" he heard Abbie say sternly. "They will save her to sell. They won't harm her. And your father will find her before she is sold. He will find her!" Her voice broke on the last words. He tried to speak, wanting to console her, but neither his body nor his mouth would move. Blackness began to envelope him as Abbie ordered Jeremy to go to the barn and see if any horses were left and to tend to them if there were. Then he felt the knife being pried from his hand. He let go reluctantly. LeeAnn! He had to save LeeAnn!

There followed two days of searing pain and semiconsciousness for Zeke, during which he often mumbled LeeAnn's name. Abbie knew he was struggling to dredge up the inner strength that came from his deep spirituality, that certain savage strength he had acquired from early days of fasting and visions and from his beliefs in the powers of the animal spirits, the strength that kept men like Zeke going when others gave up the fight. By the third day he was sitting up and meditating when she went into the bedroom that afternoon to check on him. When he looked at her, she felt as though a sword was being driven through her middle. His eyes were wild and bloodshot, his usually handsome mouth set in rigid determination that made him look like the vicious, painted warriors who had stolen away LeeAnn. Their eyes held for just a moment and she swallowed back her terrible sorrow, wondering how many things one person was supposed to bear.

"You'll go after her, of course," she said quietly.

His fists were clenched, and he deliberately worked his badly bruised right wrist, wanting to feel the pain, wanting to suffer for failing his daughter and, in his mind, for failing his wife too.

"Tomorrow," he replied.

Her heart tightened. "You aren't ready to travel, let alone fight Comanches. There's a terrible stab wound in your right shoulder and you probably have a concussion and your wrist—"

"Tomorrow!" he growled. "I feel no pain from my wounds! I feel nothing but revenge—and shame!" He raised his right arm and worked it up and down, beads of sweat breaking out on his face. Any delay was too long.

Abbie's eyes widened. "Shame! There must have been twenty of them! How can you feel shame?"

"I should have sensed their presence in the first place!" he hissed. "I have been too long away from living wild and free like the animals! At one time my keen senses would have warned me that Comanches were nearby! Because I have lost that sharp edge, my brother is dead and my daughter is gone, and so are my horses, my only livelihood. How am I to care for the family now?"

"We'll manage. We've always managed!"

He breathed out a disgusted sigh. "First I must find LeeAnn. Never has my heart been so torn or my mind so confused. I cannot even grieve for my brother because my heart is so heavy for my daughter!" He swallowed and looked away from her, clenching his fists again. "There will be time for grieving when I return. There will be much more than my brother to grieve over. I have lost more than my brother and horses and my daughter."

She frowned. "What are you talking about?"

He looked up at her, a terrible sadness in his eyes, as though he were telling her good-bye. "How much more can I put you through? It has already been too much. I want you to pack a travois. Are there any horses left at all?"

"Two pregnant mares, and"—she swallowed—"and Lance's horse."

She saw a strange resignation and a new, different determination come into his eyes, as though he had made up his mind about something gravely important to both of them without consulting her first. "That's it?"

She nodded, her eyes tearing.

"Then pack clothing, whatever books you need, anything special to you. Have the children help you make up a travois. We'll let Lance's horse pull it. It's important that the two remaining mares have those colts. You'll need them."

She sighed and came closer, trying to quell a building, unknown fear. "What do you mean, I'll need them?"

"We'll discuss it when I get back. I'm taking you and the children to Sir Tynes. The man is always offering to help us. Now he can do it. There isn't time to take you

192

to Fort Lyon. Besides the fort is swamped with soldiers and scouts, some of them might not be very trustworthy, not when they learn that you're married to a half-breed!" He spat the word as though he disliked it himself. "You can't stay here, of course, not with Lance dead and no man on the place. Tynes's place is much closer and I can get a quicker start in finding LeeAnn. We'll board up the cabin until I get back. Then we'll decide what's to become of the Monroes."

"I have no doubt what will become of the Monroes!" she answered quickly, her heart pounding with fear. "They will go on and survive as they have always done!"

He just looked at her then, the strange resignation on his face. His eyes dropped to gaze at her slender form. Abbie. His Abbie. Still lovely. Still desirable.

"We knew twenty years ago that our lives were too far apart, Abbie," he said coolly.

She put a hand to her stomach. She wanted to reach out and touch him, but she feared that he might bolt away like a wild animal. She was never sure what to say to him when he was like this. Her throat hurt, she wanted to cry. She needed him now more than ever, yet he was strangely removed from her. "You . . . made a decision once before . . . a long time ago . . . after I almost died from having Jeremy. Without discussing it with me, you decided you would no longer share my bed and risk another pregnancy. That decision nearly destroyed us both."

"Then we'll have to be stronger this time, won't we?" He met her eyes, deliberately ignoring the desperation he saw there. "We'll talk about it when I return. For now you will go to Sir Tynes and his fortress of a home, as he calls it." His eyes moved over her again. "I doubt that the Englishman will mind. He would like nothing better than to have you under his roof. Perhaps it is time you had a taste of the life you could have had if you had not had a heathen husband. At least, you deserve to live in comfort and without fear while I am gone. You would not do so at Fort Lyon. The only answer is Sir Tynes. He is not a bad man. He will take care of you and treat you honorably." He met her eyes boldly. "But I do not doubt he will tempt you dearly. If I did not trust you as I do, it would be harder for me. However, at the same time I want you to consider strongly what you wish to do with the rest of your life."

Her eyes widened with anger. "The rest of my life? Are you saying I have some kind of choice? Well, I most certainly do not! You are my life! This family is my life! It will be no other way. Without you I would have no purpose for existing, except to make sure my children make it to adulthood, after which I would have nothing."

"Right now you have nothing with me either." He turned away from her, his long, shining hair falling over his wounded shoulder. She knew the terrible pain he was in and wanted to comfort him, but she knew he would not let her. "Zeke—"

"Start packing!" he said curtly. "We must leave sometime today."

"But I can't be ready that quickly."

"You must! Each moment that goes by is a moment lost in finding Lee Ann. As it is, it will be very difficult."

She stepped back, shaking with the fear of the decisions he had made, knowing how stubborn he could be when he thought he was doing what was best for his Abbie. "All right," she said quietly. She left the room with a heavy heart, and Zeke watched her go. How he loved her! How his heart ached at the thought

194

of losing her forever!

Sir Tynes was more than happy to "help" the Monroes in their hour of need. He was truly sorry about LeeAnn, yet could not hide his exuberance at the fact that Abigail Monroe would be under his roof for weeks, perhaps even months. He quickly ushered all of them inside his great stone mansion, part of which was still not finished. The basic living quarters were done, however, and as he showed them those rooms, the children all stared in amazement at the rich mahogany furniture and woodwork, the four walls of books in the massive library, the polished hardwood floors, the expensive paintings on the walls, and the fancy Oriental vases placed in just the right places. The children walked carefully, afraid of breaking something, and they talked in whispers, as though they were in a king's palace.

Zeke accepted Tynes's hospitality stonily, his dark eyes flashing constant warning looks at the Englishman, looks that told Tynes to treat Abigail Monroe as the married woman she was. On the one hand, he wanted Abigail to live this life for a while, perhaps even to have the chance to enjoy it forever. On the other, he wanted to grab Sir Edwin S. Tynes about the throat and slam him against a wall, to cut his eyes out so he would stop looking at Abigail like a man in love. But Zeke had no choice. This was the best place for his family while he was gone. There were plenty of men on the vast Tynes estate, and the house itself was like a fort. His wife and children would want for nothing.

Tynes brought them to the kitchen, where he offered Zeke and Abbie tea and coffee, the children fresh milk, along with cookies just baked by a hired cook. The children ate the sweets with relish, their warmth helping to ward off the damp chill they felt because of the sleet storm they had walked through on their way to the estate.

Zeke did not sit down, but paced like a caged animal while Abbie told Tynes what had happened. The Englishman watched Zeke, amazed at his ability to recover so quickly and awed by his appearance—all Indian on this day, in dress and countenance—and impressed by the fact that Zeke Monroe was perfectly willing to ride after marauding Comanches to rescue his daughter.

"Why don't you have the soldiers help you?" Tynes asked.

Zeke stood near him and sneered down at him. "Soldiers don't go riding after one small band of Comanches to rescue the daughter of a half-breed," he replied coldly. "Besides, right now there aren't enough men to handle all the bigger skirmishes going on. Indians are making war from Texas to Montana, Tynes. My one small problem is of no concern to them."

Tynes scanned Zeke's large, menacing frame, hoping he would never have to go at it physically with the man. "Well, at least you're Cheyenne. You must understand some of the ways of the Comanche. An Indian is an Indian, is he not?"

Zeke's nostrils flared with anger. "Yes. I suppose to men like you we're all the same, but there are differences. White men never try to understand them. Because of that lack of understanding, my son is somewhere in the north, God knows where, or whether he is even still alive. Indians are making war everywhere on the plains. And now I must leave my family because my own kind have robbed me of my

196

horses and my child. My son fights whites in the north, while I go to fight Indians in the south!" A smirk twisted his lips. "It is strange the things this land makes men do, is it not? I have an Indian brother in the north riding against the whites, and a white brother in the same place wearing a blue uniform and fighting Indians. My children have Indian blood and don't know which way to go. My woman"—he stopped and swallowed, his heart heavy—"my woman is left with the biggest burden of all, caring about the whites, but loving an Indian, and raising children with both bloods. It has been hard for her. Perhaps for a while she can relax and feel safe here, stop working so hard and have access to books so the children can learn more."

"Of course." Tynes rose. "Zeke, I will take good care of them. I am honored to have the opportunity, and I wish you Godspeed in finding your daughter." He put out his hand, his eyes sincere. Zeke took the hand firmly, squeezing hard.

"I will owe you for this." He held up his chin proudly. "I will work for you when I return. I have lost my horses, and if I do not get them back I will have no way of repaying you."

Tynes started to tell the man repayment was not necessary, but he'd heard that Indians never accepted gifts without giving something in return and he'd seen the hurt pride in Zeke's eyes. "We'll figure something out when you return," Tynes told him.

Zeke nodded. "I wish to be alone with Abigail. Do you have a room where we can go?"

Tynes fought a searing jealousy, still finding it difficult to picture the gentle Abigail with this man. "Of course. Follow me." He led them from the kitchen and Zeke reached out for Abbie, taking her arm with sudden gentleness. He looked at the children. "I will see

197

you once more before I go. Be honorable and respectable while you are here. Obey Sir Tynes and treat his belongings with respect. Help in any way you can."

They all nodded, some of them still stunned by the horrible events of the last few days. Little Lillian sniffed because of a runny nose, then coughed. The trip through the sleet storm had been hard on the sickly child. Zeke turned and led Abbie out of the kitchen after Sir Tynes. They had spoken little since he'd first announced she must pack and leave. There had only been time for the packing and the uncomfortable trip and then the explanations to Sir Tynes.

They followed the Englishman up a grand staircase to a carpeted hallway in which there were several closed doors. Tynes opened one of them, ushering Zeke and Abbie into a huge bedroom. The carpeting, wallpaper, bedding, and the canopy over the grand fourposter bed were all a soft, pleasant green.

"This is one of my finer guest rooms," he told them. "It shall be Mrs. Monroe's room while she is here."

Zeke looked around the room, almost as big as their entire cabin. He met Tynes's eyes then, and the warning look in his Indian eyes chilled Sir Tynes's blood.

"I trust you will never come into this room," he said flatly.

"Zeke!" Abbie gasped, putting a hand to her chest and reddening.

The two men held each other's gaze. "Your trust is proper," Tynes replied. "I have nothing but the deepest respect for your wife, Mister Monroe, and I am aware that this is a trying time of mourning for her. I will simply see that she enjoys complete peace and comfort."

Zeke nodded. "We will all have much to talk about

198

when I return," he told Tynes. The Englishman frowned, curious, then he shrugged.

"I suppose we will." He glanced at Abbie, who had turned away. He wasn't sure he should leave her alone with her husband at the moment; Zeke looked so savage. But during the year he had known these people, he had realized that their affection and loyalty seemed indestructible. Abbie had lived with her Cheyenne man for twenty years so apparently she loved and trusted him. Tynes envied the deep love they shared. Still, he sensed that something was amiss, but Zeke Monroe's mood warned Tynes not to question him. "I'll . . . uh . . . leave you two alone now," he said quietly, turning to exist and closing the door after him.

For a moment, Zeke stood there quietly, listening to Tynes's footsteps go down the stairs. Then he walked up to Abbie and grasped her shoulders, turning her. "I want to make love to you. Perhaps it will be the last time," he told her.

She choked back a sob and turned her face away. "Stop talking that way!" she whimpered. "I . . . don't know you, Zeke. I don't know what to do, what to say to you . . . except that I love you . . . and I hate it when you talk this way!"

He began unbuttoning the back of her dress and she jerked away. "I can't! Not when you act like this!" She wiped at her eyes and walked wearily to the bed to sit down on the edge of it. It was luxuriously soft. Zeke pulled off his painted buckskin shirt and threw it to the floor; then he unlaced his winter moccasins and pulled them off. He walked over to her, kneeling in front of her, two red stripes of vengeance painted on each of his cheeks. He took her hands.

"Look at me, Abbie girl."

She met his eyes. A brawny masculinity emanated

from the hard muscle of his arms and shoulders, but there was a blueness about his right breast. Apparently the wound at the back of his shoulder had caused some internal bleeding. He had refused a wrapped bandage so there was only a patch of gauze at the wound, held there by one strip of gauze wound around his chest. Besides the blue skin near his breast, there were numerous cuts on his chest and back and arms, cuts made by the jabbing Comanche lances. Most of these were superficial. His face was bruised and his wrist was still swollen.

"You shouldn't leave yet," she told him. "You aren't ready."

"I am very ready. Besides, I have no choice." He put a big hand to the side of her face. "Many things are going through my mind, Abbie girl, and it is difficult for both of us to think about making love, our minds are so heavy with sorrow. But I may not return. And if I do, things might be different between us."

"Things will never be different between us!" she whispered, searching his dark eyes.

He reached behind her and finished unbuttoning her dress, pulling it down over her soft, white shoulders. Then he leaned forward and kissed them lightly. "We do not know," he told her. "Everything is changing, Abbie. Even you and I."

"No. Not me. Only you. You're inventing things in your mind that are not true, Zeke."

He studied her honest, loving brown eyes. "Perhaps. But I don't think so." He pulled the dress down to expose her breasts, touched them with the back of his hand, lingering for a moment on the scar at one breast left by the arrow wound she'd received when she was only fifteen. He remembered removing the arrow himself. "I have always loved you, Abbie, but perhaps

200

we have lost too much this time."

He put both hands to her face then, grasping it firmly and leaning up to kiss her, devouring her mouth hungrily, searching with his tongue, suddenly kissing her almost painfully as he laid her back and began moving more urgently, as though he might never make love to her again.

He kissed her over and over, moving his lips from her mouth to her cheek, her throat, her breasts; tasting the full pink fruits willingly offered only to Zeke Monroe. Bringing his lips back to meet her mouth and stifle her whimpers of sorrow and to quell all objections, he kissed the tears that flowed gently across her temples and into her ears. He continued to kiss and caress her and to whisper her name until he felt her relax; then he sat up and quickly removed her clothes. After he worked his way out of the buckskin leggings and loosened his loincloth, he pulled her farther onto the luxurious bed, pressing against her, grasping her tightly, and kissing her almost savagely as he bent one leg up to force hers apart.

She was barely able to breathe as he pressed her breasts against his bare chest with firm possessiveness, seemingly unaware of his injuries or of the pain they brought him.

"Abbie, my Abbie! What have I done to you!" he groaned, his hands and lips seeming to be everywhere, searching, gently loving, tasting, caressing, as though he must enjoy every inch of her and do everything possible with her so that he could remember her forever.

How long they ravaged one another she wasn't sure. Visions of him clinging to LeeAnn and fighting desperately for his daughter tore at her heart. Her mind seemed ready to explode, so laden was it with fear of what might happen to her precious LeeAnn, named after her own sister who had died at the hands of cruel renegades. It didn't seem right to be making love now, yet this man had suffered terribly over the abduction, both physically and mentally. He needed this one last moment. She knew he would draw strength from it, but more than that, she sensed a terrible desperation about him as he moved over her, a sense of finality that made her give in to him simply because she, too, knew this could be the last time. He could die at the hands of the Comanches, yet she knew that was not the real threat. The real threat was that something had already died inside this man. His son was gone, all of his brothers except Dan and Swift Arrow were dead, and his daughter had been stolen away, along with his precious Appaloosas, his very livelihood. A great deal of his pride had also been stolen, and Sir Edwin S. Tynes posed a threat to him much greater than that of the land and its elements. She felt almost as though he were saying good-bye. He could not seem to get enough of her, and when he planted himself inside of her it was with painful force.

Minutes after he'd finished with her, it started all over again. Very little was said, but his own tears fell on her cheeks as he took her again, this time more gently. Then he simply held her, pulling up the luxurious quilts around them and holding her close while outside a gentle but cold rain splashed against the windows.

She wasn't sure how long she lay there in the comforting warmth of his arms before she fell into a deep, badly needed sleep, and only a few hours later she awoke. At first she snuggled down under the warm quilts. It took a moment for her mind to come back to reality. Then the horrible vision returned—LeeAnn!

Her beautiful LeeAnn being whisked away by the cruel Comanches. What would happen to her lovely daughter? LeeAnn! She sat bolt upright, calling for Zeke, realizing with even harsher reality that he was not in the bed, not even in the room.

She quickly rose, hurrying to the nearby washbowl to wash herself before dressing. She picked up the brush lying on the washstand and ran it through her long, thick hair; then she twisted the locks into a bun, securing it with the combs that had lain scattered on the pillows and sheets since Zeke had undone her hair while making love to her. She put her hands to her still-flushed cheeks and was embarrassed to go out. Surely Sir Tynes would know what had taken place. She breathed deeply for composure. What did it matter? She and Zeke were husband and wife and they had a right to say good-bye in whatever fashion they chose. Zeke was probably ready to go, and she must see him once more before he left. She was devastated that she had not awakened when he'd gotten up.

She hurried out the door and down the stairs, calling his name. But the house was still and cold. She looked around the large entranceway in confusion, unsure where to find her husband in the huge house. Then Sir Tynes came rushing in from one of the many rooms.

"Mrs. Monroe!"

"Where is he? Where is Zeke?"

The man's eyes softened with pity and he frowned. "I'm sorry, Mrs. Monroe. Zeke is gone."

She grasped her stomach. "Gone!"

Tynes's eyes ran over her body. He longed to have been the one to have so recently bedded her, but only Zeke Monroe enjoyed that privilege.

"Yes. He came down perhaps an hour and a half ago

203

and told me I must not wake you under any circumstances, that you needed your rest and that . . . that it was better this way. It was his wish, Mrs. Monroe."

Her face paled and she shook her head. "No!" she whispered.

His heart ached for her. "I'm sorry. It was his wish. He did tell each of the children good-bye. I took all of them upstairs and insisted they all lie down and rest. The little girl—Lillian I believe you call her—she's feverish and should stay in bed I think."

Abbie wondered how much longer she would be able to breathe. Her throat was so tight from the need to scream and cry that she felt she was being strangled, and her heart hurt. She ran to the huge oak door that led outside and opened it, walking out onto a porch that overlooked the vast expanse of prairie that led south, an endless horizon into which Zeke Monroe had ridden. In her last memory of him, she lay in the warmth of his protective arms. Now he was gone, perhaps forever, and for some reason he had decided not to wake her, as though to say that this time it was too hard to say good-bye, perhaps because something had been lost between them that might never be regained.

She stared out at the cold, rainy horizon. Poor Zeke! He had ridden off alone into the dreary November day to risk his life, and just before he'd left his precious pride had been broken.

"He's not even . . . healed yet," she said desperately as Sir Tynes came up and stood beside her. "And he's so . . . alone! So alone!"

"Please come inside," Tynes told her. "You'll take sick, Mrs. Monroe. I'm sure he'll be back. Men like Zeke are survivors, are they not?"

She stared into the gray mist. If only she could have

held him once more, just once more, and told him how much she loved him . . . She hung her head and wearily walked back inside. Miles away Zeke Monroe was well on his way south, the cruel, stinging sleet mixing with the warm tears on his face and making the red war paint run and smear.

Chapter Ten

Wolf's Blood bit off a piece of cooked beef and threw a fatty piece to Wolf. The animal swallowed it so swiftly he seemed to inhale it.

"This white man's beef is not so good as buffalo meat," Wolf's Blood complained. "Not even as good as deer meat. There is too much fat, and no flavor."

Swift Arrow nodded and swallowed, taking his knife then and slicing another piece off the large roast that hung over their tipi fire. "The flavor is better when you remember it is free, my nephew," he answered.

Wolf's Blood met his eyes and they both laughed. "It was a good day!" Wolf's Blood then said between bites. He swallowed. "By the time the miners' wagon train gets to Montana, there will be no cattle left at all. Our bellies will be full and theirs will be empty—or they will die of Cheyenne and Sioux arrows and bullets before they get there!"

Both chuckled again, and Swift Arrow threw a bone to Wolf. "This is a good time for the Sioux and Cheyenne," he told the boy. "Together we are almost eight thousand strong. With leaders like Roman Nose—his great medicine helps him from being killed—and Red Cloud and Sitting Bull and Dull

Knife, we will not lose this fight for Paha-Sapa, Wolf's Blood. The Black Hills are all we have left. Here is the center of the world. Here is where we belong. I have been so long with the Sioux that I feel I am Sioux somtimes. This is how it is for many of the northern Cheyenne. We are strong now. Those Bluecoats at Fort Connor are dying of starvation and sickness because we have them surrounded, and while they waste away, we fill our bellies with white man's cattle and feed on the buffalo and antelope that they cannot escape the fort to find. By next spring they will give up this country. If not, even more will die."

"That is why I am here, Uncle. To see soldiers die makes my heart happy. It feels good in my blood. After Sand Creek I will never get enough vengeance." He threw his own bone to Wolf and wiped his hands on the knees of his pants, recalling with amusement that his mother would chide him for doing such a thing. The thought brought a longing to his heart, for he missed his mother and father fiercely. Still, his mission here was more important, and it felt good to live in the Indian way.

Swift Arrow watched the boy. He looked so much like Zeke that it made Swift Arrow miss his brother very much, yet there was an element of Abbie in the boy too, an element that Wolf's Blood struggled against constantly, a soft, mannerly side that sometimes surfaced in little ways. Swift Arrow had no doubts about Wolf's Blood's ability as a warrior. Zeke had taught him well, and Swift Arrow himself had taught his nephew many things. Right now, the boy's heart was hurting badly. That made it easier for him to raid and kill, but Swift Arrow wondered if the boy would go back to his home, once time healed some of the wounds. The boy refused to recognize that he had any white blood, but the fact remained that he did. He could not forever deny it. For now, Swift Arrow was happy to have the boy with him. He was good company, and family. And he was struggling to become a man.

Swift Arrow wiped his own hands and stretched out against a pile of robes. He was a handsome man, forty years old now but still a strong, fighting man, hard-muscled and powerful, but shorter than Zeke. Yet he was a lonely man. His Cheyenne wife and son had died many years ago of a white man's disease, and Swift Arrow had not chosen to marry another. Instead he'd put all his energy into fighting the white man. He was an honored Dog Soldier. Dog Soldiers did not marry.

The fire crackled quietly while Wolf's Blood lit a thin cigar and puffed it, feeling manly as he did so. He breathed deeply of the smoky smell of the tipi and leaned against a backrest of chairlike design, made of woven willow shoots laced together with buffalo sinew and covered with skins. Wolf curled up and sighed, closing his eyes in sweet happiness, his wild belly full and his master close by. Outside there was laughter. Some of the men were recounting tales of battles, others gambled, and a few drank whiskey.

"I think tomorrow we will go on a buffalo hunt," Swift Arrow spoke up. "It is good here. We are still free. Would you like to go out tomorrow and ride down a buffalo? It is very dangerous, but exciting for a man who enjoys danger."

Wolf's Blood grinned. "I will go." He sighed and puffed the cigar again. "Father took me sometimes. He loved riding down the biggest cow he could find. He would talk about how her wild eyes looked up at him when he got to her side and they were running full out. Father always said to look into the eyes of a buffalo when she is right beside you, her great bushy head almost even with your own, is like looking death right in the face and laughing. I have felt the same. It took me five hunts to finally kill my first buffalo. Once I shot one and she kept right on running, as though the bullet were no more than a rock being thrown at her."

"You did well. It takes many a man more than five hunts to get his first buffalo. The buffalo is the greatest beast in the land. He belongs to the Gods. He was put here to sustain God's People of the Plains." The man sat up then. Picking up a stick and poking at the coals of the fire, he reached for more wood to build it up. "But now the white man is destroying the buffalo, Wolf's Blood. I remember the first time I saw a great bull lying dead on the prairie, only a little of the meat taken, and the hide and head and all the usable parts left there to rot. It was a bad sign. I never forgot it. Now the white hunters come with their big guns to take more, and the iron horses are creeping across the land, scaring away the herds. Those that are not frightened away are shot by the white hunters to feed the men who build the roads for the iron horses. It is a sad thing to see. But we will fight to keep the whites from spreading into this land." He tossed his long, black hair behind his shoulders, and a tiny bell tied into a hair ornament tinkled. He crossed his legs and stared at the fire. Wolf's Blood smoked and watched his uncle, a handsome man, still hard and strong.

"Why did you not marry all these years, Uncle?" the boy asked. "I mean, I like girls." He frowned. "I loved Morning Bird. I would have married her one day. I would have given many horses for her. Never will my heart stop hurting for her. Yet I know that one day I will probably love again, as my father said I would. I want to be a good warrior, but one day I would like to have sons. And I do not wish to go forever without a woman."

Swift Arrow grinned. "There are plenty of loose

Arapaho women in camp, and some Cheyenne widows are willing to give a brave warrior his pleasure in return for food he has brought from a hunt or from a raid. There are ways for a man to find satisfaction without marrying. Good Dog Soldiers do not marry."

"But what about a family? After your first wife died, did you never love another woman, never want sons?"

Swift Arrow's smile faded and he stared at the fire, thinking of Abbie. Beautiful Abbie . . . The first year Zeke had brought her to live among the Cheyenne, Zeke had left for a while, and Abbie had been placed in Swift Arrow's care. He had taught her many things about the Cheyenne that summer, had taken her along to the north for the Sun Dance, had protected her. At first he had highly resented Zeke bringing her to the People, for he'd hated all whites even then, especially white women. But Abbie was different. She was strong, determined, brave. She had already killed three Crow Indians, and later she had saved Tall Grass Woman's daughter from the deep waters. Slowly his attitude toward her had changed, but too much the other way. For he had learned to love his brother's white woman, secretly, respectfully, but with great passion, passion that could never be fed. Never would he speak of his love or do anything about it. Abigail Monroe belonged to his half brother and she had eyes for no other man.

"You are my son," Swift Arrow said to Wolf's Blood. "You are my family. Yes, I have wanted sons, but my desire to wipe out the whites is greater. Once in a while a widowed squaw or one who likes all men comes and lives with me for a while, but I have not wanted to take a wife." His dark eyes met Wolf's Blood's, and the boy saw a strange sorrow there, not just sadness because of the wife he had lost so many years ago. "Tell me, Nephew, how is your mother . . . truly? You said when you and your father found her, after those white men

211

took her, she was very sick in body and mind. Is she truly recovered?"

The boy took the cigar from his mouth and studied it. "She seems to be, but only my father could really tell you. I think it was hard for him to . . . touch her. He was afraid he would frighten her after what those men did to her. I think it was . . . a long time."

The boy was surprised to see that his uncle's hands were trembling. Suddenly, the man gripped the fat stick he was holding and snapped it in two. "Bastards!" the man growled, throwing the stick into the fire. Wolf's Blood watched the stick burn, thinking how fat it was and how difficult it would be for any man to break it with his hands unless he was enraged. "I wish I had been there to help you kill those men!" Swift Arrow hissed. "Tell me again how they suffered!"

Wolf's Blood grinned. "All I had to do was think about my mother being touched by them, and it was easy. Father and I tasted the sweetest revenge. We cut them many times, laughing at their screams. They died slowly, Uncle. Their filthy manparts went first, and we stuffed them into their own mouths to stop their screaming. Neither of us has ever regretted what we did to those men. And you know my father, what he can do with his knife. I learned many ways to torture a man that night. Winston Garvey's body lies in many pieces, buried deep in the mountains north of Denver. He will never be found, nor will the two men who helped him torture my mother. For many weeks the Denver papers spoke of the disappearance of the rich man Winston Garvey."

"And you are sure it was Garvey's son you saw at Sand Creek?"

Wolf's Blood nodded. "I have seen him before. He is ugly, and an Indian hater. He rode with Chivington that day. He injured me, but before I went down I sunk my lance deep into his thigh. It scraped the bone so loudly I could hear the sound above the noise of the fighting, and as I fell myself I could hear his terrible screams. It was a good sound. I hope that he died, but I do not know."

Swift Arrow reached over and picked up a rawhide shield with a beaded fringe and arrows painted on it. It looked very old and was quite faded. "Your mother made this for me, years ago," he told the boy. "She made it so well that I can still use it." He held the shield out to Wolf's Blood, who took it, wondering how the conversation had changed so quickly from his encounter at Sand Creek to his mother. "Your mother is an honored white woman among the Cheyenne," Swift Arrow was telling him. "Some of the younger ones do not understand why, and I worry that she might be hurt by some of the very Cheyenne she loves. But perhaps not. She speaks our language, understands us, and she has a goodness that shows in her eyes, a love that shines there for all men. She is without the hatred and scorn most white women show those who do not have white skin. And she is brave, strong. She is not like any white woman I have ever known. The first year your father brought her to us, I taught her many things, and Tall Grass Woman gave her a beautiful white tunic and my mother, Gentle Woman, painted your mother for the Sun Dance ceremony. Her lovely white skin was covered with many colors. Flowers were painted on her arms; a tiny horse was painted on one side of her face, an eagle on the other—your father's signs. Her hair was braided, and she sat through the Sun Dance and did not faint as other white women would do if they witnessed that ritual. I was proud of her that day. I—"

He stopped suddenly when his dancing eyes met Wolf's Blood's. The younger man was staring at him knowingly. Swift Arrow had allowed himself to get

213

carried away, and now his smile faded at the look in Wolf's Blood's eyes.

"You love my mother," the boy said quietly. "That is why you never married, isn't it?"

Swift Arrow held the boy's eyes steadily. "It is true. This is why I came north so many years ago. It was better that I was not near her. It only made the hurt in my heart much worse."

"My father knows?"

Swift Arrow nodded. "He knows. We talked of it many years ago, when he saw the look in my eyes that you have just seen. Your mother is sweet and honorable. There were never any such thoughts in her heart for me. I was simply her husband's brother, and I would not hurt her by telling her my true feelings. I think she suspects, just a little, but she does not know how deep the feelings are."

Wolf's Blood studied the faded war shield. "Now I understand many things—why you did not come and see us more often, why you seemed to abandon the southern Cheyenne. I thought you just loved to make war." He handed the shield back to his uncle.

"That part is true, Wolf's Blood. I have fought the white men settling in this land all my life, and I will continue to fight them. I have many wounds, but I will not be stopped unless a white man's bullet enters my heart or my head. But I pray and fast and feel no fear. I will fight for many years to come."

Their eyes held. "I . . . do not know how to feel, Uncle. She is my mother."

Swift Arrow raised his chin. "And a beautiful and honorable woman. There is no reason for you to feel any different about her, or me. Abigail is the same as she has always been . . . and so am I. The only difference is now you know that I love her. That changes nothing. It will be our secret, my Nephew.

Now we both understand why we are here. We both have a love to forget and a vengeance to take, for we both hate the white man. That is all that is important now, to be good warriors and to die like men—in battle—not like women, not on the hated reservations." His eyes were watery. "She is . . . happy now? She is well?"

The boy nodded. This was Swift Arrow, his favorite uncle. He loved him nearly as much as his father. "I think she is. My father is good to her. He was kind and patient after what happened to her, and their love is very strong."

Swift Arrow smiled sadly. *"Ai.* This is true. Everyone can see their love, and my brother is a good man, also honored among the Cheyenne, one of the most skilled, one of the bravest. And he is a very lucky man to have found such a woman. But it has been hard for him, for sometimes he wants to ride with his red brothers."

"Yes. But he does not like to leave my mother, especially now." Wolf's Blood picked up his rifle to clean it, and Swift Arrow studied the boy's lean, hard body. The young man was exceedingly handsome, and the available Sioux and Cheyenne girls often whispered about this newcomer who was supposed to have white blood but who certainly did not look as though he did. Wolf's Blood had already proven his prowess. He had taken two white men's scalps, and he could ride, hunt, shoot, and raid as well as any of the Sioux and Cheyenne men. Yes, he could have his pick of any of the young maidens. But his heart still longed for Morning Bird, and Swift Arrow understood that longing.

"We will speak no more of my feelings for your mother," Swift Arrow told him. "It is over. I have honored you by trusting you with feelings that are sacred and private. Do not disappoint that trust by betraying that honor and speaking of it to someone else or bringing it up to your father."

Wolf's Blood held the man's eyes. This was Swift Arrow, his beloved uncle, a respected Dog Soldier. He put out his hand and grasped the man's wrist and Swift Arrow grasped his in return.

"I am only here to fight the white man and be Cheyenne!" the boy told him. "I am honored to share such sacred feelings over your fire. If you love my mother, it is only with the greatest respect. She is a woman who would be easy to love. We will speak of it no more."

Swift Arrow nodded. "Tomorrow we hunt buffalo. Perhaps the next day we will join the braves who surround the soldiers at Fort Connor and share in the game of watching them die."

Wolf's Blood grinned and nodded. Then each man lay back to think his own thoughts for a moment, while drums beat outside.

"Do not forget what I told you about the loose squaws," Swift Arrow said then. "I can tell you the best ones if you have not learned that part of being a man yet. They will teach you without laughing at you."

Wolf's Blood smiled. "I will think about it awhile."

Young Margaret walked to Tynes's stables to check on Sun and Dreamer, the only two remaining Monroe Appaloosas. These horses represented the future for her father, for both mares were pregnant, and she knew they must be well cared for. All the children took turns tending them, but Margaret spent more time with them than the others. Being near the mares made her feel closer to her father and to Wolf's Blood. She missed them both, and was afraid for them.

She entered the stall where Sun stood and picked up a brush, walking to the front of the horse and talking softly to her. "You eat up, Sun, and don't be kicking out stall doors and running away like you did last year." She began brushing the animal gently. "You are carrying the beginnings of a new herd in your belly and you must take care of yourself."

The horse whinnied and nodded as though she understood, and Margaret laughed lightly before she absently began to hum a hymn she had often heard her mother sing softly while at work. She was worried about her mother. Abbie had been so quiet and withdrawn after their father had left. She seemed somehow broken, and Margaret wondered if something had happened between her parents. She was upset because she did not like the way Sir Tynes watched her mother and doted on the woman. The girl sighed heavily as she brushed the horse, and her thoughts went to her little sister Lillian, who was very sick. She began to hum the hymn again, feeling that it would make her feel better. She hummed for several minutes until a startled gasp cut off her singing. A man bobbed up from the next stall. He had apparently been there all the time, on the other side of the wall where she couldn't see him.

He was quite handsome, one of the new breed Sir Tynes had spoken of, a cowboy. Sandy hair was scattered every which way beneath the old, leather hat he wore, and his face was tanned, a reddish tan not a dark one. His eyes were a dancing blue, and his teeth were straight and white when he smiled at her.

"You have a pretty voice, matches your pretty face."

She stared back at him with dark, suspicious eyes, ready to dart away. She had heard so many things about strange white men and what most of them thought of Indian girls that she wasn't sure what to think of this man staring at her now, even though his blue eyes were friendly. Several months earlier, when she'd been barely fifteen, a white Confederate soldier had been about to rudely show her what squaws were made for, and if it were not for Wolf's Blood's intervention, something terrible might have happened. She knew that, although she didn't fully understand what would have happened to her at the hands of the pawing, cruel soldier.

"Now I know you speak, because I heard you singing," the man told her, coming from his stall to stand at the gate of her own. "And I know you speak English, because you're that white woman's daughter, and because I heard you talking to your horse there."

She backed up, clinging to the brush, watching him warily. He was tall and lanky, with slim hips and waist but broad shoulders. She guessed him to be in his mid-twenties. His eyes were still kind as he put a piece of straw in his mouth and leaned against a support beam near the stall, careful not to enter it and frighten her.

"Which one are you? You have so many brothers and sisters, I get mixed up. You Ellen?"

She swallowed. "Margaret," she managed to choke out.

He grinned more, pushing back his wide-brimmed hat. He studied her exquisite form and provocative face, her full, innocent lips and wide brown eyes. She had the enticing beauty that only girls of mixed blood were privileged to have. He was struck by it. He wanted the dark beauty that was looking back at him now.

"Well, Margaret, my name is Sam. Sam Temple. I work around here—herd cattle, tend to horses and such. Sir Tynes pays well." Margaret still did not offer any words other than her name, and he folded his arms. "Have you looked at Sir Tynes's horses?" he asked.

She only nodded.

"He's got some mighty fine quarter horses. They make the best kind for cutting out calves and such. Quick on the hoof, you know? And he's got some of them fancy thoroughbreds from England. But I gotta say, these two Appaloosas your father brought in are beautiful animals. Beautiful animals. A man doesn't see many Appaloosas in these parts, mostly quarter horses and roans. Your father must be real good with horses. 'Course most Indians have extra talent that way, with breeding and riding. You a good rider?"

She swallowed. "I'm pretty good."

He smiled warmly. "I'll bet you are. Will you go riding with me sometime?"

She shook her head. "I . . . don't know you."

"Sure you do. I just introduced myself. I'm Sam Temple and I'm from down Texas way. I'm twenty-five and I came to Colorado just to see something new. I think I'll stay on here. Ought to be a longstanding job. Sir Tynes has a good idea. Soon as the railroads reach Denver from the East, we'll be able to ship beef eastward real fast to provide fresh meat there, instead of herding them to places where they can get loaded onto trains. Without that long walk, the beef will be a lot fatter and they'll bring in more money."

She frowned. "Will a railroad come all the way to Denver?"

He laughed lightly. "Sure it will. The Kansas Pacific is almost to Fort Rilely now, and the government has given them permission to head on west. You just wait. In ten years there will be railroads all over the plains and all the way to California."

She fingered the brush nervously. "My father and mother say the railroads are bad for the Indians. They scare away the buffalo, and they bring more white people."

"Well, that's probably true. But it can't really be

219

stopped you know. I think they probably know that. How did we get on the wrong subject? I still want to know if you'll go riding with me sometime."

She put an arm around Sun's neck and petted the horse. "Not right away. I would have to know you better, and you would have to talk to my mother."

"All right. That's fair. How about the next few days I just come to the house. We can sit on the veranda and have coffee on the better days. Sometimes in Colorado it can get right warm this time of year—then whammo! There comes another blizzard. On those days we can sit in the kitchen."

"You don't have to tell me about Colorado weather. I've lived here all my life. I suppose we could do that."

He nodded. "I'd be honored. I can't say when I'll be able to come. I have a lot of work to do around here. Probably in the evening." His eyes quickly scanned her voluptuous form. "How old are you, Margaret?"

"Sixteen."

He nodded. Yes, this one was worth the effort. She was the prettiest thing he'd seen since coming to Colorado—and she was Indian. A man didn't need to make commitments to pretty little squaws. He kept the friendly smile, aware of his own good looks and his easy way with girls.

"You got an Indian name, Margaret?"

She nodded. "It's Moheya, Blue Sky."

He winked. "Well, now, that's right pretty. You go ahead there and tend to your horse, Blue Sky. I've got chores to do." He started to walk away.

"Mister Temple," she spoke up. He turned to look back at her. "When will you come?"

He grinned. "How about this evening?"

He was so handsome and seemed so sweet. He made her feel strangely warm and excited inside. "All right. I'll tell my mother, and I'll be waiting."

He tipped his hat, wondering with an ache how long it would take to break down her resistance.

Abbie put a cool cloth to little Lillian's fevered brow. The girl had gotten steadily worse since the trip to the Tynes estate. Abbie was worried. Lillian was not strong. She had been sick many times, but she'd never been this bad. Her chest was dangerously congested, and her fever would not go down.

Sir Tynes knocked softly and entered at Abbie's bidding. Lillian slept in Abbie's bed so that Abbie could be near the girl at all times. He came and stood near Abbie, who sat on the bed beside her daughter.

"Would you like me to send to Denver for a doctor?" he asked Abbie. "I can get you the best available."

"I . . . can't really afford—"

"Nonsense! I'll pay his fee. It's the little girl's health that matters. Please let me send for someone."

She nodded, her eyes tearing. She wondered how much more she could take. If only Zeke were here to hold her, share this terror. But he was experiencing his own terror, searching through Comanche country to find yet another daughter who had been stolen away. Abbie fought to keep from thinking about poor LeeAnn, for beside her lay Lillian, who might be dying for all she knew. To think of them both at the same time was overwhelming, yet she could not help doing so at times. Being unable to do anything for LeeAnn filled her with an apprehensive black feeling. She remembered watching the poor girl being dragged off by the renegades, remembered her terrified screams.

Abbie suddenly burst into tears, covering her face with her hands. In addition to her worries about Lillian and LeeAnn, she knew that Zeke could be killed. And if he was not, what would happen when he returned? He seemed changed, almost determined that they could never again go back to the ranch and live happily. She felt her whole life slipping away; everything she had struggled to build, everything she loved was being swept away from her.

Tynes put a gentle hand on her head. "Poor Abigail. I wish I could do more for you." How he loved her! But he had been purely cordial to her, strictly a good host and nothing more. She was suffering so that he could not truly woo her or explain his feelings. He had no right to do so, yet he longed to keep her there, longed to promise her peace and comfort for her remaining years. And she looked so much like his own Drucinda, the lovely young wife who had been taken from him after only one year of marriage. For fifteen years after that loss he had wandered the world, seeking one adventure after another, trying to forget.

"You've ... done too much ... already," Abbie sobbed, taking a handkerchief from the pocket of her dress and wiping at her eyes. He studied the plain blue cotton dress she wore and pictured her in some of Drucinda's magnificent gowns. Drucinda would have been about Abbie's age if she had lived. "We'll never be able to repay you," she was saying. "And I'm afraid I'll be terribly spoiled by the time we leave here." She sighed deeply and forced a smile. "You must let me do some of the cooking and such." She blew her nose.

"Nonsense! I have a cook and I have people to clean. You are not here as a servant. You are here as a guest. And God knows you have many things on your mind, enough burdens to shoulder without worrying about such trivialities as cooking. I shall send for a doctor right away."

She looked up at him, her feelings for the man mixed. She knew he dared to be interested in her, even though she was married. She could see it in his eyes, hear it in his voice. Yet he had been so kind and helpful, she didn't have the heart to be rude or to chide him about it. He hadn't done anything or said anything that he shouldn't. Under normal circumstances she would have put him in his place, for she was not a woman to have eyes for any man but her husband. With a husband like Zeke Monroe she had no cause to look elsewhere. But now she felt that the one man she did love, her one source of strength and courage, might be taken from her. She rose and walked to a window, looking out at a gray day. A few snowflakes struck the window.

"That's very kind of you, Sir Tynes."

"Please call me Edwin. You allow me to call you Abigail, but you won't call me by my first name."

She nodded. "All right." She watched the snowflakes, longing to gather her children and ride into the horizon, for beyond it lay the Monroe ranch and her warm little cabin where she had known so much happiness and hardship. She wondered if she would ever go back there again.

These books worth almost $20, are yours without cost or obligation
when you fill out and mail this certificate.
(If the certificate is missing below, write to: Zebra Home Subscription Service, Inc.,
120 Brighton Road, P.O. Box 5214, Clifton, New Jersey 07015-5214)

Complete and mail this card to receive 4 Free books!

YES! Please send me 4 Zebra Lovegram Historical Romances without cost or obligation. I understand that each month thereafter I will be able to preview 4 new Zebra Lovegram Historical Romances FREE for 10 days. Then if I decide to keep them, I will pay the money-saving preferred publisher's price of just $4.00 each...a total of $16. That's almost $4 less than the regular publisher's price, and there is never any additional charge for shipping and handling. I may return any shipment within 10 days and owe nothing, and I may cancel this subscription at any time. The 4 FREE books will be mine to keep in any case.

Name _____

Address_____ Apt. _____

City _____ State _____ Zip _____

Telephone ( ) _____

Signature _____
(If under 18, parent or guardian must sign.)

LF1096

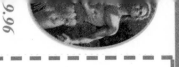

4 BOOKS FREE!

9.96
...te...
utely
EE
 no
tion to
ything,
er!

Chapter Eleven

Zeke hunkered down under a heavy buffalo robe, his back against a large boulder, the front of him soaking up the heat of a campfire at his feet. He closed his eyes to the splashing sound of the nearby Red River as moonlight danced on the crest of each rivulet. It was a quiet place, a lonely place. But then, most of Texas was lonely. He stuck his nose under the robe to warm his face. This part of Texas was reasonably mild in winter, usually in the fifties. But the nights were cold, falling into the teens. He wondered how many more cold and lonely nights he would spend away from the warm cabin on his ranch, away from his family, away from Abbie.

Perhaps he would never know those things again, for he felt certain that he must give Abbie a chance to live the kind of life she could have if she were not married to Zeke Monroe. She had given him twenty good years, twenty loyal, hard-working, dedicated, sacrificial years. He would not blame her if she wanted to give it all up now. Life seemed to continually plague her with heartache. Her own abduction nearly two years ago had been bad enough. Now her daughter had been abducted, and he wasn't sure how he would tell her if he found LeeAnn dead, or raped and enslaved. The thought of men cruelly using his innocent daughter set his mind to reeling with thoughts of the worst kind of revenge; then he again felt responsible for bringing his wife heartache. He loved Abbie so much. He hoped he loved her enough to get out of her life when this was over.

He was not sure in which direction to head next. This was certainly Comanche country, but most of the Comanches were in southern Kansas, preparing to abide by the latest treaty. He had checked at Fort Elliott and Fort Sill on the eastern edge of Comanche territory, after first going almost directly south from Colorado to Fort Union in New Mexico, then on down to Fort Summer, more Apache country than Comanche. He had thought the renegade Comanches might be running with the Apaches, but the men at the forts had had no indication that this was so. When he had headed east across the vast Texas plains to Forts Elliott and Sill, he had gleaned no useful information. The men had kindly said they would keep their eyes and ears open for rumors of a white captive among the renegade Comanches, but Zeke knew they would not go out of their way to help her, for LeeAnn was also part Indian.

The trip over the Texas plains had been devastatingly lonely. This was big country, endless country. Now, as he camped on the Red River, he felt somewhat less lonely, just because the nearby river made noise. The splashing sounds made him feel that he had company. The roan mare beside him bent its head and nudged him lightly, and he patted the horse's nose.

"You feel lonely and out of place too girl?" He sighed, his heart heavy. This was the horse Lance had been riding the morning of the raid. He wanted to cry for his brother, to let blood, but he was unable to vent his grief. He was too full of something else. Vengeance.

He must find his daughter! He would not give up until that feat was accomplished. He would not return home without LeeAnn or without at least knowing if she was dead or alive. If it took him a year, so be it. But he could not forget the horror of feeling her ripped from his arms that day, nor the sound of her screams. Zeke Monroe did not like being helpless or defeated. If he had not had to cling to her that morning, perhaps he could have beaten his adversaries, but with only one arm free, it had been hopeless. Still, he was grateful that because of his brave fighting the Comanches had let him live. He would prove that gesture to be a mistake. His biggest worry now was that the Indians might have already sold his daughter to white slavers. It had already been nearly a month since the girl's abduction, and his heart was breaking because of his desperate fear of what could have happened to her. She would be a prize in any villainous man's eyes. Her body was developed beyond her thirteen and a half years, her skin was fair and flawless, her white blond hair was long and thick, and her eyes were wide and blue. He had always known he would have to keep an eye on the young men who wooed her, but he hadn't planned on something like this. If he found the girl dead or violated, it would kill Abbie, and it would destroy his own pride and will to live.

He tried to force himself to sleep. It was difficult, for there was so much on his mind. And worse, he had a haunting feeling, the kind that had tormented him when he'd been back East and felt something was wrong with Abbie. When he'd returned, he'd discovered that she'd been kidnapped by Garvey's men. Now he had that feeling again. Something was wrong at home, something other than LeeAnn's capture and his own departure and the words he had had with Abbie. What had gone wrong? He could not go home to find out, for he must stay in this desolate country and search for his daughter.

He shook away these thoughts, but he knew he would get no sleep this night. His face had aged from lack of sleep, from being exposed to the elements twenty-four hours a day, and from the terrible stress of his ordeal. Again he closed his eyes. He would think of Abbie, his precious Abbie girl, and that last moment he had spent with her, that moment of soft lovemaking and delicious kisses, the wonderful satisfaction of being one with his Abbie. He thought of how she'd looked when he'd left her lying there asleep, in his eyes still pretty and young looking. Perhaps he would never see her that way again, lying naked in his bed, sleeping off the satisfaction of having been one with him.

A cold wind penetrated the heavy fur coat that Sir Tynes had insisted Abbie wear, and whispers of snow brushed across her feet as she stood beside the lonely grave. The horrible hurt in her heart was worsened by the fact that her daughter could not even be buried on the Monroe ranch. It was obvious a winter storm was coming so Sir Tynes had insisted they stay put. She knew he was right, but still . . .

Lillian! Again the horrible blackness swept over her, and she knew the chill she felt came more from the inside than the outside. It mattered little how many children a woman had. In losing one's only child or one of many, the hurt was the same. Her little girl had struggled to hang on, had taken the medicine the Denver doctor had brought; but his long trip had been for naught. Sir Tynes had wasted his money paying for the man's long trip. Little Lillian was not designed for this land—this cruel, harsh land. And on January 2, 1866, Lillian Rose Monroe, little Meane-ese, Summer

228

Moon, had died, at the age of eight and a half.

The girl's life had been so quiet and uneventful she might never have existed. She was not a girl to speak loudly, she was never naughty. Her coloring was plain, her countenance thin and frail. Abbie had always felt she could never give the girl enough attention, maybe because she was so often sick and maybe because the rest of the family seemed to go about their business without really noticing Lillian. As the sixth child, Lillian had received little acclaim, being overshadowed by her oldest brother's strong personality, by her sister Margaret's unusual beauty, and by the interest LeeAnn's blond hair and blue eyes attracted. Even her brother Jeremy, the second son, got more attention—boys usually did. She did not have Ellen's good looks or intelligence. Ellen was very smart and often read to the other children. Even the third son, Jason, not only a boy but the baby of the family, received special attention.

Now, all the Monroe children stood around the grave crying. A messenger had been sent north to tell Dan what had happened, in the hope that he could find Wolf's Blood somehow and let the boy know. Wolf's Blood . . . If he would come home, Abbie was sure she would feel a little better. The boy seemed more like Zeke all the time. If he were here . . . No. It was Zeke she needed. Zeke. How would she tell him about this? What if he returned to tell her that yet another daughter was dead? How would they bear the loss?

Sir Tynes stepped close to her. He had spoken Christian words over the little girl who lay in the plain wooden box. It was over now. She would not come back to life, and a piece of Abigail Monroe's heart had also died. Tynes put an arm around her shoulders.

"You should come inside now, Abigail."

She shook her head, beginning to tremble. "I . . .

can't leave her here . . . in the cold. She always hated the cold."

"She's fine now, Abigail. She's free of pain and sickness. She's free of this cruel land. She was not made to be long here on earth."

Abbie nervously twisted the necklace she held in her hand. "My mother . . . was always sickly," she told him. "She died—back in Tennessee . . . before we left for Oregon." She held out her hand. "This was her necklace. I'd like to . . . lay it beside Lillian. My children never knew their grandmother. She died before I met Zeke . . ." The horrible blackness engulfed her again and she bent over in a wrenching sob, grasping her stomach. Tynes grasped her arms and pulled her close, holding her tightly.

"It will fade a little . . . the worst grief," he told her. "When I lost my first wife I thought I would never again see the sun. She was so young . . . and I had only had her for a year. Come. I will help you to the casket and you can lay the necklace there and say good-bye one last time. Then we must leave and get you and the other children inside. The snow is coming down harder now. My men will take care of things here."

He helped her to the grave. She felt old, suddenly old. Her arm seemed to weigh a hundred pounds when she reached out to place the necklace on her daughter's frail body. Never had Lillian looked prettier. Some of Sir Tynes's help had dressed her in the pink dress he'd instructed them to make from material he'd had at the house. Her hair was neatly braided, with pink ribbons tied at the ends, and a light rouge had been put on her pale cheeks.

Margaret stood nearby, weeping bitterly, held by Sam Temple. She had grown to love Sam, grown to trust him. They had gone riding several times, had talked for hours; and he had kissed her. His sweet, warm, gentle kisses had stirred new and exciting feelings in her innocent body. He never touched her rudely or said crude things as the cruel Confederate soldier had done that awful day when he'd tried to force himself on her. Sam was different, and her young heart was truly in love for the first time. She had sometimes thought about Indian men, but she had wondered what future there would be in marrying one. With her looks she felt she belonged with the Indians, but she had been raised as a white girl and she knew that to have a home and children, she should marry a white man. However, she also knew that most white men had no respect for Indian girls. Then Sam Temple had come along. He was different. He respected her. He had not said that he loved her, but she was sure he would. Sam was her hope for a happy future.

But right now she was temporarily saddened by her sister's death. She watched her mother put the necklace into the casket and she wept harder, turning and burying her face against Sam's chest. She wondered if this terrible grief would be made worse when they found out what happened to LeeAnn. And what of her father? What would happen to Zeke Monroe? Would they ever live happily at the ranch again?

The snow came down harder, and now Sir Tynes was dragging Abbie away, against her protests. "I can't leave her there alone! It's too cold!" Abbie kept saying. "Oh, God, where's Zeke? If only Zeke were here! Zeke and my son!"

The words echoed in Margaret's ears and she wept harder, standing there in the blowing snow with Sam's arms around her while the rest of the weeping Monroe children filed after their mother toward the Tynes mansion. Sam kissed Margaret's hair.

"Come on, honey," he told her softly. "Let's go to my cabin. You're better off not being around your ma right now. Come to my cabin and I'll warm you up and we'll talk." He led her in the opposite direction as men began to lower the small wooden coffin into the ground.

Margaret sipped the hot chocolate, the heat of it burning her throat, warming her stomach, and helping her heavy heart. She set the cup on the crude wooden table in Sam's cabin. He walked up behind her and patted her hair. "Feeling better?"

She sighed deeply and wiped her eyes. "A little." She turned to look up at him and he touched her cheek. "I must look terrible," she told him.

He knealt down beside her and leaned up to kiss her cheek. "Now how could a beauty like you look terrible? You're beautiful, like always." He handed her a big, clean handkerchief and she blew her nose.

"Oh, Sam, I'm so scared." She began shaking and new tears wanted to come. "Father might never come back, and we don't know what's happened to my poor sister. My brother is in the north, maybe dead from some raid, and—" She met his eyes. "Hold me, Sam."

She wrapped her arms around his neck and he enfolded her in his own, pulling her out of the chair and hugging her tight. He kissed her hair. If ever she was vulnerable enough for him to take her, it was now. He had gained her trust. Every girl had to take her first man sooner or later, and this one was Indian, so it didn't matter if they weren't married. Sam Temple was not about to commit himself to any girl. He liked many girls, and he did not intend to lose his freedom. But now he was with Margaret—beautiful, young, unsuspecting Margaret who was frightened and lonely. He moved his lips from her hair to her cheek, then to her full, sensuous lips, kissing her in a seductive, almost demanding way. He had never kissed her like that before. He parted her lips hungrily, then moved a hand down to press against her slender hips when he felt her responding out of her confusion and fear.

Leaving her lips, he kissed his way to her throat, then her ear. "Let me help you forget all your sorrow, Margaret. Let me make you feel alive and happy." He rubbed his hand over her hips and kissed her again before she could reply, pressing his hardness against her flat stomach. He felt her stiffen then, and her heart beat so hard he could feel it against his chest. "Don't be afraid, Margaret. Don't I mean anything to you? Don't you love me?"

He released her slightly then, and she met his eyes—so true and kind. "You know I love you, Sam. But I've never . . . I mean . . . we aren't married."

He smiled. "We can always get married. I just don't want to wait. It would take time to get a preacher. I want you now, right now. I need you, Margaret. You've seen how easy it is for life to slip away in this land. I could get killed on a roundup tomorrow, be attacked by renegades, who knows? You know better than anybody all the things that can happen out here. I'm scared too, Margaret, scared something will happen to you or me and we'll never have known each other that way. I want to be your first man, Margaret, your only man. I won't hurt you, I promise. Every day I wonder if this is the last day we have together."

He had chosen the right words for a frightened girl who was in love. She felt flushed and confused, and her heart pounded furiously. "I . . . I don't know what to do."

"You don't have to know anything. I'll teach you. And I won't hurt you, truly. I just . . . I want to make love to you, Margaret. I want you to be my woman. Don't you want me to be your man? Don't you want to make me happy, like your mother makes your father

233

happy? You've told me how much they love each other. We can be like that too. I ought to get your father's permission before I marry you, and who knows when he'll be back. I don't want to wait that long. We can be one now, right now. And when your father comes back, we'll be married. If he doesn't get back within a month or so, we'll just get married anyway."

"Sam, I . . . I've thought about you . . . that way. But I felt ashamed of doing so."

"Ashamed? Why? Don't you love me?"

"You know I do."

"Where's the shame in that? We've been together almost every day now for better than six weeks, Margaret. It's not like we're strangers anymore. We're good friends. I want to be more than that. I want to be lovers. You're so beautiful, Margaret. You drive me crazy."

He kissed her again, groaning suggestively.

"But, my mother—"

"Don't worry about your mother. She's grieving right now, Margaret. Don't worry her about it. Don't tell her. You're a big girl. You can make your own decisions, and you know when you're in love. Your mother can't decide that for you."

He kissed her again; then he reached down and picked her up in his arms, carrying her to his bed. She wanted to protest, tried to think of an argument against it but could not come up with a reasonable one, not when she thought about how much she loved him. It did not enter her mind that he still had not told her he loved her. After all, he had talked of marriage, hadn't he? He had talked of needing her, of wanting to be her first man and her only man. He had been kind to her, never touching her wrongly all this time. He had stayed beside her through her sister's last hours and through the funeral. How could she doubt his apparent fidelity and love, ignore his gentle touches, his warm smile and his true blue eyes?

His hand moved up under her dress and fire leaped through her veins at his touch. She had never been touched this way, had never wanted someone to touch her this way. Yes, she wanted to forget her confusion and sorrow. How she wanted to forget! He touched her gently in that secret place no man had ever touched and she gasped with excited pleasure, her womanly instincts awakened for the first time.

She started to object again, and he cleverly and quickly took his hand away, being careful not to move too quickly and frighten her. Instead he stopped her objections with a kiss as he gently moved the hand over her tender young breasts. She was soon lost in him, for Sam Temple knew how to handle girls and he knew just the right words to use to get the ones who didn't understand these things to submit. He was going to have a pleasant time of it, he was certain of it, for this one had never known a man. Slowly but surely he worked off her clothes and his own, and he smiled when she kept her eyes closed to his nakedness and tried to curl up to hide her own. In time she was letting him kiss her breasts, letting him touch that secret place that set her body ablaze. Her eyes widened in startled pain when he finally had his way with her and she started to push at him, but it was too late.

"Relax, honey," he told her, bending down and meeting her lips. "It only hurts the first time, sweet Margaret. It's all right. You're going to be my wife, remember?"

Of course. A woman had to suffer these first pains when she gave pleasure to the man she loved. Her mother had explained some of this to her, but she had explained it from the standpoint of husband and wife, explained how beautiful this thing became once the pain was over. Margaret believed that, but it didn't help the pain she was feeling now. Perhaps it would feel better if Sam was her husband and she didn't have to wrestle with pangs of guilt as well as physical pain. Yet she loved him so! She wanted so much to make him happy, to have this special moment, to feel alive and in love and unafraid.

It was soon over and she lay there in his arms, damp with perspiration, curled up against him.

"You all right, honey?" he asked her.

"I think so."

He patted her bottom and hugged her close. "It's always that way. You'll get over that part of it. Every time we do this from here on, it will get better and better, and you'll get more pleasure out of it than I get."

She wondered for a moment how he knew it was always this way. How many other young girls had he done this to? She brushed away the thought. He was too kind, too true. This was her Sam.

"We . . . we shouldn't do this too much, Sam, not before we get married."

He moved a hand over her flat belly, then bent down to kiss it, and she felt a flutter of desire again. His lips moved to her breasts, then her lips. "I don't think I can keep from doing this as often as we're together, but don't worry about that. We know we're getting married, so what does it matter?" He kissed her gently. "You were wonderful, Margaret. I never felt like that before. You'll make a hell of a wife."

"Will I truly?" she asked, her innocent brown eyes searching his own.

"Do I look unhappy?" he asked.

She smiled. "No."

He kissed her hungrily. "Let's do it again, honey."

"But it hurts."

236

"All the more reason to do it again. The more we do this early on, the faster the pain will go away." He moved on top of her, devouring her mouth and refusing to let her voice an objection. She wanted to resist, for she was afraid of the pain, but he was more insistent this time. She suddenly felt a wave of deliberate abuse, as though any concern for her own feelings had suddenly left him, but, loving him, she attributed that to his being a man, to his needs. It was a woman's duty to fill those needs if she loved her man. She didn't want to disappoint him, didn't want him to think she wouldn't be a good wife. She relaxed more and allowed him his pleasure in spite of the pain, for she did love him so. But she didn't feel the same warmth from him that second time, and she felt strangely removed from her body, as though there were two Margarets. An intuitive voice deep within her was trying to tell her this was wrong, that there was something untrue about Sam Temple; but she refused to listen to that voice, for the damage had already been done and she loved him. She had to believe the best of him, for he had earned her trust and had said over and over that he would marry her.

The small wagon train headed slowly along the White River, the small band of emigrants from Minnesota making their way toward the Bozeman Trail for they were headed for the Montana gold fields. Wolf's Blood and the others smiled at the stupidity of these white people, who thought that some Divine grace was going to keep them from harm, as though just being white would save them from the elements and the Indians. But wagon trains meant supplies, and they also meant more settlers moving through Indian lands. They must be stopped. The war party waited on the ridge until they were spotted; then they laughed at the sight of the wagons quickly forming a circle and at the frantic shouts of the people preparing to defend themselves.

There were at least ten of them, all white, all men, all headed for the gold fields. The miners were the worst of the lot, Wolf's Blood thought, the most notorious for ignoring treatries and invading Indian lands. Up to now he had only raided soldiers and forts, but this was something new and exciting. He let out a war whoop and joined the others in swooping down the ridge toward the train, his well-earned eagle feathers dancing in the wind at the base of his braids, his rifle in hand and ready to fire. He and the twenty Indians with him, including Swift Arrow, began to circle the wagons, yipping and firing, enjoying the fear in the eyes of the white men.

The Indians danced in and out of the range of fire daringly, sometimes riding behind rocks and dismounting to take better aim. Some shot flaming arrows into the wagon canvases, and soon two wagons were burning, their white tops turning to roaring orange, black smoke billowing high into the sky. It was not long before half of the white men were dead. With so few left to fight, there were now openings through which the warriors could break through the circle.

Wolf's Blood, high on the thrill of the attack, was enjoying the chance to wreak more revenge on behalf of poor Morning Bird. He charged into the inner circle of wagons. He wanted a scalp today. He wanted to do something different, something to prove there was no white in him. It was then he spotted her, a young girl huddled behind one of the wagon wheels.

The rest of the Indians charged inside the circle and

busied themselves with killing off the rest of the white men and looting the unburned wagons while Wolf's Blood urged his horse toward the girl, dismounting and walking over to stoop by the wheel and grin at her. Her eyes were wide and frightened, her hands clinging to the spokes to tightly that her knuckles were pure white. She was perhaps eighteen, with reddish hair and green eyes. Wolf's Blood felt a sudden urge to take the ultimate revenge for being denied the warmth of his own Morning Bird, and he darted beneath the wagon, grabbing the girl about the waist and yanking her away from the wheel, a difficult task for she hung on for dear life. She began to scream so he grabbed her wrists and wrenched her arms behind her back, throwing his weight on top of her so that she could barely move. Then he kissed her, savagely, determined to do this one thing that would forever prove he had none of the gentleness of his own white mother left in him. When his lips left hers, she stared at him with pleading eyes from which tears ran.

"Please don't hurt me! Let me go!" she begged. "Please!"

He said something to her in the Sioux tongue, making her think he did not understand her language. In response she wriggled fiercely, trying to get away, but he held her tightly, kissing her again, moving his head to keep contact with her lips as she tried to wrench her mouth away from his, feeling his own excitement build as she struggled. Finally his lips moved to her neck.

"God no!" she wept. "Someone help me!" She went suddenly limp and wept pitifully, and much as he had tried to ignore it, the softer side of Wolf's Blood began to assert it self, making him almost angry. He raised up and looked at her. This could be his mother—or one of his sisters.

"Katam!" he swore in the Cheyenne tongue. He raised up slightly, shifting her wrists which he had pinned beneath her into one of his strong hands to free the other. Then he grabbed the bodice of her dress and ripped, partially exposing one breast. She screamed again. He let go of her then, but stayed on top of her pushing on her shoulders. "Stay down!" he warned her. "They must think I abused you! It is important they do not know I let you go!" She stared at him in amazement, surprised at his good English. "I will take you back to camp with me and tell them you are mine. But somehow I will let you escape."

She tossed her head and started to scream again.

"Shut up!" he ordered. "Do what I tell you and they won't abuse you or kill you. Do what I tell you! I am trying to help you! It is the only way!"

She stared at him, her chest heaving in frightened pants. As he started to move off her, she bolted away, crawling out from under the wagon and wrenching her foot free of his hand when he tried to grab her. Then she ran, screaming like a maniac, and he cursed her stupidity as he scrambled after her, but it was too late. Another warrior had spotted her. Letting out a war whoop he charged up to her, grabbing her hair as he leaped from his horse and knocked her down. Three more gathered around her, but Swift Arrow held back, not interfering but not participating either. When he saw Wolf's Blood running toward the men, he started to call out to the boy not to try to stop the warriors for fear of his own life, but there was no time. Wolf's Blood charged into the men, drawing his Bowie knife, and to Swift Arrow's surprise, the boy plunged it into the girl's heart.

There was a moment of complete silence. The four warriors backed off in surprise, staring at Wolf's

Blood, who knew he was in a bad situation.

"She was mine!" he told them, trying to sound authoritative. "I found her. I chose to kill her. I only want her scalp!" He bent down and deftly cut away part of her scalp, holding up the long hair. "Go and get your own scalps!" He walked boldly away and mounted his horse, tying the fresh scalp into his horse's mane and riding out to Swift Arrow. Their eyes held, and Wolf's Blood's had tears in them. "I tried to stop her from going out," he told his uncle.

Swift Arrow studied his nephew. "You were going to help her?"

Wolf's Blood swallowed. "I was going to . . . use her for my vengeance, but something my mother had said stopped me."

Swift Arrow smiled with understanding. "There is another side to you that cannot be denied, Wolf's Blood."

"I hate it!"

"But you cannot deny it, not fully. Do not feel ashamed. You are a proven warrior, proven in skill and bravery and in your knowledge of the Indian ways. You have suffered the Sun Dance, and you have taken soldier scalps. I will tell you something. I almost took my pleasure with a white woman once, but instead I helped her too. Because she looked like your mother. You see, I do not even have your mother's blood in me, yet she has influence over me. That shows the power she can have on people."

Wolf's Blood gripped the handle of his knife and turned to look back at the dead and bloody body of the young girl. If she hadn't been so foolish, he could have helped her. But she had run. So he had helped her in the only way he knew how, for he knew what the other men would have done to her. He did not blame them. They, too, had vengeance to exact. They had lost wives and daughters to needless slaughter, and their blood was hot with anger. But he could not bring himself to watch them violate the frightened girl. He had simply and quickly put her out of her misery. Now he felt ill.

"I wish to be alone," he told his uncle. He untied the scalp and threw it to the ground and rode away, suddenly longing to have his father to talk to.

Chapter Twelve

Abbie sat near the hearth of the great stone fireplace, her Bible in her lap, her eyes staring at the flames. Jeremy sat nearby, studying a painted wooden train he'd taken down from the mantel on which a number of scale-model trains were perched, some of wood, some of pewter, some of brass—all intricately designed and suitable for Sir Tynes's fascinating collection, a "frivolous but fun" hobby, as he put it.

"That one was hand-carved in New York," Tynes was telling Jeremy.

"Really?" The boy took note of the colorful designs painted on the sides of the woodbox. "I've never seen a train. Are they big?"

Sir Tynes smiled. "Oh, quite big and quite noisy. See that gadget on the front of the engine?"

Jeremy touched the slanted grate. "What is it?"

"That is called a cowcatcher."

The boy frowned. "What's a cowcatcher?"

"Well, my boy, a cowcatcher is exactly what it says it is. It catches and deflects any cattle or other animals that get on the track, knocks them off so they cannot be caught under the wheels and cause a derailment."

Jeremy giggled. "I bet it can't knock off buffalo!"

Tynes laughed with him. "No, I don't think it can, Jeremy. The buffalo would give any engine a good run, wouldn't it? They're such fine, great beasts. I admire the buffalo. It is as magnificent as the elephant."

Jeremy looked up at him, wonder in his eyes. "Have you seen an elephant?"

"Oh, of course—in India and Africa."

Jeremy watched the man light a fancy pipe. "You've been to those places?"

Sir Tynes nodded. "And Australia. Have you ever seen a picture of a kangaroo, Jeremy?"

The boy shook his head.

"They're delightful animals, boy. They're like giant rabbits, and they hop around, straight up, on powerful hind legs. The mothers have great pouches on their bellies. They carry their babies in them, sometimes for several years. Marvelous animals! Marvelous! I shall have to find a picture of one for you in my library."

"I'd like to see it." The boy looked at the train again. "You have a lot of trains, don't you?"

"They fascinate me, son. That one you're holding is called a 4-4-0, meaning it has four wheels under the lead car—the four small wheels at the front of the engine there—and four drivers, the very large wheels that are driven by steam—those actually push and pull to make the train move—and no wheels under the cab. Thus it's a 4-4-0. That engine up there on the mantel is called a 4-4-2, and a later model is called the 0-8-0. It has eight large driving wheels with no small wheels on the front and no wheels under the cab."

"Where do they come from? What makes them go?"

"Well, the engines are built in great factories in the East. Someday when you are grown up you should go east and see the wondrous things that are there, tall buildings and brick roads and miles and miles of railroads. There are steamships and theaters and all sorts of wondrous things." He glanced at Abbie, worried about her depressed state. He wished he could see her smile again. How he would love to take her around the world and show her the things she had never seen! "As far as what makes the engine go," the man continued, looking back at Jeremy, "it is powered by steam. A fireman takes wood from the woodbox, that pretty painted car just behind the engine there, and he throws it into a huge furnace deep in the engine, keeping a hot fire going which heats the water inside the engine. The water boils and turns to steam, and the steam is trapped and driven through special pipes and instruments that make a drive shaft move back and forth. See that there?" He pointed to the shaft and wiggled it back and forth. "When the shaft moves, it causes this bar that is attached to the wheels to move, and that makes the wheels go around. The hotter the fire inside, the more steam and the more powerful the engine—the faster it goes. Its speed is controlled by the amount of steam, and if the engineer wants to stop the train, he simply releases the steam through a special valve so that it can't go to the wheels. Quite marvelous, don't you think?"

Jeremy sighed, working the wheels again. "I sure would like to see one."

"Well, I think you will in a few years, Jeremy. The locomotive is on its way west. Some day East and West will be linked by trains. There'll be no more stage coaches."

"Do you really think so?"

"Oh, I know so. It's inevitable." He glanced at Abbie again, noted the tear on her cheek. "Jeremy, why don't you take that train to another room and play with it. Be a good chap now and let me talk to your mother."

The boy rose. "Thanks!" He ran off with the train in his hands.

Sir Tynes tamped out his pipe and walked over to kneel beside Abbie. "You must stop suffering, Abigail," he told her. "Lillian has been dead for six weeks, and you have six other children, four of them right here with you. All of whom need their mother. Soon your husband will be back with the fifth, and I will wager that the sixth, your son in the north, will come home eventually. You must be strong. You must be ready to help those who are gone and those who are here."

She moved her eyes to meet his. "It isn't just Lillian. It's your talk about railroads and such." She looked back at the fire. "I came out here with my father in a covered wagon, Edwin. There was no Denver. There was no talk of gold. The buffalo ran in great, thunderous herds so thick one could almost walk across the prairie on them, and the Indian was happy and peaceful. Men like Zeke could live free and wild, could make their own laws and deal their own justice. I see all of that disappearing." She looked at him again. "Did you know I killed a woman once, a vicious Indian woman who loved Zeke. She was trying to kill me."

He frowned. "You shot her?"

She shook her head. "I stabbed her with scissors. She had attacked me, hurt me very badly. Then she'd turned on Wolf's Blood. He was just a small boy then. He'd come into the room with his lance, thinking he could save me, but he wasn't strong enough to really hurt her. She took the lance from him and was going to kill him, so I grabbed my scissors, the only weapon nearby, and I stabbed her. I'd never thought I was capable of such a thing." She held out her hand. "I still have a scar. She cut me badly." He studied it and took her hand gently. "I don't know why I suddenly thought to tell you that. There have been many times when Zeke and I have both had to do what was practical, despite what refined whites would think was right. One of the

246

first things Zeke taught me about this land was the necessity to be practical, like the day I had to sit and watch those Comanches take my little girl away. If I had run outside to help, they would have killed me, or taken me too. I might have drawn their interest to the house and the rest of the children. I had to protect them." She studied his eyes. "Do you understand that?"

He squeezed her hand. "Of course I do."

She shook her head. "I don't think you fully understand. You haven't truly suffered. You've been to many places in the world, but you've always had what you needed for survival." She looked down at his hand. "On that wagon train, my little brother fell under a wagon wheel and was crushed. He suffered terribly from wounds that would never heal. He was dying slowly, horribly. Maggots were crawling in his wounds. I"—she swallowed and her eyes teared—"I asked Zeke to quietly end my brother's life with his knife. I knew that if anyone could do it quickly, and with little pain, Zeke could. He agreed, even though it's totally against his grain to hurt a child. But we both knew he would really be helping Jeremy, putting him out of his misery. That was probably the hardest thing Zeke has ever done. But he did it, and it was our secret. That was when I knew how much Zeke Monroe loved me."

"Why are you telling me all these things, Abigail?"

She stared at the fire again. "I don't know. I just . . . need to talk about them. Suddenly my past is dancing through my mind. It's as though I'm trying to figure out how it all started, how I got here. If someone had told me, when we started out from Tennessee, all the things that would happen to me, I wouldn't have believed it. Actually, I probably would have been terrified. I've been through so many things, Edwin, but I've survived them. I've survived because I had Zeke."

He squeezed her hand again. "You also survived

because of your own inner strength, Abigail. You are a remarkable woman, you know. You must realize your own strength and courage, for it is possible that you won't always have Zeke. He is a man who lives by rules that are changing now, a violent man who grew up in a violent land that is now being tamed."

She sighed. "The strange part is that despite all I've been through, I don't really want this land to change. I like to think about those early years: migrating with the Cheyenne, watching the great buffalo hunts, helping dry the hides and make tipis from them, making pemmican. I like to wear tunics—they're quite practical and comfortable—but I don't dare wear them in civilized places anymore for fear of laughter and ridicule. And I can see that my children who do not look Indian are going to try to keep their Indian blood hidden. That hurts. It's so difficult . . . watching all these changes."

"Of course it is." Tynes rubbed the back of her hand with his thumb. How he wanted to hold her! "Can I get you something, Abigail? Coffee? A little wine, perhaps?"

She sighed deeply. "Tea. I wouldn't mind some tea." She met his eyes again. "I've seen so many people die, Edwin. My own parents, my sister and brother; Zeke's Indian parents and two of his Indian brothers; Dooley, a good friend and our ranch hand; Lance, Zeke's white brother; and so many more. And now my own daughter. Somehow I thought my own family was immune from death, that it only happened to those outside our close circle. Now it has come to my little girl, and I suddenly realize it could come to more of my children . . . it could come to Zeke." Her eyes teared again. "And even if it doesn't, something has been lost between us . . . and I don't know what it is . . . or how it happened." She choked back a sob and put a hand to her face.

He reached up and patted her hair. "You must stop dwelling on sad things, Abigail. You won't know about Zeke until he gets back, and I'll wager from what I know of the man that he'll most definitely come back— with your daughter perched on his horse, unharmed. You'll see." He squeezed her shoulder. "I'll go get that tea for you."

He left reluctantly, wishing he could do more for her, wishing her love for Zeke Monroe would be given to him instead. But she was a loyal woman, and getting her to look at any other man would be a monumental task . . . unless Zeke Monroe should, for some strange reason, leave her. He walked to the kitchen and ordered the cook to set up a tray of tea, which she did quickly. Then he returned with it to the drawing room. Abbie took a cup and sipped it quietly while he sat down across from her.

"Now then, Abigail, I want you to tell me more about your past—tell me about living with the Indians, about their customs, how they use the buffalo, that sort of thing. I should like to take notes for my book. I think it's good for you to talk. And when we are finished, I have some lovely dresses that belonged to my wife and I would be delighted if you would wear while you are here. I am exceedingly curious to see you in an expensive dress, and they are just hanging in the closet."

"I couldn't—"

"I insist. I am your host and you should please me. I ask you sincerely to wear them, and I thought perhaps you might like to prepare supper this evening. You are accustomed to working, and much as I am against it, I think it would be good for you. You have far too much time to think right now, but it isn't good to sit and dwell on sad things. If it makes you feel better to cook and bake and do some cleaning, I shan't stop you. I want you to be happy."

She looked at him curiously, seeing in his eyes what she did not want to see—love. She looked down at her tea then. "I am deeply grateful for your kind hospitality, Edwin. I would dearly love to cook and bake for the children." She met his eyes again. "If you have any material, I would like to make new dresses for Margaret and Ellen, and perhaps one for LeeAnn, to surprise her when she comes back. And . . ."

Their eyes held, and Sir Tynes smiled. "There. You see? Already you are thinking about her return, thinking positively."

She smiled a little and he grinned and leaned forward, his elbows on his knees. "You have no idea how good that smile looks, Abigail. You are such a beautiful woman. I wonder if you realize just how lovely you are."

She looked away again. "Don't say that."

"Why? It's a simple fact, you know. There is nothing wrong with my admiring you. You are a rare woman, and Zeke Monroe is a lucky man. I have no doubt he realizes that. I see it in his eyes when he looks at you. And I'll tell you something, Abigail. I would gladly give up my wealth to trade places with your husband, if doing so meant I could have you. I don't mean that I would try to steal a man's wife. I only mean I wish I could find a woman like you for myself, and if I had to give all this up to do it, I would. That is why Zeke Monroe is a much richer man than I."

She looked at him again. His handsome dark eyes were sincere. "I . . . I guess I should thank you," she said softly. She smiled then, almost bashfully. "Zeke has told me many times he's a lucky man, but I feel I'm the lucky one. I didn't even think I was pretty when I first came out here at fifteen. But when Zeke stepped into the light of my father's campfire, and looked at me"—she closed her eyes—"I felt like the prettiest girl who was ever born. And even though to others he looked mean and wild, I saw something in Zeke's dark eyes that spoke of loneliness. He was the finest-looking man I'd ever seen—still is. I knew what I wanted, right then and there. But I had my work cut out for me because I was just a child in his eyes, and I wasn't sure of how to go about hooking a man like that onto my apron."

She smiled fully then, and when she opened her eyes they glittered with love and remembrance. Edwin Tynes knew at that moment that there was no room in her heart for another man, but he still hoped that somehow he could have Abigail Monroe for himself.

"Tell me more," he urged. "Keep talking, Abigail. If it makes you smile like that, then tell me more. What happened on your trip?"

"Oh, my. I'd keep you all day if I covered that and the past twenty years."

He leaned back. "I have nothing else to do today. It is snowing outside and I don't feel like going out. We'll just sit and talk today."

She turned her eyes to the window. Yes, it was snowing. She wondered about Zeke. Was it snowing wherever he was? And what about little LeeAnn? Was she warm enough? Were they feeding her? She thought of poor little Lillian, lying out there in the cold ground!

Tynes saw sorrow come back into her eyes. "Ah-ah," he said quickly. "No bad thoughts, Abigail. Talk to me."

She met his eyes again. "You're so very good to me, Edwin. Thank you." She sipped her tea again. "There were a lot of different people on that wagon train, all with different reasons for going west. My sister, LeeAnn, she was looking for a rich man to save her and take her away because she didn't want to go to that place called Oregon . . ."

Zeke rode boldly into the camp of the Comanche renegades, realizing there were too many of them for him to fight and that they respected courage. His best bet was to bargain with them. He couldn't be certain these were the ones who had stolen his daughter; he saw no sign of her and no sign of his horses. Soldiers at Fort Wichita had told him they'd had word of Comanche renegades along the Brazos River, but they had been unable to locate them. Zeke had been sure he could. He knew how to track Indians, but he didn't tell the soldiers that. He was aware of how such men went after Indians, charging in without a plan, attacking first, bargaining later. Zeke was well aware that the worst thing he could do was bring a force of military to attack the camp. The first one to be killed would be his daughter. Captives were always killed rather than given up. It was the Indian way of winning by not giving in to the whites.

The camp was sheltered under a huge overhanging rock that was surrounded by Yucca bushes and prickly brush. An inexperienced person would ride along the ridge above and never realize there was a camp there. But Zeke could read tracks, that ability and a sixth sense had led him here. He removed his jacket in the warmth of the afternoon while several Comanche men stood up to stare at him as he rode in, amazed by his audacity. A couple of dogs barked and then nipped at the heels of Zeke's horse, and a couple of women peeked at him from behind their men. The Comanches looked hungry and haggard, and he saw only three children, all with swollen bellies and hollow eyes. When he reined in his horse and dismounted, one of the sturdier-looking Comanches marched up to face him.

The Indian looked Zeke over and frowned; then he turned to the others, grinning. "It is he! It is he!" the man yelled out in his own tongue. Zeke understood and his heart pounded with hope. "It is the one who fought us to protect the girl!" The man laughed and the others joined him. They were all amazed that this Indian man had traveled all the way to the middle of Texas and had searched them out. They gathered closer. Zeke rested his hand on the handle of his knife. "So, you come all the way here to take back your own little captive, huh?" the apparent leader said loudly.

Zeke held the man's eyes steadily, his own gaze cold and daring. "She is my daughter," he replied in the Comanche tongue.

The man laughed and the others joined him. "You are an Indian! She is fair!" the man guffawed. "Why do you insist on calling her your daughter?"

"Because she is," Zeke replied, no smile on his lips. "My woman is white. The girl is our daughter."

The Comanche man's smile faded. He looked Zeke over again. "You are a very unusual man," he commented. "And how did you find us?"

"I've been hunting all through Texas for weeks," he answered. "And I did you the honor of not telling any soldiers where I thought I might find you. I have kept your whereabouts a secret. You can repay me by giving me back my daughter."

The Comanche stepped back a little. This Indian man was not one to deal with lightly. He had already seen how Zeke could fight, and the look in the man's eyes made him swallow dryly, even though there were plenty of Comanche braves about. He studied Zeke's painted face and his fringed buckskin clothing. A tiny copper bell tinkled slightly when Zeke's long black hair blew in the wind. There was an aura of power and determination about the man that impressed the

Comanche leader.

"We do not have to repay you for anything," he answered, feeling challenged. "We can simply kill you if we choose."

"The Comanche don't just kill a brave man outright. They honor that man's bravery by letting him fight for his life. And if he wins, they owe him what he asks."

The Comanche man eyed him with a sneer. "You are Cheyenne?"

"Half. My father was white. But I lived among the Cheyenne. They taught me how to fight, taught me the Indian ways."

The Comanche grinned. "A half-blood? A white belly?"

Zeke ripped out his knife and held it up. "Try me!"

The Comanche man sobered and slapped Zeke's horse out of the way. The rest of the Comanche men came closer, and their leader signaled two of them to step forward, both of them wielding knives.

"You have your wish, white belly," their leader told Zeke. He pulled his own knife and the three of them circled Zeke, while the others watched with great glee, enjoying this piece of entertainment that enlivened an otherwise quiet day. Most of these Comanches had no family left, but they were determined not to live on a reservation. They raided whenever and wherever they could, in a futile effort to stop the flow of whites into Texas. They were constantly hiding, often hungry, always waiting and hoping for the day when more warriors would join them and they would wipe the whites from the face of their land. In the meantime they built up their store of guns and ammunition by trading horses and women to white men. But their life was lonely and lean, and now they looked forward to a good knife fight. Already they planned to take Zeke's clothing and weapons, his supplies and his horse as soon as he was dead.

One of the Comanches came at Zeke then from behind. Sensing the movement, he whirled, swinging his leg high in the air and landing a foot across the side of the Indian's face. The man's knife glanced off Zeke's calf as he fell. Zeke felt the stinging cut, but he kept whirling, lashing out with his own knife as he came around, slashing it across the cheek of the second Comanche, who spun sideways, grasping his face. Zeke sucked in his belly and arched back as a third man stabbed at him, while the Comanche leader quickly darted in and jabbed Zeke in the side with his blade, then leaped out of the way as Zeke swung around.

Zeke stood crouched then, waving his blade and waiting for the two assailants to come at him again. The first man appeared to be knocked out, and blood ran dangerously heavily from the second man's cut cheek. Zeke's was on fire, but he sensed that they were toying with him. The leader could have sunk his blade much deeper, but apparently he had decided to prolong the fight.

The two men came nearer, joined by two fresh men. Zeke's defensive senses came fully alert, and though they were four against one, he could see some fear in their eyes. He moved fast and they could already see that the blade was probably his best weapon. One man came at him them, slashing wildly, but Zeke kept backing up, letting the man slash at him, even taking one slash cut across his shoulder. Then he grabbed the wrist of the man's knife hand and jerked the arm up high, sinking his blade deep into the Comanche's belly and ripping upward before yanking it out. He let the body drop and faced the other three.

"Come on!" he sneered. "I am ready for you!" He cursed them then in the Comanche tongue. Two of them charged, but the leader hung back. Zeke ducked and rammed his head into the gut of one, pushing his blade into the man's groin as he did so. He felt several stabs to one leg when he first bent over to ram the man. They had been dealt by the second Comanche man, who couldn't quite get at Zeke because he had moved so quickly. Zeke rose up and the attacker he had stabbed fell headlong over his back. Zeke flipped him off. Then he whirled, oblivious to his bleeding, painful leg, aware only that these men intended to goad him and torture him before they would give him his daughter.

The second Comanche man jabbed at him then— short, hissing jabs that kept missing because Zeke darted this way and that, his sharp fighting skills coming back to aid him. Zeke waited for the right moment, and as the Comanche man made a slash at him, Zeke ducked back and waited for his arm to swing wide, the man's knife narrowly missing Zeke's eyes as it whisked past them. As soon as the knife arm was around, Zeke charged forward and sunk his blade deep into the man's side, high up, where he would surely penetrate a lung. He shoved the man then, yanking the blade out as he did so, not even waiting for the man to fall before turning to face the leader and whoever else might be called forward. But the leader held up his hand and slowly put his knife away. He studied Zeke intently, frowning.

"What are you called, white belly?"

Zeke remained ready to kill, his shoulders hunched forward, his knife tightly gripped, his breath coming in heavy pants. "Monroe. Zeke Monroe."

"No. What do the Cheyenne call you?"

"Lone Eagle. Some call me Cheyenne Zeke."

The Comanche man nodded. "Just as I thought. I have heard of you, but I did not know if you were still alive. You are known for your skill with the knife." He studied Zeke's bleeding side and badly bleeding leg. "You can put your knife away. We honor your bravery and skill, Cheyenne Zeke. We would fight you until you are dead, but it would be useless. Your daughter, if she is that, is not here; and if a man is to die, it should be for a good reason. Save your strength and skills for the men who have her now."

Zeke felt weak and his heart tightened. "What men? Where is she? What have you done with my daughter?" He stepped toward the man menacingly, angered that he had suffered his wounds for nothing.

"She is sold . . . for many rifles. She is sold to Comancheros, who take her south to sell to a wealthy Mexican for much gold. They also have the horses. But perhaps most of them have already been sold. We traded them for more rifles and ammunition. We need these things to keep fighting. They gave us some of their horses, which were not as fine. But we would rather have the guns and give up the fine horses for lesser ones."

Zeke wanted to scream at the man, to drive his blade deep into the leader's belly. "Where in God's name did you sell her? How long ago? Where would the Comancheros be now?"

"They will go south and east to Mexico, probably along the foothills of the Blue Mountains. We sold the girl and the horses right from this camp, perhaps five days ago. They had trouble getting here so we had her and the horses with us longer than we'd planned."

Zeke stepped closer, his teeth gritted, his body afire with hatred and revenge. "And how many of your men had their turn with her?" he hissed.

The Comanche leader stood firm, his broad shoulders straight, his black hair blowing in the wind. "None," he answered firmly. "She was saved. The fresh ones bring more rifles. The Comancheros will do the same. The Mexicans pay much gold for the untouched ones."

Zeke wondered if he'd ever be able to breathe again; his chest was so heavy. LeeAnn! His precious, innocent LeeAnn in the hands of such men! It was his fault. Somehow he should have been able to save her.

"Why did you bother fighting me at all!" he growled at the Comanche man.

The man grinned. "To see if you were worthy of the information. Now you have it. Leave our camp."

Zeke straightened, wishing there was some way he could kill them all. But he had to think of LeeAnn. He was escaping with his life and was being given a chance to find his daughter. Now that these men had the rifles they needed, they had given him the information he wanted. He stooped to wipe his knife clean on a dead Comanche's clothing, then rammed it into his sheath and walked to his horse, mounting painfully. He wondered how badly his leg was hurt as he turned the horse.

"Cheyenne Zeke!" the leader called out. Zeke glanced back at him. "You understand the Indian. You know what is happening to your own. You know about Sand Creek. We did not believe she was your daughter, so we took her. We needed the guns. Do you understand this? Do you understand in your heart why we must keep fighting?"

The man held Zeke's eyes, and for a moment they were Indian and Indian, sharing one cause. "Yes. I understand," he answered. "That is one of the reasons why I didn't bring the soldiers here."

The man nodded. "And because of that I have given you the information you need. If you ride fast you will catch them. But be careful. There are many of them and only one of you."

"They have my daughter. One of me becomes many

when I am angry!"

The Comanche smiled and nodded. Then Zeke turned his horse and rode through the rugged underbrush and out of the camp, just as one of the Comanche women began to wail for a child that had just died from hunger.

Margaret walked to Sam's cabin, carrying the biscuits she had made for him. She wondered again if she should tell her mother what had been happening between herself and Sam Temple, for she didn't feel right about sharing the man's bed this long without marriage. Sam continually promised her he would marry her, but he had made no attempt to get a preacher to come to the ranch or to take her to the city to find one. Nor had he said anything to Abbie about wanting to marry Margaret. Margaret had mentioned marrying Sam once to Abbie, and the woman had given the girl a warning look.

"Has he actually asked you?" she'd said to her daughter.

"Yes. But he wants to wait until father returns."

Abbie had studied the girl closely then, suspecting that Margaret and Sam were closer than she wanted her daughter to be with a man. But Margaret had picked the right time to begin seeing a man, for Abbie was so absorbed in the death of Lillian and the abduction of LeeAnn that she hadn't the energy to be overly concerned about an older daughter who could take care of herself. Still, Abbie sometimes worried. Hadn't she been only fifteen when she'd fallen in love with Zeke, and hadn't he made her his woman out in the middle of nowhere, before they were married, in a land where there were no preachers? She began keeping a closer eye on Margaret, but she didn't have the determined motherly instinct or the sternness she would normally have had at her command. She had too many other things on her mind, and after a couple of weeks of keeping a tighter rein and seeing for herself how kind and mannerly Sam Temple was, she gave up worrying about Margaret. She couldn't bear the extra burden. Still, there was something about Sam that made her uneasy. Yet how could she tell Margaret? The girl would only defend him more.

On her part, Margaret was caught between her conscience and pleasing Sam Temple, who had become more demanding. She feared that if she didn't continue coming to his bed, he would be disappointed in her and think she wouldn't make a good wife. And she did love him so!

She knocked on the door and he opened it, his jacket and hat on. He looked surprised. "I thought you weren't coming until tonight," he told her.

"I wanted to surprise you," she answered, pushing past him and going inside. "Aren't you glad to see—" She stopped short. The mattress of the small bed was bare, and saddlebags and a bedroll lay on it. She frowned and looked around the room. His small personal things were gone. She met his eyes, her heart pounding with dread. He sighed and walked to the bed to pick up his things. "I'm going to Denver," he told her.

She swallowed. "To get a preacher?"

He looked her over. "No," he said quietly. "I'm just . . . going."

She clung tightly to the basket of biscuits. "I . . . don't understand."

"I think you do. We've had our fun, Margaret. I'm not the settling type. It's time for me to move on."

She shook her head, her eyes widening as they held

his blue ones. "You can't go! We're supposed to be married!" she told him in a shaking voice.

He laughed lightly and shook his head. "Margaret, grow up. You've been around Indians and whites a long time. You know that most white men will sleep with Indian girls, but they don't marry them, Margaret."

Her chest hurt so badly she felt as though a knife had been pushed into it. She wondered if she was having a nightmare. Surely that was it! She would wake up soon!

"How can you . . . say that?" she squeaked. "I didn't sleep with you for the fun of it. I made love with you because I loved you, and I thought you loved me."

He stepped closer. "Did I ever say I loved you, Margaret?"

"You said you'd marry me!"

"That isn't what I asked you."

Her whole body began to shake, and she looked him up and down as though she were seeing him for the first time. So, it was true. Because she appeared to be totally Indian, white men would only use her, never love her, yet she had no future with the Indians. Where did that leave her? She had given her virginity to this man, only to have it smeared in the mud. She had lost her purity and innocence and had been rudely awakened to real life. Her starry-eyed love for this man had been destroyed in one moment, along with her pride. She backed away, her eyes taking on the wildness that only an Indian's could express. How she hated him! How she suddenly hated him!

"I should kill you!" she hissed.

He just grinned and shook his head. "Don't take it so hard, Margaret. You have known a man. Someday you'll make some Indian buck a fine wife, I expect. But

261

don't bother with the white boys. Look at your own grandparents. Your father's father was white, and he only lived with your father's mother. He never married her. You told me so yourself. A white man has to be with his own kind. That's why the man went back to Tennessee and married a white woman. And your Indian grandmother went to her own people and married an Indian man. That's how it is, Margaret."

"She was forced to be with my white grandfather! She never loved him as I loved you! She was sold to him! I gave myself to you willingly, because I loved you and because you promised to marry me! You won my friendship and trust first! You betrayed me! And if I get the chance I'll kill you! Better than that, I'll send my father after you!"

He felt a slight chill at these words. "Don't be so dramatic. You'll get over it in time." He picked up the rest of his gear and started for the door.

"You'd better keep an eye out behind you, Sam Temple!" she hissed. "Zeke Monroe will be looking for you!"

He looked back at her for a moment, then turned and quickly left. She ran to the door and watched him mount, turn his horse, and ride out. Then she looked around the little cabin where she had known her first love, where she had lost her precious virginity. It wasn't supposed to be this way. How could he have made her trust him so implicitly? She shuddered from the shock of it, then threw the biscuits on the floor and ran out. She couldn't go to the house, not yet—not now. Great sobs of sorrow mixed with vengeful hatred engulfed her as she ran, yet she kept running until she could barely breathe. She finally stumbled and fell, and just lay there in the snow, crying. How she hated Sam Temple! How she hated the white world! And the worst part was she hated herself for her stupidity, and she hated her dark skin for the first time. She stared down at the back of her hand, then scratched at it, wondering if somehow she could scratch the color off so it would be white. She tore at it until it bled; then she fell back into the snow and sobbed, deep wrenching sobs that made her stomach sore. She would never love again— not even herself.

Chapter Thirteen

Abbie knocked on the door to Margaret's room. The girl had not been downstairs all day. She and Margaret had become close over the years, even closer since LeeAnn's abduction. Margaret had always been the quiet one, the solid dependable one, more like a friend than a daughter.

"Go away!" The response was unexpected.

Abbie frowned and knocked again. "Margaret, it's your mother." She heard footsteps, and then the door was suddenly flung open. Abbie's eyes widened at the look of the girl. Her hair was disheveled. Her eyes, red and swollen from crying, were mean and dark, almost like her father's when he was out for vengeance. "Margaret? What is going on? Why haven't you come downstairs today?"

"I was down—earlier!" the girl snapped, turning and walking back into the room. Abbie followed her inside.

"But I didn't see you."

"I used the back stairs and went to Sam's cabin," the girl interrupted.

Abbie studied the girl, her heart aching at the realization of what must have happened. "What is it, Margaret? Tell me what's wrong. Did Sam try to make love to you?"

The girl laughed lightly; then she whirled, her eyes fiery. "Make love to me?" She laughed again. "My God, Mother! He's been making love to me for weeks!" Tears started to fall again. "I . . . loved him! We were supposed to be married!" She noticed the mixture of anger and disappointment in her mother's eyes and choked back a sob. "I wanted . . . to tell you. But you had so much to think about already . . . I didn't want to bother you with it."

Abbie sighed and walked closer to the girl, reaching out and hugging her, but Margaret quickly pulled away. "I'm sorry, Margaret," Abbie said quietly. "I appreciate your not wanting to bother me, but for something as important as giving yourself to a man—"

"Oh, mother, I think I'm going to be sick!" the girl wailed, sitting down on the bed. "I feel so ugly and . . . spoiled! It was so beautiful at first." She sobbed so hard for a moment that she couldn't talk; then she breathed deeply, fighting the tears, hating Sam all the more for making her cry over him. "I was . . . so happy with Sam. We were good friends. He didn't . . . make any advance . . . right away. How can I . . . ever trust anyone . . . again?"

Abbie walked to the foot of the bed, wanting to cry for her daughter. "Where is Sam? I'd like to talk to him."

"That's just it. He's gone! He's gone to Denver! I went to see him . . . this morning . . . and he was packing and leaving. He was going to leave without even telling me, but I went over before he could get away!" She sniffed and wiped at her eyes. "And he told me I was stupid to think . . . he'd really marry me. He said Indian girls were good for . . . sleeping with, but white men . . . never marry them! My God, Mother, what does that make me? And where do I turn? I've never hated being Indian . . . until now!" She wept harder, putting her hands to her face and bending over. Abbie noticed the scratches on her hand. She walked over to kneel in front of the girl.

"What happened to your hand, Margaret?"

The girl took a deep breath and flung back her head. "I tried to scratch the color off!" She sneered.

There was something frighteningly ugly about her now, something changed. "Margaret, believe me, it will pass in time. Not all white men are like Sam, and a lot of Indian men are starting to settle like white people. You can marry an Indian man without living on a reservation."

"Oh, Mother, stop it!" the girl growled, getting up and walking away from where Abbie knelt. "You know as well as I do there is no future for any Indian who tries to do anything but live on a reservation! And there is no future in that either, so we all might as well be dead!"

Abbie's heart was pounding. She desperately needed to get through to her daughter. It was too frightening to think that she had lost her in one day. "Margaret, wait until your father gets back and talk to him. You've been close, and your father understands."

"He's a man! He doesn't understand! It's different for a woman. A man is strong. He can choose his own way!"

"That isn't so. Are you forgetting what happened to him in Tennessee, what happened to his wife and son just because his wife was white and Zeke was Indian? Your father knows more about suffering because of his race than you'll ever know!"

Margaret walked to a window. "Perhaps he does. But apparently my turn is coming." She turned back and faced her mother. "You told me you were with my father before you married so don't look at me as

267

though I'm bad." The girl's eyes were cold and accusing.

Abbie rose, anger rising in her heart. She struggled to stay in control. "I never said you were bad, Margaret. I never believed you capable of being bad. If you think I look at you that way, then it's your own eyes you're seeing looking back at you. You're accusing yourself of being bad, not me. I fully understand why you did what you did. But I do not like the way you speak about me and your father! Yes, I gave myself to him. I was fifteen years old and had lost my whole family! We'd been on the trail for weeks and weeks and we already knew one another well. I knew what a lonely man he was, and I knew he loved me but wouldn't touch me because he felt he had no right. I let him. I let him because I wanted him and I loved him. He had already proven his love for me when he did as I asked and killed my little brother out of mercy because the boy was dying of horrible wounds! He ended my brother's life, at my request, even though it gave him nightmares for a long time after that! Our love had already been proven in many ways, Margaret Monroe! Even at that, I gave myself to your father fully knowing he didn't feel he had any right to marry me, fully knowing he might go on to Oregon and leave the train and I'd never see him again! There were no promises of marriage. It was strictly an act of love that we both knew might have no future at all. Yes, I was with your father, if you want to put it that way. But he didn't seduce me or force me or make any promises, and I never felt bad. Not once! Being with your father was the most beautiful experience I'll ever know, and it is to this day!"

Abbie choked on the last words, the necessity of having to remember the past now, when she knew Zeke might not return, tortured her heart and mind. She

268

turned away. "How dare you speak of my love for your father as though it were something ugly and wrong! Zeke was my whole world! I had nothing—no one—and he saved my life, more than once. I didn't have to wonder if he was sincere. I didn't have to wonder if he loved me." She sucked in her breath in an effort not to break down. How she needed him now, right now! He would know what to say to Margaret. They could talk to the girl together.

Margaret looked back out the window. "I'm sorry, Mother. I know it wasn't like that for you, but it was for me." Her voice was bitter. "And you are white, Mother. You had choices I will never have. That's where we are different. That's what you'll never understand."

Abbie wiped at her eyes and stepped closer. "Margaret, I lived among the Indians for years. How can you say I don't understand your problem?"

"Back then it was Indians among Indians, and whites among whites. The Indian was free to live as he wished. It isn't that way anymore, and the whites won't let the Indians mix. They shove them onto reservations. People like me are caught between. Father is already grown and established and knows his way. But I am seventeen, and I already see that there is no future for me, whatever I choose. I have few options, Mother."

Abbie frowned. "What do you mean by options?"

The girl gave her a sultry, mean look that reminded Abbie of another Indian woman she had known, the dark and jealous Dancing Moon, who had once tried to kill Abbie because of her desire for Zeke. Dancing Moon had been vicious and wild, and Margaret's look frightened Abbie. The girl was changed. This was not her daughter.

"I am not sure myself what I mean, Mother," she said coolly. "I only know that there are other things for girls like me besides getting married. There are other ways

269

of surviving." She shrugged. "Perhaps if I went away, to a place where there were more people, perhaps I'd find the right man after all. Who knows? But it will be hard. I'm already spoiled, thanks to Sam Temple."

"Margaret, you're talking foolishly. Sam didn't spoil you. You're only spoiled if you allow yourself to look at it that way. You loved Sam. You gave yourself to him out of love, thinking that he was going to marry you. You did nothing bad, darling. You're a beautiful, sensible girl, and you have us. You're only seventeen, Margaret. It isn't the end of the world."

The girl folded her arms, her eyes hard. "Isn't it? You don't know how I felt, Mother. You don't know how I felt when he said that to me and you never will." She held out her scratched hand. "This gives you an idea, and I have my father to thank for that. He knew what it was like for him. He never should have had children!"

Abbie just stared at her for a moment; then she walked to the door. "I'll not answer such a remark. You can live with it if you wish. Your father and I love you more than you will ever know, and you are an exceedingly beautiful girl. I'm sorry if I was too upset by Lee Ann's abduction and Lillian's death to see that there was something very wrong in your life. But a woman can only handle so much, Margaret. I can only say that I love you, and I will be here when you have gotten over your grief and are ready to talk."

She left quietly, and Margaret immediately began to pack a carpetbag.

Abbie spent half the night in prayer, then fell into a deep sleep brought on by exhaustion. She had slept little during Lillian's illness, even less since her death. Weariness was setting in, and each day it was more difficult to get up. She awoke late the next morning, and her first thought was of Margaret. She put on her robe and hurried to the girl's room. When there was no answer to her knock, she walked away. Thinking the girl was only exhausted after her bad experience, Abbie went back to her room to wash and dress, then down to the kitchen for coffee and biscuits. But there was a fear in her that she could not explain. She went back to Margaret's room and knocked again. Still no answer. She quietly opened the door to look inside, then rushed in when she saw that the bed was made. She glanced around the room, noting the absence of Margaret's few possessions. She ran to the dresser, pulling open empty drawers.

"Dear God!" she exclaimed. She ran out, hurrying down the stairs to the kitchen. "Where is Sir Tynes?" she asked the cook.

"Why, he's gone to the stables, ma'am."

Abbie dashed off before the woman was quite finished with the statement. She ran down the back steps and across the field to the stables, oblivious of the cold wind and darkening skies. She was screaming Edwin's name, and he came out of the stables, hurrying to her. "She's gone! Edwin, she's gone! Someone must go after her!"

He grasped her arm. "What are you doing out here with no coat! You'll be sick, Abigail!"

"She's gone! Margaret's gone! She's run away, I know she has! That Sam Temple got her to his bed and then ran off on her, Edwin! She's so hurt! She's only seventeen, Edwin! Only seventeen! And she's run away, I know it!"

"Calm down and get back to the house!" he ordered, taking an arm and hurrying her back.

"But she's gone! My God, I've lost three daughters all of a sudden! Three daughters, and my son is in the north and might be dead! LeeAnn might be dead! Zeke might be—"

He jerked her around and shook her. "Stop this!" he

271

barked. "You are Abigail Monroe and you do not panic and go to pieces! You're strong, Abigail, so just stop this! You know your husband will come back— with your daughter! And I shall find Margaret for you!"

She stared at him wide-eyed, and his heart ached for her. So much suffering, but he could not relieve it, only make life as easy for her as possible.

"Come back to the house, Abigail, and we'll talk about it."

She nodded, sniffing back tears. He took advantage of the moment and lightly kissed her forehead. "Sometimes I look at you and you seem only seventeen yourself," he told her. He sighed deeply. "And I would give you the whole world if you would let me, but it wouldn't mean a thing to you. You would never be happy, and that's the hell of it."

He began walking with her again, taking her back inside and forcing her to sit down while he ordered some tea. He sat down across from her. "Now, what is all this about Margaret?"

Abbie wiped at her eyes, suddenly conscious that she hadn't combed her hair yet. "She's been seeing that Sam Temple."

"I know that. And you say Sam wooed her into his bed?"

She nodded and rubbed her forehead. "Oh, God, Edwin. Last night she was so distraught. Yesterday morning she went to see Sam and he was packing to leave. He wasn't even going to tell her good-bye. And he told her that white men . . . white men sleep with Indian girls, but they don't marry them. She was so devastated! So bitter! I'm afraid for her, Edwin! She's run away!"

"Are you sure?"

"I should have known by the way she acted last

272

night, so bitter and hateful. She told me there were . . . other options for girls like her." She put her face in her hands. "God only knows what she meant by that. I only know that when I went to her room this morning, her bed hadn't been slept in and all her things were gone."

The man sighed and leaned back in his chair. "I'll have every building and room on the premises searched and all the men questioned. She would have needed a horse and some help to run away. Someone would have had to take her to Pueblo. And she would have needed money. Where would she have gotten money?"

Abbie looked at him as the cook set more tea in front of her. "I don't know. I had some money in a drawer in my room, money Zeke gave me. We'd had it hidden in the cabin. She knew about it."

"Then drink a little of that tea and we'll go up and see if it's there."

She held his eyes. "Thank you, Edwin. You're so understanding about all of this. We've been a great burden to you since we came here."

He smiled sadly, wondering if she fully realized how much he loved her. Her whole being was wrapped up in Zeke and her children, so much so that for another man to tell her he loved her was almost totally useless. "You haven't been a burden. I've enjoyed your being here immensely, and you know it."

She sipped more tea, and then they went up the stairs to her room. Abbie hurried to the dresser and pulled open the drawer to rummage beneath some clothing. She pulled out some money and counted it, then sighed deeply. "Apparently she would have felt guilty about taking it all," she said dejectedly. "There is fifty dollars missing. Margaret must have taken it. There's no other explanation."

"You never heard her come in?"

She closed her eyes. "No. She must have done it while I slept." Abbie put the money away. "It's the Indian in her, I suppose, so quiet when necessary."

Edwin walked up to her, grasping her shoulders. "We will find her, Abigail. And if we don't, you will hear from her. There is too much love in your family for her to stay away forever."

"But she's only seventeen! She knows nothing about the world out there. And worse than that, she looks Indian! You know what could happen to her because of that. Dear God!"

When her knees began to give out, Edwin enfolded her in his arms and lifted her. "You are to lie down if I have to tie you to the bed," he told her. "You've hardly slept for weeks. You can't keep this up, Abigail. You rest, and I will do everything I can to find your daughter." He led her toward the bed.

"Zeke," she said weakly, her head on Edwin's shoulder. "If only . . . Zeke were here." She thought of her last beautiful moments with Zeke, of falling asleep in the warmth of his arms. It seemed her happiness had ended with that moment.

Zeke urged his horse to the edge of a massive mesa, to look out at the valley that stretched before him and into the mountains ahead. This was big country. The cry of the coyote could be heard from miles away, and things that looked close could be sixty miles off. He had been traveling for nearly three weeks, sticking to the route the Comancheros would most likely take to Mexico. He had little to go on but his own Indian intuitiveness, his ability to smell out a man, and his experience at surviving in this country. They would stay away from the open country and stick to the foothills whenever possible. They would head southeast toward Mexico. They would stay away from forts and cities.

He bent down to rub his aching leg. The stab wounds he had suffered in the knife fight with the Comanches had festered badly, and he shuddered at the pain he had suffered when ten days earlier he had held hot coals to his own leg to burn out the infection, drawing on all of his strength, knowing that if he did not do something, he would lose his leg or die from infection and never be able to help his daughter. The wounds he had suffered on his side and across his shoulder were superficial and had healed, but his leg seemed to be taking a very long time healing. It still pained him greatly.

If he didn't find LeeAnn within another month, he didn't know what he would do. It was already February, and he had been gone ten weeks. He still had a wife and family back in Colorado. There were things left undone there. They must be seen to, for he was more and more convinced that Abbie was better off without him. That must be settled when he returned, but he did not want to go back without LeeAnn. He couldn't bear to see the look on Abbie's face if he returned empty-handed.

He had new hope that he was on the right trail when he came across a burning barn and ranch house. He had ridden down to find a man and boy dead, the livestock apparently stolen. Only a few chickens and sheep had been left behind, the sheep grazing near the bodies and the smoldering ruins. He'd been certain the Comancheros had been there, and he'd wondered if there had been a woman at the ranch and she had been taken. Most likely. He'd shuddered when he'd realized the things his daughter must have witnessed. Then he had spent the rest of the day circling the ranch, checking tracks, wanting to be sure that when he headed out he followed the right ones, and hoping they would lead him to the Comancheros and not to a band of renegade Comanches or Apaches. There had been no arrows in the bodies, no signs of an Indian attack, which indicated the Comancheros were to blame. After four days, the tracks had led to the base of the mesa where he now was perched. He had ridden to the top to see what he could see.

His keen, dark eyes scanned the horizon, and he thought he saw a tuft of smoke curl up from a crevice in the distant mountains. It was difficult to tell. The mountains seemed painted against the sky, and the day was sunny but hazy. He studied the green and purple, velvety-looking peaks that thrust skyward, never feeling more alone than that morning as he sat atop the mesa, a tiny dot in a great, massive land. There was no sound, not even a breath of wind. He saw the smoke again, and his heart pounded with hope and anticipation that it might be from someone's morning campfire—perhaps the Comancheros'!

He had prayed to Maheo all through the night, begging for the wisdom and skill to find his daughter. He'd wished that Wolf's Blood were with him, as he'd been when they'd rescued Abbie from her abductors. The boy would have been a tremendous help. But Zeke Monroe had taken on outlaws single-handedly before, and he would do it again. He turned his horse and quietly urged it down the mesa to the trail he'd been following, occasionally coming across old campfires and garbage, signs that several men had made camp along the way. He reached bottom and kicked his horse into a faster gallop, heading toward the velvet mountains.

With a shaking hand, LeeAnn handed the coffee to the leering Mexican. She had learned soon after her capture by the Comanches not to struggle and fight, for that only meant beatings and the awful rawhide tied tightly around her wrists, making them bleed and hurt. It was better to be a willing, cooperative slave than to be constantly tortured. She remembered her mother saying that one had to do what was practical to survive and that helped her now. Once she had determined after several days of captivity that the Comanches were not going to rape her, she had opted simply to live, trusting that somehow, some way, her father would come for her. She hoped her father was alive, for he'd been badly beaten when the Comanches had pulled her away from him. Since then she had been tied and beaten, forced to do hard chores with the other Comanche women, taunted by those women, and teased and looked over and terrified by the men. But they had not touched her. She suspected they were saving her for something worse, and her suspicions were realized when the outlaws came for her, a mixture of renegade Indians of various tribes, several Mexicans and a few white men. She had just begun to calm down and understand what the Comanches expected of her when the new men came and bought her and her father's horses for rifles. These new men were more ruthless than the Comanches. Her hands had been kept tied to the pommel of her saddle almost constantly, and they rode hard and methodically, giving her little to eat, allowing her little rest. They, too, had inspected her, humiliated her. They had not raped her, but they had seen her and touched her, and she knew with horrible dread that she was most certainly being saved for something—someone. She could only pray that her father would help her before they reached wherever it was they were going.

The Mexican who took the coffee from her laughed and rubbed a hand across her bottom. She jumped away. She had long ago lost the dress she'd worn the day of the raid, and she was clad in a Comanche tunic now, under which she wore nothing. She lived in constant fear of what these men might decide to do with her, especially since she had been forced to witness them rape a white woman they had captured from a ranch three days earlier. LeeAnn's thirteen-year-old mind had been rudely and graphically awakened to the intricacies of what men and women did. She knew there had to be a nicer side to it or there wouldn't be happy husbands and wives, but she wasn't sure she could ever forget this or ever love a man and let him touch her. She wondered what kind of torture was in store for her when they reached their destination, wondered how anyone would ever find her in this desolate land—even her father? And what about the woman? She was kept tied to a travois during the day, completely covered, and taken into a makeshift tent every night. She was there now, and men kept going in and out. Laughter and horrible grunting sounds came from inside, but the woman's sounds had long ceased. She wondered how long it would take the men to tire of the woman and turn their attention to herself. She vowed that somehow she would find a way to escape if someone didn't come for her soon . . . or perhaps she would simply kill herself rather than face whatever it was they had in store for her. Her father's horses had been sold to another group of men not long after they'd first left the Comanches. The men looked Mexican and had paid in gold. The only horses left now were two mares and Kehilan, her father's prized stud. She was glad the horses were still with them, for watching them made her feel closer to her family, and gave her hope that the man who owned them would find a way to come and rescue her.

278

But that hope was fast dwindling. How she hated this land now! It was wild and ugly and full of bad people. Everything about her hurt, and her ribs stuck out from hunger. She was dirty and tired and terrified, and she vowed that if she got away, she would leave this land when she was old enough. She would go East, go to school and become a fine lady. No one would know she had any Indian blood at all. People would look up to her. She would marry a rich white man and live where people were civilized and cultured, live in places she had only read about. A hard slap to the side of her face knocked her down then and brought her back to reality.

"You sit and dream, huh?" a Mexican growled at her. "Stop wasting our time! Clean up the mess around here and be quick about it. We must sleep soon and leave in the morning!" He yanked her up by the hair of the head, holding her little body close to his own. "Not many days now you will be at the home of a wealthy Mexican who will pay much gold for the likes of you! He will tame you, huh?" He ran a hand over her hips again and she struggled against tears. "Oh, I wish I could be the one to do that. It would not be long before the hate in those blue eyes would turn to desire, little one. Never have we had a prettier captive, and I am tired of that used-up woman in the tent." He laughed and shoved her down, then walked away.

LeeAnn finished clearing up with shaking hands, trying not to sob too loudly for fear they would hit her. Then she walked to the juniper tree where she was to be tied for the night, subdued again and determined to cooperate for fear of being beaten or raped. One of the men came and tied her wrists together, then he tied her bonds to the slender trunk of the tree. She curled up next to it, and he threw a blanket over her. More men

279

entered the tent, and she turned her face away and tried to block out their laughter and grunts.

The day had been long for Zeke, for he had been forced to watch from his hiding place as his daughter had been abused. He could not move in too quickly. He intended to do so that night, after most of them were sleeping. He would have to do everything with his knife, for to start shooting would rouse all of them at once. It must be done quickly and quietly. They would not suspect that one man would come after them in such country.

Zeke's blood ran hot with vengeance now. He was glad LeeAnn was tied. She could not run if all hell broke loose and get caught in crossfire. He moved like a cat in the night, making no sound as he came up behind the first of two guards, quickly clamping a hand over the man's mouth and sinking his big blade into the man's spine. He stood that way for a moment before letting go and hanging on to the man until he was on the ground, so there would be no noise from his fall.

There was one other guard on the other side of the camp. That man had heard nothing. Zeke ducked back into the shadows and hurried around to that guard. He watched the man for a moment, then stood up out of the light of the fire and tossed his knife. It landed with a thud in the man's heart. The guard let out only a light grunt, then sank to his knees. He tried to go for his gun, but Zeke dashed out of the darkness and yanked out the knife, quickly slashing it across the man's throat and pushing him to the ground.

There were seven left now. He had taken a count that day while he watched them. Two slept nearby. He had

280

to move fast, very fast, before any of them awoke and realized what was going on. The element of surprise was always a man's best advantage. He crouched down and deftly slashed his knife across their throats; then he moved to where LeeAnn slept. The girl was not even aware of what was going on, for Zeke Monroe knew the Indian ways of making no noise. He crept up to her and clamped a hand over her mouth before fully waking her. She began to struggle, thinking that one of the men had come to rape her. She tugged at her bindings and Zeke grasped her tight, keeping his weight on top of her to stop her struggles.

"It's me—your father," he whispered in her ear. "I'm going to cut you loose, LeeAnn. Go into the shadows, out of the light of the fire, as soon as I release you. Understand?"

He raised up to meet her eyes, and the look of relief and joy he saw in them was worth a million lives to him. He put a finger to his lips, indicating that she should make no sound whatsoever when he took his hand from her mouth. She nodded and he took the hand away. In the light of the fire, disheveled as she was, she was still beautiful, still his LeeAnn, and from what he could determine from the movements in camp that day and the talk he'd heard, still untouched. There would be time to talk about that, time to start helping her forget the horrors she had seen and suffered the past several weeks. First he had to get her out of here alive. He quickly sliced through her rawhide bindings, releasing her hands, and she hugged him around the neck.

"I thought you were dead!" she whispered.

"I'm too mean for that," he whispered back, pulling her arms away. "Get going, LeeAnn."

She turned and ran into the shadows, just as a huge,

281

fat Mexican man came out of the bushes from relieving himself. He spotted Zeke rising from where LeeAnn had been and looked up just in time to see the girl running into the bushes.

"Hey!" he shouted.

Zeke spun about to see the big man running toward him. He threw his knife and it landed in the Mexican's chest, but the fat man kept coming and drove into Zeke's middle, bashing Zeke to the ground. The man was yelling something in Spanish as Zeke wrestled with his massive weight, finally rolling the man over. Suddenly, the Mexican weakened from the terrible stab wound, and Zeke yanked out the knife and stabbed again, this time more directly into the heart.

By then the remaining four men had been aroused. Two had been sleeping in the tent, two outside. The two outside were sitting up by now and rubbing their eyes, one already reaching for his gun. LeeAnn put a hand to her mouth when he drew his gun and fired. Her father ducked sideways, drawing his own gun and getting off four shots which ended the lives of the two men outside the tent. Then he yanked his knife from the fat man's chest and rolled onto the ground into the shadows as a man came out of the tent, brandishing a rifle. He approached the bodies around the campfire, not sure if they were dead or sleeping. All he knew was that he had heard yelling and gunshots.

LeeAnn watched in terror, unable to see her father now. Had he been shot? Should she run? She heard a soft thud and the man with the rifle fell forward, a huge knife sticking out of his back. She gasped and felt ill; then saw Zeke dash to the tent. Several shots were fired, and a moment later her father exited. He pulled his knife from the outlaw's back and wiped it off on the man's shirt, then put it in its sheath.

"LeeAnn!" he called out. "It's all right, honey. It's over."

The girl dashed from the shadows and ran to him, and he swept her into his arms. "I'm getting you away from here right now. Don't look at the bodies, LeeAnn. I'll get you to my own camp and come back for Kehilan and the mares in the morning."

"Father, don't let go of me!" she cried.

"I won't. I won't let go of you again, LeeAnn." He held her so tightly she could barely breathe. She noticed then, as he carried her quickly through the underbrush and across an open stretch, that he seemed to be limping.

"Father, are you hurt?" she asked.

"Just my leg—a little gift from the Comanches. I had a little trouble getting information out of them."

She cried against his shoulder then. She would never understand this wild man that was her father. Within moments he had killed nine men and yet now he carried her gently, like a man who had never known violence. She would miss him terribly when she left this land— but leave it she would. Her mind was made up.

"Father, the woman! The woman in the tent! They did . . . terrible things to her!"

"Hush, LeeAnn. Your young mind should never have been exposed to any of that. I could die thinking of it. I hope you can forget."

"But the woman!"

"She's dead, honey."

She clung to him tightly. "I'm glad. She suffered so badly!" The girl cried harder. He had found her! Her father had found her!

Zeke walked silently. He would not tell her that he had killed the woman himself. What he had seen inside the tent told him she was better off dead. That was the

283

way it was in this land. A man had to be practical about such things. The woman had begged him with her eyes to end her life, and he had put her out of her misery. He was only glad he had not found his daughter in the same condition. He would get Kehilan and his two remaining mares and leave this place, but what had happened here would probably always haunt his daughter's mind.

Chapter Fourteen

Bonnie picked her way through old, crusted snow, the cold rain turning it into mud and slop. Fort Laramie was alive and teeming, for the Sioux attacks were growing worse, much worse. Getting through to Montana along the Bozeman Trail was almost impossible, for Red Cloud had announced he would kill every white man who set foot upon the Sioux hunting grounds, and he was doing a very good job of keeping his word. With the Civil War finally over, more soldiers were being sent west to build up the troops for a new war—with the Indians. She made her way up the wooden steps at the front of the officer's quarters, stomped the mud and slop from her feet, walked along the porch to the door to Dan's living quarters, and tapped on the door.

She waited a moment until a supply wagon rattled by; then she tapped again. A soft voice responded, "Come in." She opened the door and peeked into the small room. Dan sat in a chair, staring at the wall, a bottle of whiskey on a nearby table and a small glass of it in his hand. Bonnie frowned in confusion, for his hair was uncombed and he wore uniform pants but only his cotton undershirt. The buttons at the top were undone, revealing a good part of his chest, and his feet were bare. She reddened slightly and stayed in the doorway. "Dan?"

He turned red, tired eyes to meet hers. "Bonnie!" He smiled a rather drunken smile. "Come on in." He poured himself some more whiskey. "Want a drink?"

She closed the door and walked cautiously toward him. "You told me you . . . had a drinking problem once, Dan, but you've not touched whiskey since I've known you. You'd better put that stuff away. . . . You'll get arrested, or kicked out of the Army."

He chuckled and slugged more down as she sat down across from him on the edge of a cot. "If I wasn't so dedicated to the damned Army, I'd not have to drink!" he anounced. "I'd have been home . . . in the place my wife called home . . . St. Louis . . . in bed with my wife where I belonged." Bonnie reddened again, then felt a strange stirring as his eyes roved over her body. "I should have married someone like you," he said quietly, "someone of strong, sure, sturdy stock."

Their eyes held; then she looked at her lap. "You make it sound like picking a horse."

His snicker of response became an all-out laugh. "I guess I do, don't I? Well"—he stopped laughing—"I didn't mean it that way." He sighed deeply and swallowed. "Bonnie, she's . . . dead. My Emily . . . is dead."

He threw down the glass of whiskey and hung his head, weeping like a child. She reached out and touched his hair. "I'm so sorry, Dan. But . . . how? She's so young."

He cried for several more minutes before he could speak. "The doctor's letter said it was her . . . heart. Said she's probably had some kind of heart condition . . . all her life . . . and that was why she was always so . . . frail and weak. And all these years I blamed her for not being strong enough . . . or brave enough to come out here with me."

She stroked his hair. "Dan, you can't blame yourself for that. Apparently no one knew, not even Emily. I'm so sorry, Dan. So sorry. I came over here to ask if you'd heard anything more about Zeke. I didn't expect this, but I'm glad I came when I did."

He began breathing deeply for control. "I haven't . . . heard. God, Bonnie, it seems like everything . . . is going to hell. Zeke's poor little girl taken off by Comanches, little Lillian dead. Zeke probably doesn't even know that yet. I just got that news, and now I find out . . . my own wife is dead." He ran his hands through his rumpled blond hair. "And I can't find Wolf's Blood anyplace to tell him any of the news. God only knows if he's still alive. The Indians are making war everywhere . . . and Zeke's people are being shipped off to Kansas. And my little girl . . . is sitting in St. Louis all alone." He took out a handkerchief to blow his nose, then put it away and started to pour himself another drink. His hands shook when he reached for the bottle, and Bonnie reached out and grasped his wrists.

"Don't drink any more, Dan. Don't you realize you have all the reason in the world not to drink? You just said it. Your daughter is still in St. Louis. You must send for her, Dan. Bring her to Fort Laramie."

He met her eyes. "How can I? With all this business with the Sioux, and with no wife, how can I take care of a little girl?"

"I'll take care of her for you."

He frowned. "I can't ask that of you. You have your hands full with Joshua and the mission, and you've been doctoring soldiers' wounds. You're busy all the time."

"I can fit her in, Dan, and I can teach her right here.

287

She'd have all the schooling she needs. She should be near her father, Dan. You're all she has now. She must be so lonely and frightened. Have her sent out here. It will be different and exciting for her. The change will help her forget the pain of losing her mother. And it will be good for you. Surely you miss your little girl."

He smiled sadly. "She's almost nine," he told her. "The prettiest little thing you ever saw, with her mother's red hair and green eyes. But she's a strong, sturdy child, not weak like her . . . her mother." His eyes teared anew. "It's strange, Bonnie. We were apart so much, it's almost like I was never really married to her. I don't even know why I married her—because she was so damned pretty, I guess. She tried to be a good wife, but Emily didn't really know how to care about anything but Emily. Her mother died at an early age, and her father spoiled her terribly. Then he died, and . . ." He studied Bonnie's soft blue eyes. "Would you really help me take care of her?"

Bonnie blinked back her own tears and nodded, fighting the terrible desires she was having for this man who was so much like Zeke. He looked so lonely, sitting there, half-undressed, his hair disheveled. She looked down for a moment to gather her thoughts. "Of course I would," she told him, meeting his eyes again. "Dan, I'm a very lonely woman. Having Joshua is wonderful, and having your little Jennifer would be even better. I enjoy children, and you're Zeke's brother. I'm always happy to help anyone Zeke loves." She smiled nervously then. "Isn't it strange? I have a child that Zeke brought to me many years ago to care for, and now his brother is asking me to do the same. I have a way of collecting children, yet I've had none of my own."

Their eyes held, and on impulse he leaned forward suddenly and devoured her lips in a hungry, drunken, lonely kiss, one that soon became demanding; for he was full of alcohol and grief, angry that his own wife hadn't come out to help soothe his manly needs as well as his emotional needs. Bonnie pushed against him, but he was too drunk and too powerful. He pushed her backward onto the cot, groaning as he lay on top of her and prolonged the kiss. Finally his lips left her mouth and moved to her neck. She drew in a deep breath, refusing to let wanton passion make her do something sinful and foolish, unwilling to let this man have her out of sheer drunken loneliness. She pushed at him again.

"Dan! Dan, stop it! You're drunk!"

"Sure I am," he replied in a voice husky with need. "And we're both lonely and you're the finest woman I know." His lips moved farther down and she pushed at his face, yelling his name loudly. He met her eyes, then rolled off of her.

"My God!" he groaned, rolling onto his stomach. "Damn!"

She quickly got up, moving back from him and pulling her shawl close around her. "It's all right, Dan. I understand what you're going through."

"It's not all right!" he growled. He moved to a sitting position. "What a damned rotten thing to do. That's a hell of a way for a man to show his grief, isn't it?" He ran a hand through his hair. "God, I'm sorry, Bonnie."

She touched her lips with her fingers. The fire was still there. No man had kissed her that way, except one—once—in a moment of similar need. Zeke. Would she ever really get over loving him? Perhaps Dan . . . but no. She must not think of him that way. This had been a momentary fit of need and loneliness. It had been painful enough loving Zeke and never being able to have him. She must not let herself have feelings for this man, for surely when he was sober he would see her differently. He liked pretty little china dolls like his Emily. But how did a china doll handle that much man?

She swallowed. All her love and desire for Zeke Monroe had been reawakened, and it hurt. Here in front of her sat his handsome brother, and her thoughts and emotions were confused. Dan stood up and breathed deeply. He walked over to stand close to her, towering above her.

"I'll never be able to apologize enough, Bonnie," he told her. "The combination of alcohol and grief—"

"It's all right," she told him, wondering if that was all it was . . . just alcohol and grief. Probably so, which was why she must not have any feelings for him. Surely next to his Emily, she was as plain as plain could be. "I fully understand, Dan. Nothing has changed." She put a hand on his arm and managed to meet his eyes, but she had to look away again for when she looked directly into those deep blue eyes she wanted him. The memory of the feel of his body crushing hers, the thought of what it would be like to be one with him rushed through her in painful waves. How many times had she thought of Zeke that way? Too many times for God to forgive those sinful thoughts. "Please do send for Jennifer, will you? Your daughter should be with you, Dan."

He put a big hand to the side of her face and forced her to look back up at him. Then he held her chin and rubbed a thumb across her lips. "Give me some time, Bonnie. It wasn't just the whiskey." Her heart tightened. "But right now I've got to get myself together, get over Emily, see my little girl again. What's hard is that I can't even go to the funeral. I'd never get there in time. Some good friends of Emily's family are taking care of everything. It's all just . . . such a mess. I'm a mess . . . everything is a mess."

She fought to keep from trembling. "I understand,

Dan, more than you know. We won't think about today. It's forgotten, all right? You just send for your daughter. I'll be more than happy to help you care for her."

He ran his hand from her cheek over her neck to her shoulder and squeezed it lightly. "Thank you, Bonnie Lewis. My brother knew what he was doing when he asked you to take Joshua. Not many women would agree to care for a crippled half-breed boy."

She smiled sadly. "It wasn't just . . . for the boy's sake," she answered quietly. "It was partly because . . . because Zeke asked me to take him."

He kept hold of her shoulder. "And you love Zeke."

She reddened deeply and looked down.

"Did you think I didn't know?" he asked.

She sighed deeply. "Well . . . we all have our burdens to bear, don't we?" She looked up at him then. Their eyes held, and he bent down to kiss her lightly.

"Maybe somehow they can be shared," he answered. "Maybe that way the burden is a little lighter." He held her arm and walked her to the door. "I'm glad as hell you happened by, Bonnie. I'm sorry for the bad news." He stopped at the doorway. "I'd better wash up and sleep this off. Then I'll see about sending for Jennifer."

"Are you sure you'll be all right? I hate to leave you alone. Promise me you won't drink any more today."

He smiled, a soft, handsome smile. "I promise. Luckily I'm not on duty today. I'll be all right. In a way I'm grieving more over our crazy, messed-up marriage than over Emily. We were never truly close, Bonnie, but I sure as hell did love her."

She took his hands and held them tightly. "I know you did. God bless you, Dan. I'll pray for you."

She turned and quickly left and Dan stared after her, watching her trudge through the slippery mud toward the mission, wondering at how lonely she must be. But with the heaviness in his heart over the news of Emily's death, he couldn't quite put together the realization that they both were lonely, yet neither of them had to be. He closed the door and went back to flop down on the cot, curling up into a pillow and pretending it was Emily. Sweet Emily! He would never hold her again. Yet sometimes it seemed he had never held her. The only proof that he had was Jennifer.

Abbie scraped snow and ice from the little stone at the head of Lillian's grave. It seemed the bulk of Colorado's snow came at a time when other parts of the country were enjoying a hint of spring, and now this early March snowstorm was bringing a new whiteness to the Colorado Plains. She wished that at this moment Tall Grass Woman was close by. She would enjoy talking to her friend; she needed to talk to another woman. Margaret had been the closest friend she had, but Margaret was gone. Perhaps she would never see her again. They had been unable to find her. She had paid one of Sir Tynes's ranch hands to take her to Pueblo—paid both money and, to Abbie's horror, her body. Sir Tynes had sent men to search all over Pueblo for the girl, and he had promptly fired the man who had taken her there. But no trace of Margaret had been uncovered, and Abbie didn't dare leave the rest of the children to try and find her.

Now she knew the "option" Margaret had meant. The young, confused girl apparently had lost all pride and dignity, and in her hurt, bitter state she had decided that she was only good for what white men had told her Indian girls were good for. Abbie wondered if she had somehow failed the girl. Surely she had. There had been so much to think about, so much on her mind, that she had not noticed the changes Margaret was going through, had not acted on her suspicions of Sam Temple. How could she tell Zeke when he returned that his eldest daughter had run off to some unknown place, probably to sell herself to men? What terrible news she would have for him when he returned . . . Lillian dead and Margaret gone. If he returned without LeeAnn, the news could kill him. At that moment she wondered how she had kept going herself. How she missed Lillian! Sweet, quiet Lillian. If only she could hold the girl once more, tell her once more she loved her. If she could change places with any of them—Margaret, Lillian or LeeAnn—she would do it.

Someone called out her name, and she turned to see Edwin Tynes trudging through the snow toward her. "You shouldn't be out here!" he called. She watched him with mixed emotions. He had been good to her, and a little voice told her he loved her very much. But she didn't want to think about that. They, at least, could be good friends, and that was what they had become. She had grown to be grateful that she was at the Tynes estate rather than Fort Lyon. Zeke had made a good choice. The fort was full of confusion and strangers, even dangerous. Here she had peace and quiet and comfort, at a time when she needed all of those things desperately. Tynes came closer, taking her arm. "What are you doing out here alone?" he asked her. "I've told you not to pine away by yourself, Abigail."

"Sometimes I have to be alone, Edwin." She turned back and faced the gravestone. "And I was worried about Lillian, out here in the cold." He felt her tremble and moved his arm around her shoulders.

"You stop that talk." He sighed deeply. "Damn, I wish I could help you more, Abigail." He gave her a squeeze. "Look, as soon as this spring snow leaves, you can plant a garden if you wish, and maybe we'll go riding. Would you like to go riding? You can take that old thing of your father's that you call a rifle and hunt if you wish. I suppose you miss those things. I don't know quite how to treat you, you know. You're so different from the frail, fainting women I've known in the past."

She looked up at him through tear-filled eyes and smiled softly. "Dear Edwin. You needn't do anything. You've already done more than we can ever repay. And these things that have happened to me were beyond your control." She turned away from him and stepped back from the grave, staring across the prairie at distant purple mounds shrouded by the thick snow, the Rockies, those stalwart pinnacles of the West that stayed the same in spite of all that happened beneath their great shadows. "Where could she have gone, Edwin? Denver? Do you know what it would be like for an innocent child in a place like Denver?"

"Don't torture your mind any more than necessary, Abigail."

She swallowed and breathed deeply. "Sometimes I think it's better to know a loved one is dead . . . than to not know what has happened to them . . . to wonder how they must be suffering. God, what has happened to Zeke and my Lee Ann?" She turned to face him, and her heart tightened at the look of utter love on his face. She reddened slightly and looked down.

"I do love you, Abigail. You know that, don't you? I've said it in my actions, in the way I look at you, the things I do for you."

"Don't say that, Edwin." She turned away. "It isn't right that you should say it. I am married, and I dearly love my husband. There can never be anyone but Zeke for me and you well know it. I daresay that if he . . . if he doesn't come back . . . I will never remarry. And I have so much to think about. I wish you wouldn't . . . say that. It only makes my heart heavier. You're a fine and good man, but I can never return any love you might have for me."

He breathed deeply and stepped closer, putting his hands on her shoulders. "Forgive me," he said quietly. "I know I have no right, but when one's heart is as full as mine, it sometimes feels as though it might burst if the words aren't spoken. I feel better just saying it. I . . . I know full well the foolishness of it—the wrongness. Yet I would trade all my possessions just to see your eyes light up when you speak my name as they do when you say his. You have shared a past of love and hardship that creates a bind between you two, one that not even death can break. But we are at least good friends . . . are we not?"

She turned around and met his eyes. How lovely she was! Though thinner and paler than usual, her beauty and strength shone through her large, brown eyes.

"You know what we are. I would never deny that friendship, Edwin, unless I thought you would do something to dishonor it. I'm deeply sorry to hurt you, but there is only room in my heart for Zeke Monroe."

He smiled, sadly but handsomely. "And what a lucky man he is." He reached out and took her arm. "Come back to the house, Abigail. I'll survive my unrequited love, my dear. I've survived other things, and I feel better for having spoken of it. You shouldn't be offended, you know. I simply stated my feelings. I've not dishonored you, and I certainly didn't expect you to fall into my arms. I know full well I can't expect miracles. Still, I daresay you'd best not tell your husband, if it's possible to keep such a thing a secret. I become chilled at the thought of Zeke Monroe coming after me in a jealous rage."

She smiled then, stirred by the thought of Zeke Monroe in action. Few men went up against her husband, and those who did were those who had not heard of him before. All of them regretted their challenge. "He wouldn't do that," she replied. "You've been too kind, and you're treated me with respect." She sighed deeply. "But I'm worried about him, Edwin. Not just what he's doing now. Zeke is capable of taking care of himself in the worst situations. I'm worried about what is going on in his mind. He said things before he left . . . things that made me wonder if he was thinking we could no longer be together, as though he thinks he has ruined my life up to this point and that I should be given a chance at a better one. He talked as though there was no future for us." She looked down at the snow as they walked. "I couldn't live without him, Edwin. Perhaps I could survive his death, but I couldn't bear being without him when he's still alive— couldn't bear his leaving me. He can be so stubborn sometimes. I'm so afraid he'll leave me, just because he thinks it's best for me. He's come close to doing that a couple of times, only because he loves me so much. Once, when I almost died after having Jeremy, he . . . he stopped sleeping with me because he was afraid another pregnancy would kill me. It was a terrible time. I got strangely ill, weaker every day until I could no longer get out of bed without help, and when he came back to me completely, I got better again. It's so strange that two people can love each other so much that they become physically ill when something comes between them. I would never want that to happen again."

They reached the steps that led to the Tudor arch at the entranceway of the Gothic mansion of Sir Edwin Tynes, and they walked beneath the carriage porch and through the doors, closing them and stomping off their boots. "I'm sure it will all work out, Abigail. It might surprise you to know that I hope it will. I want your happiness above all things, even if it means I can never have you."

She met his eyes and pulled a hood off her hair. "You are a remarkable man, Edwin."

He shrugged. "No more remarkable than Zeke Monroe—or yourself." He waved his arm. "Look around this mansion. I would give it all to you in a moment, yet I can tell you are anxious to get back to your cozy little cabin and be with your husband and children. I hope that happens for you, Abigail." He took her hooded cape, one that had belonged to his first wife, and handed it to a maid who approached them then to take their wraps.

"You have a letter, ma'am," the maid told Abbie, handing her an envelope as she took the cloaks.

Abbie glanced at Edwin, then back at the maid, taking the envelope. "A letter? Perhaps it's from Dan." She looked at the return address, a number and a street in Denver—no name. Her face paled. "Edwin, it might be from Margaret. It's from Denver. There's no one else in Denver who would write me, except . . . but no. She wouldn't write. She has no reason."

"Who?"

She looked up at him and reddened slightly. "Just . . . someone." She walked toward the drawing room. Edwin followed her, ordering tea to be brought to them. Abbie sat down beside the fireplace, carefully opening the envelope with trembling fingers.

"Do you want me to open that and read it first?" Edwin asked.

"No. It's all right." She removed the letter, quickly looking at the back page first. "My God, it's from Anna Gale!" she exclaimed, her heart tightening. Why on earth would Anna be writing to her?

"Who is Anna Gale? Is she the woman you meant before?"

Abbie stared at the name. "Yes," she answered

297

quietly. "She's a . . . rather infamous prostitute . . . in Denver." She began reading the letter and Sir Tynes frowned, wondering how someone like Abigail Monroe would know a Denver prostitute. He watched her face pale more as she read, and after several minutes she handed him the letter and just stared at the flames of the fire while the maid brought them tea and Sir Tynes read the letter.

Dear Zeke and Abbie,

Normally, for obvious reasons, you would never have heard from me again. I have, unknown to you both, sent messengers your way to find out how you both are doing, for I have worried ever since the night Zeke came to me to see if I knew where you, Abbie, had been taken after you were kidnapped. I will not mention those details, as we all know I cannot in case others should see this letter. But to my great relief, my spies, so to speak, informed me that you were, indeed, rescued, Abbie. I knew Zeke would find you. It seems he can do anything. My biggest concern was your condition, and I am told you are doing well. I was also relieved to learn that neither of you had been involved in that horrible massacre at Sand Creek, and that your oldest boy was there but recovered from his wounds. See how clever I am at finding out about people I care for, even though I am not worthy to set foot on their doorstep?

It was several months ago when I learned about Sand Creek, and that was the last I heard. So you can understand my shock and surprise when I discovered your eldest daughter, who is really but a child, here in Denver. I passed her on the street, and although I had never met her, she looked familiar, very much like her father and older brother, I suppose. I stopped her and spoke with her and discovered who she was. I almost fainted when she told me. I told her I had known her father at one time, but I did not go into any details. I asked her about his well-being, and she told me the terrible news of LeeAnn and Lillian. That is how I knew where to write you. I am so very sorry, Abigail. Part of the reason for my letter is to inquire whether Zeke has returned yet and whether LeeAnn is all right. Zeke is such a capable man. Surely he will find her. What a terrible time you must be going through, Abbie.

I also want to inquire about Margaret. I know how you must be suffering, but Margaret seemed so bitter. When I asked why she was in Denver and where she was staying, she told me she had come there to make money, that she lived over the Golden Saddle saloon. She didn't go into any further details, except to say that if her father ever came looking for her, I could tell him exactly where she was and that she was perfectly happy. Then she promptly walked off. I sensed that something terrible must have happened to her, and I knew that you didn't know where she was or what she was up to. I know about places like the Golden Saddle, even though I have personally quit the business of prostitution. I run a "respectable" boarding house now. Don't laugh. I'm trying. Not that I will ever equal the likes of Abigail Monroe, but the older I got the more I hated myself and what I was doing. So I figured, what the hell, I'd give honest living a try. I made my bundle during the first big gold strike, and although I've been lucky and the years have not yet taken a terrible toll, I'm not getting any younger. The time will soon come when men *won't pay so much for a woman of my age, I realized then it might be too late for me to get into anything else and straighten out my life. So, here I am.*

I don't want to step in where I don't belong, Abbie. Perhaps none of this is any of my business. I just thought you should know where your daughter is and what she is probably doing. She is very beautiful and will undoubtedly get rich, but she is too precious to be doing this to herself. She is, after all, a Monroe—much too special to destroy her life. I think she wants you to know where she is. She almost dared me to tell you, which means she is secretly asking for help, so there is still hope.

I will gladly talk to the girl for you and try to get her to go home if you wish. But until I hear from you, I will simply keep informed as to her well-being. From personal experience, I know how rough some of those men can be, and the fact that she looks all Indian means they will be even less considerate. I have a feeling you don't know where she is, and I am sure that with all you must have on your mind, Abbie, this was a problem you simply could not handle. I am so sorry, and will do whatever you ask. I will stay out of it completely if you tell me to do so. I have no doubt that Zeke Monroe will never allow this to continue when he gets back. If he or anyone else is coming for her, have them see me first and we can talk to Margaret together. Lord knows I am familiar with all the bad things about prostitution—all the reasons why it is a road to nowhere—but then I had many reasons for getting mixed up in that business whereas a girl like Margaret had no reason to at all, not with all

*the love she has waiting for her at home. How
lucky she is to have a family, parents! That is
something I never had. If there is anything I can
say to her that will help her while she is still young
and able to turn her life around, I will gladly do it.*

*My love to all of you, and, pardon me,
especially to that big half-breed Indian who so
rudely interrupted my life and my heart more
-than once. Forgive me, Abbie, for sending such
sorry news. I will wait to hear from you. I give you
one little warning. In view of the mood Margaret
is in right now, if you send me to drag her away,
she will only become more bitter and you might
lose her for good. She would probably only run
off again. It is better to give her a little time, in
spite of what you know she is doing. Let her learn
a few lessons on her own. Of course, you can't
leave her there forever, but I wouldn't rush in
immediately either. Trust me to watch out for her.
If anything dire happens to her, I will help her and
see that she is not harmed. But being almost a
stranger to her, there is little I can do, and without
your permission, I cannot really tell her the details
of how I know you both. So I will simply keep an
eye on her and leave the rest to your discretion. I
know I will hear from you or see one of you on my
doorstep soon. Come to me at the address shown
on this letter.*

I pray for you. God bless.

Yours, Ann Gale

Edwin looked over at Abbie. "Dear God, I'm sorry,
Abbie."

She met his eyes, her own clear and proud. "She'll
come back. She'll soon learn her folly. She isn't born to
endure such a life. Somewhere along the way her

Monroe pride will bring her home. Anna is right, you know. I can't go and drag her out of there. I'll have to be careful."

"You're amazingly calm."

She smiled, almost bitterly. "I have expected it, after what she did to pay her way to Pueblo. Besides, there are times when I have to be cold and hard, Edwin, or go crazy. This is one of them."

She picked up a cup of tea and sipped it, and his heart ached for her. He knew full well the torture she was silently suffering. "Do you want me to send someone to Denver to try to talk her into coming home?"

She sighed deeply. "I don't quite know what to do. I don't want to lose her completely, Edwin. I don't want to be accusatory or to embarrass and demean her. I think perhaps I will write to Anna, have her keep a watch on Margaret, maybe even talk to the girl. Then, if Zeke isn't back within another week, I'll make the trip to Denver myself. There isn't much else I can do. But this looks like a bad storm. I won't be able to get a letter through for the next couple of days so maybe one of your men could make it as far as Pueblo and send a wire to Denver over the telegraph lines. The way it's snowing right now, he might not even be able to get that far." She rose and paced. "Damned weather! Why couldn't it have kept thawing?" She folded her arms. "I have to think about this. I have to be very careful, Edwin. Very careful. Margaret and I had something special. I don't want to lose that."

"I'll do whatever you ask."

She turned to face him. "I know you will. I'd like to reply to Anna right away, if you have a pen and paper I can use."

"Certainly." He took out a pipe. "How on earth do you know this Anna Gale?"

He began stuffing his pipe. She didn't answer right away, but turned and walked to the window. "When I was telling you about Zeke's and my past, I left out Anna." She stared at the long icicle on the overhang. "I left her out because to tell you the whole story about her would mean telling you something that no one knows about me and Zeke, Wolf's Blood, and Anna."

"You said you were abducted a couple of years ago, but you couldn't tell me by whom or why because you would have to tell me something no one must know about. Does it have to do with that?"

"In a way. Years ago Zeke was searching for his Cheyenne sister-in-law—she had been sold for whiskey—and his search led him to Anna. That was when she was deep into prostitution down in Santa Fe. She owned her own place. Only Anna could give Zeke the information he needed. By then he'd been through hell. He'd been wounded, had been away from home a long time. He was tired and desperate. Anna was well guarded. If he had beaten her or hurt her to get his information, he'd have been arrested and hung, for he was Indian. Anna was more wicked then, younger, wilder. She . . . wanted Zeke. She demanded only one price for the information . . . and he paid it." Abbie stared out the window for several silent seconds. "I'll tell you how much Zeke loves me, Edwin. The Cheyenne believe in making personal sacrifices for their loved ones, usually when they die. Relatives have been known to slash themselves several times, to let blood, over lost loved ones. I have seen Zeke do it himself. And when he was untrue to me, the Indian in him made him want to suffer. He seemed to think he had to show me how sorry he was by making a physical sacrifice, by letting blood, so to speak. He slept with Anna Gale to get his information, and after he left there, he cut off the end of a little finger. He wanted to feel the pain, hoping it would relieve the pain in his heart, because he was afraid his white woman would never forgive him for what he had done." She smiled softly. "He did not have to tell me everything, but he did—because that is the kind of man he is."

She sighed and walked back to her chair. "Ironically I met Anna a few years later when we went to Denver to see a doctor about my dangerous pregnancies. Some white men picked on Wolf's Blood, and Zeke went to the boy's rescue and landed himself in jail. Anna saw it all. Zeke had not given her a thought in years, thought she was still in Santa Fe. She saw me standing there, helplessly watching those men drag Zeke off to the jail, and she hurried to my side, offered me a place to stay. I didn't even know who she was, and when I found out I hated her at first. But she helped get Zeke out of jail— he could easily have been hung—and she gave us a free place to stay when we learned I needed an operation. I'm not sure what we'd have done without her help. We were forced to talk, got to know each other, discovered we were not so different, except that our lives had been led in different directions by fate. We actually came to like each other, even though I knew she loved Zeke. She told me she'd never forgotten that one night with him, in spite of all the men she'd known. She said he'd made her wish she had lived differently, and that she greatly admired me. I learned about her past, came to understand a little better why she had become the way she was. But she said then that she wanted to live a better life someday, in spite of the great deal of money she made. She's an exceedingly beautiful woman. I'm glad she has the boardinghouse." Abigail sipped some more tea. "A few years later she helped us again. She had information that helped Zeke deal his own form of justice to my abductors . . . and it also helped him find me. We owe her a great deal."

304

He puffed quietly on his pipe. "So . . . Anna Gale loves your husband . . . and I love you. Yet you and Zeke have eyes only for each other. What bad news for me and for Anna Gale. I wonder how many others have loved each of you secretly?"

She stared into her tea and thought about Swift Arrow. There was a time . . . but she had not seen Swift Arrow in years. She knew why he stayed in the north with the Sioux, however, that was another matter better left buried. And, of course, there was Bonnie Lewis, who loved Zeke.

"Zeke told me once there are many kinds of love, that he realized other men at different times would love me, other women love him. But we seldom find that special kind of love that must be quenched, a love that cannot be broken, one that transcends the temptations others might offer. We love them back in a grateful sort of way, but we never really love them in that one special way."

She met his eyes and saw that he was studying her. "So I am just one of many who have admired you deeply," he answered. "Is that it?"

"Yes. I suppose so. I don't mean to sound cold, Edwin. You will always be very special to me."

He leaned forward and tamped out his pipe. "But I am not Zeke Monroe," he said with resignation.

Her mind flashed to that first time she had set eyes on Cheyenne Zeke, his dark eyes glowing in the night campfire, his long, black hair hanging over shoulders clad in a buckskin jacket with long, dancing fringes; his waist adorned with an array of weapons; his physique commanding and almost frightening. His aura of power and manliness had struck her hard, and he'd been in command of her whole being when his eyes had first met hers and he'd flashed that broad, handsome grin. She set down her cup and fingered the diamond ring he had bought her years before in Santa Fe.

"Zeke is Zeke," she answered. "There is no other like him." She closed her eyes. "I just pray to God he comes home soon, with LeeAnn, but I don't know how I'm going to tell him about Margaret and Lillian." She breathed deeply, and Edwin could tell that even apart, Zeke and Abigail Monroe were together.

Chapter Fifteen

The early dawn was extra cold, and Zeke noticed
that the snow was getting deeper as they entered
Colorado. If he were alone, he would have been up and
on his way, for they would be home soon if they
hurried. But LeeAnn was sleeping so hard, buried
under all the blankets, that he hated to wake her. Zeke
wore only his sheepskin jacket. He had given LeeAnn
all the blankets, wanting to her to have all the warmth
she could get. He was used to the cold and the elements.
He didn't mind sleeping huddled under his jacket, his
head on a saddle, pine branches beneath him to keep
him from the wet ground. But it irritated him that every
old wound and every joint ached now in the early
morning, worse when he was cold. They never used to
bother him quite so much, and now he had the
additional pain in his right calf. It had healed slowly
and still pained him.

He looked out at the brilliant colors of the winter
morning. There were wispy clouds in the sky, pink and
yellow and blue, depending on how the rising sun hit
them. They hung just above the Sangre de Cristo
Mountains, and Purgatoire Park loomed above the
lesser peaks, ascending into the clouds. There was no

sound, yet he knew that the mountains and foothills teemed with life: deer and elk, bear and eagles, streams full of fish. The mountains were topped with snow, gray and purple rocks jutting out from beneath the white. In the distance, they looked like a painting, hanging there for him to view. On mornings like this it seemed this land was at total peace. It was difficult to realize the violence that could take place here, violence he himself had often dealt out. It was so vast, this country, that he wondered why there was not room for the Cheyenne to stay. But no, the whites had to have it all—every last bit of it. The Indians had been forced into worthless land they didn't want, and those who refused to go and chose war would have to run and hide and starve until they surrendered. He wondered how Wolf's Blood was getting on. He missed the boy so badly that at times his absence was a physical hurt. Maybe he should leave Abbie and the rest of his family to Sir Tynes and join the warring Sioux and Cheyenne in the north—ride free one last time and die in battle. That was what he was meant for, not civilization. But he had chosen civilization, for his Abbie girl.

He closed his eyes and thought of her. The struggles they had been through were too many to think about all at once. He knew how much she loved him, and he loved her more than his own life. But Sir Tynes loved her too. He was sure of it. If there was any possibility of her making a life with Tynes, maybe she should. She deserved to live the rest of her life in comfort, yet he knew she would not choose it for herself. He would have to convince her that it was best for her. His mind reeled with confusion, his passion for Abbie making these thoughts seem absurd. The mere suggestion that any other man might touch her brought a killing jealousy to his soul. No man but Zeke Monroe had touched her in love and desire, and with her willing.

308

Her rape was different. That had been cruel, forced on her against her will, and he had avenged it. They had abused his Abbie, had hurt her. But what about a man who truly loved her? Could she learn to love another somehow, if it was best for her? All his life he had suffered guilt for marrying her, even though she had wanted that more than anything else. Life could have been so different for her if she had stayed within her own race. Yet what would his own life have been like without Abbie? He'd probably be dead by now, for he would have lived like the wild grizzly and would probably have been killed in battle or died from exposure to the elements. Abigail Monroe was the only thing that kept him somewhat civilized. She was the only woman who stirred aching needs in him that made him restless and frustrated when they were apart. How could he possibly live out his life without her? Yet how could he deny her a chance at the peace and comfort she deserved? She had given him so many good years. Still, the thought of her lying in another man's bed . . .

Angrily, he snapped the stick he was holding and got up, stirring the fire. He would heat it up before he roused LeeAnn. He was worried about the girl. She had spoken little since he'd rescued her. At first she had been almost hysterical with relief at being saved, had clung to him every moment, begging him never to leave her alone. He could see that she was going to be afraid of everything and everyone for a long time, and her normally happy, carefree spirit was destroyed. LeeAnn had never been one to think too seriously about anything; she had lived one day at a time and enjoyed it. But she was different now, and he hated to see that. She was another casualty of this land, another reason for him to feel guilty, and he would forever live with the nightmare of how it felt to have her torn from his arms. He had been unable to help his wife once. He'd been gone when she'd been abducted. And he had been unable to help LeeAnn. That was devastating to a man like Zeke. It ate at him, feeding his feeling that his whole family would be better off without him.

He added more wood to the fire, then stooped over LeeAnn to tuck the blankets closer around her neck. His long, black hair brushed against her cheek and she started awake, screaming and grasping the blankets about her, then scooting back.

"Don't touch me!" she yelled.

He frowned, his heart breaking. "LeeAnn, it's just me—your father."

She stared at him with wide, blue eyes, her breath coming in short gasps, her face still that of a little girl, for that was all she was. It sickened him to think of the horrible way she had learned about the realities of life, the side of life he'd hoped to keep from her a little longer, the cruel side.

She choked in a sob. "I'm . . . sorry," she whimpered. "All I saw was . . . an Indian."

The words cut him deeply. Their eyes held for a moment; then he turned to go to his saddlebags and get out some beef jerky and coffee. "Since you're awake, we'd best get moving," he told her. "I didn't mean to wake you. I only meant to make sure you were warm."

As she watched him make coffee in an old tin pot, she could not stop her tears. She loved her father, but she hated all Indians now and she wished she were old enough to go East, where she could be free of the terror in this land, where she could pretend she knew nothing about Indians, pretend that she herself had no Indian blood. None of the children looked less Indian than LeeAnn, with her flowing white blond hair and fair skin.

She stepped closer to the fire, and Zeke looked up at her. "I'm sorry, Father. I have . . . bad dreams. I

310

remember those awful Comanches . . . dragging me away from you . . . beating on you. When you leaned over me and woke me . . . my first thoughts were of them."

He nodded. "I know. It's all still fresh in your mind." He stood up, towering over her. "You half grew up with the Cheyenne, LeeAnn. You know that not all Indians are bad. And you know why they're doing what they're doing now. They're desperate and starving."

She hung her head. "I know. But now I don't care. I just don't care, Father. Maybe someday I will again."

He touched her hair gently, hoping she had told him the truth when she'd said she'd not been raped. She probably was. It would be like the Indians and the Comancheros to save her so they would get more money when she was sold. But she had been badly abused, and had seen and heard things that had affected her deeply. She had been humiliated and inspected and touched, he was sure of that. He could not blame her for hating those men or for connecting all Indians and this land with her misery and terror. It would take her a long time to forget . . . if she ever could. He would have to leave the right words up to Abbie. He wasn't sure how to talk to a thirteen-year-old daughter just budding into womanhood who had been so cruelly awakened to reality. Abbie would know what to say to her. Abbie always knew what to say to the girls.

"Sit down by the fire, LeeAnn," he told her. She sighed and did as he bade her, and he got out a small frying pan and set it over the flames. He took two potatoes from his parfleche, along with a small jar of melted pork fat and a spoon. He scooped some of the fat into the pan, then set down the jar and picked up a potato, pouring a little canteen water over it to wash it. Then he whipped out his huge knife and in seconds

311

dashed it through the potato many times, cutting it into tiny slices. As he picked up the second potato, he glanced at LeeAnn, who was staring at the knife. He hesitated, realizing she was thinking of his own capacity for violence. Her eyes teared.

"How can you kill men . . . and slice up a potato . . . with the same knife! It's like . . . like killing those men was . . . nothing to you."

He washed off the second potato. Irritated now, he quickly sliced it. "A knife is a knife, LeeAnn. At home your mother uses her own favorite knife to clean rabbits and other animals, the same knife she uses to cut vegetables and bread. You simply wash the knife and use it."

She closed her eyes and looked away. "You're . . . like them, aren't you? Sometimes you're just like them. You can kill . . . so easily."

He frowned and shoved the knife angrily into its sheath. "What was I supposed to do? Let them carry you off to some Mexican because I didn't want to dirty my knife, or because I might feel guilty about killing them? You've been forced to see the real side of life, LeeAnn, one you didn't know existed. As long as you had to learn that lesson, then learn the lesson of survival. Understand my violent side. When it comes to protecting my own, I don't give a damn if I have to kill fifty men! They mean nothing to me! That's right. Nothing! I lost count a long time ago of how many men I've killed, but I've always done it in self-defense, or in vengeance for my loved ones." He rose and limped away from her to look out at the mountains, inwardly cursing the pain in his leg. "Yes, LeeAnn, I am just like them. I wouldn't harm innocent people like the desperate ones are doing now, but otherwise, I am just like them—in spirit, LeeAnn. And you have some of that spirit. You just don't realize it yet. Someday you will." He turned around to look at her. "I am Indian, LeeAnn. Half of me runs wild and free with the wind. I love the Cheyenne. I love this land. My name is Lone Eagle, and for years I lived with my Cheyenne mother and brothers. I fought other Indians, hunted the buffalo, lived in a tipi, slept with Indian women. Then I met your mother, and she pulled at the other half of me, the white boy from Tennessee. Your mother keeps me civilized, LeeAnn. But she never asked me to deny my Indian blood, and I have never wanted to and never will! I am Cheyenne! I am proud of it. So don't look at me as if I were some kind of worthless savage!"

She started to cry then. She could not forget the way he'd clung to her and fought for her the day she was abducted, nor the fact that he'd risked his life with the Comanches and the slave traders to get her back. Lucky for her he was the way he was, or she would be in the hands of some cruel Mexican by now, suffering untold horror. He'd been badly hurt by the Comanches, his leg still pained him badly.

"I didn't mean it that way," she sniffled. "I'm . . . confused. You're just like them . . . but you're my father. I didn't mean to sound ungrateful." She looked up at him with her blue eyes, eyes that made him so unnaturally soft. "I love you, Father. Don't be angry at me."

He sighed and walked over to her and knelt down, petting her hair. "I'm sorry, too. It's been a bad day for both of us, hasn't it, little Ksee?" She dropped her blankets and hugged him around the neck, and he embraced her tightly. *"Nemehotatse,"* he whispered, his dark hand petting the nearly white hair. "Let's eat and head home, little girl."

Margaret brought a tray of drinks to the table of

well-dressed men who were gambling. She wore a low-cut Indian tunic, at the request of the tavern owner. "You're an Indian, might as well dress like one. That will be your come-on," the man had told her. "Some of the wealthier men who come here have never had a try with a squaw. You'll be right popular. Do a good job of serving drinks and you can keep what you earn any other way. No matter to me." He'd puffed on his fat cigar. "You look a mite young, though. How old are you?"

"Nineteen," she had replied.

"Well, seems to me you're lyin', but who cares if you want to be here. Most men like the young ones." He'd put out his cigar. "I . . . uh . . . I usually get first turn though, seein' as how you'll be working for me and all." His eyes had roved her body then, and she'd felt ill. Yet her rage and bitterness were too strong.

"Sure. Show me where I'll be sleeping," she had replied.

His grin still haunted her, his foul breath and his sweaty body. She hated white men, and only slept with them to take their money. After all, wasn't that what Indian women were supposed to do?

As she set down the drinks, an older man in a dark, silk suit smiled at her and rested a hand on her hips, signaling her to bend closer. She thought about the rich white man who had abducted her mother, thought about what her father thought of men such as this one, but she banished those thoughts and smiled prettily for him. He was wealthy. He would pay a high price. She bent closer.

"You're about the prettiest thing I've ever set eyes on, even if you are Indian," the man told her. "I don't suppose you have a room upstairs? You do more than serve drinks, don't you?"

Her face was close to his, which was red from

whiskey and desire, making his white mustache look even whiter. She thought about how nice it would feel to stick a knife him and watch his eyes bulge out in pain.

"Yes, I have a room upstairs, and I do more than serve drinks," she replied, smiling enticingly at him.

He patted her bottom. "That's what I thought," he said with a chuckle. "You're a smart girl. This beats the reservations, right? Here you can get rich doing what Indian girls are best at doing. What's your name, anyway?"

She straightened and tossed her long, dark hair behind her shoulders. "I am Moheya, Blue Sky," she told him, holding her chin proudly. She remembered then the day her mother had made them go around the table saying their Indian names and telling them to be proud. Pain stabbed at her heart. Sometimes she wanted to go home, but she couldn't do that now. Not now. She remembered Sam Temple's words, and her bitterness and hatred returned. She had hoped that she would see Sam, that he would know what she was doing and feel badly about it, perhaps ask her to stop. But that was probably a foolish dream. "I get off at midnight," she told the man in the suit. "And I prefer not to know your name."

He winked, drinking in her voluptuous young body and wondering how he could wait until midnight. "That's smart too. Makes it all easier." He frowned. "You seem too intelligent and well-spoken to be a squaw. There's something about you that doesn't seem all Indian."

Her eyes flashed. "I am all Indian!"

"Hey, squaw, you'd best tell your Indian friends to stay on the reservation," another of the men spoke up. "The iron horse is coming through, and the Indians had better be out of the way. You know what an iron horse is, little squaw?"

She glared at him. "I know what it is. It is a train."

"And trains mean the end of the Indians. You're one of the smart ones. You know your place." He winked at her, thinking perhaps he'd return the next night for some of what his friend would be getting tonight. "Yes, ma'am, investors like us have bought up Indian lands and we'll be making quite a bundle off the railroad. Someday the railroad will stretch from the east coast to the west. Denver will be connected with both. Hang around, honey, and watch this city grow like it never has yet. We won't need gold to keep us going. We'll be the center of trade."

She picked up their empty glasses. "That warms my heart," she said sarcastically. "I am sure my friends will be happy."

They all laughed. "Well we showed your 'friends' what will happen to them if they get in our way—at Sand Creek, right?"

She froze for a moment, and the look she gave the man chilled him. "Yes. You showed us, all right. I had relatives at Sand Creek." Her eyes held his boldly and he swallowed.

"Well . . . uh . . . you ought to know there were a lot of investigations into that affair," he told her, trying to get out of the hole he had dug. "Why, Governor Evans himself was forced to resign, and that Chivington fellow dropped out of sight. Now that the Cheyenne are off to their new reservation in Kansas, there won't be any more trouble. Something like Sand Creek won't happen again."

She straightened and smiled bitterly at him. "Sand Creek was only the beginning!" she snapped. She whirled and carried the tray back to the bar. The men all turned to watch the gentle curve of her hips beneath the soft tunic.

"Do you think it's true they don't wear anything under those buckskins?" one of them commented.

"I'll find out later tonight," the first man answered, putting a cigar in his mouth.

They all chuckled. "She's a wild-looking one. Better be careful, Stu. She might sink a knife into your belly."

"Ben wouldn't have her working here if she was dangerous," the man replied. "And I'll tame her down fast enough."

"Beats going home to a wife with a headache, right?"

They all chuckled again. "A wife for social appearances, a whore for a good time in bed," the first man answered.

Margaret stood at the bar, waiting for another tray of drinks. A well-built, dark, and very handsome man sat on a stool beside her. She felt his eyes on her, and she turned to meet his brown eyes. He was older, perhaps thirty-five, with dark wavy hair and a lean, provocative look about him. He flashed a wide, handsome smile, his teeth straight and white. There was something warm about his smile. He did not leer hungrily like the others. "Hello," he said softly.

When she nodded, he glanced back at the table of men. He had watched her conversation with them. Then he looked back at her. "You're awful pretty to be working in a place like this," he told her. "Why aren't you with your people?"

Her smile faded. "My people are dying. There is no future on the reservation, and no future in the white man's world. There's nothing left for me but this. I make a lot of money."

"That I do not doubt." Their eyes held.

"Are you interested, or are you just making conversation?"

He leaned back and looked her over. "I might be interested. But you seem kind of . . . special. I think I'd

317

rather have you because you want me, not for my money."

She felt a gentle stirring of desire, something she had not felt for some time. She turned away to set drinks on her tray. "Then I guess we can't do business. Pay me enough, and you can come to my room. You think about it."

He put on a wide-brimmed hat. "I'll do that. Name's Brown. Morgan Brown. And something tells me you have a white name—a Christian name, they call it."

She kept her face turned away from him. "I have no white name," she answered. "Why would I have a white name?"

He shrugged. "The way you talk, I guess. There's just something about you that doesn't belong here."

She met his eyes defiantly then. "Believe me, Mr. Morgan, I belong here!" Taking the tray, she walked to another table of customers. He watched her. Perhaps he would do business with her after all, if that was the only way he could have her.

Abbie dismounted from the sleek thoroughbred Edwin had given her to ride and walked to the little stream where they had gone to talk. Edwin dismounted too, tying both horses as Abbie removed her cape. A sudden spring thaw had arrived; the temperature was in the sixties. Another snowstorm was likely, for it was only mid-March, but they enjoyed this break in the weather, during which the heavy snows of the past week were swiftly melting.

"I must go to Denver, Edwin, now that I can get through," she told him as he walked up to stand beside her. "Another storm could come at any moment and I've lost too much time already. I have sent a letter to Anna, telling her to expect me."

"I will go with you. You shan't go to that place alone."

She sighed and stooped down to pick a tiny flower making its way through the snow. Then she rose and looked at Edwin, twirling the flower in her fingers. "I'd rather you sent one or two of your hired help with me. I don't think it would look right if we went. I'm afraid your love . . . shows too much, Edwin. People might get the wrong idea. There is nothing between us, and I don't want people to think otherwise."

His eyes moved over her, handsome dark eyes that belonged to a handsome dark man, wealthy and titled. She wondered why it was so easy for her to walk away from what he was offering, while he suffered the pains of not being able to have what he wanted—for the first time in his life. "I wish it were the 'otherwise,'" he answered.

She looked down at the flower. "I'm sorry, but it can't be . . . even if Zeke doesn't come back . . . not for a long time." She sighed and blinked back tears. "Oh, Edwin, I have so many decisions to make. I must decide what to do about Margaret and the ranch. I don't know what has happened to my husband and LeeAnn. Should I send men searching for them? What will I do if something has happened to Zeke? I don't know where my oldest son is right now, whether he's alive. And if Zeke is dead, how will I be able to go on living?" A tear slipped down her cheek, and she breathed deeply to control herself. "Edwin, I need you to help me for I must make up my mind soon. Yet I feel guilty for seeking your help when I know how you feel. I can't return your feelings, and I have no right to be here under those circumstances."

He put his hands on her shoulders. "You will always have a right to be here, and I will help you all I can. I expect nothing in return, Abigail."

She shook her head. "No. I've been here too long already. I'll . . . I'll go to Denver and try to get Margaret to come home. Then I'll take the children and go to Fort Laramie where Dan is. He will help me find a place to live. Perhaps I can do mending or washing for the soldiers, baking and such. I would be near the Cheyenne again . . . and near Zeke's Cheyenne brother Swift Arrow, and our son." Her eyes lit up a little. "Yes! Why didn't I think of that before? I could be among the Indians again, and near two of Zeke's brothers and our son."

He shook his head, smiling sadly. "You really would be happy around the Indians again? Don't you realize it can't be the way it was, Abigail? If you approached the Indians now they would probably scalp that beautiful hair from your head, after they did worse things to you."

She reddened. "Not Swift Arrow."

"It might be impossible to find him. It's been a long time since you truly lived among them, Abigail. Many of the Indians don't even know you anymore. You must understand that it would be as dangerous for you to go north as it would be for any other white woman. I couldn't let you do that."

"I don't care! I'll go. If I go to Fort Laramie where Dan is, I'll be safe, and at least I'd be close to the Indians. I'd have a chance to see Swift Arrow and my son." Her lips quivered and she put a hand to her mouth. "I have to go, Edwin!" she whimpered. "I have to do . . . something. I can't just sit here the rest of my life!"

He frowned. "Is it that bad here? That boring?"

She met his eyes again. "Oh, no! I didn't mean it that way."

He laughed lightly. "Of course you did. You actually can't stand all this luxury, can you? You'd rather be

320

baking and scrubbing and hunting, making your own fires and teaching your children and planting a garden. You'd have Indians camped on your doorstep if they weren't gone now. And you'd rather be sleeping on a bed of robes with Zeke Monroe than in one of my luxurious, fourposter beds—with me." His smile faded at the words, and she reddened deeply, turning away.

"I'm sorry, Edwin."

"Oh, don't be sorry. Don't ever be sorry, Abigail. I love you for what you are. But why choose hardship over the things I can give you, Abigail? And I can offer so much to your children."

She shook her head and turned back to him. "My children will be just fine. In fact, Margaret might be better off up north. The change might be good for her. I don't know why I didn't think of it before. I could put the ranch up for sale. Perhaps you would want it, Edwin. I'll go north to Dan and Swift Arrow. You could . . . you could just watch over the ranch for a while, like you've been doing, until I know for sure what has happened to Zeke. And if he's . . . if he's . . ."

A black shudder rippled through her body at the very real possibility that Zeke would not come back this time, nor would her daughter. How could she handle that truth, with Lillian's death so fresh in her heart? Breathing became difficult, and she dropped the flower and grasped his arms. "What if he really is dead?" she whispered, staring past him at the water. "My God, Edwin! All my strength comes from him. All my reason for living."

"You have a strength of your own. And your reason for living will be your children. You will survive, Abigail."

She shook her head, her eyes wide, and she stepped back from him. "No!" Never before had she realized so clearly just what losing Zeke meant. "You don't

321

understand . . . what we have. I couldn't . . ." A terrible pain swept through her chest and she put a hand to her heart, turning and walking farther away. "Zeke!" she whimpered. Edwin rushed up to her, grasping her arm.

"Don't do this, Abigail. Don't tear yourself apart. You must go to Margaret, remember?"

She hunched over, almost gasping for breath. Zeke! How much longer must she endure not knowing what had happened to him? Edwin pulled her into his arms, holding her tightly as though if he did so he could keep her from going to pieces. "Hang on, Abigail. Take deep breaths now. Think of the good things."

She nodded, breathing deeply. How he wanted to comfort her! To kiss her! To make love to her! He helped her to a sitting position. "You sit there and relax a moment, Abigail. I wanted this ride to be enjoyable for you, but it seems there is nothing I can do to comfort you. I'm sorry about that." He patted her hair. "Get control of yourself. I won't have you mounting a horse until you've settled down. If you want to go north, then you shall go north. I will help you get there safely. Then I will wait, Abigail. I will wait here in the hope that you will come back. I will—" He stopped and looked over the broad horizon. "Someone is coming— riding hard," he told her.

She threw her head back, breathing deeply, struggling not to think about the possibility of Zeke Monroe being dead. The pounding hooves came closer and she turned to see one of Sir Tynes's men on a lathered horse.

"I've been trying to find you, sir, thought you might have come here."

"Ah, you know I like this spot, Frank. And what is it that makes you get that horse so lathered trying to find me?"

322

The man looked from Edwin to Abbie. "Your husband is back, ma'am—with your daughter. They're both fine, except your husband has a wounded leg."

Abbie gasped, then let tears of relief fall. Edwin felt the pain of jealousy and resignation. Surely his hopes were dashed now. "Thank you, Frank. We'll be along right away."

As the man nodded and turned his horse, Edwin walked over to help Abbie up. She said nothing to him, but let out a strange guttural sound of total joy and let go of him, running to her horse and mounting the sidesaddle. She did not like this new form of riding she had recently learned. She'd rather ride on a normal saddle or an Indian saddle, which was the next thing to bareback.

"Use your head, Abigail!" Tynes shouted as she turned her horse. "Don't ride too hard in your eagerness and get hurt before you see him."

She rode off, ignoring his warning, not caring that he had to mount hurriedly and try to catch up. Abigail Trent Monroe knew how to ride and how to ride hard. She wasn't worried. Zeke was back! Zeke was alive! And so was LeeAnn! LeeAnn! He had brought her home! Great sobs of relief swept through her, and she breathed deeply of the sweet spring wind, enjoying the feel of it in her hair, loving the look of her horse's flying mane. Perhaps living with Zeke had made her more wild and a more a lover of freedom than she realized.

Chapter Sixteen

As Abbie rode up to the mansion, LeeAnn ran down the steps toward her. Jumping from her horse before it came to a halt, she hurried to LeeAnn, scooping the girl into her arms. For several minutes, they embraced, saying nothing, only crying. Tynes, who had ridden up, looked around for Zeke but saw him nowhere.

"It was so terrible, Mother!" LeeAnn finally choked out, clinging to the woman. "I thought I'd never see you again. I kept praying Father would find me, and he did! He found me!"

"Of course he found you!" Abbie replied, finally releasing the girl and wiping her eyes so she could take inventory of her daughter. "Zeke Monroe can do anything." They both hugged again, laughing and crying at the same time.

Then LeeAnn's mixture of laughter and tears turned to just tears. "Mother, Jeremy said Lillian died," she sobbed. "And Margaret has run away!"

Abbie held her, stroking the girl's long, blond hair. "It's true, dear." Her heart tightened. "My God, did he already tell your father?" She pulled away again and LeeAnn nodded. Abbie let go of the girl for a moment. Pulling a handkerchief from the pocket of her cape, she blew her nose and wiped her eyes. "Where is he, LeeAnn?"

The girl sniffled and wiped at her eyes with her arm. "He asked . . . where the grave was. I think he went there."

Abbie looked up at Edwin and the man frowned. "You'd better go out there, Abigail." She could see the pain in his eyes. She turned back to LeeAnn.

"First I must look you over, LeeAnn, and later we must talk." She smoothed back the girl's hair, studying her face. The girl wore a simple cotton dress that Zeke had taken with him in case her own clothing were torn or gone when he found her. The fact that the girl wore the dress brought a sick feeling to Abbie's stomach. She well knew the horror of rape, but for a thirteen-year-old girl who knew nothing about men . . . "What did they do to you, LeeAnn?" She put an arm around the girl's shoulders and walked her away from the others.

"They hit me . . . made me do work for them." The girl put a hand to her stomach. "The Comanches weren't so bad, but they hit me a lot and the women were mean to me. Then they sold me—to Comancheros."

"Comancheros!" Abbie held the girl closer.

"They were awful men!" LeeAnn whimpered. "I would rather have stayed with the Comanches. They . . . undressed me . . . and looked at me." She wrapped both arms around her stomach. "They raided a ranch and took a white woman and did . . . cruel things to her. Every minute I was scared . . . they'd do that to me. But they didn't. They kept saying I was worth more if they left me alone."

A wave of relief swept over Abbie, even though she knew her daughter had seen and experienced things that would surely haunt her forever. She kissed the girl's hair and hugged her close. "We'll talk more later,

LeeAnn. We'll talk a lot . . . as much as you want to talk. You must remember that there are good people, and good men like your father. Being with a man can be wonderful and beautiful, LeeAnn. And you're such a beautiful child. Don't let this destroy that."

"Sometimes I just want to go away, Mother—go East where everything is different . . . civilized." She leaned back and looked at her mother, already as tall as the woman who bore her. "Do you think when I'm older I could go East to school, mother? Could I?"

Abbie's heart was pained at the thought of her children growing up and going away. "We'll see. Perhaps Bonnie Lewis could give us some advice. I haven't been back East since"—she thought about Zeke, and how they'd met—"since my father brought me out here from Tennessee. She looked out in the direction of Lillian's grave, which she could see now from where she was standing. She could see a horse, and the figure of a man kneeling under the huge cottonwood tree that shaded the little grove. She felt as though someone were pushing a sword through her heart. "I must go to your father, LeeAnn."

"He's hurt, Mother, but he's healing."

Abbie frowned. "Hurt? How? Where?"

"The Comanches. He had to fight them before they would give him information. He got stabbed in the leg many times—his right calf. He told me it got infected and he had to burn it himself."

Abbie closed her eyes. "Dear God!"

"He said he had to, or he might have lost his leg. He suffered so much to find me, Mother. And he attacked the Comancheros' camp and killed them all! I never saw him like that before."

Abbie sighed deeply and stroked the girl's hair, studying her, hardly able to believe she was standing there in front of her. "What happened to the poor white

327

woman the Comancheros took?" She shuddered at the thought of it, her own memories of captivity making her feel ill.

"Father said she was dead when he found her in the tent where they kept her, after he'd killed them all. But I know she wasn't dead before that, because there were men in there with her." The girl swallowed and held her mother's eyes. "I think . . . I think Father killed her himself. He acted funny . . . when he told me she was dead."

Abbie's eyes teared. She remembered when Zeke had ended her little brother's life to stop the boy's suffering, knowing the child couldn't possibly live. She could imagine the condition in which he had found the woman, and her chest ached as she walked LeeAnn back toward the house.

"You go inside and take a bath, LeeAnn, and change and rest. You can have whatever you want to eat. Just ask the cook. Enjoy the company of your brothers and Ellen."

"What about Margaret?" the girl asked with concern.

"Now that your father is home, he'll go after her and bring her home. I'm sure of it." She banished the jealousy that streaked through her at the realization that Zeke would have to see Anna Gale. It didn't matter. The important thing was to get Margaret home.

"You won't go, will you, Mother? Don't go away! I want to be with you for a while. Don't go with Father. He can get her himself."

She wanted desperately to go with Zeke, to be with him now for a while, to help him face whatever he must in Denver. But how could she leave LeeAnn? He would have to go alone. She wondered if the family would ever be together again, ever be normal. "I won't go,

LeeAnn," she told her daughter.

As LeeAnn walked up the steps to rejoin her sister and her brothers, Abbie looked at Edwin. "He was badly wounded. Will you help LeeAnn find her way around? Give her a room and have someone help her prepare a bath?"

"I'll watch after her. You'd better go to Zeke now." Their eyes held for a moment and he smiled sadly. "Go." He walked closer and helped her onto her mount, and she rode off toward Lillian's grave and the lone figure who knelt beside it.

Within a few feet of the grave, she halted her horse. Zeke was shirtless, his buckskin jacket on the ground beside him. She knew why, knew what she would find when she walked closer, for he had lost a daughter. His long, shiny, black hair blew loosely in the wind, and the tiny bell he wore in his hair ornament was tinkling softly.

"She should be buried on our own land . . . beside Lance," he said gruffly, his back to her.

She studied his muscular shoulders, the scars on his back from the whipping white men had given him many years ago. It seemed she had to strive for breath. "It was very cold . . . beginning to blizzard. It would have been a dangerous trip. I didn't want to risk one of the other children getting sick. If it were possible, I'd have taken her there."

He turned to look at her, quickly scanning the magnificent thoroughbred she rode, noticing she sat sidesaddle and wore an expensive yellow dress. Obviously it had been given her by Sir Edwin Tynes. Her hair was drawn up at the sides with fancy combs but hung long at her back. There was a reddish glow to it in the sunlight. She was beautiful, more beautiful than he had ever seen her. Apparently the Tynes estate had been a good place for her. But she was thinner, paler. He could imagine the hell she had been through.

Their eyes held for several seconds, saying many things without words. "It was . . . pneumonia," she said finally in a shaky voice. Would he ever cease to overwhelm her with his virility and animal-like grace?

Blood trickled from a self-inflicted wound on his chest. She was not surprised or appalled. She had expected it. It was the Cheyenne way of mourning.

"We did . . . everything we could," she continued. "We even sent for a doctor from Denver . . . but she couldn't hang on. She was never strong." She struggled to stay in control. "We picked this place because it was high and shaded."

"We?" There was an odd, cold sadness to his voice. She realized how she must look to him. He must think she had easily adapted to this new life and was enjoying it. When he returned she had been out riding with Edwin Tynes. She wore a fancy dress and a cape, and was perched on one of Sir Tynes's grand horses.

"Don't look at me that way, Zeke Monroe! You know me better!" she said, suddenly angry. "I've been slowly dying day by day without you, and if you don't hold me quickly, I'll faint—right off this horse!"

He rose and walked to her, his dark eyes steady but bloodshot, his face tired—so tired. She noticed that he limped. "I'll get blood on that pretty dress."

"I should care at a moment like this."

He reached up and she let go of the reins and bent toward him. In the next moment she was in his arms. She broke into wretched sobbing, a mixture of renewed mourning over Lillian and utter relief at having her husband and daughter back. He held her tightly, the feel of her against him making him wonder how he would ever tell her she was better off without him. Yet he felt that he should leave her at this place where there was comfort and safety and beauty. His heart was torn between what he knew was best for her, and his own need. This was where she should be. He could see it, just by the way she looked now. She was all elegance and beauty. It was difficult to remember her wearing a tunic and sleeping beside him in a tipi. Yet doing what was best for her would mean that Sir Edwin Tynes eventually would make her his own, and the thought of any man touching her that way filled him with rage. He held her tightly, hoping there had been nothing between her and Tynes, knowing there had not been. His Abbie girl was incapable of it. If she were not the way she was, it would be easier to turn away from her.

"It's all right, Abbie," he told her, running a hand through her hair. "Things will work out somehow. I just . . . poor little Lillian. If I just could have seen her again."

She felt him tremble, knew he was weeping, and they remained in an embrace for several minutes. Then he slowly released her, kissing the top of her head. She sensed something different now, and fear gripped her heart when she finally met his eyes. He was somehow removed from her.

"Why did you leave the way you did, Zeke? When I woke up you were gone."

"You needed to rest. I had to get going and I didn't want to disturb you."

She pulled back, running her hands over the hard muscles of his arms and shoulders. "No. It was like . . . like you were saying that was the last time you would share my bed."

She choked back a sob and he grasped her wrists, pulling her hands away. "There's no time to talk about any of that now. I have to go after Margaret."

She hung her head. She needed him to hold her—they had been apart so long—yet he didn't seem to want to hold her. "Do you blame me . . . for her

331

running away?"

He frowned. God how he loved her! How he wanted to hold her again! How was he going to be able to do what was best for her? She was his life's blood. "Blame you? Why would I blame you?" He took her arm and helped her sit down, sitting down beside her and crossing his legs Indian style. The fringes of his buckskin pants danced in the wind. Everything about him was raw and rugged, a part of the wind, from the dancing fringes of his buckskins to his streaming hair and the soft tinkling bell. When he had held her she had breathed deeply of the familiar scent of leather and fresh air. "Tell me what happened, Abbie," he said.

She wiped at her eyes and turned to grasp his arm, bending and kissing his shoulder. "First I want to know how badly you were wounded. LeeAnn said the Comanches stabbed your leg."

He picked up a stick and traced it along the grass. A spring wind had already dried off the hill where they sat. "The Comanches have a strange way of making a person pay for information. I'll be all right. It's healing. I burned out the infection myself."

She closed her eyes and rested her head on his shoulder. "Dear God! I wish I had been with you. What about LeeAnn? How was she when you found her?"

He sighed. "She was wearing a Comanche tunic. She'd been treated roughly—rudely—but she wasn't raped. I'm sure of it. She'll have some pretty horrible things to forget, though. She's a smart, tough little girl. She cooperated, knew it was best to do so if she wanted to survive. I think she'll be all right in time. But she hates the Indians. Even I frighten her. I've not been much good to this family lately, have I?"

"That's foolish talk."

They looked at each other, and it seemed to her that he wanted to kiss her. But he didn't, and she realized

332

with surprise that he hadn't kissed her yet. He turned away then. "Tell me about Margaret."

She took a handkerchief from her cape again, untying the wrap and laying it beside her. Then she reached around and dabbed the handkerchief along the cut on his chest, worried by his strange, stubborn mood. It was as though she had just met him and didn't really know him. How she wished she could say something to make him smile. But she had only bad news for him.

"She became interested in a young man here on the estate—a ranch hand named Sam Temple," Abbie told him softly. "He was very good to her, or at least put on a good show of it. They became fast friends. Sam is young, handsome, nice enough—or so I thought. There was something about him I didn't trust, but I couldn't put my finger on it." She sighed deeply, refolding the handkerchief and dabbing at a few spots that still bled. The rest of the cut was beginning to scab. So many scars, inside and out! "I love you, Zeke," she said, suddenly feeling an urgent need to say it, suddenly aware of how much he was hurting.

He turned and met his eyes again. How handsome he was! It seemed aging had only made him more so. His skills had not lost their sharpness, his strength and hard-rock muscle were still intact. But how much suffering did he bear without telling her? Surely he was often in pain, but he never showed it. Again came the fear. Again he did not kiss her. The look on his face at that moment reminded her of the way he used to look at her when she was fifteen and crazy in love with him, when he'd argued that they should not marry because he was part Indian and it could be bad for her. He had been so stubborn then, so hard to convince that she loved him and didn't care that he was Indian, didn't care about anything but being his woman. Was he thinking now, after all these years, that they should not be together?

"I love you too," he answered quietly. "More than my own life. That's why I can't stand being responsible for your suffering."

"But with you at my side it doesn't matter."

He turned away again and stood up, walking away from her. "What happened with Margaret? Did this Sam Temple hurt her?"

She looked at the bloody handkerchief. She had lost him again. Why was he so elusive now, harder to hold than ever? "I was so . . . so upset over LeeAnn, and Lillian was so sick after you left. Then she died. I guess with all those things happening, I didn't notice the changes Margaret was going through. She said she didn't want to bother me with her problems. By the time I found out, the damage was done."

"He slept with her and then he left her—because she's Indian and that's all Indian women are good for, right?"

She looked up at him in surprise. "Yes! But how did you know?"

He smiled, a sneering smile. "Come on, Abbie. I grew up in Tennessee among whites, remember? White men murdered my first wife and our son, just because Ellen was white and she had slept with a half-breed! I know how they think!" He drew out his knife and threw it hard. It stuck in the cottonwood tree with a thud. "I'd like to get my hands on Sam Temple!" He turned to face her. "You have any idea where Margaret went?"

She wrung the handkerchief she held in her hands. "That's the hard part." She swallowed. "She was . . . so hurt, Zeke. He was her first man, and he had promised to marry her. She was so sure of him. And then he just . . . left. He told her Indian women were great for sleeping with, but white men didn't marry them. It made her hate herself, Zeke. She scratched half the skin off one hand, trying to scratch off the color, she told me. She was so . . . bitter. So full of hate. She got a wild look to her. I couldn't talk to her. It was as though she wasn't even Margaret anymore. She had a wicked look, like Dancing Moon had sometimes. And then she sneaked off in the 'night—even took some of our money. She paid a ranch hand to take her to Pueblo, paid with money and . . . and her body."

He threw his head back and clenched his fists. "Damn!" he swore. "God damn all of it! How much is a man supposed to take!"

Abbie's body jerked as she choked down a sob. "She told me before she left that she couldn't live on a reservation but no white man would want her for a wife . . . so she'd have to seek other options." She sniffed and wiped at her eyes. "And then a few days ago I got a letter . . . from . . . from Anna Gale."

His eyes hardened. "She went to Denver? My daughter went to Denver?"

She nodded, breaking into harder tears. "Edwin had men search . . . all over Pueblo, but they found no sign of her, nor did they turn up a trace of where she might have gone. Then I got the letter. I was getting ready to go there myself before you came . . . to try to talk her into coming home. We had a terrible snowstorm right after the letter came, and I wasn't able to go. But Anna said she'd keep an eye on her, that whoever comes should see her first. She said she'd help . . . talk to Margaret . . . because she knows what the girl is going through and because she can tell her how unhappy she will be in the end if she lives a life of . . . of—"

"Prostitution," he said quietly, the word almost a groan.

She cried harder. "Oh, God, Zeke, I feel so . . . responsible! I should have seen what was happening. I might have been able to say something . . . to stop what was happening, but Lillian—poor, sick Lillian . . ."

He was suddenly there, sitting down and facing her, pulling her into his arms and holding her tightly. "Stop it, Abbie. How can a woman who has just lost a child to death be aware of everything happening around her?" He rocked her gently. "Lillian was sick and dying, and for all you knew LeeAnn was dead too, or suffering. You can't blame yourself. If anyone is to blame, it's me."

She rested her head against his shoulder, glorying in being able to share the burden, taking strength from him and giving it back to him. But his last statement alarmed her, and she tilted her head back to meet his eyes. "How on earth are you to blame, Zeke? You've been a good father to her."

The slight sneer came back when he smiled at that remark. "That's just it, Abbie girl. I am her father. I gave her that dark skin and those Indian looks that have her so confused. I don't doubt the rest of the children have equal doubts. I should have listened long ago when a voice told me you belonged to your own kind. I had no right to drag you into this life, and now it's affecting the children. Our little Lillian is dead because she wasn't strong enough to bear this land; LeeAnn was taken from us by Comanches and her head is full of nightmares now; Wolf's Blood is riding with the Sioux; and Margaret is selling herself to strangers just because a white man has told her she's worthless." The words stuck in his throat like stale bread, and he gently pulled away from her and stood up to pace. "I should wring her neck! Yet when I think about why she's doing it, my heart bleeds for her, and I want to hold her and ask her to forgive me—ask all of you to forgive me."

Abbie frowned and got to her feet. "Forgive you? What for?"

He stepped back from her. "You know what for. For allowing myself to weaken twenty years ago and marry you, just because I loved you so damned much and wanted you so bad!"

Her heart pounded at the words, as he walked to the tree and yanked out his knife. What was he telling her? He turned to face her, shoving the knife into its sheath. "The worst part is I still want you." His eyes roved her body, seeing clearly what she could have been. "I will go and get Margaret. I will bring her home if I have to drag her by the hair of the head! Then we will make some decisions. I will make sure you are taken care of."

She shook her head. "What are you talking about? We'll go home, Zeke."

"Home! We have no home! Face it, Abbie. It's all gone to hell! Even Tall Grass Woman is dead!"

He hated himself immediately for saying it. She paled and stepped back. "But you said—"

"I found her at Sand Creek, Abbie," he said in a more subdued voice. "I'm sorry. I shouldn't have told you now . . . not this way."

She turned around, staring out over the open plains where once the Cheyenne migrated on summer hunts. Tall Grass Woman! Her good friend, so jolly and happy and loving. She felt Zeke's strong hands on her shoulders then.

"I'm sorry," he repeated.

She turned to look up at him. "Why do you say we have no home? Why do you talk as though there is no future for us?"

He studied the lovely face he loved so much. "Look at you," he told her, stepping back slightly. "You're dressed the way you should be dressed. You fit this place. This is the kind of life you should be leading. I

337

don't want the second half of your life to be as hard as the first half has been. Tynes loves you. Don't deny it. I knew it when I left. I can't imagine that he hasn't told you so by now."

Her eyes widened. "I don't give a damn if every man in Colorado loves me! I love Zeke Monroe. Do you honestly think I could just forget you and go on with a new life and a different man after twenty years with you? After all we have been through together? After struggling to build that ranch, after agreeing to live out here with you—even among the Cheyenne those first years—after bearing seven children by your seed? How can you possibly talk this way? Do you want me to die, inch by inch, without you?"

He grasped her arm. "You won't die. You have everything here. I want you to have peace and comfort and happiness, Abbie. I want you to have an easy life for your remaining years."

"It would be no life at all, and you well know it! I don't give a damn about comfort and an easy life! I don't feel any differently about you now than I did twenty years ago. You're still my Zeke. I can't survive without you."

He squeezed her arms. "That's the whole point!" he said urgently. "Look at the death all around us; then look at me! I won't live to be an old man, Abbie. Can't you see it? I've been damned lucky up to now, but violence and death stalk me constantly. You have a chance for safety and comfort here. You will be secure and cared for, and I won't have to worry about what the hell you'll do if something happens to me."

"And just what would you do? Where would you go?"

He let go of her and turned around, rubbing at his eyes. "I don't know. It doesn't matter what happens to me. Maybe I'd just go north and join Swift Arrow."

338

"And ride into some battle where you know good and well you'll be killed, because that is what you'll want, isn't it?" Her heart raced with aching love for him, hurt for him, yet she didn't know how to help him. He was giving up! Zeke Monroe was giving up! She had to stop him somehow! If only Wolf's Blood would come home! She suspected that would help.

He only shrugged. "Why not? It would be an honorable way to die."

"Zeke, the children love and need you. Margaret is the only one who has had a real problem with her Indian blood, but we can work that out with her. She's simply young and hurt. We all love you. You know how much I love you." Her voice was breaking and she struggled for control. "Zeke, remember that day we were riding back to meet the wagon train, after you rescued me from those renegades? We made love the night before, and you were telling me good-bye then. I just realized it was almost the same when we made love before you left this time. You're feeling the same way again—that you have no right to keep me. Do you remember what I called you that next day when you said we had no future and you were ending it once and for all?"

He remembered the day well, could still see her sitting on her horse screaming at him as he rode away from her, telling him what a coward he was, scared of loving again, scared to stand up to the challenges they would face. But memories of his first wife's murder had haunted him then. He had not wanted to drag little Abbie Trent into a life like his. He turned to face her, a slight grin actually passing over his lips at the memory of her shouting at him, screaming that he could go against Indians and outlaws and fight several men at once, but that he was afraid of a fifteen-year-old girl.

"I remember," he told her. "You said it could be

different out here, that a half-breed could marry a white girl and they could live happy and free." His smile faded. "But I warned you how bad it could be for you. And you failed to realize that the whites back East would come here, Abbie, bringing their barriers with them."

"And I said there are those who are strong enough to prove it can be different. I said you were that strong, and so was I. And we have been. We've survived many things, Zeke. We can survive this. I told you way back then that I didn't care about a fancy house and fancy clothes, that I would live anyplace and put up with anything to be with you. I asked you even then what good a fourposter bed would be to me if I had to sleep in it with a man I didn't love."

He drew in his breath and she saw jealousy flash in his eyes. It was practically the only tool she could use to keep him—make him angry, make him jealous. That always stirred a fire in him. But this time he was even going to fight that. She could tell. Still, she was not going to let him give up. "Is that what you want Zeke? To ride off alone and lonely, while some other man takes his pleasure with your wife, and she continues to suffer because there is only one man she wants?"

"Stop it!" he growled. "I know what you're doing. It won't work this time."

She stepped closer. "I told you way back on the day we argued that I wouldn't let you out of my life. I belong to you, Zeke Monroe, and I won't let you go now. I was fifteen years old when you branded me, and you can't change that fact, nor can you deny our love. You tried once before, after Jeremy was born. It almost killed both of us. What makes you think it would be any different this time, that either of us could survive without the other!"

He swallowed and stepped back from her. "Maybe

340

we have to try."

"Stop talking that way!" she said, her voice rising in panic. "I can't believe what you're saying. After all we've been through these past months, we need each other more than ever, Zeke! You're my last remaining strength and hope—my last reason to go on living! My God, Zeke, we're standing at our daughter's grave! You've just brought another daughter back from hell, and Margaret is alone and afraid in Denver! If you intend to destroy me, you certainly picked the right way to do it. Your timing is . . . absolutely perfect!" She choked on a sob and hunched over, and then he was pulling her into his arms.

"Jesus, Abbie, I'm not out to destroy you. I want to save you. I want you to have the good life you were meant to have."

"But it's been a good life—a wonderful life! I have never regretted one moment of it!" She wept bitterly against his broad, muscular chest, against his self-inflicted wound. There it was. The Indian in him again. The side of him she could never fully reach. Indians had a way of doing what was right, foregoing all personal feelings. That was what frightened her. She could not be that way. He was turning to the Indian side of himself that was telling him it was best to leave her. And he might do it. But he was half white. There was a softer side to him that could not let her go. She knew that. She was sure of it. She must appeal to the Tennessee man who had settled down like a white man just for her, the Tennessee man who played the mandolin and sang mountain songs. She would find a way. She was sure she would find a way.

He stroked the long, thick hair that hung down her back and she felt him trembling as he tried to stay in control. She looked up at him and he pressed her close, meeting her lips with groaning hunger. She returned

341

his kiss with equal fervor, reaching up around his neck. How easy it was to be lost in him, to want him, to be hypnotized by his dark eyes and spellbound by his sweet lips. The kiss was long and heated, saying many things, expressing great sorrow and hurt, deep love, desperate needs. How good it tasted! How delicious! How comforting it was! He would take her to the house and make love to her, she was sure of it. Everything would be all right then.

His lips left her mouth and traveled over her cheek to her neck. There were tears on his cheeks. "I'll leave right away, Abbie," he told her, his voice strained. "There is no time to lose in getting Margaret." His head rose and he kissed her eyes. "And it's best I go before I . . . before we . . ." He kissed her again, and she could taste his tears. Then he released her mouth and just held her. "I'm sorry, Abbie. I don't want to hurt you. But it seems like I will, whether I stay with you . . . or go."

"You'll stay with me," she wept. "We have to be together." She looked up at him. "Don't go, Zeke. Don't go without making love to me. Surely an hour or two—one night—won't make a difference. We need that. We get our strength from it."

He shook his head. "No. It will only make it harder if . . . if you should want to consider staying here."

"But I thought that was settled! I don't want to stay here. I want to go home."

She saw him changing again, giving up again. "Home to what? I managed to save Kehilan and two mares that had been mistreated and probably won't be worth anything now."

"We still have Sun and Dreamer, Zeke, and they're both pregnant."

"That's a far cry from a full herd. It takes ten months for a mare to deliver. Sun and Dreamer will deliver soon, but you're talking another year before they can deliver again. That gives me two mares that I can't sell because I need them, a stud I can't sell for the same reason, two other nearly worthless mares, and two foals. Who knows if the foals will even survive? I don't have any horses to sell, and I won't for a long time."

"We've been in worse shape."

"Not with a whole brood of children to feed." He walked toward his horse. "I'm leaving today, Abbie. You'll think more clearly if I don't touch you now. I want you to think very hard about a lot of things while I'm gone. Let's go back to the house. I want to see Anna's letter."

Anna! Her heart pounded with dread. She could not let him go this way, especially when he would be seeing Anna Gale! He was hurt, lonely. He was trying to prove to himself that he could survive without his family. Anna Gale was the last person he should see right now. Anna had been good to them, she cared about them; but if she knew for one minute Zeke Monroe wanted her, needed to relieve his needs with her, she would surely let him, for her heart and body wanted Zeke Monroe!

She met his eyes as she walked to her horse and grasped the bridle. She held her husband's gaze. "You think too, Zeke. Think about the fact that if you leave for good you'll be killing me."

Pain passed over his face and he reached out and touched her cheek. "I should have ridden out of your life when you were fifteen—when it would have been so much easier."

She took his hand and kissed the palm. "Don't leave this way. Please. Stay with me one night." She kissed his hand over and over, talking meanwhile. "You must . . . be to tired . . . and you're wounded. And I . . . need you, Zeke. Please stay . . . just one night."

343

He pulled his hand away. How he wanted her! How he longed to take her, ravage her, devour her. But he thought about her abduction nearly two years ago, how he had found her, what she had suffered. If she had not been married to him, none of those things would have happened.

"No," he answered quietly. "But I will come back, Abbie. That's a promise. I will come back before we make any final decision—and I'll have Margaret with me. We'll talk about it then, all right?" She nodded, holding back a sob. "Tell me true. Is Tynes treating you all right?"

She nodded again, unable to meet his eyes because she wanted him so. "He's been . . . wonderful," she answered. "Very respectful. He is a gentleman, and he is very concerned about all of us."

He fought his torturous jealousy. "And he loves you."

"Yes," she answered quietly. "But he hasn't been disrespectful. He is like a good friend . . . that's all."

He studied the woman he had loved for so many years. "I'm sure it didn't take long for him to know that he loved you. You're easy to love, Abbie girl. That's the hell of it."

He turned and eased up onto his horse in one graceful movement, the tiny bell tinkling again. The only thing that made the thought of his leaving bearable was knowing he would come back. He would not break that promise. But how would he feel when he returned? Perhaps Anna Gale would help him make the final break. She must rely on Anna's common sense and the brief friendship they had shared. Perhaps Anna could convince him that he must stay with his family. Perhaps seeing Margaret would help.

"Zeke, you can't go to Denver looking like . . . like that." How she hated having to say it. "You'd be hung before they'd let you in any establishment."

He looked down at her proudly. He was all Indian, from the tinkling bell to his buckskin moccasins. His eyebrows arched. "Shall I cut my hair too?"

Her eyes teared more. "No. Please don't ever cut it."

He grinned rather sarcastically, but a bitter grin was better than none at all. "You read a story to the children once from that Bible of yours, about a man called Sampson. I think I would feel a little bit like he did if I cut my hair. It would take away some of my strength."

A tear slipped down her cheek. "If it would make you weak enough to stay with me, I would cut it off myself." Their eyes held, and Cheyenne pride shone through his.

"Then it's best for you that I keep it. I'll braid it neatly for the white men, though." He snickered. "Perhaps your Edwin has a suit I could use."

"Don't call him that. He's not my Edwin. There is only my Zeke."

He looked at her almost as a raiding Indian would look at a white woman, sitting tall and proud, looking down at her as though she was at his full command. "Perhaps I only loaned myself to you, Abbie. Perhaps I belong only to the land after all."

She shook her head. "You're trying to hurt me, trying to make me hate you. It won't work."

His bronze shoulders glistened in the sun. "I'll just go to Anna's first," he told her, ignoring her statement. "She'll let me in no matter how I look. She can help me find the proper clothes."

Her heart raged with jealousy. "I am sure she can! I am sure there are a lot of things she can do for you, except give you back twenty years of your life and give you seven beautiful children!"

His horse pranced in a circle, seeming to sense that his master was ready to ride again. "What about Wolf's

Blood?" he asked. "Has there been any word of him?"

She wanted to hit him for avoiding a response to what she'd said. "None."

He gazed across the plains, dotted with melting snow. "Perhaps when I get back I should go north and find out what has happened to my son. I'm worried about him."

If only she were stronger! . . . She would pull him from his horse and tie him and make him stay until he was himself again. "If you went north, you'd join the Sioux and never come back, not in the mood you're in."

He smiled proudly down at her. "It is the only way for a man like me to die, Abbie, and without you I would have no reason to live. You would have the children and all of this, and a fine man who loves you. You would survive."

"I have never heard you talk so foolishly in my entire life!" She climbed up onto her own horse. "I'm telling you right now that wherever you go I'll follow you! I'll never let you go! Never!"

He was staring at Lillian's grave marker, his jaw flexed in an effort not to soften. She knew a terrible struggle was going on inside of him. She couldn't hate him or be angry with him. She knew him too well. He looked at her with softer eyes then, but just for a moment. "We must get to the house. I want to see the letter, and I have to restock my supplies while it is still daylight."

"Zeke, you must rest! You must!"

"No! Every moment I rest some man is putting his hands on my daughter! My Moheya! She has a pride deep inside her that she does not even realize she possesses. Indian pride! I'll shake it out of her if I have to! But I won't come back here without her, even if I have to tie her and drag her behind me!"

346

"Zeke, be careful. You're right. She is proud. So, be careful how you treat her or we'll lose her forever. She's still so much a child."

He looked at her, the love in his eyes obvious as they moved over her. "When you were seventeen you had already given me a son. You were a woman."

"I was white. I had choices Margaret will never have. And I had a man who . . . loved me."

Their eyes held. "I don't mean to hurt you, Abbie."

She rode up closer to him. "I know that." She drew her cape back around her shoulders. "Please be careful with Margaret, Zeke. She must come back of her own accord, or she'll just leave again. It has to be her decision, her desire."

"I will try, but it will not be easy." He turned his horse and she followed. They headed toward the grand Tynes mansion.

It seemed ironic that she had wealth and luxury at her fingertips, that she could grasp it at any time, yet all she longed for was to be back in her little cabin, with all of her children around her and with Zeke Monroe beside her at night on a bed of robes. Love has a way of making everything else seem unimportant. They rode side by side, he in all his Indian splendor, she on a grand thoroughbred, the yellow skirts of her expensive dress flowing in the wind, each a stark contrast to the other, bound by only one thing, one delicate bind— love. She had always thought that bind was made of very strong material. She could only pray now that it had not been weakened to the point of breaking. Zeke Monroe was suffering, and she did not know what to do about it. Somehow, while he was gone, she must think of a way to reach him. She was losing him! She was losing Zeke Monroe! It would be better to lose him to death than to lose him this way!

347

Chapter Seventeen

Dan ducked down into the rifle pit as another bullet sang past him. If he weren't in command of this platoon of cavalry sent out to scour the southern portion of the Bozeman Trail, he would gladly down some whiskey. If he was going to die, maybe with some liquor in him, he wouldn't feel the pain of the Indian tomahawk or lance that would take his life.

They were surrounded by hundreds of Sioux, who darted in and out teasingly, taking turns badgering the bluecoats, laughing at them, cursing them, waiting in the surrounding hills for the forty soldiers to die slowly from thirst and starvation. For two days and a night the Sioux and Cheyenne, who had surrounded and attacked them near a tributary of the Powder River, had continued to harass them, belting out war whoops, dancing and drumming nearby at night, enjoying the advantage of their numbers.

Dan cursed his superior officer, a greenhorn from the East, who had ordered the patrol. He had told him the dangers involved in the mission, had tried to impress upon the man that there were thousands of Sioux roaming the Powder River and Bozeman Trail territory, not just a handful. But orders were orders.

349

The settlers and miners headed for Montana insisted that the trail be kept open, no matter how many men had to be sacrificed to do it. They didn't even have a cannon along, and most of their horses had been shot by the Indians to keep the soldiers from getting away. They had crouched behind the dead bodies of their mounts for protection until Dan had ordered trenches to be dug.

He wasn't certain how many of his men had been lost, perhaps five or six. Several others had been wounded. The Indian casualties were probably greater than that, but there were so many of them it didn't matter.

He cursed their vulnerable location, in a ravine near a creek, with hills all around them, hills dotted with large boulders that made good hiding places. His own feet were soaked, for in digging the trenches they had hit water just two feet down in the boggy ground. Two more mounted platoons were to have started out from Fort Laramie two days after their own departure, but there had been no signs of them yet, no sign that they would be saved from their present predicament.

There was a lull in the fighting, and he used it to rest, leaning against the side of the rifle pit, wishing he could sit down but unable to because of the water. He thought about Bonnie. He had thought of her often, wondering if he was foolish to consider marrying her so soon after his wife's death. But Emily had not been a wife to him for a long time, and Bonnie was alone. They were both alone. Out here in this land, people married who hardly knew each other. A woman might be widowed with children, and a settler would marry her because he needed a woman for all the things a man needs a woman for. Women remarried quickly because in the West a woman needed a man. It was done for practical purposes, but the marriages were usually good, often leading to genuine love. He was sick and tired of being alone. He wanted someone like Abbie, and Bonnie was as close as he would come. He had no doubt she'd make a good wife, and she was already accustomed to this land and its dangers and hardships. But maybe she wouldn't want to marry him. Maybe there would be some religious reason why she couldn't. And the fact remained that she loved Zeke, but she could not have him.

A private crept over to him, crouched low. The boy reloaded his rifle with shaking hands. "You scared, Lieutenant?" the boy asked.

Dan pushed his hat back, studying the boy, remembering his own first days in the Army and the Mexican War. "Sure I'm scared. A man would be a fool not to be. I've seen what the Sioux do to some of their captives. But help is coming, Private. Don't you worry. It's good to be scared. Keeps you alert like you ought to be. There's a difference between being scared and being a coward, Private."

The boy grinned a little. "I suppose." He finished loading his gun. "You married, sir?"

Dan pulled a last cigar from his pocket. "No," he answered quietly. "I was. My wife is dead."

"Oh. I'm sorry."

Dan lit the cigar. "You couldn't know." He puffed on the smoke for a moment. "I have a little girl. She's coming out next month with a Regiment out of St. Louis."

The boy grinned again. "That's real nice. I hope she makes it safely. How old is she, sir?"

Dan stared at the cigar he held between his fingers. "Jennifer is almost nine."

The boy turned to peek out over the trench. "I have a girl back in Illinois that I'm going to marry. I've been wanting her to come out, but with the Indians at war like

351

they are, I'm afraid for her."

Dan puffed the cigar again. "Don't be, Private. Send for her. Believe me, a few years of being with your love is a lot better than many years apart. More and more wives are coming out all the time. Send for the girl and marry her. Don't waste your time leaving her back East when you're out here."

The young man frowned. "I don't know. She could die young out here."

Dan lightly pressed out his cigar, wanting to save as much of it as he could. "She could also die young back East like my wife did."

A bullet hit the dirt just in front of them, sending sand and tiny rocks flying. They ducked.

"Do me a favor, Private, and get around to all the others if you can. Give me a count of the dead and wounded, and tell them to guard their ammunition. I don't want them wasting it on targets that can't possibly be hit. We must make every shot count."

"Yes, sir." The boy scooted off as a new band of Sioux and Cheyenne swooped out of the hills for another attack, screeching and war whooping and raising their lances. Some braves had crept forward ahead of them, and they let off a volley of shots to keep the soldiers down and unable to fire as the mounted Indians circled closer, shooting arrows in arcs so they came down like rain on the soldiers. The painted warriors shot the arrows while riding, sometimes hanging from the sides of the horses facing away from the soldiers so that the horses provided protection for them. Dan never ceased to admire their riding ability and the feats they could perform while on a fast-moving pony. He had seen Zeke perform similar tricks, and Swift Arrow and Wolf's Blood. He wished the days of peaceful visiting had not ended.

The thundering hooves came closer, charging in

when they knew most of the soldiers had fired and had to reload. They were getting braver now. They wanted to ride in close and count coup—touch their enemy. This was considered an act of bravery by their kind. Now a young warrior charged toward Dan's trench, his face painted, feathers of conquest tied onto his long, black hair, his Appaloosa sure-footed. The boy looked familiar, and Dan's eyes widened with surprise. Could it be? He called out without thinking.

"Wolf's Blood!"

The warrior stopped short, his horse's hooves digging into the soft earth as he stared at Dan, who rose up slightly from his trench. A shot rang out and a hole exploded in the boy's upper left chest. He was hurled from his mount, grasping at the reins as he fell and bringing the horse down with a crash beside him. He lay still.

"Jesus Christ!" Dan swore. "Cover me!" he ordered the sergeant several feet from him. He set down his rifle and scrambled out of the trench, crawling on his belly toward his nephew, memories of Shiloh reeling in his mind, of the terrible belly wound he had suffered there. He prayed he would not feel that pain again. The Appaloosa reared and stood up, running off. Wolf's Blood lay panting and bleeding badly, his eyes wide and staring when Dan reached him. He pulled his knife when he saw the bluecoat moving toward him. He tried to rise but could not. The most he could do was raise his arm, in a determined effort to plant the knife his father had given him into the white man coming toward him. But the man's hand grasped his wrist and pushed the arm down. Wolf's Blood was too badly wounded to resist.

"Don't struggle, son!" Dan ordered. "You're badly hurt. It's me, Dan, your father's brother."

The boy just stared at him, the wound making his

mind hazy and confused. Dan carefully took the knife from the boy's hand, while bullets and arrows sang past him. He put the knife in its sheath and placed an arm under Wolf's Blood's shoulders, wrapping another around his chest. "It's all right, Wolf's Blood," he assured the boy. "I'll get help for you."

He began pulling, and the boy groaned pitifully. He uttered something in Cheyenne, and Dan recognized the word for father. Dan wished Zeke were there. He wondered if Zeke was even alive, whether he had found LeeAnn. He had not heard. He struggled backward, pulling the boy into the trench, holding him with one arm while he dug at the dirt sides with the other hand to cover over the water so there would be a place to put the boy without getting him wet. The private was returning then, and he stared at the young warrior wide-eyed, while the sergeant also looked on. The private pulled a pistol.

"No!" Dan ordered. "Don't shoot him!"

The private frowned, still pointing the gun. "But, sir—"

"No! He's my nephew!"

Both soldiers showed their surprise. They looked at each other, then back to their lieutenant. "Nephew!" the private exclaimed.

Dan removed his neckerchief and pressed it against the boy's wound. "I have a brother who is half Cheyenne. We share the same white father. This is his son."

The private crept closer to have a look at the wild Indian in the lieutenant's arms. "I'll be damned!"

"Help me get my blanket under him," Dan ordered. "And give me your neckerchief. I've got to stop this bleeding! This boy means everything to my brother."

The private moved quickly to his officer's command. Dan prayed inwardly that he could help the boy, but unless they could get back to the fort and a doctor soon, he knew Wolf's Blood would not live.

"Damn!" he kept swearing. "I shouldn't have called out to him!" His eyes teared. He hadn't seen the boy for a long time, but Wolf's Blood could be Zeke's twin, in younger form. He had known instantly who he was. It was like seeing Zeke again.

The firing continued for several minutes, then the Indians suddenly drew back and things quieted down. Several minutes passed before the sergeant crawled over to Dan.

"Sir, some of them are riding off. I don't understand it."

"One of them is coming in!" someone shouted. "He's carrying a white flag of truce!"

Dan frowned. Why this sudden change? He looked down at Wolf's Blood. The change had come after the boy was shot. "Swift Arrow!" he whispered to himself. Of course! Where Wolf's Blood's was, there would be Swift Arrow. He rose from the trench.

"Hold your fire!" he ordered loudly. "Any man that shoots will be shot by me!" He climbed out of the trench, and the other men stared at him in wonder as he removed his weapons and walked toward the approaching Indian. The Indian man rode a grand Appaloosa—one of Zeke's, no doubt. The handsome warrior came closer and stopped before Dan. "Swift Arrow." Dan put out his hand and Swift Arrow took it. They grasped wrists, brothers through Zeke, but not blood brothers. Zeke and Dan shared the same father; Zeke and Swift Arrow shared the same mother.

Swift Arrow studied the blue eyes of Zeke's white brother. They were honest. "My nephew's horse returned without him," he spoke up.

"I saw him go down. I have him, Swift Arrow. He's badly wounded. Let us go and I'll take him to the fort where he can get help. It has to be soon or he'll die."

Swift Arrow nodded. "My heart is heavy. I will be a broken man if he dies. Take him. We will let you go. I am a leading Dog Soldier. They will listen to me."

Dan nodded. "Thank you, Swift Arrow." The man didn't seem any older than he had when Dan had met him years before at the signing of the Laramie Treaty in 1851. He wondered how some Indian men remained so strong and solid in spite of aging. The man was about forty, but he looked no more than thirty, if that, still hard muscled and handsome.

"Tell me quickly. How is my brother . . . and Abigail?"

Dan frowned. "I don't really know, Swift Arrow. I got a letter that LeeAnn, their blond daughter, had been stolen away by Comanche renegades and Zeke had gone off to find her. I have no idea if he found her or if he got back. Then I recently got a letter telling me another daughter, Lillian, had died of pneumonia. Needless to say, Abigail is suffering."

Swift Arrow's eyes softened. "She is a woman born to suffering. She does so because she will bear anything to be with my brother." How his heart ached for her! What burdens she had to bear! "Do not tell her her son has been wounded. It would be too much. Make him well first, so that you can send her good news, not bad."

"I will. There's no sense worrying her until I know how the boy's going to fare."

Swift Arrow breathed deeply, his chest aching. "Save him!" he said in a voice gruff with sorrow.

"I'll do my best."

Swift Arrow nodded. "In one moon, I will send a runner to learn of the boy's health and to find out if you have heard from Zeke. I will pray to the spirits for my brother and his family. The boy should go to his father. It will relieve Zeke and Abbie's suffering some, for the boy and Zeke are close. Convince him he should go home for a while."

"I'll do my best, Swift Arrow, and I'll get word to you. Zeke and Abbie are always inquiring about you, but I can never find you to tell them how you are. Now I am glad I can tell them you are alive and well."

The man backed his mount. "Tell Abigail . . . I think of her often. Tell my brother I am with him in spirit, but I cannot come and see him. Not now. It has gone too far. I will let you go, bluecoat, because you are blood to my brother and because I know you to be an honorable man. You have good doctors at the fort. You can help my nephew. Go now."

As he turned his horse, Dan noticed the Z branded into the animal's rump. He turned and walked back toward his men, again shouting at them not to fire. Swift Arrow rode hard, his long, black hair flying, the feathers tied onto his horse's mane dancing in the wind. Soon he disappeared over a low hill and everything was quiet.

Edwin Tynes walked into the kitchen, where Abbie was already ordering things prepared for Zeke's trip to Denver. He frowned and watched quietly, studying the savage-looking man who stood near his tiny wife eating a piece of venison. Tynes noticed that Abbie's hair had fallen free of the combs, and when she returned, her face was stained from tears. Zeke followed her gaze to meet the Englishman's eyes. There was a moment of quiet, and Tynes wondered what sort of torture Zeke Monroe was considering inflicting on the white man he stared at. Zeke had put his buckskin shirt back on, but it was not laced, and part of the raw, red line from his self-inflicted mourning wound showed. Tynes glanced at the handle of the huge blade at Zeke's weapons' belt;

then he swallowed and stepped a little closer.

Zeke finally nodded. "Tynes."

Edwin looked at Abbie's sorrowful eyes before he returned Zeke's gaze. "I'm glad you made it back, Zeke, glad you found your daughter. From the looks of things, you are planning to leave again."

Abbie turned away, picking up some potatoes and putting them into Zeke's parfleche.

"I'm going to Denver to get Margaret," Zeke answered.

Edwin frowned, concerned for Abbie. Something was amiss. "Surely you will wait until morning."

Zeke began to lace his tunic. "No. There's some daylight left. I'll leave as soon as my gear is ready and I've talked to all the children again."

Their eyes held. "Then at least come to my game room and let me share a drink with you."

Abbie turned to look at them both, her eyes resting on Zeke pleadingly. He reached out and put a hand to the side of her face. "Go on up with LeeAnn," he told her. "Then bring all of them to the kitchen. I'll be back in a few minutes."

She grasped his hand. "Zeke, please wait until morning."

He shook his head. "Go."

She blinked back tears and rushed past both of them. Zeke watched the way Edwin looked at her when she went by, with great pity and concern. Tynes looked back at Zeke, running his eyes over the Indian's magnificent frame, well aware that he must be very careful about what he said. He turned and went out of the room, and Zeke followed him to a huge room where a pool table and a chess table sat. Tynes went to a buffet and removed the stopper from a bottle of bourbon, pouring two shots. He turned and handed one small glass to Zeke, then held his own in the air. "To

358

Abigail," he said quietly.

Zeke stared at him silently for a moment and Tynes held his breath. Then Zeke raised his own glass. "To Abigail." They both drank down the whiskey.

"Another shot?" Tynes asked.

"Just one. Whiskey and Indians don't mix, remember?"

Tynes grinned a little. "Yes, I have heard such stories." He walked back and poured two more shots, handing Zeke's back to him. "I am trying to figure you out, Zeke. The way you look at me makes me wonder if you intend to sink that blade into me."

"The thought has occurred to me." Zeke slugged down his second shot. "But circumstances prevent me from doing so. I owe you a great deal, Tynes. I can never repay you for the way you've watched over my ranch and my family."

Tynes smiled. "Payment is not necessary. Just having the children around has been a great pleasure."

Zeke walked to the fireplace and set his glass on the mantel. "Tell me, Tynes"—he turned and faced the man, his power filling the great room in which they stood—"just how much do you love my wife?"

Tynes's arm froze as he was raising it to down his second shot. He lowered it slowly, meeting Zeke's eyes squarely, suspecting the best way to deal with Zeke Monroe was honestly and openly.

"Look around you," he answered. "I would trade all of this for that little cabin of yours, if I could have her. I have offered her all of this, and she doesn't even want it. I must say, she's not like any woman I have ever known. I envy you."

Zeke studied the man. He was handsome, tall and well built but not quite as big as Zeke, a worldly man but not a coward. "Have you touched her? Kissed her?"

Tynes's eyebrows arched and he cleared his throat.

"Do you expect me to tell you if I have? I'm too young to die, and I know I'm no match for you."

"I want the truth. I have no intention of harming you."

Tynes frowned, confused. "The truth is I have held her a couple of times, only in friendship and because she was suffering. That's all. But she knows how I feel. I have told her, fully knowing it would be of no use. But when you love someone that much you have to try, right? I tried." He nodded toward Zeke and drank his second shot. "My best to the better man. You chose well. Considering what I have waved under her nose, her love for you is greater than I imagined."

Zeke walked to a huge window that was draped with red velvet curtains. "I want your promise on something, Tynes."

The man folded his arms. "If it has anything to do with Abigail, I will gladly make it and keep it."

Zeke sighed deeply. "If I should for some reason . . . be killed"—he swallowed—"I need to know she would be . . . looked after, that my children would be cared for. I need to know she won't be alone and vulnerable in this damned land. I need to know someone will see that she gets settled someplace in the East, or if she stays here, someone will care for her."

Tynes dropped his arms and stepped a little closer. "If you want to know whether I would be willing to do those things, I most certainly am. If she would have me, I would marry her. If not, I would never let anything happen to her. But I fail to understand why you are talking this way. You just came back from a foray against Comanches and outlaws. You are safe now. What do you think is going to happen?"

Zeke turned to face him. "I'm not sure I'll stay once I return from Denver." He looked around the room. "Here she would have all the things she deserves, a good life for her remaining years. She has suffered enough from being married to me."

Tynes almost laughed. "Do you think that with you alive she would ever come to me—ever be happy anywhere with anyone but Zeke Monroe?"

"If I were dead, she would have no choice but to try."

Tynes studied the pain in Zeke Monroe's eyes, realizing to his utter amazement just how deeply this man loved his wife. "Why would you be dead?"

Zeke smiled sadly. "Death has been at my doorstep all my life, Tynes, and I have always worried about what Abbie would do if she were left alone out here. When I get back, I may go north to see about Wolf's Blood. I might even join Red Cloud and Swift Arrow. I want to die the only way a man like myself can die—in battle."

Tynes shook his head. "Much as I love her, Zeke, I would ask that you not do that to her. For however many years you might have, let her have them. She will always belong to you, in life or death. It won't make any difference. I have come to know her too well. I can only say that if such a thing would happen, I would do all I could to help her, and I would give her a home here if she would have it. But you aren't thinking clearly, Zeke. Take her home when you come back. She has suffered enough."

Zeke walked toward the door. "That's just the point. She has suffered enough." He paused, meeting the man's eyes. "I was only feeling you out, Tynes. And I am trusting her to you, trusting you to respect the fact that she is married to me. Normally I would kill any man who looked at her with desire, but your look is one of love and respect. You needn't fear me if I should come back to find that she wants to stay here."

"That, my friend, will never happen. I am no fool, and neither are you. You know full well where she wants to be. She will still be yours when you come back, and I daresay you will want her as much as you have always wanted her. A man cannot easily give up that which makes him walk and breathe, can he?"

Their eyes held, Zeke's dark and flashing with Indian pride and great passion for his wife. "When an Indian village is attacked, the men go forward and fight as quickly as they can grab a weapon," he said quietly. "Often some of them deliberately expose themselves to to the line of fire, drawing off the enemy's attention so that the women and children can flee to safety. The women and children must be protected at all costs and a warrior will die to do it. In a sense that is what I am doing now, Tynes. I am fighting—dying—for their protection. Indian women run to the hills or to cover. I need to know my woman can run to you and that you would give her refuge, but that you would not take her to your bed unless she was willing to go. That is the only circumstance under which I would kill you, and you would suffer long before you died." His nostrils flared with repressed jealousy, and Tynes fully understood how difficult it was for the man to consider giving up his wife.

"A woman like Abigail can't be had any other way but willingly, but she would have my eternal friendship and protection." He watched Zeke struggle for composure. "But I must tell you I think you're very wrong to be thinking the way you are, Zeke. You are a fighter, and above all you want her happiness. Without you she will never be happy. So you'd best do some serious praying to whatever Gods you pray to, and know in your heart what is really right to do."

Zeke swallowed. "Thank you for the drink—and the promise. I treasure your friendship. I have brought back my prize stud, Drinker of the Wind. He is yours

362

if . . . if anything happens to me. So is my land, except that you should consult Abbie on her wishes. The land is in her name." Anger came to his eyes then, a sneer to his lips. "Indians cannot own land! Not even a man who is only part Indian!" He turned and quickly left.

Bonnie straightened, looking down at a replica of Zeke Monroe. Five days had passed since Wolf's Blood had been shot. She turned to Dan. "The doctor has done all he can. I'll keep a good eye on him, keep his bandages changed."

Dan walked closer, putting a hand on her shoulder. "He has to live, Bonnie. My God, he has to live! I'll not tell Zeke Monroe that his son is dead."

She blinked back tears. "I know. Oh, Dan, he's so young! What is he now? Twenty at the most?"

"Something like that. Nineteen, I think. How bad is the wound itself? I know the greatest danger was the loss of blood. If I could just have got him here sooner!"

"The loss of blood is why he's so weak, and why he lost consciousness. His left collarbone was badly broken. It will take some time to heal. And he lost a piece of his left shoulder blade. That was quite a hole someone blew in him. I wish Zeke could be here, but we don't even know if he's back so I hate to write to Abbie and give her such sorry news. She couldn't bear it right now."

"We'll keep it to ourselves and hope we never have to tell her anything but that he's fine and coming home."

She sighed deeply and turned to look up at him. "What about you? You look terrible, Dan. It must have been quite an ordeal. Are you all right?"

"I'm fine. Just a little weak from hunger."

"I hope they don't send such a small platoon out on

a patrol like that again," she told him. "What if it hadn't been Swift Arrow? You'd all have been killed." Their eyes held. "I don't want anything to happen to you."

They were alone in her bedroom, where she had insisted Wolf's Blood be brought so she could nurse him. Dan could not resist the urge to kiss her. He bent, meeting her lips warmly, gently. This was not the rude, groping kiss he had given her when drunk and sick with grief for Emily. He felt her shiver and he pulled her close, pressing his hand into the small of her back, kissing her harder then, on fire when she gave a light whimper. Her arms moved up around his neck and he embraced her tightly, enjoying the feel of her breasts against his chest.

Finally, he released her and held her close, and she breathed deeply of his manly scent. In all her years with Rodney Lewis, she had not felt this way about a man. She had never felt fulfilled.

"What would you say if . . . if I asked you to marry me, Bonnie?" His voice was gruff with passion. "I know it's awfully soon for both of us, but I'm tired of being alone. I want something soft in the night, after drilling men all day—something warm and gentle waiting for me when I come back from patrols. You're going to care for my daughter. You might as well be her mother."

Her heart pounded in excited joy, and her breath seemed to have left her. "Oh, Dan! Would I be foolish to say yes?"

Their lips met again, this time more hungrily. He moved his lips to her cheek, her neck, holding her tightly so that her toes barely touched the floor. "No more foolish than I am to ask. Out here people do crazy things, don't they?"

364

They both started to laugh, and their eyes held. He saw the sorrow in hers then, and he released her slightly, still holding her close. "I know you will always love Zeke, Bonnie, but—"

"No! Don't say it. That was a long time ago, Dan. It's over. I knew in the beginning that was impossible. Don't ever think you would be a substitute, Daniel Monroe. I have grown to love you for you, and you're more man than I dreamed I could ever have. Yes, I will marry you. I will love Zeke, as a dear friend and a man who is very special to me, but I will love you as a wife loves a husband, with all my heart, all my devotion."

He pressed her against him, and she knew one night with Dan Monroe would far excede all her nights with Rodney Lewis. "When in hell is your father supposed to get here?" he asked. "He could marry us."

"Two days! I almost forgot! Just two days, Dan, and we can be married!"

"Well, let's hope nothing happens to him. I'm not even sure I can wait the two days. I suddenly realize very clearly what I want, and I'm going to be a very happy man."

She felt her body flush and tingle. "And I will be a very happy woman."

Wolf's Blood groaned and the spell was broken. Dan released her and she bent over the boy, who was only moaning in his unconscious state. He had not been totally awake and alert since he'd passed out shortly after he was shot. "I just hope he'll be all right, Dan. I couldn't be truly happy for a while if he doesn't make it." She gently caressed the boy's forehead, and Dan knew that looking at the son of Zeke Monroe brought back painful memories for her. She would always love Zeke and he knew it, but she was aware that was an impossible love. Dan didn't care. He would make her his wife and love her, and he knew she would love him totally, never again mentioning her feelings for his brother. In two days he would share the warmth of a woman's body again, have someone who would care about him, care for his little girl. That was all that mattered. A man needed a woman in this land, and a woman needed a man. They would be happy.

Chapter Eighteen

Anna opened the back door to the kitchen in answer to the knock. Then she gasped and stepped back, her heart pounding with instantly awakened memories and desires. "Zeke!"

He came inside in one quiet, graceful step, dressed in buckskins, looking all Indian. She quickly closed the door.

"What on earth—" She stepped around in front of him. "I was expecting Abbie. She had sent me a letter saying she'd come as soon as weather permitted."

"I got back since she wrote. I came instead. LeeAnn needs her."

Their eyes held. It had been a long time. She was as beautiful as ever, her black hair showing no gray, her blue eyes painted lightly, provocatively, her full figure enticing in a simple dress that showed the gentle curve of her ample breasts and the smallness of her waist. How many years ago was it she had used her deviltry to force him to her bed in exchange for the information he needed about his sister-in-law. But that had been a different Anna Gale. She had changed, yet he imagined that after all those years of lying with men, she still had a harlot's heart and a harlot's talent for pleasing a man.

She, in turn, was struck by the fact that he never seemed to change. He had the same brawny power, the same provocative dark eyes and finely chiseled lips, the same Indian spirit that had stirred her desires. But she had long since learned it was impossible to have this man, for she knew he loved Abigail Monroe.

She tried to control the flush that was coming to her cheeks, and to her dismay she felt like a young girl who has never been with a man. Her palms were sweaty and she rubbed them against her skirt nervously. "Well . . . sit down, Zeke! How long have you been riding? Are you hungry? Would you like coffee or something? It's well past supper time, but I can heat something up for you. I—"

"Where is she!" he demanded. "Show me the place!"

She frowned, studying his appearance. "No. Not yet. You sit down and get your thoughts together. You go storming over there looking like that and someone will shoot you before you walk through the door." She became her old, sure self again when she realized how angry and upset he was. "Besides, you'd be going after your daughter in the wrong way. Make her want to come home, Zeke, don't drag her there."

He just stood there, rifle in hand. "I'll drag her anyplace I want! She's my daughter! I'll not have her whoring around!"

She flinched slightly and reddened a little. "I can understand how you feel, but let me help you think this out, Zeke. I understand what she's going through." Her eyes hardened a little. "When I was raped as an orphan child back East, I reacted the same way. I felt dirty and ashamed, and good for only one thing. Orphans were looked down upon as Indians are today. They still are in some places."

She turned away and set a large coffeepot on her iron

368

cookstove, opening a little door beneath to stir the embers. Then she took a few pieces of coal from a nearby bucket and added them to the fire.

Zeke sighed and sat down at the table. "I'm sorry, Anna. We both appreciate your writing us." She turned around to face him, her eyes glistening with tears. "Damn it, she's my daughter!" he hissed.

She swallowed. "I understand," she said quietly, sitting down across from him. She breathed deeply. "Zeke, please do as I say and think this out. Stay here tonight. I'll give you a free room for as long as it takes to talk her into going back, and I'll get you some civilized clothing tomorrow. Get some rest and gather your thoughts, and don't make a scene when you go, no matter how difficult it is for you to hold yourself in."

His jaw flexed and he grasped a salt shaker, squeezing it nervously. "I'll do my best."

She studied him lovingly, then reached out and touched his hand. "How is Abbie? I never heard from you after I told you about Winston Garvey and how you could get your hands on him."

He let go of her hand and leaned back in the chair, his long legs and big frame seeming to fill the small kitchen. Momentarily, she had the sensation that a wild animal was loose in her house.

"I won't go into detail about Garvey and his men. Only Wolf's Blood and I know what happened to them." A chill swept through her at the realization of what this man was capable of doing. "We found Abbie in a deserted mine." He stared at the table. "She was in a bad way—almost dead from starvation and beatings."

"Poor Abbie! I'm so sorry, Zeke."

He turned the salt shaker in his hand. "It took her a long time to get over it. She could have handled the neglect and beatings. It was the fact that other men had

369

used her that made her not want to live at first. She thought I wouldn't want her anymore." He smiled bitterly. "What a foolish thought!" He met Anna's eyes. "She finally came around."

Anna smiled, an almost wicked smile. "With you to turn to, what woman would stay estranged forever? If any man can help a woman get over something like that, I felt you could. Your love is so strong. You two have something few people ever find."

His eyes saddened and he set the salt shaker on the table. "True. But maybe we love each other too much. Things aren't so great now, Anna. Too much has happened."

She frowned, resting her elbows on the table. "What do you mean?"

He stared silently at the salt shaker for a moment. "I don't know if I can stay with her after this. Because of being married to me, she's suffered so many things, more than any good woman should." He breathed deeply and stood up, pacing like a restless cat. "I'm thinking of going north after I get Margaret back—maybe joining the Sioux and getting it over with."

Her chest tightened. "Getting what over with?"

He stopped and grasped the handle of his knife nervously. "My life. With me gone, she'd be free to live the kind of life she deserves. She'll not consider it while I'm alive. But there's an Englishman who bought up thousands of acres adjoining our land. He's handsome, wealthy, worldly. He's a gentleman, well schooled. Lives in a mansion that looks like a castle. And he loves her. Without me in the picture, she can have it all and live in luxury for her remaining years. Ever since her abduction and rape I've suffered from an unbearable guilt. The things that have happened over the past few months have only made it worse."

She rose, anger in her eyes. "I've never heard

anything so ridiculous in all my life! Do you really think she could just casually take up life with a new man after being with you for twenty years? And I always thought you were a wise man! You're a fool!"

He straightened, anger appearing in his own eyes. "You don't understand. You've never loved this way."

She met his gaze. "Haven't I? What would you know? I think I fully understand why Abigail Monroe doesn't give a damn about riches, not when she can have you beside her in the night!" She whirled and walked to the coffeepot, which was beginning to heat up. They both stood quietly for a moment. "I'm . . . sorry. I had no right to say that," she finally said. "But don't tell me I don't understand about love, Zeke Monroe. I wish to hell it was Abbie who had come and not you."

"I can stay someplace else if you want."

She shook her head. "No." She turned to face him. "I wouldn't think of it. Besides, you need to talk—a lot. Something has happened to you, but you will get over it, Zeke. Don't do something foolish now and leave your Abbie. You're just suffering from so many things that you can't think straight. Leaving her would destroy her, Zeke, not help her. Do you really think she could go to another man, or that you could bear the knowledge that another man was bedding her?" She smiled at the flash of anger and jealousy in his dark eyes. "Just as I thought." She laughed lightly. "Sit down, you big, stupid buck, and have some coffee. Do you want something to eat?"

Somehow he suddenly felt better; some of his anger and depression were leaving him. "Maybe just a biscuit, if you have any."

She nodded. "Coming up." She walked to a bread box, and he watched her graceful movements. "Have you heard anything about Wolf's Blood?"

371

"No. That's one reason why I need to go north. I can't stand not knowing. I love him."

"God knows you do." She brought two biscuits to the table, and a wooden bowl of butter and a knife. "For him you must keep going, Zeke. He might be making war up north, but he still needs and loves you."

Zeke broke open a biscuit and buttered it. "I've never been so confused in my life, Anna. The memory of those Comanches ripping LeeAnn from my arms still haunts me. I rode out to find her—finally did . . . with Comancheros. Thank God she hadn't been raped, but she'd been treated badly and she'll have nightmares for a long time to come. Then I came home to find little Lillian dead and my oldest daughter run off to Denver. In addition, Comanches stole my whole herd. I don't know if I can start from scratch and make it all over again. My brother was killed when the Comaches raided, and—" He set down the biscuit and looked at her strangely. "My God, Anna, my brother is dead! Lance is dead! I haven't even been able to think about that! It's as though . . . as though I just now remembered!" He closed his eyes and leaned back, putting a hand to his forehead. "I feel so tired and beaten, Anna."

She rose and walked around behind him, putting one hand under his chin and the other at his forehead and resting the back of his head against her waist. "Maybe you just haven't grieved enough, Zeke. Not just for Lance, but for what happened to Abbie, for Sand Creek, for all of it. Maybe if you went someplace alone and truly let go, you'd be able to think more clearly. You'd get rid of that terrible load of guilt and sorrow you're carrying—for your family, for the Cheyenne."

Her hands were cool and soft, relaxing. "Maybe you're right," he said quietly. "But it won't come out, Anna. It's like a bunch of explosives are bottled up

372

inside of me, all lit and about to go off, but they never do."

She moved her hands to his shoulders, massaging them. "Eat those biscuits. I'll pour you some coffee, and when you're through, I'll give you a room. Sleep tonight. Sleep as long as you need to. Tomorrow is soon enough to see to Margaret. You'll do her no good going over there angry and exhausted and confused like you are tonight. It's a long ride from where you live to Denver, and I don't doubt you made it in half the time it would take a normal man." She patted his shoulder and walked back to the stove, pouring him some coffee. Then she struggled to think of a way to change the conversation to something more light-hearted. Finally, she smiled. "How do you like my new business? Kind of a change, isn't it?"

He smiled in return then, and his dark eyes roved over her voluptuous body. She belonged in a spangly dress with a plunging neckline and sparkling jewelry. He almost wanted to laugh, seeing her standing there in plain clothes with hardly any makeup, her hair drawn into a prim bun. But she was trying to change her life, and he knew that meant a lot to her.

"I'll agree it's quite a change," he answered. "I'm happy for you, if it's what you want. So is Abbie."

There was a strong hint of the old Anna about her. She had been hardened by years of scratching for survival, years of groveling in bed with men who were not always pleasant to be with, years of living out the bitterness of her treatment as an orphan.

"Well, it is what I want," she answered, moving to the table with the old saunter he was more accustomed to seeing. "Pretty funny, isn't it? Anna Gale, notorious prostitute, running a proper boardinghouse. I'll have you know that nothing illicit goes on here. I run a respectable place, believe it or not. Of course, some of

373

the 'proper' ladies about town still won't have anything to do with me, but I've won a few friends. It's kind of nice. The best part is being completely alone at night, without some cowhand pawing me." She met his eyes then, her deep blue ones flaring with sudden remembered love. "But not every man was difficult to lie with. There was one I wanted very badly. He could still have me if he needed me." She smiled a provocative smile. "But then I'd be breaking my rule of no hanky-panky in my very proper boardinghouse, wouldn't I?"

Their eyes held. "You don't play fair, Anna. You know I'm in a bad state right now. I didn't come here for that."

There was a long moment of silence. "Didn't you?"

He put a biscuit in his mouth and chewed. His eyes dropped to her full bosom as he swallowed and then washed the biscuit down with black coffee. "I came here for Margaret," was his only reply. He swallowed more coffee. "And tell me about Charles Garvey. He around?"

"No. He's East—at college. Wants to get into politics. You can imagine what that would mean for Indians!"

His eyes hardened. "He's alive then."

"Yes. What made you think otherwise?"

"He was at Sand Creek. My own son sank a lance into his leg."

"Wolf's Blood?" Her eyebrows arched and she grinned. Then she laughed. "Wonderful! No more fitting person could have done it! I hear Charles has a bad limp that will always be with him. He even has to use a cane sometimes."

"Good. I'll be sure to tell Wolf's Blood." His face darkened and he sipped more coffee. "If he's alive . . ."

"He's your son. You can bet he's alive." She sighed as he finished the other biscuit. He had avoided her

374

question, but she'd had no right to ask it. Deep inside, in spite of her regard for Abigail Monroe, Anna Gale knew that she would take Zeke Monroe on any terms, even if just for one night to release his needs and pent-up emotions. "Get your gear and come upstairs. I'll give you the best room in the house, unless you want mine."

He grinned. He knew her well. Her remarks did not surprise him or fluster him. He was his own man and took a woman on his own terms. And right now his whole being was filled with Abbie and what he should do about her. "I'll take a room of my own for now, thank you."

She winked and rose, picking up his plate and cup. "You haven't changed, Zeke Monroe. That's good. There's still a lot of the old Zeke left, which means you'll go back to your wife eventually."

"You think so, do you?"

She met his eyes again. "I know so, much as it pains me to say it. Now go get your gear, and don't worry about your horse. I'll take care of it. I have a shed out back with several stalls for customers. I usually make them care for their own animals, but I'll make an exception with you."

He chuckled. "You haven't changed either, Anna Gale, in spite of those prim and proper clothes."

She sauntered up close to him. "Now don't say that, Zeke. I'm trying. Really I am."

He grasped her shoulders. "I know that." She looked up at him, and he was tempted to kiss her. But he knew he didn't dare—not now. "I love her, Anna. I don't know what to do."

She patted his chest. "You will sleep—that's an order—and tomorrow you will go and see Margaret. But you will do as I say and tread lightly. Now, go get your gear."

She pulled away, feeling almost faint from wanting him, and headed out of the kitchen to prepare his room.

"Anna," he called.

She turned and waited.

"Thank you, Anna. What would I have done without your help in the past? I never could have taken care of Winston Garvey—never would have found Abbie. You're a good woman, Anna, no matter what others say about you and despite the fact that you pretend to be otherwise."

She smiled sadly. "Well, it's a little late for me all the way around, isn't it? But that's all right. Just knowing that one person sees me for what I am is satisfaction enough." She left the room.

Abbie stared out the screened door of the kitchen. It had gotten even warmer, and though it was early morning she was not cold. She breathed deeply of the luscious spring air with the smell of rain upon it. A black cloud in the distance hinted of a coming storm, and it was already sprinkling. Spring storms could be very frightening on the plains, and damaging. She smiled at the sweet memory of other storms she and Zeke had weathered, remembering when they had run out frantically to get the horses back into the barns and then had scampered back to the house, laughing at how wet they were. Sometimes the children had huddled around them, afraid of the violent thunder and lightning. At others, Zeke would get out his mandolin and sing them funny songs to make them forget the storm.

Her smile faded suddenly and her heart tightened. Those were good days. But now a storm had come that they might not be able to weather. How she missed having her family together, missed the little cabin and the room where she and Zeke slept. They had had such happy times there, and moments of ecstasy she might never enjoy again. She was tempted to gather the children and leave the Tynes mansion, to go back to the cabin and wait for Zeke. But LeeAnn wasn't ready to travel yet. She needed a good, long rest. To go back now, without her father nearby for protection, might bring back unwanted memories. No. They must all go back together—all of them, including Zeke. She was sure that if she could get him back to their own place, he would feel better, be his old self again, want to stay.

She heard footsteps behind her and turned to see Edwin. She reddened slightly, for she wore her flannel gown and a bathrobe and her hair was still uncombed. She walked to the table and set down her cup, nervously pulling her robe closed and tying the sash.

"I didn't think anyone would be up so early," she explained. "I couldn't sleep, so I came down here and made coffee."

She smoothed back her long, lustrous hair with her hand as Edwin watched her, amusement and desire on his face. She looked as though she had just gotten out of bed, which made him think of her in bed. Her full breasts filled out the soft robe enticingly and he reflected on how ironic it was that only two thin layers of material hid that which he so longed to touch.

"Don't worry about a silly robe," he told her. "You look just fine. In fact you look beautiful . . . with your hair in disarray."

She smiled nervously. "I'll go upstairs and dress."

She started past him, but he put an arm out and caught her about the waist, suddenly and unexpectedly drawing her to him, unable to control the temptation to feel her body close to his when she wore no underthings. "Abbie," he whispered. He had never

377

called her that before. It had always been Abigail.

She looked up at him in surprise, and in an instant his lips covered hers hungrily while one arm embraced her tightly and his other hand moved over her hips. She wasn't sure what to do, he had been so good to her. She didn't want to hurt him, but neither did she want him in this way. She pulled her mouth away and pushed at him.

"Edwin, don't."

"It's such a quiet, rainy morning, Abbie. A good morning to linger in bed, to talk, to make love." He kissed her neck and she pushed harder, finally wrenching herself away. She just stared at him for a moment, her eyes wide with surprise and humiliation. Then she ran past him and up the stairs.

"Abigail, wait!" he called out to her, cursing himself for that sudden moment of uncontrolled passion. Even if it were possible to have her, he had gone about it the wrong way. He kicked at a chair. Abigail Monroe was the first thing Edwin Tynes had wanted that he could not have.

He hurried up the stairs after her. At the door of her room, he started to knock, but he remembered LeeAnn was also there. The girl suffered from nightmares and Abbie wanted to be close to her at all times, so she had been letting the child sleep with her. Tynes sighed, the reality of the situation hitting him all at once. Even if Zeke Monroe were dead, he would come between any relationship Tynes might be able to have with Abbie. There were seven offspring who would always remind Abbie of other days, happier times, and of the man who had fathered them. Between her children and her memories he could never have Abigail Monroe totally, which was the only way Edwin Tynes wanted anything. He did not like sharing.

He turned and went back down to the kitchen,

378

pouring his own coffee and sitting down at the table to drink. The rainy smell in the air made him miss the green hills of England, reminded him of foggy London days, of home. With piercing clarity, he knew Abigail Monroe could never be a part of that. His heart would one day take him back to England, and she would not fit there. She would be unhappy. In spite of all she had suffered, Abigail Monroe belonged right here, on the Colorado plains, in a warm cabin with her children and her half-breed husband, in a land as wild and free as the man she had married. Perhaps if he went back to England, he could forget her, find someone there who fit him the way Abigail fit Zeke.

Moments later he heard the rustle of a dress behind him, and Abbie walked in, wearing a mint green day dress, its full skirts giving her the appearance of floating. How odd, he thought, that this woman could look so normal in a simple tunic, and in turn look equally at ease in the lovely dress that so enticingly fit her slim waist and the lovely curve of her breasts. Her hair was drawn into a bun.

She poured herself more coffee, and at first neither of them said a thing. Then she turned to meet his eyes. He saw no malice in her brown ones, but she held her chin proudly.

"I am sorry, Edwin. But I simply do not desire any man but Zeke, in spite of all that you keep offering me. I truly am sorry because I know what I am giving up and because I know how you feel. You have been a cherished friend, a very big help in so many ways. Whatever happens to me, I will remember you— always. But only as a good and kind man, an interesting man, a friend. God knows I couldn't have made it through all of this without your kind support, and for that I am eternally grateful."

He sighed deeply and leaned forward, resting his

elbows on his knees, and she came and sat down at the table near him. He pressed his hands together. "I came up to your room . . . to apologize. But then I remembered LeeAnn was there, and I didn't want to say anything in front of her." He met her eyes again. "I humbly beg your pardon, Abigail. To a man who has been long without a woman, one who loves the one he is looking at, you looked very . . . inviting. And Zeke did say that if you chose to stay here, you could. I have to try, don't I?" He smiled apologetically.

She looked at her coffee. "I suppose. But it's no use, Edwin. Even if Zeke were to ride north and get killed, it wouldn't change anything. I would go to Fort Laramie then, where I could be near Dan and have the company of Bonnie Lewis; where I could be near Swift Arrow, even though he would be almost unreachable. If I were to take on a new life, I would feel like a deserter, Edwin—not just of Zeke, but of the Cheyenne, of all the Indians. If there is any way Zeke and I can still help them, any way that I can help them by myself, I will do it. You weren't here in the days when they lived free, when they were happy. All of this belonged to them. I think I know what's wrong with Zeke, with both of us. We miss them. We miss the Cheyenne. Maybe when he gets back and we get things in order, we should go to Kansas and see if there is anything we can do. I won't let Zeke go north alone. I'll go with him. We can see Dan and Swift Arrow."

The rain started coming down hard then, the morning sweet and alive. He reached over and took her hand. "I think perhaps I shall go back to England, Abigail. I was sent here to get things started. My brother and a nephew will be coming later this summer. This is just one of my enterprises. I thought for a while I might stay here, but I realized this morning just how much I love England, how lonely I am for it."

She met his eyes. "We are both meant for very different things, aren't we?"

He smiled sadly. "Yes. I suppose we are."

She squeezed his hand. "I will miss your friendship. All of us will. It would be nice if you could stay, but if you go, we will understand. We know what it is like to miss home."

He rubbed the back of her hand with his thumb. "I would not be going just because I miss home. Surely you know that."

She blushed again. "I know." She sighed deeply. "But England does sound so beautiful, and you have family there. I think if you went back you would forget me quickly enough."

His eyes took in her beauty. "Forget you?" He gave a light laugh. "No. One does not forget an Abigail Monroe. When I write my memoirs of this wonderful land, I will devote many chapters to women like yourself who have braved things many men would not. It will make interesting reading for some of my pampered friends. I daresay they'll find it most entertaining, none of them suspecting that I am writing about a woman I fell in love with."

She looked at the hand that held hers. "I'm sorry, Edwin. When will you go?"

"I'm not certain. Sometime after my brother and nephew arrive. But I won't go until things are right again between you and Zeke. I promised him I'd watch out for you, under any circumstances, at least until you are settled in some way. And I will not easily give up the fight to make you my own."

She met his eyes sadly and rose, walking to look out the door again. "That would be useless, Edwin, at least for a long, long time, even if Zeke were dead." The realization that Zeke was in Denver now, with Anna, caused her pain. "What will I do, Edwin, if he sleeps with that woman, if he lets her convince him he can get along without me? Anna can be a good person, and she has helped us, but if she can get Zeke Monroe into her bed, she'll do it, for she worships him."

He leaned back and folded his arms. "I am sure Zeke can not be lured into any woman's bed. If he goes to her, it will be of his own accord and for his own reasons. But I am not so sure that would be such a bad thing, Abigail." She turned in surprise. "Take it from a man, Abigail. It might be good for him to bed this Anna Gale."

He saw her stiffen, and her eyes teared. "Look, Abigail, I'm only saying that perhaps that would make him miss home more—the quiet of your ranch compared to that noisy jungle called Denver. I'd guess if he lies with some other woman, he will want you more than ever. He will know no woman can please him like his Abbie girl, and he will get something out of his system, something that has been eating at him."

Her chest ached with dread and jealousy, and she looked away. Anna Gale! He would be seeing Anna Gale at a time when he was so vulnerable.

"Abigail, look at me," Edwin ordered. She met his eyes again. "I am a man. I am telling you that if he sleeps with that woman, it can do nothing but enhance his love for you. Perhaps the two of you have loved too hard for too long. Perhaps you need to be apart this way, each of you looking at alternatives, each of you learning to appreciate what you've had together."

She put a hand to quivering lips. "I can't bear it, Edwin! I can't bear the thought of him being with her, especially after the way he left here!"

He rose and walked to her, putting his hands on her shoulders. "Yes you can. You can bear anything that means he might see things more clearly, might want you more than ever. Remember one thing, Abigail.

Jealousy can work two ways."

She sniffed and wiped at her eyes. "What do you mean?"

He grinned and walked to the table, picking up his cup and drinking more coffee, making a face. "I'll never get used to this stuff. Tea is so much better." He set the cup down, smiling at the anxiety in her eyes. "Abigail, when Zeke talked to me, asked me if I loved you, he was so damned jealous I thought he might burst. What if he thought there really had been something between us? What if he thought you had truly taken his suggestion and had considered another man, perhaps had even . . . made love to another man out of your loneliness?"

Her eyes widened. "Edwin! I could never—"

"I'm not saying it has to be anything literal. Why not tell a lie, Abigail, if it would bring your husband back to his old self?"

She sniffed and half smiled. "Edwin, he would kill you!"

Tynes chuckled. "I daresay he would want to. But he made me a promise, and Indians don't break promises. He said if I took you against your will, he would kill me. But what if he thought you had come to me willingly? The man would be absolutely beside himself with rage. My bet is he would want you more than he has ever wanted you."

She put a hand to her chest. "Oh, Edwin, I don't know. I wouldn't want him to think that of me."

"Abigail, you are a woman who is not afraid of risks. He needn't think it forever. Only long enough to make him see what he really wants." He smiled, a boyish eagerness in his eyes.

"Edwin, that's terrible!"

"I know," he replied, still smiling. "Quite daring, isn't it?" He turned to leave the room. "You think about it. Soon he will return with Margaret. Don't let your hope dwindle if it takes him awhile. He said he would return, and you say he never breaks his promises. When he comes, don't make leaving you an easy thing to do. Make it difficult, Abigail, as difficult as you can make it. Use the only tool that seems to rouse him from his own self-pity and sorrow. Use his jealousy—his possessiveness of Abigail Monroe."

He left the room, and she walked back to look out at the storm. Denver. Anna Gale. Margaret. What a mixture for Zeke to walk into. He hated Denver, hated busy places full of laws and white men. He would have to face the horror of finding his daughter inside some saloon, selling herself, and his only refuge would be Anna Gale. Anna would help him, keep him out of trouble. But she would do more than that, for Zeke would be wanting to prove that any woman would do, that he could go off alone and leave Abbie to what he thought was best for her. Perhaps Edwin was right. Perhaps Zeke's possessiveness, which he was struggling to bury, was the only tool she could use to keep him.

Chapter Nineteen

Margaret closed her eyes, preparing to shut off her mind and senses so she could bear the pawing hands of her customer. His breath was foul with whiskey and his whiskers hurt her chin. His calloused hands moved roughly over her body. The man thought he was showing the pretty squaw a good time, for her eyes were closed, surely in ecstasy, but she seemed a bit stiff and quiet. No matter. Indian women were easy to please. She would relax soon.

The door suddenly burst open, slamming against the wall. Margaret and the man with her both jumped to a half-sitting position, startled to see a huge man standing before them, apparently an Indian but wearing a white man's suit.

"Father!" Margaret gasped.

Her customer's eyes bulged. Father? "What the hell?" he grumbled.

"Get out!" Zeke growled.

The man slowly rose, staring at the fiery dark eyes of the Indian. He picked up his long underwear. Margaret trembled at the look in her father's eyes and pulled a sheet over her nakedness. Her customer hesitated before he began to put on his clothes.

"Look, mister, I already paid for this damned squaw! I don't know who the hell you are, but—"

His words were cut off when Zeke whipped a huge blade from under his suit coat, holding it out menacingly. "Get out of here right now, or I'll cut off something that will make it impossible for you to lie with any woman!"

The man swallowed and quickly put on his long-johns, gathering up his other clothes to finish dressing in the hallway. He kept a careful eye on Zeke as he eased past him, picking up his gun and hat, and then hastening out. Zeke followed the man with his eyes, grabbing the door and slamming it shut as soon as the man was gone. Margaret jumped again at the loud bang the door made. Zeke shoved his knife back into its sheath and struggled to stay in control. He wanted to beat her, strangle her, throw her out into the street, and then drag her home. But this was Margaret, his first daughter, his Blue Sky, so he also wanted to grab her and hold her and tell her he loved her. Abbie and Anna had both told him to be careful or he would lose her forever. He turned his eyes back to her, and she cringed against the head of the bed, looking small and childish.

"How dare you do this!" she hissed, hurt and sorrow in her voice.

"Dare?" His anger rose again. "I am your father! I'll do whatever I damned well please! You're my daughter—Abbie's daughter. I've come to take you home! Get dressed."

Her dark eyes flashed, reminding him of his own. "I'm long past taking your orders, Father!" she said, a challenge in her voice. "I'll get dressed when I feel like it! And I don't want to go home. I'm perfectly happy here."

"Are you now?" he sneered sarcastically, his eyes roving over her curving form beneath the sheet, making her feel embarrassed that he knew she was naked beneath it. "Where is your pride, Margaret?"

She tossed her head. "I lost it in the bed of a man who said he'd marry me—a man I loved, one who turned around and told me squaws are for sleeping with but not for marriage! The dark skin I inherited from you, dear Father, has branded me for life! I have you to thank for that. A dark beauty they call me. Oh, yes, I am beautiful! But my kind of beauty is meant for all men, not just one!"

Her heart ached at the look in his eyes, yet she could not stop herself from hurting him. If it hadn't been for him, she wouldn't be torn inside herself. She had said the very thing that would hurt him most; right now she wanted to hurt him.

He stepped closer to the bed, studying her. She could tell he wanted to hit her but was holding back. His jaw flexed with repressed anger as he took in the satiny dark skin of her shoulders and arms. "Do you think you shock me, sitting there naked in front of your own father?" His eyes suddenly softened. "All I see is my little girl . . . my little Blue Sky . . . the shy one . . . the scared one. You were always afraid of strangers. Now you sleep with them. This isn't you and we both know it. You got hurt. A lot of people get hurt, Margaret. I lost count of my own hurts a long time ago."

She looked away. "Please go away, Father."

"Not until I've had my say. You can fight me all you want, but behind your defiant eyes I see my Abbie. The goodness of her soul runs in your own veins. Half of you is me, Margaret, but the other half is Abigail Monroe, the best woman who ever lived, as far as I'm concerned. And you can't deny the good side of you forever. Part of you wants to be like your mother, and there's enough good left in you to do that—to come home and make some man a good wife, to

387

live respectably."

Her eyes welled with tears and she could not bring herself to look at him. He sat down cautiously on the edge of the bed. She was like a wild kitten that might dart off at any moment.

"Even the other half, my half," he continued, "the wild, savage half of you, even that can be strong and proud." He reached out and touched her hair gently, but she jerked away. He sighed and rose from the bed. "Damn it, Margaret, you're part Indian, but you look all Indian, just like I do. So face it, admit to it, and be proud of it. You have every reason to be proud of that part of you. Come home with me and be what you are!"

Her body jerked in a sob, but she quickly swallowed back the tears and met his eyes with her red, tear-filled ones. "How can I be proud . . . when everyone around me with white skin continues to remind me that I should be ashamed? When they tell me I'm only good for one thing? It's easy for you! When someone smears your name or throws insults at you or attacks you, you can wield your knife or pull a gun or use your fists. You're a man—big and strong! But what can a woman do? What is there left for me?"

"Yourself! You have only yourself, Margaret! That's all any of us have in the end! How do you think I felt back in Tennessee? I was a small boy, helpless, like you are now. The kids constantly picked on me at school. I got in a fight nearly every day. I was made to sit in the back of the room—at school and at the church full of pious people. My stepmother always dragged me there because she hoped the 'devil' would be preached out of me! I was called stupid. 'Look at the dumb Indian!' they'd say. They'd laugh, sometimes throw rocks. My stepmother detested me because I was the offspring of the Indian 'squaw' my father had lived with. That 'squaw' was your grandmother, Gentle Woman, a

388

beautiful, generous woman who fit her name perfectly! I quit going to school and spent most of my time in a nearby swamp—alone. That was the only way I could be happy! But I never lost my pride, Margaret. I knew I was Indian, I knew I was intelligent, and I knew they were wrong! I was Cheyenne and I was proud! Don't tell me about hurt! Don't tell me about that swine you thought you loved and who hurt you! I'll tell you hurt, Margaret! Hurt is when the woman you love with your whole being is raped repeatedly and tortured and murdered, her head shaved and her arms cut off! Hurt is seeing your baby son lying in a bloody heap on the floor with his head cut off, because his father was Indian! That's hurt, Margaret! That's what Tennessee did to me, and that's the kind of risk your mother took when she married me! She doesn't deserve the treatment you're giving her. She's brave and good and she loves you! She's lost a daughter to death and perhaps a son for all we know! And you haven't even asked about LeeAnn!"

She looked at him, eyes wide, realizing he was right. "I—"

"She's all right." He sneered. "She went through some terrifying moments and was badly abused, but she wasn't raped."

She looked away again. "I'm glad she's all right . . . and I'm glad you're all right. But I'm not going back, Father. I . . . I can't yet. Not now. Maybe not ever. The damage is done."

He moved closer again, bending down and grasping her arm. "That's foolish talk, Margaret! It's never too late, not when it comes to your parents—to home! We love you! We want you away from this place! We don't look at you any different than we ever have. All Abbie wants is to see you come home with me."

She kept her eyes averted. "I can't yet. Please let go

of me!"

He crushed her arms tighter. "You're coming with me, and you're coming now, Margaret Monroe, if I have to drag you naked through the streets!"

"No!" She struggled, desperately clinging to the sheet. "If you make me go now I'll run away again, I swear!"

"Don't be a fool, Margaret!"

"Let go of me! If you don't, I'll scream and men will come and arrest you!"

He stiffened, then let go of her with a jolting shove. He walked to the door. "I'm staying at Anna Gale's boardinghouse. She says you've met. She also said she's talked to you about stopping this foolishness before there really is no turning back."

She met his eyes, her own burning with defiance. "She just told me those things because you're her friend. I've talked to others in Denver about Anna Gale. She was the richest prostitute in the city, and she loved it! She got rich doing what I'm doing. She has no right to tell me I'm wrong."

"She's also a lonely woman who wishes she could change it all."

"Does she? And just how well do you know her, Father? Does mother know you're sleeping at that woman's house?" Her lips curled in an ugly sneer, and he felt that a knife had been plunged into his heart.

"If I were sleeping with Anna Gale, it would be to help convince myself I don't need your mother. I've already decided that once I get you home, she'll be better off without me, Margaret. Living with me has only brought her pain and sorrow."

"What are you talking about, better off without you?"

"When you come to your senses I'm taking you home. Then I'm going north, and if all of you are lucky,

I'll be killed in a Sioux war and that will be the end of this hell!" He opened the door. "I'll be at Anna's. When you're ready, you come. If I have to wait a week, then I'll wait. If it's a year, so be it. But I promised your mother I'd not return without you, and I'll be damned if I'm going to break that promise!"

He turned and left, this time closing the door quietly. She stared after him. There was a certain hopelessness about him she had never seen before—a giving up. He seemed to be holding a gun to his head, ready to pull the trigger. She shuddered and curled up under the blankets, crying bitterly, wanting to run after him. But her shame was too great, as was her childish refusal to admit she was terribly wrong. She had dug a deep hole for herself. Perhaps she could never climb out of it.

Wolf's Blood heard arguing in the outer room. He rubbed at his slowly healing shoulder, wondering if he would ever again have full use of his arm as Bonnie Monroe had promised he would. It felt strange to call her Bonnie Monroe, but he was glad to see the happiness in his white uncle's eyes. Wolf's Blood had little use for whites, but he knew that Dan Monroe was his father's favorite white brother and that there was great affection between the two men. He also knew that Bonnie was the woman who had taken little Crooked Foot, the half-breed boy born of Zeke's dead sister-in-law and the hated Winston Garvey. He had seen Crooked Foot, called Joshua by his adoptive mother. The boy had had several operations on his club foot and now walked rather well in spite of a brace from ankle to hip. Wolf's Blood liked the boy, who often came to visit with him, full of questions about the Indians. The boy didn't seem to know a thing about his origins, and Wolf's Blood suspected he was not supposed to tell. Watching the boy made Wolf's Blood miss his mother more than ever, for it was to keep Joshua's identity hidden that Abigail Monroe had suffered the rape and torture when Winston Garvey had wanted to locate the boy so he could kill him. Wolf's Blood knew how proud his mother would be if she saw the boy now, how glad that she had not given away his whereabouts. For Joshua was pleasant and intelligent, and he had an air about him that made one suspect that here was a great man in the making. Already the boy spoke of going East to school, to study law and get into politics and do what he could to help the Indians. The lad had a natural sympathy for Indians, although he did not realize he was half Indian. Wolf's Blood knew the day would come when the boy would be told about his true identity, but that was up to Bonnie and no one else.

The door opened, and Dan entered. Wolf's Blood could see an officer in the outer room before Dan closed the bedroom door. The boy didn't like being at the fort. There were too many soldiers around, all ready to hang him. His only protection was Lieutenant Dan Monroe and the fact that they were related. Dan walked to the bed and sat down on the edge of it.

"I'm having a time keeping them from throwing you behind bars or shooting you, Wolf's Blood. I nearly lost my commission when I brought you back here to heal."

"I am grateful," the boy told him. "I do not want to make trouble for you."

"I know that." Dan studied the heavy bandages around the boy's upper left chest and shoulder. "Wolf's Blood, the best I could get out of my senior officer was an agreement to let you go free, as long as you promise to go back home to Zeke and Abbie and not to return to Swift Arrow and make war."

The boy sighed, turning to gaze out a window, past the wooden buildings of the fort to the freedom of the hills beyond. "I cannot make such a promise. I know I should go home. My sister Lillian has died, and my parents are suffering." He met Dan's blue eyes with his dark ones. "Have you heard yet if my father came back from searching for LeeAnn?"

"Not yet."

The boy made a fist in anger. "I should be with him! I should have gone along to help him! Now it is too late. I can only pray he will be all right and that my sister will not be harmed. But when I think of how it is for the white women my own people attack . . ." He thought about the girl her had killed. "Poor LeeAnn. It can only be bad for her. Perhaps my father does not want me to come back. He may be angry. Perhaps LeeAnn could have been saved if I had been there to help."

Dan grinned. "One thing I can guarantee, Wolf's Blood: Zeke Monroe wants to see his son again, under any circumstances. He would most definitely love to have you come home, and so would Abbie. I'm sure she needs you right now, Wolf's Blood. I wish you'd give it serious thought."

"I have vowed to fight with my people."

"Fine. But you're badly wounded anyway. It will take time for you to heal, even after you're well enough to travel. Go home to do the healing. Then you will have helped me keep my end of the bargain. My senior officer doesn't need to know if you head north a few months from now. That's up to you. But I can't save you much longer without a promise that you'll go south. Even at that, you'll risk running into other soldiers who won't know what has happened here and who might shoot you on sight."

Wolf's Blood gazed out the window again. They

both heard the long, lonely cry of a wolf somewhere in the distant hills. Wolf's Blood sat up straighter, and there was a wildness about him that suddenly filled the room. "Do you hear it?"

"That wolf? We've been hearing it for a couple of weeks. It's giving the men the jitters."

Wolf's Blood looked at him and grinned. "Good. It is my soul they are hearing, crying for my people."

Dan frowned. "Your soul?"

"My soul is in him, in that wolf you hear. He is mine, my pet, as you white people call such things." He looked back out the window. "He waits for me. It all waits for me—the land—the wind—the wolves." The lonely wail came again, and the boy's wild, dark eyes flashed back to Dan. "I will think about what you have told me. Perhaps the lonely call of my wolf is also the voice of my father, calling for me." His eyes teared. "If something happens to my father, much life will go out of me forever."

Zeke paced the kitchen while Anna put away some dishes. "I don't know how much longer I can keep from going over there and tying her to my horse," he grumbled.

She turned and went to a drawer, taking out a small piece of paper and a pouch of tobacco. "Hang on, my friend. I'll go talk to her again if you'd like. I don't know how much good it will do. Besides, she probably hates me because she thinks something is going on between us." Anna smiled enticingly. "I wish to God she were right."

She liked his wild restlessness, was touched by his need to get free of Denver and its suffocating effects. That was what she loved about him, he was so different from other men, unaffected by the whites around him. Conversations around the supper table with her other boarders were always interesting, they asked endless questions about Indians, sometimes arousing Zeke's ire by their ignorance and misconceptions. A few times she had thought Zeke would explode and hit someone, and occasionally a guest would suddenly excuse himself or herself, afraid of the long-haired, dark man whose handsome face revealed a hard life and an experience beyond their grasp. Whenever Zeke was gone, he became a conversation piece, and two guests had left because they feared to stay in the same house with an Indian.

He stared out a window now, apparently not even aware of her last statement. "You'd better calm down or I'll lose more guests," she declared, sitting down at the table. "Come over here and I'll show you something new."

He turned and looked at the paper and tobacco. She sprinkled some of the tobacco onto the paper as he walked over and sat down. He watched her as she rolled the paper, licking its edge and pressing it firmly so that the tobacco was packed tightly in the middle.

"There," she said. She held it out to him. "Try it."

He frowned. "What is it?"

"It's a cigarette. Something new—getting pretty popular. A lot of men like them better than cigars. Go ahead. Light it."

He took it and studied it, then put one end to his lips. She shivered with desire at the manliness about him, the fine line of his lips as he held the cigarette and then lit it. He puffed on it curiously, and she wanted to laugh, charmed by his curiosity.

"You don't puff them. You inhale the smoke. It's not a pipe or a cigar. It's a cigarette."

He frowned, then took another puff, this time sucking a little in. He blew the smoke out. Her eyebrows arched. "No cough?"

He shrugged. "I have inhaled the Indian pipe many times. It is a sweeter taste, better than this. But something this small is handy, and I like it better than a cigar. Besides, Abbie doesn't like cigars. Perhaps she would like this—" He stopped short. How easy it was to think of her.

Their eyes met. "She's under your skin like your own blood, isn't she?" Anna said quietly.

He took another drag on the new cigarette, this time a deeper one. "I'll have to get her out from under it then," he answered. "The more I think about that, the more I know I am right."

"You'll never do it."

He studied her lovely eyes, his eyes dropping to her full bosom. "Perhaps I haven't tried hard enough."

He met her eyes again and their gaze held for a long time, her blood racing with heated passion. "Perhaps not. But I am saying you'll never get rid of your need for Abbie, and you'll never truly leave her. You're a strong man in all other ways, but when it comes to her you're weak."

His eyes flashed and he ground out the cigarette in a saucer. "I am going riding. I feel the walls closing in on me." He rose and walked to the door, turning back once to look at her again. "You're probably right. Perhaps I need to find out for myself just how weak— or strong—I am. I will think about it."

He left her sitting there wondering what he had meant by that remark. Would he come to her bed after all? She sighed and looked at the cigarette, touching the end his lips had touched, hungering for those same lips to touch her own in passion and desire, yet hating

396

herself for wanting him and for not caring whether she betrayed Abbie despite how much she respected the woman.

"Once a harlot, always a harlot, Anna Gale," she muttered to herself. She turned down the lamp and walked out, going up the stairs to her bedroom, and the empty bed that awaited her. Yes, her life had certainly changed.

Margaret carried the tray of empty glasses back to the bar, feeling awkward in her new red satin shoes with the raised heels. She was not accustomed to such painful footwear, nor was she good at keeping her balance on something that wasn't flat. But the shoes matched her low-cut red satin dress perfectly. The dress was fitting for a saloon girl and should have made her feel less conspicuous, but instead it made her feel more so. To make matters worse, Morgan Brown was back, and she had felt his eyes on her all evening. She had deliberately avoided him, not certain why, for he was exceedingly handsome. He was a tall, strong-looking man, with eyes that aroused feelings in her the other white men did not. As she waited for the order of drinks, she felt a presence close behind her.

"What happened to the tunic and moccasins?" came the gentle voice.

She felt a shiver, and turned to look up into Morgan Brown's dark eyes. "I got tired of the game," she told him. "Playing the squaw. I decided to dress like the white whores."

"But you aren't white. And you aren't a whore—not inside."

Her eyes flashed and she turned around again to pick up the tray. "How would you know? And why do you keep watching me? I wish you would stop. I should have you thrown out of here."

He chuckled, putting a hand on her shoulder. "Since when is it illegal for a male customer to watch the prostitutes, especially when he's figuring on doing business?"

He gently rubbed her arm and to her anger and dismay his touch excited her. Lying with this man would surely be satisfying, so why did she want to fight it? Because he was so sure of himself! Yes, that was it! He took things for granted. "I have already promised another," she told him.

"Then I'll pay twice his fee—three times as much if we go upstairs right now." He moved his hand to her shoulder. "In fact, I'll pay in advance. I'll be your only customer for the next week or so. I don't like the others touching you."

She turned again, confused. "Why on earth should you care?"

He held her eyes. "Deliver your drinks and let's go upstairs." He smiled warmly, his dark eyes dancing with an almost teasing look. A quiet sureness emanated from him, a masculine command. In some ways he reminded her of her father, for he had the same proud look about him, that of a man unaffected by others, afraid of no one, his own man. She tore her eyes from his and ducked around him, setting the drink on a nearby table and bantering with the men who shot insulting remarks at her and pawed at her. She wanted to ignore Morgan Brown but could not, and again her eyes were drawn to his. She suddenly felt as though they were the only two people in the room. She had never felt this way, not even with Sam Temple. This man was much more of a man than Sam, more sure of himself, more mature. She found herself obeying blindly, turning and going up the stairs, aware that he followed.

She went to her room, and he came in behind her, closing the door. She turned to face him and he came closer, placing his hands on her shoulders and bending closer, captivating her, meeting her lips in a tender kiss that brought out passion she had not felt since first lying with Sam. He searched her mouth, while his hands deftly ran down the buttons on the back of her dress. She felt it fall away, felt his hand come around and gently push down the lacy front of her undergarment and caress a firm, young breast. She shivered and whimpered, reaching up around his neck and returning his kiss with heated desire. Then she was in his arms, carried to the bed, lying beneath his broad frame, letting him undress her. She breathed deeply as his lips left her mouth and traveled over her throat to a breast, lightly tasting it. Then she whimpered with ecstasy, and he moved back to her mouth.

"Little Margaret," he said softly. "I am going to be your customer—tonight and every night for a long time. I told you I would come to you as a man you wanted, not just as a man to lie with for money. You cannot deny that you want me, truly want me, just as I truly want you."

She reached up and touched his face. "Why do you talk that way?"

He only grinned and kissed her again, and the next hour was one of unbridled passion. After all the men she had been with, this one stirred feelings she hadn't known she had, touched places none of the others had touched, brought out a wild need she had never felt before. He took from her, and she didn't mind the taking. She wanted to give, more than she had ever wanted to give. His movements were rhythmic, beautiful, demanding yet gentle. And when he finished with her she was totally exhausted yet rippling with satisfaction . . . or was it love?

But how could that be? It was impossible! She barely knew this man, yet suddenly she loved in a way she had never loved Sam.

He sat up, leaning against the headboard and reaching down to caress her hair. "Who was the man who came storming up here a few nights ago?" he asked. "The Indian who wore the white man's clothes?"

She frowned and looked up at him. "My . . . father. Why?"

He nodded. "I thought so. A well-spoken man. I heard him ask the bartender which room was yours. He had a slight Tennessee accent. He's a breed, isn't he? And you aren't all Indian, just as I suspected in the first place."

She sat up straighter. "Why do you care, Morgan?"

His eyes held hers steadily for several seconds. "I am a mulatto. Do you know what that is?"

She frowned. "I . . . I think it's kind of like being a half-breed. Only part Negro—dark people. I've never seen one. I've only heard of them. But father knows of them, and so does mother. There are many of them in the South."

He snickered sarcastically. "They're free now, if you want to call it that. They're going other places. You'll see one. I'm surprised you haven't already." He sighed. "My mother was a Negro slave. She was forced to go to bed with her white master or get a severe whipping." He looked at her. "I was the result. What do you think of that, Margaret?"

Her eyebrows arched. "I don't think anything, I guess. Am I supposed to think badly of you?"

He chuckled and pulled her close to him, letting her nestle into his shoulder. "Of course you are. Don't

400

people think badly of you?"

She rested a hand on his hard-muscled stomach. "Yes."

"Well, it's the same for me, so we're a lot alike, aren't we? Both of us have torn souls, so to speak, living in two worlds. Tell me, Margaret, why are you here in this place? You're so pretty, so young, and it's obvious you're educated and intelligent."

"If we're so much alike then you know why I'm here. I . . . loved a white man. He told me he'd marry me. Then he left me—said squaws were only good for sleeping with. He was my first man. He meant everything to me. I gave him what was most important to me, trust and love. And then he made me see there was no future for me. No white man would want me for a wife, and there is no future for me with an Indian man, for I would have to live on a reservation or be constantly running from soldiers. Besides, I was brought up white. I cannot truly live as an Indian, although I know their ways, their language. I care for them, yet I do not feel I am really one of them."

He kissed her hair. "There, you see? It's the same for me. No white woman is going to marry me. I won't lie about what I am, and when they know they scorn me. Yet I don't really desire Negro women. I've wandered all my life, Margaret. I was torn from my mother's arms when I was eight and she was sold and taken away. I've been through a lot, but I've worked hard in spite of it all—kept my pride. I'm thirty years old and lonely. I want to settle down. I have a good amount set aside, quite a bit by most standards. I want to share it. I came to Denver to see what I could find here in the way of work and, I guess, to see this wild land called the West. Then I walked into this saloon, and I saw a little girl with an innocent look about her, a girl who looked out of place—maybe as lonely as I was. And she was

Indian, but only part Indian, I suspected. She was the first Indian I'd seen that wasn't wild or on a reservation. I wondered: Is that little girl as mixed up as I am? Is she here because she's lost like I am, because she doesn't know whether she's white or Indian and she's given up? And then I saw the light. Maybe this was the kind of girl who'd consider settling down with me, in spite of what I am. Because she's in the same predicament, maybe we'd make a good match."

She pulled back and looked at him in surprise. "Are you crazy? I hardly know you!"

His eyes dropped to her full, firm breasts. How beautiful she was, with milky brown skin of a distinctive color—not white or red, just as his was not white or black. Why did they have to be anything in particular? They were after all just people, needing the same things all people needed.

"Of course you don't know me," he answered, meeting her eyes. He leaned forward and kissed her forehead. "That's why we're going to spend a lot of time together the next few days . . . and nights. You tell me all about yourself, your parents—everything. And I'll tell you more about me." He pulled her closer again, laying her back down and moving on top of her, kissing her eyes. "And we'll see what happens."

Never had she felt so overwhelmed by anyone. She put her hands against his shoulders. "Surely you're not saying you love me!"

He frowned sternly. "Of course not. I only like you—and want you. When I think I love you, I'll let you know. Maybe love isn't what we think it is. Maybe it isn't always something that happens quickly. Maybe it takes some people years to build a really great love."

Her brown eyes widened and suddenly became innocent and childlike, the way he knew she ought to look. "Morgan! What if we did end up together? What

402

if we had children? What on earth would they be called? Is there a name for such a mixture?"

He smiled sadly. "Yes. They're called people. Just people." He covered her mouth with his own and she soon forgot about everything but the fact that Morgan Brown was making love to her again.

Chapter Twenty

Anna was starting to blow out her lamp when a light tapping sounded at her door. It was so faint she wasn't certain at first that she had heard it. She pulled a robe back on and went to the door, opening it softly, a surge of hot desire rushing through her when she saw Zeke standing there. He wore the cotton pants he had been forced to don while in Denver, but he was shirtless, and his hair hung long and loose. He seemed the epitome of manhood, and her heart ached at the numerous scars on his muscular chest—from the Sun Dance, from past battles and old wounds, from self-inflicted wounds of mourning. He was a man beaten and battered by the hardships of the land and the prejudices of mankind.

He held up a bottle of whiskey, and she could see he had already drunk some. "Want to share a drink with me?" he asked. His face was oddly cold and determined, as though he were angry at the world and intended to do something about it.

Her heart raced. If ever he was susceptible, it was tonight. Or was he the one challenging her? What made her think Zeke Monroe would be had on her terms? He moved past her, walking inside and gazing around her bedroom, decorated in lavender. She quietly closed the door. His huge frame with its wild countenance seemed totally foreign in the room—a man of animal grace and instincts standing amid lavender and lace. She grinned. "Where's my drink?"

He turned to look at her, his dark eyes running over her voluptuous and available body as she removed her robe to stand in a thin gown that revealed the soft points of her breasts. He poured some whiskey into a glass he had brought up with him and handed it to her.

She took it, feeling fire sweep through her at the mere touch of his fingers. In a flash of remembrance, Zeke visualized Abbie handing him a cup of coffee when she was fifteen and seeing him for the first time. The memory brought a piercing pain to his heart and he turned away, his throat tight. He took a slug of whiskey and Anna sipped hers.

"To what do we owe this occasion?" she asked.

He turned, the bottle gripped in his hand. "To forgetting. If I am going to leave my wife to better things and go off and die, I might as well have one good time with the infamous Anna Gale first, right?" He stepped closer, grasping the back of her neck in his free hand. "A woman is a woman. I don't need any particular one." He drew her closer but she stiffened.

"Don't you? How long do you intend to lie to yourself?"

He reached over and set the bottle on a nearby table, still grasping her neck. "As long as it takes."

"For what?"

"For my wife to understand what's best for her. Edwin Tynes is a charming man. He can't offer her the world without her surrendering sooner or later. I intend to make it easy for her." He bent closer, meeting her lips savagely, deliberately. She wanted to tell him to leave, but knew she would not.

Their breathing grew heavier as he pressed her close

in the strong arms she had dreamed about for years, his sweet lips searching her mouth, bringing out desires other men had failed to stir. Her arms were limp, her drink still held lightly in one hand. She was not seducing him after all. He was seducing her. He always had, without even trying.

He released her slightly then, running one hand over her throat, his fingers then lightly touching the softness of her breasts through the flimsy gown. "I want to sleep with you, Anna," he told her. He took the drink from her hand and set it on the table. "I'm tired—tired of death and failure, tired of watching loved ones suffer, tired of waiting for Margaret, tired of fighting and killing. I want to make love to you, want to get my daughter home, and then I just want to get out of Abbie's life and end my own."

She pulled away slightly. "And you don't want to make love to your wife before you say farewell to this world, after twenty years and all she's put up with to stay with you?"

He picked her up in his arms and laid her on the bed, then removed what clothing he wore. Her desire grew at seeing him in his masculine glory, a man whom the years seemed only to bless with more virility.

"If I made love to her again, I'd never be able to leave her." He moved onto the bed, lying over her and resting on his elbows, studying her beauty, winding his fingers into her dark hair. "It's easier this way."

She smiled sadly. "Of course it is. You're using me, damn you! You know I can't resist you. It's wrong and I know you'll leave again, but I've wanted you ever since that one night we had years ago in Santa Fe. You've always known it, and I'll be here for as long as you need me. You can sleep with me every night if you want. I know you'll go eventually, either to Abbie or to your own death, but you'll not go before I have you once more!"

He came down on her then, hiding her body beneath his huge frame, beginning her ascent to the heights of ecstasy. It was as though he were the harlot rather than she, for he seemed to know the right moves better than she did. Somehow her gown disappeared, and their skin touched in heated desire. It had been so many years since he had done this to her, but she had not forgotten. Then he had been angry and cruel to her for forcing him to bed her. This time it was different. It was his choice.

His glorious body moved over hers, and she knew the act was made sweeter by her knowledge that this could not last for long. Everything about him groaned for his Abbie girl and she knew it, but it was not Abbie who lay beneath him. It was Anna Gale, who was prepared to take him on any terms.

Zeke's every move originated from sorrow and despair, in his mind a vision of Edwin Tynes doing these things to his Abbie. But he must do this. He must forget. He must get Abbie out of his system, take Margaret home, and go! Go! Die! Die and leave them all to a better life! First he would make the parting easier by doing the one thing that would hurt Abbie the most. He would sleep with Anna Gale and he'd make damned sure Abbie knew about it when he went back home. He would give her good reason to turn to Edwin Tynes for comfort, for security, and for a better life. Tynes would—

He suddenly thrust himself hard into the woman beneath him. No! No other man must do this to his Abbie! How could he bear the thought of her taking pleasure in someone else, of someone else penetrating the private places that belonged to Zeke Monroe. But bear it he must. He must!

Their bodies moved rhythmically, damp skin warm-

408

ing the bed, Anna's voice whispering his name ecstatically. Yes. This would hurt Abbie, and it would prove to him that any woman could satisfy his manly needs. This would help him make the final break. He smothered Anna's mouth with his own, and she was again the prostitute she was good at being, the kind of woman she was meant to be. She arched up to him, determined to enjoy every precious moment she might have with him. It would be a good night for both of them.

Anna awoke to see Zeke already up. He was staring out a window at the busy streets of Denver. How she loved him! How lonely and heartbroken she was going to be when he left. But leave he would, for she knew him well. She stretched, surprised that she felt sore all over. A woman like herself should be accustomed to nights like the last one, but then her other nights had not been spent with men like Zeke Monroe. She moaned with soft pleasure, stretching again, and he turned to look at her.

"You aren't thinking of doing something horrible again, are you?" she asked, "like cutting off another finger in remorse for what you've done?"

He walked back to the bed. "No. The reasons are different this time. I want to hurt her, even though it wrenches my heart to do so." He stretched out on the bed, putting his head in her lap, and she stroked his shiny black hair.

"I still don't really understand why you're doing this, Zeke, even though it pleases me to have you in my bed. Why are you so determined to end everything? You know Abbie loves you. You have everything to live for."

He closed his eyes. "I can't start over again, Anna.

We've been down so many times, and we've always gotten up again. This time I feel that I can't. I've lost everything I built, my little Lillian is dead, my son is gone, and Margaret is selling herself to men because she hates her dark skin. Who knows how LeeAnn will be affected by her experience with the Comancheros? And Abbie . . . my poor, devoted Abbie. I think it started when Garvey's men abducted her. When I found her, raped and nearly dead from sickness and neglect, I knew then she had suffered more than she could stand, all because she had married me. Twenty years ago, I came very close to not going back to Fort Bridger to get her. She'd suffered that arrow wound and I had left her there to mend, had married her there, and then had gone on with the wagon train to Oregon. I was to come back in the spring for her, but I was tempted to send someone else, with a letter of divorce, so she'd be free to make a better life for herself. I came so close, Anna. So close. Then I couldn't do it. I just couldn't envision my life without her. Because of that selfishness she has suffered badly. Why didn't I just let her go back then, before so much damage was done?"

"Because you loved her—needed her."

"If I'd loved her enough, I'd never have gone back. That's why I'm doing this now, because I love her too much."

She sighed. "You can't turn it all around now, Zeke. Perhaps you could have then, but not now. You've shared too much. You say you're going off to die. Well, what about Abbie? Have you ever considered that she might die before you? What if you left and she became ill. It's you she'd call for, you know, no matter who she might be with. You brought her here, planted the seed of life in her belly, sustained her, supported her, protected her, loved her. Would you want to be absent in her greatest moment of need?"

He frowned and sat up, facing her. He remembered when Abbie had nearly died of an arrow wound. That was when he'd first realized he didn't want to live his life without her. He remembered how frightened she had been, how she'd looked to him for comfort and help. "I . . . I never thought—"

"And think about something else. If she should happen to bear your leaving or your death and if she should happen to turn to another man, Tynes perhaps, she would be giving him what belongs to Zeke Monroe. Another man would take your place in her bed. Another man would take his pleasure in her. Another man would raise your children."

"Shut up!" He got up and went back to the window. "I'm going to get Margaret today, whether she wants to leave or not. I've waited long enough. It's time to get all of this over with."

Her heart fell. "You mean this is all I get? One night?" She studied the hard muscles of his hips and legs. He wore only a loincloth. He turned.

"I'm sorry, Anna, but I've waited long enough. When something needs doing, it's best to do it and not to let it fester in the mind. It's spring—a good time of year to ride north." He walked to his clothes and began picking them up off the floor and putting them on. Her heart pounded with dread. He was leaving. This was it! She might never see him again. He would go back to Abbie or ride north and do his best to get himself killed. He was a stubborn man and now his mind was made up.

"Zeke!" she said softly, watching him with pleading eyes. He buttoned his pants and sat down on the bed, pulling her into his arms, letting her cry.

"I love you, Anna, in a different way. Not like my Abbie. You have been good to me—and to Abbie. For this we are both grateful. I used you last night, and for

411

this I beg your pardon. We both knew it had to happen once more, didn't we? Now it is done."

She straightened suddenly, tossing her hair and wiping her eyes. "Don't be feeling sorry for the likes of me," she told him. "I knew what you were doing, and I didn't care. I wanted you. That was all that mattered." She moved off the bed and put on a robe. "Anna Gale doesn't get hurt so easily. You know that. I'm too crusted. I've been around too long. You had something to prove and I hope you proved it." She folded her arms. "But I'm putting my money on Abbie—on the love you two have. You won't be able to leave her, not to Edwin Tynes or anyone else." She grinned. "I wish I could be there to see you surrender to her. You will, you know."

He rose and began to finish dressing. "I won't. I know what's best now."

She laughed lightly. "So do I, and it isn't what you think. You're so strong, so proud, so skilled. How many men can you handle at once, Zeke? How many have you killed? What was it like, suffering the Sun Dance ritual? Everything about you is strength and Indian spirit, wildness and recklessness . . . except when it comes to Abbie. That tiny woman makes you as weak as a kitten! It's almost humorous."

He scowled. "I don't find it humorous." She laughed lightly and he glowered at her. "I'm going to get Margaret. Will you prepare some food for me and bring out my horse? I'd appreciate it."

She shrugged. "Sure." He turned to pull on his suitcoat. "No kiss good-bye?"

He sighed and walked up to her. "Damn it, Anna, what can I say? I don't seem to know my own mind anymore. I shouldn't have come here last night."

"Of course you should have." She put her arms about his waist and pressed close to him. "I won't

412

forget it for the rest of my life." She looked up at him then, and he bent to kiss her, enfolding her into his arms. When his lips left hers, she rested her head against his chest. "It's been nice having you here. Three weeks of Zeke Monroe. Too bad I couldn't get you into my bed sooner. I could have had you for much longer. I just hope the nice old ladies I've made friends with don't suspect. I wouldn't want my reputation ruined." She looked up at him again and they both smiled. "You can't wait to get out of this city, can you?" she added. "It's been hell for you being here. You're ready to go out on the plains and feel the wind in your face and a horse beneath you. You want the sun on your back."

"You know me well."

She sighed. "Oh, yes. Well enough to know I'll probably never see you again once you leave here." She pulled away. "Thanks for the glorious night. Prostitutes don't usually enjoy a night in bed with a man who really cares." She put on a cold air, tossing her head and lighting a thin cigar. "What are you going to do if Margaret won't leave with you?"

He sat down to pull on his boots. "She'll leave with me. She'll have no choice. This has gone on far too long. Abbie has been going mad from worry while men have pawed at my daughter. I shouldn't have listened to any of you. I should have dragged her out of there the first day I got here."

"It would have been a mistake, believe me. And if you drag her out of there today it will still be a mistake. She has wounds that have to heal, lessons to learn. She'll come around to the way she was brought up in the end."

"I don't have forever. It's been a long winter, and there are decisions to be made." He turned and their eyes held. "Thank you, Anna. I know now what I will do."

He left the room. "Good-bye," she whispered. She glanced at the bed, then walked to it and stretched out on it, running her hand over the place where he'd lain. Then she curled up into a pillow and wept.

Zeke walked through the muddy streets of Denver, dodging horse dung and the mud splattered by passing wagons. Sometimes women stared at him, but most people stepped back as though they feared for their scalps. Men tended to eye him suspiciously or to make hostile remarks: "There should have been more incidents like Sand Creek"; "Why aren't you on the reservation with the rest of the red bastards?" A child emitted an Indian howl. A few people were pleasant and courteous, seemingly unaffected by his heritage—a few.

He walked into a general store, thinking about Anna. He knew he had hurt her, but he seemed to be hurting a lot of people lately and Anna was Anna. She had seen a lot and done a lot. She had no fantasies about there being anything permanent between them. She would survive. He was glad Winston Garvey was out of her life. The man had held her indebtedness over her head for years. He'd been a senator then, and a steady customer of the young Anna Gale. But that was a long time ago, and Winston Garvey was dead. Zeke grinned at the thought of how horribly the man had died. He would never cease to derive pleasure from that memory.

He approached the store clerk. "You got any tobacco and some of those papers for the new smokes, cigarettes?"

The clerk cleared his throat and swallowed, wondering if the big Indian had come to rob him. "Yes, sir," he answered quietly. He was reaching for the tobacco when a young, sandy-haired man asked him for a canteen.

"Maybe I should just leave this list with you, mister," the young man told the clerk. "I'm heading back to Texas and I'm low on supplies, but I'm in a hurry. Can I leave this and come back later?"

"That'll be all right. And the name?"

"Temple. Sam Temple."

Zeke turned to study the man. He fit the description, and he was from Texas. According to what Abbie had told him about the young man who had ruined their daughter, this had to be the one . . . and he had said he was going to Denver. Temple left, and Zeke looked at the clerk.

"Get my tobacco and papers. I'll be back in a minute." He hurried out and glanced up the street to see Temple head for a hotel.

He walked quickly after the man, glancing around to be sure no one noticed. People went about their business as Zeke followed Temple into the hotel lobby, where a few men sat reading papers and conversing. The clerk was busy signing in a new guest. Zeke watched Temple go up the stairs; then he followed, speaking to no one, making himself look as though he belonged there and was simply going to his room. He reached the top of the stairs just in time to see Temple go into a room and close the door.

Quietly, Zeke went to the door and knocked. "Come in!" came the reply. Zeke gladly obliged, and when Sam turned to see him he froze momentarily, remembering a tall Indian who had come to the Tynes estate with his family. Zeke closed the door, his dark eyes burning into Temple, who swallowed and stood up straighter, his hand resting on a gun. "Monroe?"

Zeke just stared at him, making his heart pound. Sam glanced at the window, then the door.

"You won't escape either way," Zeke hissed.

Temple began to shake. "Look, Monroe, your daughter was willing! I did what any red-blooded young man would do!"

"She was willing because you won her friendship first, then her trust, then you promised to marry her! You ruined her! Destroyed her pride! Robbed her of something precious! You deliberately led her on. You had no right to take advantage of her innocence." The words were hissed.

"I didn't hurt her. She learned a good lesson, that's all! Now get out of my room before I yell for help and get you thrown into jail."

In a flash a big hand grabbed Temple around the throat. The hand was amazingly powerful, for Zeke Monroe squeezed not just with his own strength, but with a fury aroused by the thought of what had happened to Margaret and aggravated by his terrible sorrow over his recent losses. This man was the reason for Margaret's despair. He had deceived the girl, deceived Abbie. He was the reason Zeke had been forced to stay in this city that he hated. All Zeke's agony and restlessness and sorrow were being vented on Sam Temple. His grip was like a vise around the man's throat.

Temple started turning red as he tried to pry the arm away; then he went for his gun. Zeke caught the movement and grasped the man's wrist with his other hand, kneeing Temple between the legs. The man's eyes bulged, and he started to crumple, but Zeke hung on, watching the color in the man's face turn from red to purple, then to an ugly gray as his body slowly slid to the floor. Zeke kept hold until he knew the life had gone out of Sam Temple. Then he rose and looked down at the dead man.

416

"Who says a man can't deal out his own justice in a civilized town?" he hissed. He felt good. Somehow he even felt relieved. He wanted to let out a war whoop, but he didn't dare. He went to the door, opening it cautiously. No one was in the hall. He closed it quietly and left by the back way.

Minutes later Zeke Monroe entered the general store again. "I'll take that tobacco and paper now," he told the clerk.

"Certainly," the man replied nervously. "I have them ready. Will there be anything else, sir?"

Zeke looked around. "Yes. Maybe a bottle of nice perfume for a lady friend of mine—and a couple of fancy combs, for my daughter."

The clerk looked around, finding suitable items. "Fine day, isn't is, sir?" he said, wanting to stay on friendly terms with the big Indian he waited on.

"It's a beautiful day," Zeke replied. "One of the best I've seen in a long time." He paid the clerk and left.

Margaret opened the door to her room and stepped back when she saw her father, allowing him inside. Zeke's eyes rested on a tall, handsome man standing in the room. A carpetbag was on the bed and Margaret was dressed.

"I was just coming to see you, Father."

He frowned and looked from the carpetbag to the man, who smiled and nodded to him. "Morning, Mister Monroe." Zeke looked at Margaret.

"You running away again, with this man? Get him out of here or I will! You're going home with me."

She smiled and took his hand. "Father, sometimes you're such a bear." She led him to the man. "This is Morgan Brown, Father, and he's my husband, We

417

were just coming to see you."

There was a moment of silence as Zeke looked from Brown to his daughter, surprise in his eyes. Morgan put out his hand. "I'm glad to meet you, sir. I saw you once before, but you didn't see me." Zeke hesitated. Margaret couldn't have known the man for long. "I know what you're thinking, sir, and you shouldn't. Margaret and I care for one another very much. Marriage just seemed like the right thing for us. I intend to take as good care of her. In fact, we have a lot to talk about."

To Margaret's relief, Zeke finally shook the man's hand. He was good at judging men, and he liked the look in Morgan Brown's eyes, the firm friendliness of his handshake.

"We have a lot in common, Mister Monroe," Morgan told him, releasing his hand and putting an arm around Margaret's shoulders. "You are a half-breed. I am a mulatto. We might as well get that cleared up right now. We were coming to the boardinghouse to talk to you, but we can talk here."

Zeke just stared at him. "Mulatto?"

Morgan chuckled. "You look as though you could use a drink." He walked to a night table and poured Zeke a shot of whiskey. "You do know what a mulatto is, don't you?"

Zeke looked at Margaret. Sheer happiness glowed on her face. She seemed totally changed. "I love him, Father. We are very close. And he's proud and independent, like you."

Zeke turned back to Morgan, who handed him the whiskey. "I know what a mulatto is," he replied. "I grew up in Tennessee."

"Well then, by your own experience, you know what life has been like for me. Margaret has told me a lot

418

about you—your family. I look forward to meeting all of them."

Zeke drank down the whiskey. This was turning out to be a strange morning indeed.

Brown rambled on about his own background, and about how he had saved a great deal of money. He'd been told of Zeke's misfortunes, and since he was now part of the family, he wanted to help.

"I've been looking to settle down for a long time, Mister Monroe, and I'm a hard worker. You have a ranch but no horses. I have money but no home. I propose to buy you a good start to a new herd, if we can use your ranch to raise them on. You have horses, I have a home, and we split the profits. I'd like to live there with Margaret—build ourselves a little cabin. It would make your wife happy to have her daughter near, and Margaret says you're good with horses, maybe the best. There's no way my investment could go wrong, and you'd be back in the business of ranching. I'd be there to replace the loss of your brother. I'm good with a gun, Mister Monroe, and not afraid of many things. Men like us soon learn to take care of ourselves, don't we? What do you say?"

Zeke looked at Margaret again, overjoyed by the eagerness in her eyes. He had his daughter back, the Margaret he knew and loved. If this man could do that for her, he had to respect him. And there was an honesty about Morgan Brown that he liked, as well as the similarity of their situations. He rose and walked to the window. This husband of Margaret's gave him new hope, more hope than he had had in months. But there was still Abbie . . . and Edwin Tynes. The fact remained that she had a chance to live in peaceful comfort for the rest of her life. Perhaps he could just give the ranch to Morgan and Margaret. Yet the thought of starting up again, having things the way they once were, excited him.

"I don't know what to tell you," he answered. "I had . . . plans. I didn't think I could start over, and even if I can, I'm not sure what's best for my wife and family."

"Oh, Father, if you're talking about that lily-white Englishman, you're being foolish. Mother is no more interested in him than she would be in a doorknob! You can't leave her and you know it. And we all"—she swallowed—"we all love you."

He met her eyes and they were wet with tears.

"I'm sorry, Father, about . . . about things I said." She rose and walked up to him and they embraced. Then she wept quietly. "I want to go home," she whimpered.

He patted her shoulder. "We'll see, Margaret. I have much to think about now. Much to think about."

He gave her a squeeze and kissed her hair. "Why don't you finish packing and we'll leave today. I had planned on it anyway. We'll all have plenty of time to talk on the way home."

She pulled away and walked to a dresser to take out some clothes while he strode to the window and glanced down at the street where a crowd was gathering. He wouldn't tell his daughter the real reason why it was best to leave right away. Perhaps she wouldn't want to know her father had ended Sam Temple's life, even if she did think she hated the man. Two men were coming back toward the saloon, and Zeke could hear them talking as they passed beneath the open window.

"Wonder when this place is gonna get really civilized," one commented.

"Out here?" The second man laughed. "Probably never. That's why I like it. I just hope I'm not one of

420

those that gets buried in some unmarked grave—probably because of an argument over an unpaid bet."

"Nobody knows much about him. The hotel clerk said he was from Texas and was headed back there. Too bad he didn't leave yesterday, huh?"

Both men chuckled and went inside the saloon.

Chapter Twenty-One

Zeke stood in the doorway of the small ballroom in which Edwin Tynes was entertaining guests from Denver. He quietly watched Abbie, his heart aching at the knowledge that she really was better off here, yet his whole soul yearning for her as never before. She was unaware that he had quietly entered the house, unaware he was even back. She wore a full, flowing gown of dark blue velvet, the material gathered in deep loops over a lighter blue silk skirt. Her hair was drawn back and held in place by jeweled combs. She looked as though she fit there, and Zeke was convinced that she did. He had half considered taking her back to the ranch and starting over, but seeing her this way, so at peace, so beautiful and pampered, living in luxury, how could he ever again make her go back to their old life?

He turned and walked back down the hallway. Two guests passed him, staring, then whispering after he went by. He walked back to the large entrance hall, where Margaret and Morgan waited, Margaret still hugging LeeAnn and both of them jabbering, wanting to share their experiences. Zeke realized it would be good for both of them to talk to each other. It would help to relieve the horrors they had both experienced over the past few months.

LeeAnn had brought the rest of the children down. They stood around watching their older sisters and staring at the man Margaret had brought home with her. Margaret looked at her father when he approached.

"Where is Mother?" she asked.

"I . . . I don't want her to see me. I'm leaving, Margaret. You go and get her."

"What do you mean, leaving? You're staying right here." She looked at LeeAnn. "Go and get Mother, quickly!"

"Damn it, Margaret, you don't understand!" Zeke growled.

"Oh, yes I do! You're being silly, that's what. If you leave without seeing Mother, you'll kill her! Besides, you have to take Morgan to the ranch—show him around. You're going to stay, Father. We're all going to be together!"

She took hold of his arm and he knew she'd make a scene if he tried to leave. He loved her for it, but it also made him angry. A moment later Abbie was rushing in, Tynes right behind her. She stopped short, meeting Zeke's eyes, each of them wondering about the other. Had he slept with Anna Gale? Did she want to stay with Tynes? Would he go away now and never return? Had Tynes touched her, perhaps made love to her? The man looked at her now with deep affection. Zeke had seen him with his arm about her waist, as though it was quite natural for him to hold Abbie. She looked beautiful, so beautiful! And to her, Zeke looked more wonderful than ever, standing there in buckskins and moccasins. He had not cut his hair; she had been afraid he might do that.

There was nothing to be said at first. They just

424

looked at each other. Then Abbie's eyes turned to Margaret. For the moment it didn't matter who the stranger with her was. Margaret was home! The girl looked healthy—happy—and she was crying now, walking up to Abbie. They embraced, and both of them wept.

Zeke met Edwin Tynes's eyes, noting the jealousy in them, the possessiveness. Zeke thought he might go mad from wondering. Not Abbie. Not his Abbie! She wouldn't. But the way Tynes looked at her, the way he'd had his arm around her when Zeke first arrived, as though they were natural together, like a husband and wife . . . Tynes held up a glass that had a drink in it.

"Welcome back," he told Zeke. "I am going to rejoin my guests. I will leave Abigail to her family."

The man turned and left, and for the next several minutes there was much commotion and talking. Morgan Brown's presence was explained, he was introduced to the rest of the children, and there was talk of Morgan investing in the ranch and buying a new herd. Abbie's face glowed with happiness, and she kept glancing at Zeke. Was it true? Would he really go back now and start over? He misinterpreted the questions in her eyes, thinking she was trying to think of a way to tell him she didn't want to go back. Suddenly he turned and exited amid the confusion, waiting until Abbie was absorbed in Margaret again so she wouldn't realize that he was leaving. When she saw that he was gone her heart tightened and she panicked.

"Zeke!" she called. She hurried to the door, only to see him riding away. "Zeke!" she screamed.

Morgan Brown took her arm. "It's all right, Mrs. Monroe. He told me on the way here he'd like to spend this night alone on the prairie . . . pray to his Gods. He'll be here in the morning."

"But . . . we didn't even speak! After all this time we

425

didn't even speak! He'll ride North! He won't come back!"

"Yes he will."

"Mother, he promised me if he went off to be alone tonight he'd come back in the morning." Margaret came up and put an arm around Abbie. "He said he'd be back to stay . . . or to tell all of us good-bye." Abbie looked at her in near terror. "Mother, we talked and talked to him, mostly about the ranch, about how much fun it would be getting things going again, all being together again, building a cabin for Morgan and me. I think he wants to, Mother, I really do. I don't think he'll go away now."

Abbie looked out at the horizon. Zeke had already disappeared. "You have to be right, Margaret. You have to be!"

The night was long and quiet, a sleepless one for Abbie. Once she thought she heard the howl of a coyote, or was it a man's cry? It seemed that morning would never come, and when it did, there was still no Zeke. She picked at her breakfast, while the children talked and laughed and ate, all anxious now to go home. But home wouldn't be home without Zeke.

Abbie kept glancing anxiously at Edwin, who only smiled reassuringly. Soon the others were through and Margaret took Morgan out to show him Kehilan. The children followed, fascinated by Margaret's new husband, trying to imagine what a Negro looked like, for Morgan Brown didn't look anything like what they'd heard about black people. But then neither did LeeAnn look anything like an Indian.

Soon the kitchen was empty except for Abbie and Tynes.

"Edwin, he isn't here yet!" she whimpered.

"He will be. Remember what I told you, Abigail. Remember his jealousy. He apparently saw us together yesterday, perhaps in the ballroom."

She met his eyes. "Edwin, you must think of a way to keep him here when he returns. If he says he's leaving for good, we must find a way to make him stay at least a few days, until I have a chance to talk to him!"

He nodded. "I've already thought of that. One of my prize thoroughbred studs is very sick. I can't think of a better man to doctor him than your husband, can you? Who else is better with horses?"

Hope came into her eyes. "Yes. He loves horses. He'll not leave one sick and dying."

"Nor will he leave you. Remember what I told you now, about letting him think for a while that you and I have been more than just friends."

Her heart pounded. It seemed everything—her past, her future—rested on the next twenty-four hours. She could keep him, or lose him forever. Her Zeke! Her beautiful Zeke! Her strength, her courage, her life.

The morning hours stretched to noon, and again the Monroes were seated round the table, some of the children now asking when their father would come so they could go home. Suddenly he appeared at the back door, his quiet approach reminding them of how stealthy an Indian could be, bringing to Lee Ann's mind the night he had so quietly entered the camp of Comancheros and saved her.

Abbie just stared, her heart racing. "Zeke!" Tynes called out. "It's about time. Come in and join us. Are you hungry?"

He quietly stepped inside, wearing buckskins, his infamous knife on his weapons belt. Abbie studied him lovingly, glad to see his limp was gone now. His sleek hair was brushed out long and clean, the buffalo hair ornament braided into one side of it, the tiny bell making a tinkling sound. She was very aware of his masculinity, which was accented by the dancing fringes of his clothes and the tinkling bell. He looked at her, more love in his eyes than she had ever seen. Was it because he was leaving? He walked closer to the table.

"I've come to spend the day . . . with my family," he said quietly, struggling to keep his voice. "Then I will leave—tonight."

Abbie paled and wondered if she might faint. She began to tremble and shook her head. Tynes grabbed her hand and squeezed it tightly. Zeke's eyes rested on their hands and his jaw flexed, but he tore his eyes from the sight and glanced around the table. "Morgan and Margaret can run the ranch as they see fit. You children can live with them, or remain here, whatever you choose. The same goes"—he met Abbie's eyes—"for your mother."

"Father, you can't be serious!" Margaret said angrily.

His dark eyes flashed to hers. "I am! I want no more arguments!"

"I am afraid you can't go, Zeke." Tynes rose, doing his best to appear angry. Zeke looked at the man and frowned.

"Who is going to stop me?"

"I am!" Tynes shot back. "Not physically, of course. A man would be a fool to try to do that. But you owe me, Zeke Monroe. I have watched over your family all these months, and watched over your ranch . . . as well as your wife!" Zeke's eyes flared and Tynes felt elated, but Abbie cringed. "I have known you to be an honest man, Zeke, one who pays his debts. You'll not leave here until you pay your debt to me."

Their eyes held challengingly. "And how do I do that? I don't have anything left, Tynes, but a small savings—pennies compared to what you have."

"You have a great talent with horses," Tynes replied. "Something that money cannot buy. I have a prize stud that seems to be dying. If you can save him, I will consider the debt payed. He is a very expensive animal."

They glared at each other, anger emanating from Zeke Monroe. He had not planned on this. He was prepared to leave—tonight. If he stayed longer, he might not find the strength to go. But Tynes was right. He owed the man.

"Where is the animal?"

"I'll take you to him."

"Then take me now!"

Tynes nodded. "As you wish. But I expect you to stay here until the animal is definitely well, not just to tell me what is wrong with him. I want you to tend to him, not some bumbling idiot."

"That could take days!"

"So be it." Tynes threw down his napkin, walking through the back door. Zeke hesitated, then glanced at Abbie's stricken face. How had this great wall come between them? Why couldn't he say anything to her? Perhaps it was the way she looked, sitting there perfectly coifed, wearing a beautiful yellow dress. He turned and walked out, angrily slamming the screen door. Margaret actually snickered.

"Did you see his face, Mother? He's so mad that he can't leave today. What a good idea! I'm glad Sir Tynes's horse is sick."

Abbie just looked at her helplessly, unsure what to do, not knowing how to approach Zeke. She turned and looked out the door, watching the two men walk to the huge barn where the stud was kept.

Outside Zeke studied Tynes's back. He had been prepared to leave Abbie to the man, yet at this moment he wanted to sink a knife into the man's spine for loving

Abbie. But he had made a promise not to harm the man if Abbie went to him willingly. Had she? They walked into the barn.

"Tynes!" Zeke barked. The man turned, waiting. "Has anything happened between you and my Abbie?"

"Your Abbie? That is a strange thing to call her if you are considering leaving her for good."

Zeke grabbed his lapels. "If I leave her, she is free. But I haven't left yet! Is she still mine?"

Tynes met his eyes challengingly. "Remember your promise, Zeke. You said if she was willing, you wouldn't harm me. I love her. If you want to know whether you should kill me, then ask her. Only she can give you that answer." Edwin's heart pounded with fear, for the look on Zeke Monroe's face was terrible. He could only rely on Zeke's honesty and word of honor to keep him from harm. Zeke's breathing was hard, his dark eyes were blazing, but he suddenly released Tynes.

"Where's the horse!" he hissed.

Tynes smoothed his lapels and ran his eyes over Zeke. "I'll have to turn my back on you to take you there. I trust nothing will be plunged into it."

Their eyes held. "Lead the way," Zeke grumbled.

Tynes turned and led him to a stall. A shining black stallion lay on its side, breathing heavily, its nostrils flaring at the entrance of the men, its eyes bulging and wild looking.

For the moment Zeke ceased to think of anything else. "This horse is in pain," he commented, immediately bending down and gently touching its back.

"Be careful, Zeke. He's been behaving wildly ever since we tried to break him. Then he started getting sick. We can't understand it."

Zeke ran experienced hands over the grand horse, feeling for anything that might be swollen or broken.

"He's a beautiful animal," he commented. The horse reared slightly, but Zeke just bent closer, putting a hand on the animal's head and talking to it in the Cheyenne tongue. As he ran a hand over the horse's neck and under its cheek, the animal reared again, as though suffering renewed pain.

"You say it all started when you tried to break him?"

"Yes. I was going to send for a doctor from Denver, but then you showed up. I thought perhaps you would be better at finding out what is wrong with him."

Zeke gently ran a hand over the cheek and lower jaw again, speaking softly in Cheyenne. The horse lay perfectly still, obedient. Tynes watched in great admiration. Zeke Monroe had a natural way with horses. He spoke to this one as though they were spiritually kin. Tynes's heart ached at the realization that he couldn't hold a candle to Zeke Monroe, in spite of his wealth. A vision of Abigail lying beneath the handsome Indian jabbed at him, but there was no other man for her. He smiled to himself as he visualized her as a fifteen-year-old girl, seeing the savage-looking scout for the first time and being unafraid. That would be like Abigail.

"Some fool didn't know what the hell he was doing!" Zeke was saying. He spoke softly to the horse while he gently pried open the animal's lips. "Someone used the wrong kind of bit—one that didn't fit properly. The bars of the mouth are badly swollen, and I think there is infection farther down in his neck. I might have to cut him to drain the infection." He looked up at Tynes. "What the hell was used for a bit?"

Tynes frowned, walking to another stall and retrieving a bit. "I believe this was used. I brought it from England. It's a British curb bit."

Zeke took it and studied it, shaking his head. "This thing must weigh two or three pounds. That's

431

miserable on a young, tender mouth. It must have rubbed the poor animal's bars raw and then they got infected." He felt around the lower jaw again. "You'll be real lucky if you can ever put another bit in this animal's mouth."

"That doesn't matter. I just want him to live. He's a prize stallion and I need him for breeding. Can you save him?"

"I'll do what I can. I'll have to go get my gear." He rose, facing Tynes, slightly taller than the Englishman. "I'll pay my debt, Tynes, and if my wife is willing to stay with you, I'll be on my way." He turned to get his horse.

"As you wish," Tynes answered with a sly grin.

Tynes watched with intense interest as Zeke knelt over the sick horse. Monroe was shirtless, and white paint streaked his chest and cheeks and chin—his prayer color. His thick black hair was wound into two braids to keep it out of his face and out of the incision he would make. Beads were wound into the braids, the hair ornament attached at one side. This was the most "Indian" Tynes had seen him. With paint on his face and chest. Zeke bent over the horse, speaking to the animal in the Cheyenne tongue while smoke from an herbal fire built in a cleared place on the dirt floor of the stall wafted into the horse's nostrils soothing the animal.

Tynes could see that there was more to Zeke's ability to heal an animal than just the physical things he could do for the horse. Apparently, no healing would take place without the interaction of spirits, and Tynes felt a chill at the closeness of man and animal. They seemed to be able to speak to each other. At that moment, Zeke Monroe was not just a man, but an animal spirit.

Zeke picked up a razorlike knife, smaller than the

one he used to kill men. He laid it in a bowl of whiskey, then started to pick it up but hesitated. Tynes followed his eyes to see Abbie standing at the stall door, her hair brushed out straight and long. She wore only an Indian tunic. Tynes could feel powerful currents fill the air as their eyes held.

"I've come to help you," she told Zeke. "I always used to help you when something like this had to be done."

Zeke's eyes ran over her body. He wanted her so badly he wondered where his breath was coming from, but the thought of Tynes touching her made him feel hot and stiff. "I can do it alone."

"No you can't. I can help keep the herbal fire going, help you keep him calm. One slip of your knife and a valuable animal will be lost."

He sighed deeply. "All right."

Tynes rose, meeting her eyes for a moment. This was the real Abbie, standing there in a tunic, without lip rouge and eye color, without a fancy hairdo. He knew this could be an important moment. "There's not enough room for all of us in here. I'll leave. One of you can come and tell me how it all goes." He walked past her, stopping for just a moment to touch her arm, telling her good-bye with his eyes. As he left, Abbie knelt down at the end of the stall by the horse's head. There was nothing to say for now. Their eyes met again, and as his moved over her, she knew he was wondering . . . wondering. . . .

"Add some of those leaves to the fire," he said quietly, picking up the knife.

For the next few moments she just watched, lightly petting the horse's forehead at times, watching the gentle hands of Zeke Monroe relieve the animal of its painful infection, surprised as always at how gentle his hands could be, hands that were brutal when force

433

was necessary.

He looked more handsome than ever to her, and she liked him this way—all Indian, the way she had known him in the beginning. When he finished he breathed deeply, then added more leaves to the fire.

"I want to keep him still for a while yet. He's not going to be feeling too good most of the rest of the night. I'll sit here with him and watch over him. Go and tell Tynes."

She sat, petting the animal. "I don't want to go yet."

He met her eyes. "He said to let him know."

"Edwin can wait. He'd understand if I . . . if I didn't come back right away. We have to talk, Zeke. This might be our only chance. I love you as I have always loved you. I want to go back with Margaret and the others—with you. I want us to be a family again. Why do you insist on leaving?"

"You know why. It's best."

"I'll die without you!" The words were said in a soft whisper, a trace of panic in them. He studied her closely.

"When I first got back I saw you and Tynes together. You looked natural in there, in those clothes, beside him. I asked Tynes if you were still mine, and his only answer was that I'd promised not to kill him if you were willing. Then he said to ask you—that only you could give me the answer. Don't be afraid to tell me, Abbie. Do you love him? Have you . . . turned to him in your loneliness?"

She could see the words almost stuck in his throat, see the desperate dread in his eyes. Even though he thought he wanted that to be true, he didn't really want it to be. "What about you?" was her only answer. "Did you sleep with Anna Gale? Did you prove you didn't need me in your bed!"

Her voice broke at the words, and his heart was

434

creaming. This was the answer to forcing her to stay with Tynes—the final hurt. "Yes. I slept with her. Anna has always wanted me. You know that . . . and she is very good at what she does."

She looked down at the horse, gritting her teeth for a moment. Everything seemed to rest on this moment. She breathed deeply, then faced him. "I am sure she is. I hope you feel good now. You have had your woman, so you intend to ride off and die in battle. You can pretend the last twenty years never happened! You can pretend I never existed, that I never loved you or gave up all my old ways to be with you—gave up ever seeing Tennessee again, gave up luxuries and civilization. You can rest easy and know that all I that I have suffered has been for nothing!"

Pain showed in his eyes. He wanted so much to hurt her, to be cruel to her and make her hate him, but he couldn't stand doing it, nor was it working. What more could he do to make her stay with Tynes?

"You didn't answer my question," he told her. "What about you and Tynes?"

She held her chin up defiantly. "What about us? You practically gave me permission to turn to him for comfort. A woman is very vulnerable, Zeke, when she thinks she has lost all that has meaning to her. A woman needs a man to hold her." She did not actually say anything had happened between them, yet she knew he thought it could have.

"I thought . . . thought you'd wait . . . till I returned."

"Wait for what! How long was I supposed to wait, Zeke? You made it very clear what you would do when you came back—very clear. You said there was no hope for us!"

She choked back a sob and he threw down the knife, grasping her arms. As he stood, he lifted her up by the upper arms, over the horse's head, carrying her to an empty stall and almost throwing her down on the hay.

"You're mine!" he growled. "I thought you would wait!"

"Why? Why did you have the privilege of making such decisions while I dangled, suffering, dying, waiting! You had no right to put me through that, not after all I've been through because I love you!"

He knelt down, straddling her legs, grasping her hair. She wondered at first if he was going to hit her. "Tell me you lie! My Abbie wouldn't lie with another man. Tell me!"

She sobbed and closed her eyes. "My God, Zeke, of course it's a lie!" Her chest heaved in great despair and she felt his painful grip on her hair lighten. "I don't want anybody else!" she wailed. "I just . . . want you!" Her broken words reminded him of how she had cried when she was a mere girl trying to convince him they could be happy together. "I don't want . . . Edwin's money . . . or that fine house. I won't sleep with a man I don't want. I just want to go home. You can't make me stay here, Zeke. You can't!"

The next thing she knew, his lips were cutting off her words. He pushed her down into the straw, his hungry lips smothering hers, his huge frame crushing her. He groaned, searching her mouth, one hand deftly unlacing the shoulder of her tunic while the other gripped her hair. He stayed on top of her so that she could barely move, yanking the tunic down to expose her breasts. Then he rose up on his elbows, moving his eyes to her breasts, making her whimper at the feel of his big hand massaging them as though to prove to himself he could still touch them. His head bent low, and his breath warmed the cleavage of the full fruits that belonged to him and no one else. He was shivering, kissing her over and over then—her breasts, her throat,

436

er mouth again—breathing deeply, groaning her name, perspiring, his movements deliberate and almost painful to her. She couldn't stop crying and she didn't care if he did hurt her, as long as she could have him again. She knew he'd not leave her if they made love. It had been so long! So long! How many months? Nearly five since he had brought her here, made love to her, and left before she could say good-bye.

"I've never wanted you so badly in my life!" he groaned, his lips at her throat, one hand pushing her tunic up to her waist. She had deliberately not worn anything beneath, hoping that this would happen. She was too lost in him even to reply as his hand moved over her bare hips and around to the front of her, searching places that had belonged only to him for twenty years, places he had searched and invaded before any other man. She was again his woman-child, lying beneath him in the wilds of Wyoming, and no one else existed. She whimpered as his fingers dipped inside that private place she had offered to no one but him, bringing out its silken moistness, then gently caressing the secret place that brought out her deepest passions.

She moaned his name, almost instantly thereafter crying out in an intense, almost painful explosion of desire. He ran a hand over her stomach, then met her lips again, pushing, searching, tasting, claiming, while his other hand removed his leggings and loincloth. "God, I need you, Abbie!" he said in a husky voice. "No one else can take your place, damn you! Damn you!"

He surged inside of her then, and she cried out at the pain of his first, possessive thrust. He kissed her eyes, her cheeks, her ears, her throat, her mouth, wanting to devour her, taking, giving, moving in sweet rhythm.

He knew every way there was to please her. After all he had been doing so for a long time. Yet it was still good, after twenty years and seven children, only because of their undying love and devotion. They fed on each other, drew from each other, gave and accepted pleasure on equal terms. A moment later his life poured into her and he relaxed on top of her, breathing heavily, his sweet dampness welcome. She drew in his wonderful scent, kissing his cheek and running her hands over his shoulders and then putting her arms around him while his face rested against her neck.

"Do you really think we can do it, Abbie? Start over?"

"Of course we can. Look how we started out. We had much less than we have now."

His body jerked oddly. "I need to . . . let go of something that's . . . bursting inside of me, Abbie. I need to . . ." He swallowed. "I never cried over Lance . . . or my little Lillian. Poor little Lillian!" He sucked in a wrenching sob that tore at her heart. She kept one arm around him, his tears wetting her neck, while her other hand sought a horse blanket close by, not caring that it was full of straw, and pulled it over them.

The morning sky was magnificent, rich in hues of pink and gold and blue, with only a few wispy clouds hanging low on the horizon. The Monroes headed home, Zeke riding Kehilan, man and horse looking wild and happy and free. The stud Zeke had operated on lived, and during the wait for his recovery, Sun and Dreamer had both delivered foals, one colt and one filly. Both pranced alongside their mothers, the broodmares ridden by Abbie and Margaret. LeeAnn rode with Abbie, eleven-year-old Ellen with Margaret. Jeremy rode proudly on his Uncle Lance's horse, and Morgan was astride his own mount, seven-year-old

Jason in front of him. Zeke rode alone, keeping an eye on the two energetic foals and the four thoroughbreds they'd purchased from Edwin Tynes. Two of them were pregnant mares, the other two younger fillies. When they were ready to mate, he would take them to the Tynes estate and leave them for a while, in order to keep the fine Arabian strain, for Kehilan was a jealous sort who allowed no other studs near his harem, and Zeke didn't want to mix the Appaloosa with the thoroughbreds.

There was hope now. Once they were settled Zeke would go to Pueblo or Julesberg and purchase more horses. Then he and Abbie would visit the Cheyenne in Kansas in the hope that they could find some good Appaloosas among his kin, horses that would be traded for money and supplies. The reservation Indians surely needed both. Somehow they would find other ways to help the Cheyenne, for they knew the battle wasn't over yet. They had already heard rumors that the war for the Powder River country was getting hotter. The Sioux and northern Cheyenne were very active, and their worry over Wolf's Blood was the only cloud that still hung over them. The great warrior Red Cloud would not give up. A Capt. William Fetterman and over eighty soldiers had been massacred at Peno Creek, and rumors were spreading of a new, fearful warrior called Crazy Horse and of a young, determined soldier called George Custer, sometimes called Hard Backsides or Long Hair by the Indians. They had heard that Congress had enacted a new bill, granting equal rights to all persons born in the United States—except Indians and women.

But Abbie refused to worry about any of that for now. They were going home. That was all that mattered. When they crested a ridge and looked down on the little cabin and the outbuildings and corral—all

439

still intact—her heart tightened and she looked over a Zeke. He looked back at her, his eyes taking in her beauty and stirring delicious feelings in her body, a body reawakened to love and passion. She felt like a young girl in love for the first time.

"Isn't it beautiful?" she commented. "We're home Zeke. There was a time when I thought—"

She was interrupted by a distant war whoop. They all reined to a halt and stared across the cabin and distant fields to a far ridge, while LeeAnn clamped her arms around her mother tightly, afraid they were being raided again.

"Zeke, what is it?" Abbie asked, her own heart racing.

The lone figure called out again, a piercing frightening cry. *"Nehoeehe! Nahoe-hootse!"*

Zeke sat straighter in the saddle, and Abbie recognized the words: "My father, I have come visiting." Her heart raced excitedly. Could it be? Suddenly Zeke let out a wild war whoop that made them all jump. He put a fist in the air and called out several more yips and whoops, and the lone figure called back. Zeke laughed.

"It's Wolf's Blood!" he said excitedly. He kicked Kehilan's sides and charged forward, the magnificent Appaloosa's mane and tail flying in the wind, as was the sleek black hair of its master. The lone figure on the ridge began riding in from the other side, a wolf running hard at his horse's heels.

"Wolf's Blood!" Margaret cried out, starting forward.

"No, Margaret!" Abbie ordered quickly. "Don't go yet. Let them be alone."

They began to ride in slowly, watching father and son gallop toward each other so fast that their horses, unable to stop, carried them too far. Sod flew and both

440

men turned, riding past each other again, now doing crazy tricks. Abbie remembered how irritated she used to be because Zeke was teaching their son such dangerous riding, but she never worried now. Could any man and animal seem more like one than an Indian and his horse? Soon Zeke and Wolf's Blood dismounted, hugging, and then falling into the grass on their backs, Wolf jumping on them, tail wagging. They were still far out in the field, and Abbie knew they would mount up again and ride off. They would be gone a long time. There as much for father and son to talk about.

She looked over at Margaret. "Let's open up the cabin," she said, a lump in her throat. "It will need airing out. And let's get a fire going in the stone oven. I want to make some of those biscuits your brother loves so much."

They rode up to the cabin, and the two foals pranced up to suckle from their mothers almost before Abbie and Margaret could dismount. Abbie stepped up and unlatched the door, pushing it open. She stared around the small cabin. Yes, this was much nicer than a stone castle. This was home.

Other Books by F. Rosanne Bittner

FROM AWARD-WINNING AUTHOR
JO BEVERLEY

DANGEROUS JOY   (0-8217-5129-8, $5.99)

Felicity is a beautiful, rebellious heiress with a terrible secret. Miles is her reluctant guardian—a man of seductive power and dangerous sensuality. What begins as a charade borne of desperation soon becomes an illicit liaison of passionate abandon and forbidden love. One man stands between them: a cruel landowner sworn to possess the wealth he craves and the woman he desires. His dark treachery will drive the lovers to dare the unknowable and risk the unthinkable, determined to hold on to their joy.

FORBIDDEN   (0-8217-4488-7, $4.99)

While fleeing from her brothers, who are attempting to sell her into a loveless marriage, Serena Riverton accepts a carriage ride from a stranger—who is the handsomest man she has ever seen. Lord Middlethorpe, himself, is actually contemplating marriage to a dull daughter of the aristocracy, when he encounters the breathtaking Serena. She arouses him as no woman ever has. And after a night of thrilling intimacy—a forbidden liaison—Serena must choose between a lady's place and a woman's passion!

TEMPTING FORTUNE   (0-8217-4858-0, $4.99)

In a night shimmering with destiny, Portia St. Claire discovers that her brother's debts have made him a prisoner of dangerous men. The price of his life is her virtue—about to be auctioned off in London's most notorious brothel. However, handsome Bryght Malloreen has other ideas for Portia, opening her heart to a sensuality that tempts her to madness.

TODAY'S HOTTEST READS
ARE TOMORROW'S SUPERSTARS

VICTORY'S WOMAN   (4484, $4.50)
by Gretchen Genet
Andrew—the carefree soldier who sought glory on the battlefield, and
returned a shattered man . . . Niall—the legendary frontiersman and
a former Shawnee captive, tormented by his past . . . Roger—the troubled youth, who would rise up to claim a shocking legacy . . . and
Clarice—the passionate beauty bound by one man, and hopelessly in
love with another. Set against the backdrop of the American revolution,
three men fight for their heritage—and one woman is destined to
change all their lives forever!

FORBIDDEN   (4488, $4.99)
by Jo Beverley
While fleeing from her brothers, who are attempting to sell her into a
loveless marriage, Serena Riverton accepts a carriage ride from a
stranger—who is the handsomest man she has ever seen. Lord Middlethorpe, himself, is actually contemplating marriage to a dull daughter of the aristocracy, when he encounters the breathtaking Serena. She
arouses him as no woman ever has. And after a night of thrilling intimacy—a forbidden liaison—Serena must choose between a lady's
place and a woman's passion!

WINDS OF DESTINY   (4489, $4.99)
by Victoria Thompson
Becky Tate is a half-breed outcast—branded by her Comanche heritage. Then she meets a rugged stranger who awakens her heart to the
magic and mystery of passion. Hiding a desperate past, Texas Ranger
Clint Masterson has ridden into cattle country to bring peace to a
divided land. But a greater battle rages inside him when he dares to
desire the beautiful Becky!

WILDEST HEART   (4456, $4.99)
by Virginia Brown
Maggie Malone had come to cattle country to forge her future as a
healer. Now she was faced by Devon Conrad, an outlaw wounded body
and soul by his shadowy past . . . whose eyes blazed with fury even
as his burning caress sent her spiraling with desire. They came together
in a Texas town about to explode in sin and scandal. Danger was their
destiny—and there was nothing they wouldn't dare for love!

*Available wherever paperbacks are sold, or order direct from the
Publisher. Send cover price plus 50¢ per copy for mailing and
handling to Penguin USA, P.O. Box 999, c/o Dept. 17109,
Bergenfield, NJ 07621. Residents of New York and Tennessee
must include sales tax. DO NOT SEND CASH.*